## Also by Anne Elizabeth

WEST COAST NAVY SEALs

*A SEAL at Heart*

*Once a SEAL*

*A SEAL Forever*

*The Soul of a SEAL*

# the POWER of a SEAL

## WITHDRAWN

### ANNE ELIZABETH

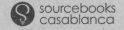

sourcebooks
casablanca

Published by Sourcebooks Casablanca, an imprint of Sourcebooks, Inc.
P.O. Box 4410, Naperville, Illinois 60567-4410
(630) 961-3900
Fax: (630) 961-2168
sourcebooks.com

Printed and bound in Canada.
MBP 10 9 8 7 6 5 4 3 2 1

*An ode to Leaper.*

*Dedicated to our men and women in uniform.*
*Thank you for your service.*

*and*

*For Rose, Hooyah and hugs!*

# Chapter 1

THE WETSUIT OUTLINED THE CURVES OF NAVY SEAL
Leaper Lefton's muscles. His body was lean, steely,
and powerful, with arms that could hold someone tight
and safe for hours on end. He was humble and most
often quiet, and he definitely didn't fancy himself the
James Bond type. But one might think he was, given
his occupation. With a hood encasing his head and neck
and the breathing apparatus and mask obscuring most
of his face, his attire was ideal for covert drops, but
at night, with additional gear and unknowable predators and random factors in enemy waters, the dive was
doubly dangerous.

In his opinion, brains, not brawn, were the key to
locking out of a submarine in the Pacific Ocean. With
less experienced newbies, it was an especially hard task.
Lights on their masks illuminated very little in the pitch-
black water, and everyone was hustling to get clear of
each other and the giant nuclear sub.

Being the last one out of the torpedo tube had advantages and disadvantages. Knowing that no one was left
behind was the primary advantage, but being unaware
of what your Teammates could see was the disadvan-
tage. Hell, no matter how many times one practiced this
maneuver, there was still a certain amount of unpredictability and chaos. Any problem meant that this mission
would be scrubbed, and no operative wanted to see that

happen. So that meant everyone was looking to Leaper, Mission Leader.

Checking left and right as he cleared the giant submarine, Leaper eyeballed his Teammates, counting heads. There were several squeakers on the mission—newbies—and Leaper looked at them first. Sure, they'd practiced locking out of subs at this depth, but being on a mission made it fresh, gave them an adrenaline rush, unlike anything an ordinary soul might experience. For all the wisdom garnered in practice, it never prepared one for the racing heart and the pumping blood that happened in the heat of the moment.

Though some might say practice makes perfect, Leaper did not believe completely in the adage. He put his trust in awareness rather than pure repetition.

*Christ!* His gut was churning. Something felt wrong. He counted again, physically touching each Teammate on a limb as his blood ran cold.

Someone was missing. *Shit, shit, shit.*

Ambient noise traveled to him slowly, like taffy being stretched and pulled. His ears picked up on something—a rumble in the water.

Hydroacoustics were tricky. Water carried sound in the strangest manner, depending on the depth, the surrounding landscape, and the proximity to everything else around them in terms of marine life. When one was suspended in the air, as in a skydive, and had just pulled the ripcord, there was an absolute silence, an indescribable hush. It was the total absence of sound. When one was in the water, it was like someone yelling at you down a long, wind-filled tunnel; the sound went out in waves that dissipated, depending on how far away you were.

In other words, it was nearly impossible to distinguish sounds clearly. Here's where experience paid off, and he had spent years familiarizing himself with this world.

Leaper turned slowly, sourcing the sound. His senses told him to move to the right.

In his periphery, he could see the sub moving farther into the darkness.

*C'mon, Hissop!* Special Operator Alvin Hissop. *Where, the fuck, are you?*

With no time for prayers, Leaper signaled with his hands—for those close enough to see it—and made a series of arm taps for those whose light could not follow as he relayed the message to his Teammates to wait near the reef.

They acknowledged him and moved off as ordered. They were quick, careful not to generate any extra current. Losing someone in the darkness was a significant and real danger.

One man stayed by Leaper's side: his swim buddy on this mission and the second-in-charge, Jollen Bell. As he came alongside Leaper, the two men retraced their steps from the origin point of their escape.

That's when they saw him. Hissop was suspended sideways, as if he were dangling on wires. Darkness framed his body, and the light on his mask flickered briefly and then went out.

Leaper was in motion before he could think.

Blood and guts surrounded Hissop's midsection, and his arms were open and welcoming. A long cut sliced down his suit where the submarine screws had cut him. The blades were so sharp, they'd sliced through the bones.

Something rushed Leaper from the side, and he didn't need to figure out what it was. He knew instinctually that it was a shark. A glance showed her to be a Great White female, at least twenty-five feet long. Leaper threw a punch at her nose. It landed, but she wasn't deterred coming back with a quick turn. That was unusual. A shark's chemosensory abilities were incredibly keen and sensitive.

Grabbing his Ka-Bar, Leaper prepared for the next pass. This time, he dug his knife into the closest target, the Great White's eye, slicing until the creature fell away. It wouldn't be coming back anytime soon.

Leaper's jaw tightened as he secured his knife. He turned back to his Teammates: Bell and Hissop. One man guarded and the other fought. Nothing would take Hissop from his Team. They would all fight to the death to return Hissop home.

Bell passed Hissop's body to Leaper and began his swim to the waiting group.

As Leaper pulled Hissop into his arms, he couldn't stop himself from searching the man's face, wishing against all logic for signs of life.

Nothing. As the current picked up, it drove the body forward and Hissop's face came closer until it was inches from his. Those normally attentive brown eyes bulged, and his mouth was open as if he had been screaming, an expression of horror frozen on his face. This man had felt pain and terror, and it had been horribly brutal.

Leaper swallowed a knot of pain. He hated the idea that his brother had been so alone.

Reaching for Hissop's mask, Leaper stopped himself, knowing instinctively there was only death there, but he could still wish for a different outcome. He was human after all, and the one who would bear witness to this tragedy.

The death scarred his spirit and his mind in ways that would never heal. How many bodies had he held, whose lives had departed too soon? Taken ruthlessly, and so completely out of his control. He couldn't process it all now. But his brain still spun with one big question: How had Hissop gotten nailed? Surely someone would have seen him get hurt and helped.

Closing Hissop's suit as best he could, Leaper cradled the man against him. Rigging his belt into Hissop's so he could move a bit faster, he swam forward. He knew it would be a long, painful ascent for the entire Team. He just needed to keep everyone focused. More mistakes happened when heads were full of grief.

With determination, he headed for his Team. They were waiting for him.

Leaper nodded at Bell. He pointed to his gauge and then to the surface.

Bell nodded his head in agreement. Signals were passed through the men until they were moving slowly upward.

The death of a Teammate was the worst grounds for scrapping a mission. And they had to be on the surface to use the fucking radio.

It was one of the longest swims of Leaper's life. Emotionally, he wanted to rocket upward and take the Team with him, but given their depth, ascending too quickly would allow nitrogen bubbles to gather in their bloodstreams. It would essentially poison them, painfully damaging and possibly killing them all on top of it.

Out of the corner of his eye, Leaper saw unusual

gestures from one of his Teammates. Arms and legs flailed, and the person's head jerked up and down.

He saw one of the guys moving erratically; avoiding the bends was a serious priority. He assessed Special Operator Koal Richter and decided that Richter's telltale panicked movements were manageable with guidance. He gestured at Jollen to partner with the eager beaver, watching as his second-in-command swam up to Richter and jerked the newbie to attention. The other man responded with instant obedience. They communicated with hand signals and then the two men slowly continued their ascent, side by side.

Leaper looked back down at the man tied to him. If only his actions could change the equation and he could breathe life into Hissop.

He bit back his frustration and pain at not being able to prevent this tragedy; it made him angry beyond words. He shouted into his mask, knowing that it would stay here in the dark waters. They were bringing up the rear, and he watched as his Teammates broke the surface of the water.

He reined in his emotions as he pulled his mask off and breathed in the salty night air. The tang of copper hit his nostrils, and Leaper pulled Hissop tighter against him.

The night sky was full of stars, one of them shooting toward the horizon. Was nature mocking him, or was that Hissop saying his final farewell?

*Christ, help*.

Leaper watched Jollen contact the submarine for pickup.

Pain nearly shattered Leaper's heart as he thought of

Hissop's young wife. What would he say to her? They trusted him—all the wives, kids, and families did—to bring their men home alive.

Tears streamed down Leaper's face, mingling with the salt water. A thousand tears could never ease this pain. Death was and always would be merciless in his world. If only he could prevent it, or give his life for theirs, but fate was cruel that way. He always survived.

—∿—

Time was an odd form of measurement. Go through hell, and the days were torturous and the nights were blobs of inky "painmares." Exist in a heavenly or blissful moment, and time rocketed by faster than you could hold on to it. In between those extremes, hours stretched on like an endless TSA line.

The Op was long over, and Leaper was back on duty rotation—yet the loss of his Teammate was still fresh in his mind. No one from that night saw the devastation, and the death had been ruled accidental. It didn't change the heartbreak of it.

The boat rocked from side to side as the water lapped at the sides. Stationary, stagnant, this felt a bit like his life right now. Leaper was a half mile off the coast of the Amphibious Base in Coronado, California. Sitting here and doing nothing might just lull him into boredom.

This was Leaper's first week back after a month of psych evaluations. Talking about the last, horrific operation was not something he wanted to do. Leaper did his best to play the part of a good sailor and give the docs what they needed, but let's get real—no one got out of battle or training unscathed. It left an indefinable mark.

Few operators shared the nitty-gritty, because what happens in the Teams stays in the Teams.

"Let's get you back out there," Admiral George had said. "We need you leading a deployment. It's just six months. Not a lot going on. You'll manage the operations from the base. Just keep everyone in line and the Teams rotating through running smoothly."

"No offense, Admiral, but I'm barely functioning. Find someone else," Leaper had replied. With that, he'd walked away from the outraged man, only to be tracked down by his Commanding Officer and told that he was going to be helping out in a different capacity for now.

Regardless of how little Leaper had shared, the Navy couldn't afford to bounce him, even if several shrinks noted that Leaper's mind had locked down the pain and he wasn't "necessarily fit." Too bad. That didn't stop Command from keeping Leaper in the game. According to the docs, Leaper was still functioning on the basic levels, but until he was ready to face the intense tragedy of Hissop's death, there was nothing they could do to assist the situation. So they stuck him on the sidelines. His current rotation was as an instructor, to teach, lead, assess, evaluate, test, and assist.

Assist. Hell, *ass* was the correct word. Leaper felt better in the field. On land, he fucking floundered like a fish out of water. Besides, most of those doctors were useless. So what! He wasn't ready to face Hissop's death, and that was life. Maybe when he was seventy-five and drinking a beer with his cronies, he'd deal with it. Until then, they could fuck off. Leaper didn't mind the fact that he was running on a single gear setting, and that mode was slow roll. His internal engine would crank up if it was needed.

A substitute instructor for Basic Underwater Demolition/SEAL (BUD/S), and for Special Warfare Combatant-Craft (SWCC), if need be—that was their answer. He'd performed this role at least a dozen times over the past twenty years. The training tended to overlap in certain areas, especially in terms of tactical intensity, gun and knife skills, and proficiency of boat maneuver skill sets. He was meant to focus on one specialty, but it wouldn't happen that way. Once you signed on as instructor, you ended up working in pretty much every area.

A ton of everything at once, and he'd do it right or not at all. That was his manner in most things—100 percent or nothing.

Leaper decided to roll with it. This duty assignment as an instructor would have to be okay for the present. Hell, he could yell at and cajole the recruits with the best of them, though it was hard to see these sailors as anything but wet-behind-the-ears kids. If he had his druthers, he'd wrap each of them in cotton padding and put them on a shelf to keep them away from the action. That wasn't an option, and certainly *not* what any of these sailors wanted. They were begging for opportunities to get in the fight and were working their tails off to prove that they had what it takes to survive and succeed for themselves and their Teammates. Leaper knew he needed to step up and prepare them for the worst, despite the pain of loss in his heart. He'd start with the basics, where he could, and coach them along further with what he'd learned from his two decades in the Teams.

The boat underneath him rocked abruptly. The current shifted, pulling the boat in a new direction as the waves grew more aggressive. They beat heavily against the sides of the boat, spraying the occupants with each thump. Leaper looked at the men in the boat with him and took control. He knew exactly where he wanted to go.

The boat slid into gear, and soon Leaper was driving it at top speed. This was one of four Reinforced Inflatable Boats, or RIBs, carrying BUD/S trainees on another phase of their training, along with four instructors. Leaper Lefton was pretty sure the BUD/S boys never imagined he would be a substitute instructor and the one leading the aquatic charge, but at the end of the day, they'd be grateful for the skills he'd teach them. Christ, he hoped it saved lives.

Murmuring voices sounded briefly behind him. Leaper looked over his shoulder and saw the other boats slowing and then stopping. He circled around and then stopped some distance away from the others.

"Listen up," Leaper said, studying the trainees. He wasn't one of those men who taught untried techniques or theories. Rather, he used his own experiences to speak about what worked and why. Being an operator with more Ops and tours under his belt than most active-duty sailors, he was pretty blunt, and his sense of humor was definitely dry, an acquired taste. His swim buddy, Declan, used to tease that if someone needed real-life input or someone to call bullshit on a situation, Leaper was the man for the job. From funnyman to leader, his honesty was legendary. There was a lot of brass who most certainly wished Leaper had had more tact training, but it was hard to criticize a man with that much sea cred. "I'm going to give you a few useful hints. You can ignore them or you can take them to heart. Your choice, but I'll only share them once."

"Yes, Instructor," the men said in unison.

Reaching his hand into his pocket, Leaper pulled out half a dozen neon bandanas and handed them out to the trainees. "Tie it around your wrist."

The trainees didn't question the order. They quickly did as Leaper bade and waited for further instruction. Eager eyes gazed steadily at him.

"Be prepared to swamp on my command," said Leaper. "Make sure the gear doesn't sink."

The men scrambled, grabbing loose fins, masks, and bags. The boat rocked as they moved hastily.

"Slow down, guys. Let's consider your actions before you take them. Make each movement count— unnecessary movements can cause harm. Water has a reaction for each action, and that's useful to know. It can be advantageous or harmful, depending on how you use it. For example, if your starboard man jumps before your port man knows, guess what's happening next?" Leaper eyed the trainees. "And I'll give you another hint on the gear. If you don't have utility belts, or any other type of belt, use something else to secure gear in a handy fashion. I always carry a bandana. Black, brown, or something that blends in with whatever outfit I'm sporting." Leaper waited for the trainees to crack smiles. Nothing.

*Damn. These recruits are too serious. Young, hungry, and scared shitless too.*

"Tough crowd," he murmured. He cleared his throat and then spoke louder. "These bandanas are yours to keep, to remind you of this swamping lesson. Now, center yourselves, and let's go slowly and thoughtfully through the process."

The boat stopped rocking as the men calmed down. The gear was secured.

"Swamping in three, two, one." Leaper cut the engine and dove over the side. Cool water rushed over his face and body. It was refreshing, and relief filled him. He surfaced faster than he preferred, but he had a job to do. He swam five feet away to gain a better vantage point.

On cue, pairs of men eased into the water. First to enter the cold Pacific water were the ones on his left. Leaving two on the right, these men grabbed the rungs on the side of the boat. They dithered for a few seconds, checking that all gear was secure, and then counted off together and jumped in. In one smooth movement, thanks to the two men from the right, the rubber boat flipped into the water. The small outboard motor propeller spun slowly in the air, as if it didn't realize it was supposed to stop moving. Eventually, all movement ceased as the men moved under the boat and breathed air together in the small, dark confines.

Leaper smiled. He swam closer and slipped underneath. He could practically feel the men grinning. They knew they had performed well. This wasn't their first rodeo. "Good job. Now, let's flip it, make everything shipshape, and get back underway."

"Aye, aye." Six acknowledgments echoed quietly inside the RIB before the trainees disappeared on the other side, righted the boat, and climbed back in. These agile men were so young. Had he ever been that shiny and new…that hopeful? God, he felt old. Was this how his old instructor, Gich, had felt about him? Damn. Well, Leaper *had* passed the big 4–0 three years ago.

Where had time gone? Maybe he should settle down like Declan, marry someone and have babies. *Who the hell would ever love a fuckup like me?* Whoever it was would have to be a lunatic like him. *If there's a woman out there like that…*

Leaper looked up. The sun was high in a cloudless sky.

He hoisted himself over the side of the boat. Looking down, he could see fish swimming below. The ocean was crystal clear. God, he'd rather be out swimming, fishing, kayaking, surfing—anything, other than teaching. Fuck, it was time to retire. Wasn't it?

"Secure. And if I can add, that was cool, Instructor," said Seaman Willie Watson. The rest of the BUD/S trainees looked on exuberantly, obviously jubilant over the ease of the experience. If there were any chance he could teach these kids something, anything, to protect them from harm…well, hell, he'd stick it out a while longer and see how he could help the next generation. They seemed like good kids. Shit, he was already calling them kids.

"Good to hear." Leaper nodded toward the other boats. "I'll bet they aren't having as much fun in those boats." He didn't agree with scaring the crap out of the recruits and making them so flustered they couldn't find their asses with a magnifying glass. Different folks had different strokes, when it came to training.

Leaper could hear several of the instructors shouting their heads off on the other boats, and one of the engines had obviously gotten loose and sunk. Bummer. Those recruits would be on the Goon Squad until graduation. Not that doing extra physical training (PT) was a negative thing, for it often had a positive effect by helping recruits make it over the hump by developing a do-or-die determination to succeed. Leaper remembered his days of running extra miles and doing hundreds of push-ups, as well as long laps around the bases and the Obstacles course. Those were the days…when his optimism was strong and his direction was crystal clear. Damn, but he was a jaded son of a bitch now.

Leaper hid his smile. "Uh, you'll notice that I depart from the regular curriculum. What I'm going to teach you are useful techniques that at some point could be lifesaving. Knowing what each person is doing—having that agreement among yourselves before you even leave the beach or the dock—will save you time. I noticed that several of you were slow to respond as the swamping began. This planning will aid you. Who is responsible for which gear or which tasks, and having a few carabineers, bandanas, and a knife with you, will be more useful than you can imagine. For example, if you're going to be MacGyver, you need to pick useful items to MacGyver with…"

Gesturing at the other two boats, Leaper added, "A few friendly tips to get you to Hell Week. Don't be a know-it-all. Share the knowledge I'm giving you. Teammates are for the Team, not the individual. If something works for you or a Teammate, pass on the wisdom. This is what the Teams are about: helping each other to the goal. We succeed as one, or we fail as one. But failure is…"

"Not an option. Thank you, Instructor," finished

Watson. "Shit. Those guys in the other boats are diving
for their gear. Has to be over fifty feet."

"It's forty-two feet. Another thing that's useful to
know is depths. Study the charts. There have been more
than a few occasions when combat swimmers have
taken advantage of the topography of the ocean floor.
Think of our underwater demolition teams, our Frogmen
ancestors, who would swim into beaches, disposing of
mines and booby traps, clearing the way for our troops
to safely land on beaches. These guys would have grease
pencils and clear plastic boards to note the landscape
of the bottom of the ocean—depths, debris, etc. This is
one type of war we're fighting, where all the areas of the
globe can become battlefields. Just because you're on
top of the water driving a boat doesn't mean you can be
oblivious to what's below you. In reality, it means you
need to be doubly aware of everything above you, below
you, and around you. Awareness, preparation, and planning means always having several contingency plans."

Leaper waved to one of the boats and gestured to
another instructor.

Receiving a thumbs-up in response, Leaper engaged
the engine on the boat and turned it away from the others
toward a group of birds diving into the water. In the distance was a small island. Farther on was San Clemente,
a training outpost they'd be visiting in the near future.
Boy, these trainees were going to hate the next stop! His
first foray into this exercise had made him wet his pants.
Luckily, he'd been in the water at the time, and no one
had been the wiser.

The sound of the screeching birds grew louder as
they neared a fish-feeding frenzy. Leaper cut the engine

about one hundred feet away. "There's a school of fish below, and most likely"—Leaper's words were cut off as the boat rocked suddenly—"dolphins."

The trainees looked eagerly over the side, almost tipping the boat.

"Easy, there. These are wild dolphins, and they are *not* necessarily friendly. Let me share a story about my time in Greenland. My former swim buddy, Declan, and I were practicing with a new type of rebreather when we met up with a pod of dolphins—mothers and their wee ones. Let me tell you, those mothers were protective…" Leaper paused as he craned his neck to the right. "What's that? Over there, I see something. Hey, is that a figure bobbing around out there?

"I'm afraid our next lesson will have to wait. This looks like an emergency. Stay put. If something happens and I go down, return to the group. Do *not* follow me into the water." Leaper didn't wait for their response. He dove over the side and swam with quick strokes to the figure he'd spied. He could feel the school of fish changing direction and moving around him. A few not-so-subtle snout bumps on his leg signaled dolphins, though sharks were known to give a not-so-subtle rub, to "taste" their prey. Fuck it—he could get rough if he needed to. Whatever came his way, he'd deal with it.

As Leaper neared the figure, he could see it was a woman—a rather pretty one too. Her movements were slow, and she looked very tired. His buddy Declan would love this. He was the chivalrous "lifeguard" type, but Leaper had pulled his fair share of men out of the drink. This could be his first time rescuing a woman.

THE POWER OF A SEAL

"Hey, are you okay?" When there was no answer, he added, "Uh, my name is Leaper. What's yours?"

"Kerry," she panted. Her large brown eyes were frantic. Her honey-blond hair was matted to her head. "My dolphin. Have you seen her? I need to secure her."

"Your dolphin? Did you ride her here? Is she pocket-size?" He moved toward her slowly. *Is she delusional? Her gaze is steady. She seems to be on the level. Or is she a good liar?*

He'd seen more than one good friend almost drowned by an emotional victim. Besides that, a person in the ocean spouting tales of owning a dolphin was worth doubting. There was a possibility this lady was unbalanced. He hoped for the best, that she was sane and easy to rescue. If not, well, here was another life lesson for the recruits.

"No. What? Are you nuts?" She spit water out of her mouth as she kept herself afloat. "I have a boat."

"Okay. Where?" He looked over his shoulder. "I don't see one. Did it sink?"

Kerry spun in a circle. "Crap! I must have swum farther than I realized. It's back there, near the far side of that island. Close to the inlet with the small rocky beach."

"That's, like, four miles away. The current must have caught you." He swam closer to her, holding at an arm's length away. "Can we give you a lift?"

"Sure. I just…need to find Juliet." She smiled as she looked down. "There she is."

A face bobbed up in front of them. The dolphin nudged Kerry gently.

"SeaWorld? Wild search and rescue? Or are you a member of the Marine Mammal Program?" Leaper nodded. "I'll bet the latter."

"*Ding ding ding*. I usually have two techs who come out with me, but there was an emergency. Juliet and I were already in the boat, so we broke protocol and ventured out alone. Normally, it's not a problem. We've done this before. But something spooked her, and she veered away from the boat, and then those guys found her." Kerry stroked the dolphin's back. When the dolphin rolled onto her side, Kerry rubbed her fin. "Wild male dolphins lure away our females. These hooligans corral our females and get them pregnant before they return them to us. The problem is, right now, there are several fatal illnesses that the males can pass on to our females, so we discourage their coupling by bringing the females quickly on board a boat, but when I'm so far from mine, well… So sometimes I just shout at the predators. Not that any wild creature is going to listen to me. Luckily, Juliet is one smart cookie, so I'm guessing she's probably avoided their advances so far. She's a very crafty and swift swimmer."

"And if she gets cornered by a group of males, what does she do, cross her fins?"

"*Pffft*. You're an idiot," Kerry said, splashing him.

"Glad you noticed. So, um, are you okay or what?" He was pretty close to her now. He could take hold of her, bring her safely to the boat.

"Honestly"—the lines on her brow deepened—"I'm getting pretty tired."

"Sorry to hear that. Ah, crap, did you ask for Juliet's friends to join us?" Leaper pointed to several fins. "They're coming."

Kerry tapped Juliet's belly and she rolled right side up. Kerry held her hand possessively on the female dolphin's back.

Swimming closer to Kerry, Leaper felt several hard bumps along his leg and back. "We need to get you both out of the water. Can you swim beside me?"

"Yeah."

The female dolphin moved protectively between Leaper and Kerry. It was a decent position for Juliet to be in, though it put the human beings in the line of fire. A dolphin's snout was a serious weapon that could cause severe pain or damage to a shark. Leaper had experienced broken and bruised ribs from the Greenland pod and didn't want to go down that path again.

His fingers brushed the hilt of his knife. With the school of fish so close, he didn't doubt additional predators lurked nearby too. But he'd didn't want to aggravate the situation, so he was going to hold off on wounding or killing one of the aggressors as long as he could.

Leaper waved at the boat and signaled to the trainees to use their paddles to bring the boat closer. They saw his signal and immediately complied. Good souls! He would be buying these trainees burgers tonight.

A young male dolphin rubbed his body along Leaper's leg. Great. Leaper froze until the sensation passed. If he pushed the male away, it would give the dolphin an excuse to respond. No one wanted to mess with a horny male dolphin!

"Don't shove the dolphins if they lean against you." Kerry advised softly. "They will meet every action with added aggression."

"Yeah, I know. I've encountered pods before, though not males, per se. I count four of them. What do you think?" Leaper did a breaststroke so he could look around while still moving. When Kerry didn't answer immediately, he asked, "Are you doing okay over there?"

She gulped air. "Yeah. Four. I'm just…spent."

Leaper came back to Juliet, put his arm over her, and gave Kerry something to rest on. "Hang in there. The boat is close."

The wild dolphins shoved their snouts against Leaper. They wanted that female. He resisted the urge to respond, though his ribs were definitely taking a beating.

His eyes continued to scan their surroundings, but the moment the boat was close enough, he hoisted Kerry in with one lift and then practically propelled Juliet on board and onto a bed of life vests and shirts. The male dolphins were highly displeased and came at him quickly with open mouths. Leaper wasn't looking to sport any scars, so he hustled himself aboard and spun his finger in the air.

Seaman Watson engaged the engine, put the boat in gear, and headed at top speed toward shore.

"Head for the mouth of Glorietta Bay," ordered Leaper. He sat up and shook the water out of his hair. Droplets of salt water flew off his head in a short barrage.

"My boat?" asked Kerry.

He pursed his lips. Though he believed she truly wanted it, the woman was totally spent. He couldn't let her operate a boat on her own. "We'll drop you off and go back for it."

"Thank you, Leaper." She put her hand on top of his. She held it there, the same way she held her other hand on the back of the dolphin. It was…nice. The way her clothes clung to her wasn't lost on him: a pair of black swim shorts hugged her shapely legs, and a bright-pink swim shirt was stretched over her breasts. Perky nipples pushed through. Probably cold. There was nothing dry on board the boat after the swamping. Otherwise, he would have offered her something to wear.

*Strange*, he noted. *I'm usually the "love 'em and leave 'em laughing" type. But this lady seems different—sweet and grateful, and sexy.*

As she looked up at him, he noticed heat in her gaze too—or was he imagining that?

"My phone number is 555-0122, in case you need to reach me about the rescue, or the boat." She smiled up at him, suddenly aware that her hand was still on his. She jerked it away. "Sorry. You're…very warm."

"Hot-blooded, I suppose," he said, and then decided that was the lamest statement ever. Christ, he was out of practice with women. When you spent all day, every day with men…you tended to lose touch.

It wasn't long before they reached the Marine Mammal area. Actually, the time had felt very short indeed. Down from the Point Loma Submarine Base and currently hidden at the back of an obscure Marine base, this place was a well-kept secret. Given that the dolphins and sea lions were mostly rescues—well protected and cared for—Leaper wouldn't mind coming back as one of these mammals if there were reincarnation. Having someone like Kerry take care of him would make life pretty interesting.

Several people waited on the docks, a swift blur of movements as they coordinated moving the dolphin into its pen. Juliet seemed pretty happy as she waved back at them with a flipper.

Kerry looked exhausted. Her face was pale, and her

legs were a little wobbly as she walked, but she held herself upright as she moved about the dock and conversed with her coworkers.

Leaper couldn't hear the conversation, but he figured it wasn't a pleasant chat. He checked his watch. It was almost time to wrap for the day, so he stepped off the boat and walked to her. Pulling her aside, he said, "I need to get going. We'll grab your boat and drop it off, and then I need to get these trainees home. Touch base tomorrow?"

She reached up and hugged him abruptly. It almost threw him off-center, but he caught her to him and held her tight. "Is that a yes?" he asked.

"Yes," she murmured against his shoulder. "Thank you." Just as quickly as she'd embraced him, she let go and headed back to the far side of the dock. The lady didn't look back, but Leaper could still feel the imprint of her luscious curves against his chest and the silk of her hair as it brushed against his neck.

Huh, he was giving her a lot of thought. Interesting. He watched her for several more seconds, and then he headed back to the boat. The moment he was on board, a voice challenged him.

"Shall we set up a smooch alert?" asked Watson.

Leaper raised an eyebrow. "Do you want to join your friends on the Goon Squad?"

"I'm just kidding." Watson sounded worried. Scratch that—he sounded scared. "Please, don't…"

"No shit, Sherlock. Hey, I like that! That's your new nickname: Sherlock." He waited for a reply. Again there was nothing. "Listen. Warriors have thick skin. What's life without teasing? Hell, it's how we show affection. I like the fact that you felt bold enough to give me shit."

Leaper patted the trainee on the back. "Don't be so scared of Goons. I did it. My brothers did it. If you let something make you stronger, it will. If you allow it to weaken you, then you've made that choice too."

He turned to the boat, speaking to all his trainees now. "Seek strength. Make choices that benefit you and your Teammates." With that, he pointed toward the horizon, in the general direction of Kerry's boat, and said, "Let's round up that boat. Heave ho."

His knees creaked as he sat. "Damn," he murmured to himself. "I'm getting too old for this shit."

No one said a word—not one smart-ass reply. *Chicken shit*, he thought. *I'll get them speaking. The Teams don't need a bunch of yes-men. These recruits all need to be leaders who know when to follow and when to stand up and voice their opinion. They're young, but they'll learn. Even if I have to drag them one by one over that damn finish line.*

# Chapter 2

Sweat gathered along Leaper's brow and dripped one drop at a time down his face and neck and onto his shirt. He'd be drenched before the day was done.

The heat index in Coronado, California, increased this time of year, especially as the day wore on. The sun's rays beat down on the occupants of the small Navy RIB. Leaper was never one to stand on ceremony or dress code, and he was the first to strip his shirt off and toss it on the heap of gear.

The recruits eagerly followed suit. Looking at their unblemished frames, he wondered what would be in store for them. If the trainees looked close enough at his chest, they'd see at least a dozen knife wounds, six bullet scars, courtesy of enemy combatants, three mis-shapen ribs from a botched HiLo jump, and one large, jagged scar from shrapnel. Leaper didn't want to scare these boys off, but the reality was…bodies entered SEAL Team one way and left another way. It was rare that anyone retired untouched, unless they only rode a desk. But even then, there were complications from endless paper cuts and the usual migraines from green gung-ho officers.

Leaper's eyes searched the horizon. Several charter boats were full of tourists out to catch something exciting on the Pacific. A few small sailboats were braving the open ocean, and in the distance a refueling ship was on its way back from filling someone up. It rode so high in the water, he could see where the hull needed to be touched up on its next maintenance docking.

Salt spray sprinkled his face. Was there any better feeling?

The wind whipped his hair as they sped through the water. He let out a long, slow breath. There was something peaceful about just riding in a boat, without some greater need for it to impart wisdom or a life lesson.

Looking at the faces of the trainees, Leaper could see them relaxing and enjoying this welcome break. He doubted any of the other Teammates were getting this treatment. Most likely those boys were toting large rocks from one place to another; getting wet, rolling in the sand, and doing leg lifts and other exercises while coated in the rough grimy sand—a.k.a. sugar-cookie drills; or running miles and miles with heavy packs. This was only a small part of the physical conditioning.

Leaper studied the recruits. "Tell me about yourselves," he said. "Why are you here?"

The fair-skinned blond boy spoke first. "Billy Coates from Boston, Massachusetts. I went to Boston University and majored in business for my undergraduate degree and psychology for my master's. My brother was a SEAL, and he served two tours in Iraq before leaving the Navy. He told me it was the best and worst time of his life. Regardless of his stories, I'm doing this for me."

Next was a tanned boy with auburn hair. "I'm Cabe Tucker, and I'm from Washington. I went to SDSU here in San Diego and graduated premed. Eventually, I'd like to be a doctor and follow that life path, but first I need to do this." He elbowed the person next to him, who was taller, with hairy arms, dark hair, and green eyes. "That's Joe Wallace. He lost his voice last night at the bar off Rosecrans. I think he's got a graduate degree in business. Yeah, he's nodding."

"Bar, huh? You'll learn that's *not* the best use of your paycheck. It's better to save your money. Wanting a car, home, and even a girlfriend or wife takes a decent amount of funds. I'm a big believer in 401(k)s and savings accounts. But to each his own," added Leaper. "What about you, Parks?"

*Was I ever that young and green*, pondered Leaper as he assessed the men. It was easy to see who would make it to next week and who would be running for the hills the minute there was a bump in the road.

"Yes, Instructor." Parks was compact and muscular. He looked too small to be in Spec Ops, and yet he was lean and agile, never missing an opportunity to help his classmates. Of course, size didn't mean anything. He personally knew a Frogman who was five foot two and served for thirty years.

"Go ahead," urged Leaper.

"Ahem, I'm Lester Parks, and I grew up in the Bronx—the rough part. It taught me to never give up on what I want. I studied mechanical engineering on scholarship at Cal Tech, and after graduating I joined the Navy. I want my life to be more than punching a clock. I like the tech part of SEAL training, and I have a few ideas for new gear. I have to believe in what I do and be a part of something bigger."

"Good to know. I agree on the 'bigger' part of a life occupation. So, on that note, let's do this as a Team

project. Could be useful in future training missions."
Leaper pointed at Watson, the boat leader, among other
things. "I know your story. You're the class leader, and
you went to Stanford, with a degree in mathematics.
You're a bit of a genius, according to your records. Isn't
that right, Sherlock?"

Watson shrugged. His face reddened and he had
large eyes, a bit googly like Leaper's, but he kept them
forward as the boat rounded San Clemente Island. "Ah,
yes, Instructor." This trainee had a medium build and
his shoulders and back were wide, but he had some beef
around the midsection. The weight would drop before
training ended. Physical endurance and peak perfor-
mance were major requirements for completing all three
phases of BUD/S training.

In the distance, Leaper could see Kerry's boat. Marine
Mammal RIBs had a splash of gray color across the
front, so no one absconded with their boats. "Watch out
for the buoys. Stay close and stay left of them, regardless of what's printed on their dysfunctional wrappers."

"Aye, aye," affirmed Watson.

Leaper pointed at the last man on the boat. "What's
your story?"

A raspy voice was cleared. "I'm Quentin Kirkland
Worthington. Naval Academy graduate. I hail from
Virginia. My father is Admiral Worthington." The boy
spoke succinctly and very fast, as if he was equally proud
and embarrassed. Hell, it was a hindrance to go through
training and be the son of an admiral and a Frogman.
Poor kid had an uphill battle ahead of him.

As Leaper studied the kid, he saw the boy's lip
quiver. He was a nervous one. *Wonder what makes*

*him tick?* Leaper had answered that particular question during his own Hell Week in a darkened room, with a spotlight on his face showing every bead of sweat. He'd been singled out by a giant Master Chief known for his handlebar mustache and tough techniques. Even his balls had sweated that day. The thing that made Leaper tick…was having something to belong to and knowing his actions made a difference.

Shit, being an instructor was not glamorous but he had knowledge to share. Basically, it was Leaper's job to do his hardest to break the trainees, but getting to know them like this, somewhat informally, had major advantages. He was actually rooting for them, though they wouldn't all make it. For instance, Leaper already knew that unless Worthington's son stepped up and showed some backbone and emotional fortitude, he was going to ring out—ringing the giant brass bell hanging in the Quarterdeck of BUD/S meant you quit training and were swept back into the general Navy, or upon rare occasion, could choose another area to apply to.

"Big shoes," said Leaper sympathetically. "Bet they're beating the piss out of you. Legacies always get an extra helping of crap, Captain Kirk—get it, Kirkland?"

"Crap juice. Crap salad. Crap steak with a side of crap fries." The boy nodded. "Any advice?" He rubbed his throat, and his nerves created a thick cloud of uncertainty around him.

Well, that's not a good sign. It was going to be the instructor's job to pick at this wavering sensation until it bled and made Kirkland Worthington—a.k.a. Captain Kirk—quit or get stronger. Leaper sighed.

"Stick with it. If this is what you truly want, hang

in there. Don't let them get in your head. Believe in yourself. The psychological tests are harder than the physical, and remember, we all went through it. Once you graduate, the challenges you face will kick your ass harder. Sure, 'the only easy day was yesterday' still rings true, but you have your Team to lean on, and they'll lean on you. So get those skills now and be proficient. Every movement and choice has a reason. Be *deliberate*. Make no decision hastily and without purpose. And remember, go through the training because you can't imagine anything else filling your life. You have to need to be a SEAL with every ounce of your heart and soul. If you can imagine any other options, then ring out and pursue them. This is an all-or-nothing experience."

"Thank you, Instructor," they answered in unison.

Leaper stood, joining Watson as the recruit steered closer to the boat. "Cut the engine, Sherlock. Captain Kirk, grab a line and jump on board. Parks, grab a line and follow. I want you remaining two to secure the boat for towing and to stay aboard the RIB in case any issues arise. If the line falters or anything out of the ordinary happens, you tell me ASAP."

The trainees hustled, making quick work of their tasks, and the two boats were soon underway. In Leaper's estimation, he'd get these trainees home in time for chow.

He scratched his chin as he glanced over his shoulder. That was a nice RIB. Too bad it was color-coded for the program, or he might consider adding it to the Team's lost-and-found collection. Nah! She was way too cute. Besides, finding Kerry's boat had been easy, in Leaper's opinion. It had been moored on the far side of the island,

and they'd had no problem setting up a series of tow-ropes and hauling it back to the Marine Mammal base, but what was he going to do when he saw her? Now, that was the hard question. Could he kiss her? Ask for a date? Ugh, he'd left his smooth-talking techniques back on base alongside his Harley.

Of course, if he'd thought to ask her for the key, that would have made things easier. Faster to drive two rather than tow one. Though he suspected the key was lost somewhere in the ocean. He supposed he could dive for it, but there would undoubtedly be duplicates some-where in her office. Shit, he was avoiding the point. He wanted to kiss her. That gorgeous mouth. Yep, that's what he wanted. Sweet and simple.

Not that he preferred simplicity, because he didn't… not in a lady. A challenge suited him better, kept him engaged longer, and he liked to give a lady a run for her money too. But he couldn't decide if he was going to pursue the curious Kerry with the shapely curves out-right or play coy.

Leaper rolled his eyes and stretched his arms over his head. Who was he kidding? He'd already spent more time contemplating this woman than any other in his life.

As the boats entered the bay, he knew the moment of truth was at hand. They pulled up to the Marine Mammal docks, and Kerry was the first to approach him. She eagerly threw her arms around him and hugged him. "Thank you."

He didn't hesitate as he leaned his head down, right then and there, and kissed her. Not a quick or congenial kiss, but a hot and heavy, I-want-to-thrill-you-to-your-core smooch.

He held her tightly to him, her body melting into his. *Well, well, well. Now this is a kiss to sear the soul!* They fit so exquisitely together, he didn't want to let go. It was as if the entire world around them had drifted away, and they were the only ones left in the universe.

Holding this lady close as the sun set behind him, Leaper never imagined this was how he would end this day. This had to be the sexiest first kiss of his life.

Too soon, reality invaded and the embrace ended. Leaper's ears finally detected the hoots of encouragement from the trainees on the boat. He breathed in Kerry's scent, memorizing it even as she clung to him, and then he slowly opened his arms and released her. As they parted, he knew he had been rash to kiss her in front of her coworkers and his recruits, but for once in his life, he just didn't give a damn about the opinions of others. This was a kiss he was going to remember.

---

The next morning, the sun struggled to shine through the heavy marine layer hovering over Point Loma. As she sat in the parking lot outside the Marine Mammal base of Operations, Dr. Kerry Hamilton wasn't sure anyone would be feeling those delightfully warm rays today. Perhaps it was an omen.

She looked in the rearview mirror again. Yep, still the same. Exhaustion traced her features, with dark circles under eyes and a pale color to her cheeks.

Oddly, though, she couldn't resist touching a finger to her lips as she thought about the kiss she'd shared with Leaper. What an incredible moment! The sensation of his mouth on hers had seared her senses all the way to her toes, and she was still vibrating with the delight of it. Oh God, how she wanted more. Infatuation was a marvelous high, and it had been ages since she had felt giddy inside.

Her cheeks were tinged with pink now, and it made her laugh softly to herself. As she sat in her car listening to the radio, she knew she was avoiding going into work. Of course, she was an hour early, but if she stayed here all day in the relative neutrality of vehicle, she would avoid any confrontation with the management.

Her fingers tapped automatically to the beat of the song on the radio. There was something special about the band American Authors' song "Best Day of My Life." It spoke to her. She wanted today to be the best day ever, yet she knew she would be taking some serious heat from her boss the minute she stepped foot onto the Marine Mammal Compound. She'd broken several cardinal rules, the first of which was *Never, ever go out alone with one of the marine mammals*. The second was *Always log your intended path of travel and the ultimate destination*.

"I better get to it. Get the worst part over with." Turning off the car, she grabbed her bag of gear and got out. She set the alarm with a press of her key fob and took slow breaths as she made her way toward the gates.

Before she reached the barrier, a slumped man who looked more scholar and scientist than bureaucrat stopped her. "Dr. Hamilton, good to see you."

"Dr. Boscher. Hi. What's up?" Kerry looked up at the tall man, noticing his disheveled clothing and the bags under his eyes. "Are you doing more research on species adaptation for our program?"

"Yes, yes. Fascinating stuff. I've narrowed my search to the tiger shark, whose intellect appears to rival that of your beloved bottlenose dolphins. Though I'm still working out how a training staff could safely work with them." Boscher waved a hand in front of his face, his gray pallor and slumped shoulders more pronounced as his moved. "I received approval from the Department of Defense for your study on dolphin environmental adaptation for our retired mammals. The funding was bumped an extra amount, in case you need additional modifications. I added that in, because I didn't see any wiggle room in your proposal. I'm not sure if you're planning on fixing up apartments for them—"

Kerry laughed. "Stop. You're too much! You know the funding is for special tanks that will allow me to change the temperature and buoyancy levels to help some of older dolphins be more comfortable without having to work so hard to swim, play, eat, and basically survive." She touched his arm. "Thank you for helping out. Having you as Special Funding Director for the Marine Mammal Program has been an incredible boon to all of us. You've added so much, and we're lucky to have you. Maybe now, Merry will perk up. She's showing signs of stress. Hopefully, the fancy new temperature-controlled tank will make a difference."

Boscher nodded his head. "Well, I have two more months before they put me out to sea…so to speak…and I plan to make the most of it. Good day, Dr. Hamilton." He stepped away from her slowly, as if his bones and muscles ached.

She wished he'd loosen up and call her Kerry, but his formality was only one of the quirks separating him from the rest of the staff. Boscher held himself apart from everyone, but she was eternally grateful for his help. She sighed. Oh well, the news of her tanks was so exciting, she could hardly wait to get started on ordering the materials and implementing them. There was so much to do.

Her mind was busy playing with the design of the tanks as several coworkers greeted her in the usual morning fashion. Maybe today wouldn't be so bad, and her mishap with Juliet in the ocean wouldn't be a big deal. Kerry started to relax. At least the rest of the staff wasn't pissed at her. Why should they be? There had been no need to rally or search for her. Instead, she'd arrived back without their knowing how dangerous the trip had been, and thankfully, the dolphin was healthy and safe. Everyone loved Juliet.

Kerry exhaled slowly and felt her lips curve into a half smile. First, she'd do a medical check on each dolphin, and then feeding—

"Dr. Hamilton." Hearing her name ground out as if it were being chewed with tinfoil made her blood freeze. She hated the sound of that voice. It was Beckstan Gellar, Marine Mammal Program Director and natural enemy to the entire staff and anyone with a hope or dream of improving anything for the marine mammals. He stood beneath the clock near the double doors to the main office like an executioner prepared to bring final judgment. His large arms were crossed, and his tinted glasses were perched on the end of his nose. "We need a meeting."

"Of course," said Kerry brightly. *Yay, management! Damn.*

It didn't look like being an hour early to work was going to impress him. Ugh. This was awful, and not how she wanted to begin her day. She needed this job. She couldn't afford to stay in her condo without it. She'd loathe having to go back home to her mother or one of her sisters with her tail tucked between her legs. And what about her beloved dolphins? She couldn't leave them, especially with the newly approved funding.

Kerry's chin dropped as she silently followed him into the main facility and through the open corral of desks to his glassed-in cube. As he closed the door behind them, she resisted the urge to claw at her throat; the sensation of claustrophobia was so keen. Instead, she held one hand with other and squeezed tight. To her boss, it probably looked as if she were praying, but she knew this was the only way she wouldn't run out of the room screaming. At least, not yet. She'd hear the man out first.

Gellar sat down behind his Nordic, minimalist desk—probably the only thing that would fit in here, she thought—and leaned on his elbows. The gray MMP hoodie lay on the side of the desk along with a pair of sunglasses. "I heard about yesterday." His voice sounded calm, but she knew the truth. This man regularly lied with his mouth and told the truth with his body. She hated that kind of duality. Didn't people like that know how easy they were to read? She supposed not—otherwise, why would they continue the masquerade?

A muscle ticked in Gellar's jaw, and his hands trembled briefly before he got them under control. His nose wrinkled as if he were breathing in something foul, and his forehead was so wrinkled with disdain, it could have been a sunshade for a family of four. "I need you to pay attention to what I'm about to say."

Kerry nodded. She didn't need to mask her emotions. She didn't give two hoots about anything the man was going to say, so she wasn't going to say a word. Nothing would make her incriminate herself. Rather, she would sit and wrestle with her true fear: claustrophobia. God, she hated cramped places.

"I know you're aware that I'm frustrated with you for breaking the rules. I need to set an example, so you're going to be on weekend duty for the next month." He waited for her to react.

After several seconds, she asked, "Days or nights?" Not that it mattered either way—she was often here long hours. The Marine Mammal Program was her entire life's focus.

"During the week, you have your normal day shifts with one rotating day off each week, and then you will be on night shift from midnight to 6:00 a.m. You can be on the water, the docks, or in the office, but you are on call." He frowned at her and shook his index finger as if scolding a child. "If I find out that you do not take my reprimand seriously and that you aren't showing up for each and every shift, well, then your pay will be docked and you will go before the Board of Directors. After that, your case will go up the DOD chain, and ultimately, I believe you will be fired."

Kerry pursed her lips. *Really? Bastard. Nothing is going to hurt me, if I have anything to say about it. Look at my record. Look at what I do around here. It's not like I stand on the dock and scratch my butt. These mammals are my life.*

Besides, she was a marine mammal vet whose area of expertise was nephrology with a specialty in kidney-stone prevention. There were only a handful of people like her in the country, and this program needed her help. Since the dolphins weren't out catching fresh fish each day, they had less hydration than normal. Thus, staff would tube-feed the dolphins with extra liquids, and the dietary changes she'd implemented would isolate the incidences of kidney stones to only a handful of older dolphins. It was practically a freaking miracle. She doubted that she would be going anywhere without the Marine Mammal Foundation pushing back on her behalf. But Kerry couldn't deny the Program Director his power or dignity, so she replied politely, "Understood."

Gellar let out a sigh of relief. Tension lifted from his shoulders, making his muscles dip and slump downward. He waved her off. "You can go back to work, Miss Hamilton."

*That's "doctor," not "miss."*

"Oh, and I saw you conversing with Boscher. Remember, he's not your boss. I am." Gellar's eye twitched.

She wanted to grab the gray sweatshirt off his desk and smack his sour face with it or maybe snap those fancy sunglasses in half. But she wouldn't. Instead, she seethed inside, silently berating him.

*Jealous? No doubt. Well, if Gellar had even an ounce of Boscher's humanity…I wouldn't be aching to wring his neck right now.* Unclasping her hands to keep herself from doing anything rash, Kerry stood. She paused as she stared at the Program Director. She wanted to say something snide, but she didn't know what. Instead, she gave him another nod. Her mother had always told her that silence is golden—or did that adage belong to someone else? Well, her mom had made it her own, and right now, it seemed like good advice. She needed to get out of trouble, not wade deeper into it.

Gellar returned the acknowledgment and then picked up a stack of papers on his desk and began sorting them. As he separated the pages, she turned away.

When she opened the door, a wave of fresh air greeted her. She waved to one of the interns and headed back through the now propped-open double doors and down to the dock. Halfway down the ramp, she keyed in the code that allowed her access and strode to the end of the gangplank, turning right and heading all the way down to Juliet's pen.

Sitting down on the dock, she placed her hand in the water and flicked her fingers.

The dolphin came gliding by for back rubs.

Kerry felt her body relax. Why could she could barely stand being around humans, for all the stress it caused, but when it came to mammals, she was at peace? *Was I a dolphin in a former life? God, I hope so.*

"I'll be back, my friend. We'll check your vitals and then feed you. You're going to enjoy my new creation. Salmon gelatin. Yum." Kerry stood.

The dolphin fluttered her left fin as if to say goodbye before swimming into the next pen to play with the juveniles while she waited. The mammals had the right idea. Play. Celebrate. Live.

If only she could master those basic choices, it would change her life.

—ww—

Standing in the shower of the locker room at the Marine Mammal base after a long day of work was blissful. Kerry wished the smell of rotten fish guts didn't turn her stomach. She rarely slipped into the waste vat. If she'd been paying better attention, and not thinking about the materials order for her new tank design or how odd a few of the dolphins were acting or the fact that Leaper hadn't called her once today… Damn, she was getting attached after only one kiss. "Turn off the brain. Steady on with the task at hand, lady," she said to herself. "Get the fish guts out of your hair and get dressed. Besides, he's just a guy—a guy with a tight ass and a lean, muscular body."

*Fudge! I'm too flipping eager. But how can I deny my primal nature? Isn't that the truth of who we all are? Food, clothing, shelter, mate…or at the very least, it would be nice to have a date.*

Adjusting the temperature setting to cold, she dosed herself with some humility and patience. She counted to fifty, felt more contrite, and turned off the tap. Goose bumps covered her skin, and her body shook as she stepped out of the shower stall.

Toweling herself dry, she was grateful for the warmth and promised herself that she would concentrate on her own well-being by treating herself to a nice dinner and a good book. Wasn't there a new Joanne Fluke book on top of her to-be-read stack? She loved murder mysteries, especially when the author made the heroine so smart and savvy.

Rummaging around in her gear bag, Kerry found a yellow short-sleeved dress with small white flowers.

She remembered adding it to the bag two months ago when she had taken a trip to Oahu. She'd never worn it. There hadn't been time. She'd worked day and night on an urgent case and had been so relieved when the dolphin survived that she'd slept for two days.

Today, this dress was the perfect thing to match her mood. *Let's celebrate me—a new me. Independent, someone who doesn't need a kiss from a handsome stud to tip my world off its axis.*

As she slipped the dress on, she knew the outfit wasn't practical for a night at home, but who cared? She was dressing to impress herself; this was a date with the most important lady in her life.

With that thought in mind, she stopped at the mirror and added a dash of pink lipstick. Now, that looked super. Fluffing her damp hair, she felt significantly better than when she'd entered the locker room.

She hoisted her gear bag onto her shoulder and left the compound with a bounce in her step. Exiting the main set of gates, it took her a few seconds to notice the man standing next to the edge of the building. As her mind registered that it was Leaper, dressed in a gorgeous fitted shirt and holding a stunning bouquet of roses, she stopped abruptly in front of him.

She was giddy with delight and found herself slightly breathless. "H-h-hi."

"Hi, yourself. Fancy some dinner?" he asked as he presented the flowers to her.

It was impossible not to beam at him. This was such a sweet gesture. Now she knew why he hadn't called all day. He'd wanted to surprise her. Well, that was certainly a very classy move.

"Yes," she replied. "I do."

———⁓———

Leaving the active base for the quiet streets was relaxing. Along the way, Kerry saw several people fishing from the bridge. They looked happy as they chatted.

Though, for a brief second, she could have sworn she saw Boscher, or maybe it was just someone with his size and shape wearing a Marine Mammal hoodie. The person handed a package to a very skinny man, who was fishing.

Wait, didn't Gellar have a hoodie just like that too?

*It's probably nothing important.*

The images sped by and she shrugged them off. What did it matter? Everyone should be able to enjoy a night like this, however it brought them joy.

Poehe's was lovely. This Coronado restaurant was designed for lovers, with its subdued lighting, wonderful smells of delicious dishes cooking in the open kitchen, and private seating. Kerry almost gasped nervously. She hoped she wasn't jumping the gun. How obvious was she being, about her interest in Leaper? She was definitely physically attracted to him, and she wanted to know him better on an emotional and mental level too. Kerry bit her lip. She didn't want to blow this opportunity, and yet if she persevered and overshared with a personal moment, and he stuck around, would it cut through the bullshit? *Why don't men come with instructions?*

"You look lovely," he murmured in her ear as they walked arm in arm.

She stopped herself from leaning into his touch. She wanted him to make the first big move tonight. That would ease her anxiety greatly. For now, she'd just go with the flow. "Thank you."

"I'm glad you were free this evening. I haven't been able to get you out of my mind all day." Leaper's voice had a sexy timbre, like a bass being plucked during a jazz solo. It sank low in your gut.

Frankly, Kerry was now grateful she had given into her whim to don the yellow dress and add a dash of lipstick. Living and working in bathing suits, sweats, or scrubs had pretty much dominated her appearance as of late, and it was nice to know she could clean up well enough to hold someone's attention.

It had been ages since she'd met anyone worthwhile. Most of the guys around the bases were meatheads looking for hanky-panky before they shipped out. Not that she was searching for a ring or even long-term commitment, but a decent chat and a strong connection would make her night. Then, if there was chemistry…well, she'd let nature take its course.

The hostess, Becky, led them to a table next to the water. It was a lovely view of Glorietta Bay.

Leaper pulled out her chair, and Kerry smiled at him as she sat down. *Good manners. You're scoring points, buddy.*

Becky filled their water glasses. "Your waiter is named Bill, and he'll be with you shortly. If you have any problems, please ask for me. Enjoy your evening."

"Thank you," said Leaper. He began cracking jokes and chatting nonstop about topical things, from food to the floral arrangement on the table. She found herself laughing easily. Though it was pleasant, she wasn't sure how to go deeper into any topic, but she craved an opportunity. "So, you work with marine mammals," he said. "Do you prefer one species over the others?"

"Dolphins," Kerry said without hesitation. "I adore them. I'm fascinated by their biology and their echolocation. The fact that they can navigate and identify so much with their unique system of clicks and echoes—it blows me away." Kerry grinned. "What about you? How long have you been a SEAL?"

"Over twenty years. I could retire, but I'm not sure what else I'd like to do with my life." Leaper drained his water glass. "So, what's your favorite color, music, or movie? Sometimes I think these answers tell us more about each other than anything else."

He really wanted to know her. This was it. The moment she'd hoped for. She knew what to say. She took a deep breath. "This might be an overshare, but it's... Well, here it goes. Otto Preminger's *Laura* is one of the most memorable movies I've ever seen. I watched it with my big sisters. It was the first time I was allowed to stay up late. We were dressed in our winter sleepwear: Lanz flannel nightgowns. Mine had red bows with bouquets of little blue flowers and a lace collar. All three of my older sisters had solid colors for their nighties, and I wanted so badly to be a big girl like them."

She tilted her head to the side, contemplating. "They were so much older back then—twelve, ten, and nine years older. At five years old, I felt so small next to them, and I wanted to be just like them. I wanted to date boys and wear pretty grown-up dresses with silky stockings. And yet when my sisters gave in to my begging and let me dress up, my mother balked. That night was the only exception, maybe because Mom didn't want to be alone. There was a storm outside, and she made popcorn with lots of sweet butter, and we all sat around watching this old black-and-white movie, *Laura*, about a supposed murder. I remember my mother saying that much of life was like the movie: perception, how you perceive an individual and an individual perceives you. Rarely do these two versions match, and knowing that early on is useful."

Her eyes filled with tears. She hastily wiped them away. "Sorry. It's just…that was the night my father was late coming home. Lightning filled the sky, and the thunder felt like it was beating directly on top of the house. I could imagine how big the waves were. Mom had this tight smile on her face when she shared how Father's boat partner, Warren Kant, had stayed home to take care of his wife, who was sick with the flu. My mom kept saying that Father was an excellent seaman and everything would be fine. I fell asleep before they came to the point in the movie where they found Laura alive. But, I do remember dreaming about my father and how he liked to read the newspaper to me and the feeling of safety and warmth it gave me."

She coughed softly. "In the morning, I learned Father had been killed. The Coast Guard wasn't sure if it was an accident or a murder. There was blood—only his— on the deck of the boat, but no other signs of foul play. To this day, no one ever explained how he died." She sighed sadly. "Things weren't the same around our house after that. My sisters didn't go out on dates any-more, and they stopped dressing me up or even playing with me. Everything…changed."

She gave Leaper a weak smile. "Maybe I shouldn't

list that as my favorite flick, but at the time I began watching *Laura*...Father was still alive, and I was a member of a happy family. Life was normal, and my childhood was untainted. After that, every experience was measured against this yardstick of definable moments from wonderful to horrible."

"Is that why you are so fascinated with sea life?" Leaper leaned forward, and Kerry could see she had his full attention. When was the last time a man truly listened to her? She couldn't remember. "Because of your father?"

"I think so. There are pictures of me in diapers, holding a fishing pole, or toddling around in the boat. I feel... more like myself when I'm in or around the water." Kerry hadn't meant to go that dark with her reminiscence, yet she was relieved Leaper could handle it. It said a lot about a man's staying power if she couldn't scare him off with that story. It screamed daddy issues, loss, grief, and pain. Some guys couldn't handle significant conversations, but Leaper seemed...different, and she liked his quirky manner. The way he had protected her in the ocean, returned the boat, and...well, tonight, he'd acted like a gentleman. The old-fashioned kind that held doors and pulled out chairs. Now, if she could just dig beneath the surface, what *would* she find there?

"I get it," Leaper said. "My old swim buddy, Declan, could spend hours in the water. I guess I feel at home whenever I'm in motion—being active, doing something. Doesn't matter where—whether it's the land, sea, or air, I just prefer adventure." His fingers toyed with the stem of his water glass. "I haven't learned to be still."

She nodded her head. "Me neither. That's something

we have in common: keep moving, and you keep in step with the changes of season and with life in general." Lifting the water glass to her lips, she took a long drink and then lowered it to the table. "What's your favorite movie?"

"*Ghostbusters*, the original one with Bill Murray. It always makes me laugh, and I appreciate laughter. I make it a point to laugh every day, or to bring a few guffaws to others." Leaper looked up at the approaching waiter. "Should we order?"

"Sure."

"Kerry, what's your pleasure?" he asked, pushing his menu toward the edge of the table where the waiter could easily retrieve it.

She placed her menu on top of his. She was not hungry for food. It seemed a shame to waste money on food when she'd probably spend the whole night toying with it. Leaper had passed her empathy test, and she wanted to experience several new things with him.

Her eyes traveled to his big hand and then up his strong arms, highlighted by the pale blue tailored shirt. Her gaze roved over that broad chest and lanky body, moving over his kissable neck to his lips, which liked to laugh. Who talked about laughter anymore? She loved to laugh and had already smiled more with him than she could remember doing in the past year. When she reached his eyes, his gaze locked with hers. He lifted an eyebrow questioningly at her.

Heat rose in her cheeks as she smiled broadly. "I'll have the, uh, seafood Cobb salad," she choked out. "No dressing. Just lemon on the side. Thank you." When she dared look at Leaper, he was folding his napkin.

"Same, and let's take that order to go."

Her eyes danced with mischievous delight as she held his sexy stare. The smile she gave him couldn't be mistaken. She was so pleased he'd taken the hint. As much as she relished sitting in this posh restaurant and chatting, all she wanted to do was strip him down and get to know him in the naughtiest sense possible.

~⁓~

In a guesthouse off First Street near the Naval Air Station North Island in Coronado, the sound of Barry White made the speakers pulse with a heady beat as eager hands caressed each other. The song "Your Sweetness Is My Weakness" filled the room.

"I like this song," Kerry sighed, cuddling closer. Leaper's rock-hard body was a solid wall of muscle, but he held her like something fragile or precious.

"Me too." His words were a caress of breath, his lips brushing against her cheek.

"Leaper, is that an entire wall of records?" she murmured.

"Yes. I take my music very seriously." He nuzzled her neck.

"Music is my vice too. I thought I had a huge collection, but this is… impressive." She could feel the outline of another impressive thing, lower down. "I like how music can strip you bare and sing directly to your soul. It can make a moment memorable or completely change the course of your day."

"Mmm-hmm." His fingers moved deftly over her clothing, heating her skin underneath.

*Who am I kidding? I want him.* And according to

evidence pressing against her, the feeling was mutual. She gave in to her need for skin-to-skin contact and tugged roughly at his clothing. Items flew in all directions, landing in disarray on the floor as Kerry and Leaper kissed passionately and wildly, falling sideways onto the bed.

They bounced lightly and stopped kissing long enough to laugh at themselves and their impatience to be naked and alone. It was a plus to have nowhere to rush off to.

Running her fingers along his pectoral muscles, Kerry's eyes held his. She could get lost in that gaze. She licked her lips, enjoying the taste of his mouth on her tongue.

His scent filled her nostrils. It was intoxicating. He smelled so good, and the appeal stroked something deep inside of her.

"God, you're so beautiful." His sexy voice stroked her senses.

"Thanks." Her hands traced the outline of his stomach muscles. "There's not an ounce of fat anywhere on you."

Leaper raised his eyebrows. "I beg to differ. Gich, my BUD/S instructor, told me I had quite a bit right up here." He pointed to his head. "He'd call me Bug Eyes, like the fat was pushing out of my brains. I think I preferred Lefty, but you can call me…tomorrow."

She frowned as she pulled his hand downward, showing him where to go. "Quit that. Stop joking. Just be here, with me."

He nodded. "Sorry. It's hard to stop a habit that's decades old. I'm the jokester. Uh, just so you know, I had a physical a month ago and I'm clean. I'm almost embarrassed to say it's been thirteen months since I was with someone." He cleared his throat. "And, for the record, please speak up. I most assuredly appreciate a woman who knows what she likes and, um, gives directions now and then."

"Good to know." *Well, that means he's open-minded. Good to hear.* "Also, I've got you beat. Two years for me, though I'm still on the pill. Too lazy to go off it. Is that embarrassing or cool?"

Leaper stroked her hair. "Cool, though you are *too* gorgeous to be single. It's hard to believe men aren't constantly knocking down your door."

"I don't make it easy for them. My work is my life," she said.

"I hear you. I have a similar circumstance, and yet here we are."

She tilted her head and looked up and down the length of him. A sculptor would have been in heaven if he could sculpt Leaper. His body was lean, hard muscle, and every ripple was a deep grove of strength. She smiled. No artist could capture the splendor of his erection, holding straight and defiant between those beefy, powerful legs. "Magnificent."

He stared at her with a quizzical expression. "Huh?"

"I'm trying to tell you that I think you're hot." She rolled her eyes. Pushing him onto his back, she said, "So I guess I'm just going to have to show you how desirable you are to me." Dragging her nails teasingly down his chest, she watched his muscles quiver with excitement.

His hands reached for her, and she pushed them away.

"My turn. You have to lie back and enjoy it. That's your mission."

"I can tough that out." He put his hands behind his head and watched her. He tracked her every movement. His attention was eagle-eye sharp, and she could only imagine what Leaper and his fine body were capable of if he didn't like what she was doing. But she had faith in her enthusiasm, even if her technique wasn't perfect.

His phone buzzed with a high-pitched tone. "Sorry. I need to get this." He grabbed the phone and listened. "Yeah, I'm on my way."

Her heart sank, and embarrassment brought splashes of red into her cheeks. How could she have been so wrong about him? She moved off the bed as Leaper quickly dressed. Why had she given in to her base urges so quickly? God, she wished she hadn't come back here.

His hands caught her to him. "Hey, don't do that. Don't pull away from me. I want to be here with you. Honestly. I have an emergency at the base with one of my trainees. If it weren't life and death…"

He kissed her. It was a deep, passionate, and heart-felt kiss that ignited her passion and soothed her bruised ego. "I understand. Go." As quickly as she spoke the words, she was staring at the empty room. "Now, that's how I really wanted to spend an evening." She gathered her clothes into her arms and went into the bathroom to dress.

———

Dropping his helmet next to his motorcycle, Leaper ran to the building and practically tore the door off its hinges in his rush to get inside. His mouth was drawn into a grim line as he made his way toward the other side of the room.

To his left, he could see three men talking in hushed tones, but he didn't even give them the time of day. He'd deal with them later.

"Lefton. Wait. You need to hear us out."

Giving them his fuck-you look for doing this exercise without him, he tugged open the far door and stepped through. His eyes adjusted quickly to the darkness as his nostrils flared at the smell. It was a mix of urine, sweat, shit, and fear. The room was filled with boxes, and there would be trainees in each one.

Spying Watson leaning against one of them and talking in hushed tones, Leaper crossed quickly to it. He nodded at the group leader to shove off, then opened the large wooden box, which, despite the air holes, released a series of noxious odors.

Leaper looked inside. "Trainee Parks. Let's talk."

"Ahh!" The trainee's screaming filled the room. His voice was hoarse, and it was obvious this had been happening for a while.

*Bastards!*

Leaper sat down on the edge of the box and said, "Parks, I'm here." When the screaming quieted, he reached down and took off the trainee's hood. "So, Lester, what's up?"

"I…I…I…" There were no words after that.

"Claustrophobic?"

"No, no, no." The trainee wrapped his arms around his knees and rocked in place. "Yes, yes, yes."

Leaper watched him. "This experience, the hood and the box… It brought something up for you…"

Lester Parks looked up, meeting his Instructor's eyes, and nodded.

"Leave your hood, get out of the box, and follow me," Leaper ordered.

Leaper didn't try to help him. The trainee had to show he could act under his own steam; otherwise, the next stop was medical care. Thank goodness Lester Parks was moving in the direction of the door. Leaper spared a glance at the rest of his group tucked into boxes. He met Watson's gaze, and the other man nodded. The unspoken command was "get your group out of their boxes."

What a fuckup! It was guaranteed that Leaper would check on all of them before he left this place and give whoever jumped the gun on this activity a piece of his mind.

Leaper opened a side door, and the two of them stepped outside. He pointed to several barrels. "Take a seat."

Standing in front of Parks, he asked, "What happened in there?"

"I had an uncle who locked me in my room when he left. There were no windows and it was small, and there was a fire. He got me out before the whole apartment building went up in flames. I don't remember him rescuing me, but I remember smelling smoke and coughing and..." Tears streamed down his face. "I can't do this. I'm ringing out. This isn't for me."

Leaper nodded. "C'mon. I'll walk with you." He escorted Parks to the BUD/S Quarterdeck where the trainee rang the bell. "Be proud of yourself for getting this far. Take the strength with you."

"Thank you, Instructor Lefton."

Two MPs appeared a few minutes later from inside the main building. They'd walk Parks back to his bunk, where he'd collect his belongings and be taken over to Naval Air Station North Island's temporary Enlisted Quarters until a new duty could be arranged.

Leaper shook his head. Would Parks have rung out of training regardless of tonight's craziness? Probably. Spec Ops wasn't for everyone. There had been "black classes"—when no trainee made it all the way through the process—before, and there would be again. He remembered seeing the specs for one recent class. Out of 171 trainees, only thirty-one had graduated.

Entering through the side door, Leaper opened up each of the boxes holding his trainees and pulled off their hoods. He pointed to a position along the wall. They seemed relieved to see him and scrambled out of the boxes and into position very quickly. So far, his guys looked okay. This night hadn't destroyed them.

Leaper pulled off the last hood. "Hey, Captain Kirk. What's up?"

"W-w-what?" The legacy trainee looked up at Leaper with wide eyes. There were tear streaks along his cheeks and long scratches along his arms. None of them looked deep enough to get medical involved, but the kid was eerily quiet. *How is it that I missed seeing this behavior or the evidence of it before? Is Quentin a cutter or into self-flagellation? None of that info is listed in his file. I need to keep an eye on this kid.* "Okay, Kirkland. Get on your feet and into line with the rest of your group."

The kid pulled down his sleeves and hastily wiped his eyes before joining the rest of the group. All of his trainees moved quickly and easily, which meant they hadn't been in the boxes very long. The expressions on their faces ranged from tired to relieved.

"Okay, release the rest of the trainees, even those not in your boat group, and form two lines. Don't worry about cleaning up this place. I know several men who are going to enjoy wiping piss and shit and puke out of boxes and off the floors. Now, move."

"Yes, Instructor."

Leaper left the room, closing the door quietly behind him. He silently studied the three SEAL Instructors— correction, two assigned SEAL Instructors and one future Rotation Instructor—as he approached them. He didn't need to ask whose idea it was to "go off book" with the trainees. He stalked toward the shortest man, a guy called Zoxt, until he was only a few inches from his face. "What gives you the right to step into our Instructor Rotation? I am doing everything in my power not to put you through that fucking wall. I know BUD/S CO Swifton wouldn't sign off on this. So tell me—why are you fucking with my men?" His voice was a low and deadly thunder. The switch had been flipped, and there was something at the back of his brain attempting to remind him that Zoxt was a brother, a SEAL. Yet there were bad apples in the bunch sometimes.

"Listen, man, this shit doesn't normally happen to me. I'm in the next rotation, and I wanted to get my feet wet. You know how it is." The idiot kept talking. There were no words of remorse or questions about the trainees' welfare. Every word was *me, me, me*! "I had the boys call you because it seemed serious. The trainee wouldn't stop screaming. Freaked me out."

Leaper's voice was like gravel on glass, low and

harsh. "You sick fuck! There's an order and protocol to how we train. The reason we do this particular exercise is to prepare the trainees for the worst of the worst, the unthinkable, which is being captured. But we're not at that aspect of training. I think you're a sadist. You were bored and wanted to feel like a god. That's not what we do here. We are training and testing these men in an attempt to save their lives. What? Do you think this is your personal playground?" Leaper's mind had clicked off the tiny voice squeaking out protests and warnings to play nice. "Do you think you're doing the trainees a favor by treating them as your own personal chew toys?"

Zoxt chortled. "Slow yourself, man. You're overreacting. Hell, I know it sure seems bad now, but it was good for a while. You should have seen them squirm. You know how it is. This is, you know, what it is."

"What I *know*"—Leaper stepped closer so that his breath was blowing onto Zoxt's face—"is that the trainees are not physically and mentally prepared to face it at this point. They don't understand themselves, let alone their link to the Team or their Teammates." It was like reasoning with a worm, trying to convince it not to crawl. "Why aren't you hearing me, that we work in a certain order? You've fucked with a very careful, tried, and safe plan. You are done, and not just for the night."

"Other people have tried to shoot me down, but I'm tough-skinned." Zoxt was attempting to look past Leaper to the other two SEALs in the room, as if looking for backup. If they were smart, and remembered that Leaper was a wild card, they wouldn't get involved.

"Look at me, Zoxt. Look. At. Me." Leaper's voice

was like ice, and if it had been a sword, it would have sliced Zoxt in two.

Reluctantly, the man met his gaze. "Feel like a big man, ordering me around because I'm shorter?"

"No, but my rank is higher, if you need that excuse. I'm telling you what to do so I don't physically twist your head off your neck. You need to read your SEAL Ethos. You need to get some basic fucking lessons in humanity, and I guarantee you that your next rotation will not be here. We do not allow egomaniacs near our training candidates. Now, tell me you're going to report to the CO of BUD/S first thing in the morning and apologize, before I lose my last thread of control."

Zoxt shrugged. "Yeah, man. Whatever. The exercise has lost its fun anyhow."

Something snapped in Leaper, and it was all he could do to watch the poor excuse for a man walk out of the building. Closing the distance to the other two men in the room, he barked out orders. "Get them fed and showered and tuck them into bed. *If* the trainees are *not* treated with kid gloves while you are doing this… I'm waking Swifton and marching you into his office tonight. Oh, and the three of you, have fun cleaning up the mess in that room. I look forward to seeing it sparkle with the cleaning power of bleach. I'll know if you bring in help."

The men stood there, eyeballing Leaper and clearly wondering if they dared to defy him. They were young, their first rotation as Instructors, with one tour under their belts and staffer positions on their resume. He didn't need diplomatic relations; he needed responsible people at this helm. As Leaper leaned in, their faces contorted into acknowledgment. They nodded and then sidestepped him, heading toward the box room.

Rage beat inside of Leaper's body. His anger wanted out. Practically every man who'd had boots on the ground and had been in significant action had some kind of beast. The longer he was in the field and the bloodier it was when he fought, the bigger and stronger the beast grew, until the feral and primal creature was only a breath away from action. But Leaper knew better than to unleash his creature. Controlling it gave him so much more focus and energy. Good decisions came out of calm. The training had taught him this fact—the very exercise those men had experienced tonight, in truth. But without the knowledge that comes from the second half of this all-important lesson, it was a useless and tortuous lesson.

It was a damn shame. The three men had cheated these trainees out of experiencing personal revelations and important combat lessons. There's power in learning from fear and pain, and learning how to move forward from emotion; as one masters the mental challenge, the skills and insights provide even more valuable information about the inner workings of an individual. Would the trainees get all of this info now, after this mess? He hoped so. But there was no doubt in his mind that all the instructors would be working double-time to give them their best.

Leaper rubbed his chin, doing something ordinary and calming and attempting to reign in his inner demon. His creature had a devilish side, and it was a ravenous and unforgiving beast. The things it had done, with his permission, were best not talked about. It was the side of him that could rip flesh open using only the strength in his arms and hands.

Stepping into the darkness, Leaper gritted his teeth and then pulled out his phone and texted Swifton. The CO was his best friend, and he needed to know about the load of crap that was walking into his office tomorrow morning. As he traded texts with Swifton, Leaper waited and watched from the sidelines…giving himself more time to cool down and to make sure his instructions were carried out to the letter.

---

The bombshell that waited for him at home was the most welcome sight of his life. Curled up in his lounger was Kerry. He was afraid he'd scared her off. This was the first time in a long time that a lady had surprised him, and he was grateful. Though it would have been a lot more welcoming if she were naked or wrapped in a towel…but maybe he was getting ahead of himself.

Kerry Hamilton was smart, sassy, and so damn sexy. She was definitely out of his league, and yet she hadn't given up on him. Wasn't it a good sign that she was still here?

His inner critter seemed to think so, because it rolled over and presented its belly in the presence of this luscious, gorgeous lady. God, he needed a little goodness in his life. She was like straight sunshine. His world had been one deployment after another until his mind felt like a gun constantly being cleaned and reloaded for the next interaction. Time to get off the merry-go-round for a while.

Giving into his urge, he sat down on the adjacent

lounger and leaned forward. His lips teased along the edge of her hand and arm.

"Leaper," she sighed. Her body was cramped, and she slowly unfolded herself from the small ball she'd curled into as her eyes opened. She blinked several times, realizing she'd fallen asleep in his lounger looking out over the water. He was smiling at her from the chair next to hers, and he looked delighted to see her. "Sorry, I must have been more tired than I realized." She pointed across the water. "I can see the Marine Mammal docks from here, and if you listen closely—"

"You can hear the sea lions." He pulled her into his arms. "I'm glad you stayed. Seeing you, after the hours I just spent… Well, it means a lot." He held her close, breathing in her scent.

"I take it that things didn't go well."

"No. It was screwed— Uh, I mean, things went sideways very quickly. Do you mind if we don't talk about it? Maybe we could pick up where we left off?"

She pursed her lips. "I've been thinking. Are we moving too fast? Should we slow down?"

His mouth descended on hers. All thoughts of protest melted away as his hands stripped the clothes slowly from her body. So much for willpower!

Leaper scooped her up in his arms and carried her into his bedroom. Placing her gently on the bed as if she were as light as a feather, he kneeled down before her. "Please…have me?" The words were spoken as a question, one that was vulnerable and heartfelt.

She couldn't stop her hand from caressing his cheek and chin. She moved closer and kissed his mouth with a tenderness that spoke volumes.

Leaper took off his clothes and lay down beside her. His hand stroked the skin of her cheeks and lips, and then he kissed her again. The delicate touch of his lips deepened to a passionate, raw emotion that was just underneath.

As he held her as if she were a fragile, precious beauty, her own needs were rising, ignited by his ministrations.

She tossed her hair over one shoulder and then cupped her breasts. Her thumbs and forefingers toyed with her nipples. She watched his pupils dilate. Slowly she lowered her chest toward his bare skin and then caressed his nipples with the erect tips of hers.

"Kerry, I never wanted to leave you. Not like that. You're so extraordinary, and from that first kiss, I knew I wanted to spend time with you—"

"Shush. No need to apologize. Let's just be... Let's connect." She kissed him and lay down on top of him.

His breath shuddered out as his hands grasped her bottom. "You're so radiant." His large hands covered her backside, gently squeezing them, and the heat from his palms was an erotic and titillating sensation.

She gyrated her hips in a tantalizingly slow rhythm against his.

He moaned with pleasure.

Kerry wasn't sure where this vixen was coming from, but this was one of her greatest fantasies coming true. She was in charge of all of this sexy muscle and heat. Thrilled by his response, she kissed her way down his belly. She teased her tongue over his skin and heard him moan with pleasure.

"Please..."

"Please what? Stop or don't stop?" she mumbled against his skin, never halting her sensual torture.

"Don't stop," he sighed. "You're so seductive. I'm totally at your mercy."

"That's right, funnyman. Who's laughing now?" She reached for his member and took him into her mouth. She felt him shudder against her tongue. Giving pleasure was, for her, one of the most intense and most personal, intimate experiences in the world.

His hands sought her, stroking her and teasing her and urging her onto the path of delight.

As his scent filled her senses, she enjoyed the heady feeling of being in control of his desire and adored the way he lost himself in the sensations. Wetness seeped from between her thighs.

He tumbled her onto her back. "May I?" His eyes were alight with fervor and passion, and she couldn't resist smiling. He growled low and lustfully.

Kerry loved it. She replied in turn, holding his head with both of her palms as she kissed him. "Yes. Yes. Yes." She punctuated each word with a more ravaging kiss until they were lost in the embrace.

Leaper's mouth was equal parts praise and plunder until she was the one begging for more.

Somewhere in the heat of their kisses, their bodies connected. His hips set an achingly slow rhythm, and she shifted her position, urging him to go faster.

Kerry's hips set the rhythm as she flew over the edge of pleasure. Her body pulsed with joy as each climax took her higher until she couldn't bear it any longer. Nothing could be greater than this moment. But as Leaper released his seed, flooding her body, he cried out her name in sheer delight. Her body drank deeply of him, and the glory of this experience gave her the biggest climax of her life. She joined his declaration as she shouted, "Leaper. Oh God. Yes!"

They clung to each other, unwilling to let go. Being joined so intimately was a rare moment; it was impossible to feel where he started and she ended. Oneness. It was the inspiration of poetry and art.

He sighed. *The bliss*.

Both of their bodies were covered with sweat as he rolled them onto their sides. Leaning his head against hers, he spoke first. "How…I mean, I'm…are *you* okay?" He was adorable.

Her lips pulled into a smile. She opened her mouth and licked at the beads of sweat on his skin. "Yes."

He shuddered against her. "Kerry."

"Hmm?"

"Can you say my name?"

She nodded her head. "Leaper," she sighed. "Leap-er." Tucking herself tight against him, she pulled a thick lock of hair against her cheek just in time to catch the tears streaming down her face.

She prayed he didn't feel or see them. This was the most intense physical joining of her life, a connection deeper than anything she'd felt before. Not that she'd had much experience, but it was enough to know that Leaper had shifted something significant inside of her. Her heart thumped loudly, and she placed their joined hands over her it.

"Mmm, that's great," he mumbled.

*God, this is… He is…so sexy. This is too much, too fast.*

Crossing her arm over her eyes, she wiped away the evidence of her emotion. It was too early to feel this way. Why was she an all-or-nothing kind of girl? She didn't sit on the fence—either she liked someone or she didn't. Damn. Maybe she shouldn't have slept with him so fast. Had her plan backfired on her? This wasn't just a fun romp or scratching an itch. She was already becoming invested.

*Right. You made your choice and you can't take it back. Unless you want to end it now.*

She was frustrated by the thought. She wanted more of him, and she couldn't let herself dwell on any negativity.

*I'll see what happens.* Uncertainty made her horribly uncomfortable, but what choice did she have? Living for the moment had to be enough.

---

Nighttime was a magical time in California. The moments before the sun kissed the ocean with brilliance were among the most profound and quiet on the planet.

Sure, sunsets and sunrises hit the top-ten list. They were stunning, with their hot colors, dark pinks and oranges, as they split the blue horizon and painted breathtaking pictures. But night was his preference, and it could be transporting. It was as if the sun melted into the ocean, sending out silence to ride the majestic waves in a rhythmic meter of peaceful lapping. It made one feel at peace, in tune with Mother Nature.

Was it any surprise that a few hours before sunrise, Leaper found Kerry standing at the window, gazing out at the ocean?

He slipped silently out of his bed and came up behind her. He wrapped his arms around her naked torso and kissed the side of her neck. "An early...good morning."

She hugged his arms. Her head nestled into the crook of his neck. "Yes, it is."

"I see you appreciate a fine view."

She nodded her head. "I certainly do."

"Do you like my home?"

"Very much. How can you afford it?"

He chuckled. "It's free, the guesthouse of a Frogman and his wife who like having me around to help now and then. They think of themselves as my substitute parents. I'll admit to having a soft spot for them. Besides, living on the water, right off First Street... well, it's pretty cool."

"What do your folks think about the Frogman and his wife? Are they jealous?"

"Don't know. I'm an orphan. Well, I was until the SEAL Team. Those guys are my brothers. Along with the couple in the big house up there, that's my entire family." He paused, and then he said, "Guess that's why I'm the funny guy."

"Making yourself likable to one and all." She touched his hand. "You don't have to do that with me. I want you to be comfortable."

"I am." He nuzzled her shoulder. "It feels...different with you."

"Yeah...for me too."

He squeezed her gently. "Hey, are you thinking about taking a swim? Maybe the kelp beds around the far side of Point Loma?"

Tilting her head back, she held his stare. "Are you a mind reader or something? I thought you might be tired."

"I don't sleep much." He grinned at her. "Who doesn't enjoy a good late-night swim? Though I'm sure you know how cold it is… Do you want to borrow a wetsuit? I think my swim buddy Declan's wife left a two-piece suit here a week ago. She's tall, but you could tuck it here and here." His hands mimicked slicking the wetsuit top around her waist.

She giggled and batted his hands away. "Stop that. I'm familiar with wetsuits. Let's go swim before I change my mind and take you back into bed."

"Huh, that idea has merit." He held up his hands and took several steps away from her naked form. The trees and shrubs blocked the neighbors' view. He knew she couldn't have any idea how hard it was not to sweep her into his arms and worship that gorgeous, supple, and curvy form right here and now. God, he could spend years learning her hills and valleys. Before he talked himself back into a horizontal cha-cha, he strode to the closet with his raging hard-on and dug through its contents. Strewing random items all over the floor—hats, boots, coats, gloves—he finally located what he was looking for on a pile of old clothes in the back.

"Got it." He grabbed the two-piece wetsuit, grateful his friends had left it here, and took it back to the bedroom. Laying them over his shoulders, he rushed into the bedroom and did his best Tarzan roar until she turned to look at him.

"Leaper!" She laughed as she took the wetsuit from him. Pausing, she swatted at his naked hip. "Very sexy. Me Jane."

He grinned, sat down on the bed, and watched her pull on a pair of panties and then cover her body with baby powder. She pulled on the pants and wiggled into the tight shirt. The suit was a little too long for her tiny frame and, in his opinion, pleasingly snug in all the right places. Thank God there would only be fish out there taking a gander at her.

She walked slowly to the full-length mirror. Rubbing the baby powder off the tip of her nose and her forehead, she nodded her head. "It will do."

Leaper donned his wetsuit, bottoms only. His body was desensitized to the water around here. Sure, it could get cold, but it was nothing like the Arctic. Somehow, that shit chilled even the nerves in his teeth. *Brrr*.

Closing the door behind them, he took her hand. It was tiny in his. He squeezed it gently and she squeezed back. His eyes caught hers, and he leaned down and kissed her.

Those tender lips, her sweet scent... It all had him wondering if they should make love again. But her smile as she pulled away from him and tugged him toward the water lured him like a Siren's call, urging him into the dark and dangerous ocean.

"Leaper," she called softly, like a whisper on the wind. The evening light silhouetted her body. Full darkness wasn't here yet. As the runes say, it was the Dagaz—a time in between the two forces, where the veil between life and death thins and anything is possible.

She pulled her hand from his and walked ahead of him.

His brow furrowed. He didn't want to let her go.

His hands snaked out and caught her. "Careful here. The rocks are sharp."

"I'll be okay," she answered.

"Allowing rocks to mangle her feet is no way to treat a lady." Leaper scooped Kerry up in his arms and carried her over the sharpest offenders. His feet were roughened by years of abuse, and nothing could penetrate his calluses. Hell, he could walk on a football field full of glass and never get cut.

"Oh!" Kerry exclaimed. "You make me feel like I weigh as much as leaf."

"You do." He smiled at her. "Maybe a little less. A quarter of a leaf."

As they reached the sandy bottom where it connected with the water, he slowly lowered her to the ground. Electric jolts zipped through his body as she rubbed against him. "Damn, you're beautiful," he said.

"You're pretty sexy too." She leaned her head against his chest and placed a kiss over his heart.

His body shuddered. He swallowed the strange lump in his throat. "Pretty, huh? I'd rather go for handsome, but if I must live with the 'pretty' label, I should probably do my hair before we swim."

Kerry pushed against his chest, and he pretended to topple over. He landed in the water with a splash, sending a wave of water her way.

They played for several moments, splashing each other and laughing, before he said, "Let's hop. I'm ready for some adventure."

She nodded her head and gave him her hand.

~~~

The boat was adorable, and so close to Leaper's home. Next to the guesthouse was a small shack with wide-open double doors displaying paddleboards, kayaks, paddles, and additional water gear. Below that was a stone wall separating the land from the stone-and-sand beach where Leaper's boat was tied to a large buoy. He could access it whenever he wanted.

Leaper helped her into a small four-person inflatable boat. He triggered the starboard and port running lights and then turned over the engine, and the boat took off. The wind picked up as they zipped past a line of carriers and ships. They went past the point of Naval Air Station North Island and the Point Loma Submarine Base and around the edge of the giant landmass until they reached the area where they could free drive and find the kelp beds.

Leaper cut the engine and tossed an anchor over the side of the boat. He set out a diving buoy and several lights before opening a small watertight chest and taking out two diving masks, snorkels, and sets of fins. After he handed her the necessary equipment, he strapped a knife to his leg, tying a bandana into one corner of the strap.

"What's that for?" Kerry asked, fingering the orange cloth with black diamonds on it. "Is it a fashion statement?"

"It's whatever I need it to be," he replied with a shrug. He gave her a mock salute and slid over the side, disappearing into the cold water.

——— ⁓⁓ ———

Lights from the buoy and boat filtered down, and Kerry could see the surface of waves above them. The eerie light permeated the kelp bed, catching the creatures inside unawares. A unique forest full of sea life skittered around, tickling her and making her giddy as they passed by. There was such a humbling feeling of grandeur in the ocean. You could know everything and nothing, but witness it all the same.

Her fingers touched the tall stalks of giant kelp— *Macrocystis pyrifera*—as they wavered in the ocean current like cornstalks in a strong breeze. She slid her fingers along part of their length. This stuff was harvested throughout the coast and used in a variety of products. It was so big here, she wondered if anyone knew about this prize cache. She certainly wasn't going to tell them.

Diving down, she felt along the rocky bottom and recognized bull kelp. A soupfin shark swam by, its tail touching her briefly. She wondered what lived beyond the light, what could sense or see her.

She shivered. Danger was never far.

Sea lions swam above her. She checked to make sure she wasn't going to step on a stingray, a common and often deadly occurrence. Relieved she was clear, she pushed off from the ocean floor. The sea lions were suddenly below her now, playing in and out of the numerous plants.

Her eyes sought Leaper. Where was that man? Just as suddenly as she started looking for him, there he was beside her, within arm's reach.

He was rolling around with the sea lions and obviously having as much fun as the pups. She wanted to warn him, tell them they often bit as part of their communication, but he dodged an avaricious mouth, proving he was already aware.

He spun and somersaulted, avoiding the twisting stalks. It was as if he understood the undulating pattern of the plants and mammals. His ability to relax in the water was so natural that she almost forgot she was holding her breath. How could he stay down here so long? His lungs must hold double what hers did. Probably all that SEAL training.

She started for the surface and kicked out with her foot

before her lungs burst, but an errant kelp plant caught her leg, winding itself tightly around it. She reached out and tried to untangle it, but her body was starved for air, and she could feel panic climbing up her spine.

*It's natural*, she told herself. *Calm down*.

Her body wouldn't obey. She struggled with the kelp, and it seemed to pull tighter with each tug.

A scream escaped her mouth, but hands on her foot forced her to look down.

It was Leaper. He cut the kelp from her foot and drew her to him. Kissing her, he forced air into her mouth. She drew it into her lungs, blowing the exhalation out her nose, and his arm held her to him as his powerful legs took them to the top.

They broke the surface. Cold batted her skin, and she gulped in fresh air.

"Slowly," he murmured. "Take it easy. I'm right here."

"I never panic. Don't…know why…I did." It took her several seconds before she calmed.

"Happens," Leaper said, watching her. Was he assessing her fitness? Nuts, had she screwed up? She wished she could read his mind.

"Is this the way things are going to be between us?"

"What?" His brow furrowed. He looked puzzled. "I don't understand."

She leaned her head against him and felt his warm hands rubbing the back of her neck. "You…having the upper hand."

His fingers found her chin and tipped her head back. "I'd say it's equal. We both have the power. I would never want to lessen who you are, only enhance it, and I'd hope you'd want the same for me."

That message combined with the massage took her breath away. "Where have you been all this time? I've lived here for years, and we're only finding each other now. Why?" She wound her arms around his neck and kissed him with every bit of passion in her soul. "Seems improbable."

His response was intense and immediate as he rolled onto his back, dragging her on top of him and heading for the RIB. "Improbable, but not impossible. Life unfolds as it does. A moment is forever and forever is nothing but a moment. My life doesn't have guarantees."

"I know, but I'll take a million nows."

"Agreed." Being the gentleman he was, he put his hand under her bum and lifted her upward and into the boat.

She couldn't stop a giggle from escaping a mouth. What woman didn't want to feel as if she weighed nothing, bouncing around with delight?

Leaper plopped himself next to her. He leaned over her and said, "How do you feel about public displays of affection?"

She poked her head over the sides of the boat. All clear. "Right now? So risky, naughty, and very, very sexy."

She'd risk it…for him.

---

He pulled in the buoy and turned off the spotlights. Grinning, Leaper turned his attention to Kerry. His eyes slid over her before he gently and methodically tugged and peeled her out of her two-piece wetsuit. When she was naked to the night air, he couldn't resist placing a kiss on the curve of her hips where they met her thighs.

The skin was so soft. He could have spent hours exploring there and the spot between those milky thighs. When she bucked wantonly against him, he hastily disrobed himself. The boat was rocking back and forth precariously by the time they were both naked.

Lying down next to her, he trailed his fingertips up her belly. "Hope no one comes a-knocking with the boat a-rocking."

"Dork!" she laughed as she pulled his head down toward her. She kissed him.

Passion surged through his body. The boat was really moving now, and water splashed inside, breaking the mood. "Uh, how about we switch places?"

"Happy to. I prefer being on top." She crawled from beneath his embrace. "Now you get the wet spot, literally."

"Ha-ha," he said as he lowered his butt into two inches of seawater. It was cold and a bit of a turnoff, but when she climbed on top of him, he couldn't stop himself ignoring the discomfort and focusing on the delight. His next sigh was one of pure spectator's delight. "Talk about a bed with a view."

Her luscious body loomed over him, and she was silhouetted by a glorious moon rising and an early sprinkling of a few stars. Hey, could he help it if he was a sucker for a gorgeous lady? Hell no!

*God, she's beautiful! Her confidence is a serious aphrodisiac.*

His hands steadied her hips as she lowered herself onto his erection. Kerry's body was slick and warm as it enveloped him. *This is…the definition of pure bliss*, he thought.

She shuddered as her body stretched to accommodate him fully, and then she arched her back and sighed. "I love the feeling of my body coming, even when it's a tiny cascade at the entrance."

Flexing his fingers, he said, "Let's see if I can turn those small moments into giant, breathtaking cries of delight."

She wiggled her hips, sending a wave of excitement through him.

He felt the boat rocking erratically, but her kisses were so enticing that he lost track of the movement.

She leaned down and caught his bottom lip between her teeth. "Game on." The kiss that followed her declaration was punctuated by some rather sexy groping and stroking, leading him to forget that they were in a rubber boat.

In an attempt to haul her down beside him, he moved suddenly and the boat rocked violently, abruptly dumping them both into the water.

Cold, salty ocean water was an unexpected wake-up call. Of course, the Pacific had no idea who it was dealing with.

Leaper and Kerry both came up laughing and sputtering. The boat had righted itself and was mere inches away. Thank God for the anchor, or they'd have been racing the current for their ride home.

Wiping drops off water off his face, Leaper drew this gorgeous, incredibly sexy woman into his embrace. His body was still primed and ready for love, and his chuckle was filled with innuendo. "Oh, how I love a challenge. A little cold water is not going to douse my excitement."

Kerry placed her arms around his neck and nuzzled

his shoulder. "Mine neither." Next, she wound her legs around his waist. "You know, I am a doctor. Maybe I should check your heart rate and stamina, SEAL man."

"Ar, ar, ar," he replied, mimicking a sea lion. His lips found hers as her body lowered onto his waiting shaft. He thrust his hips forward, and their bodies found a slow, sensual rhythm.

Shudders of intense pleasure raced through him. Hell, he could tread water for hours, days even. In his opinion, the toughest part was already out of the way— there was no disrobing of wet clothes in the ocean. Being naked and being alone… Well, that definitely had its advantages.

# Chapter 3

*WAITING FOR CHANGE CAN BE A DRAG, AND OFTENTIMES, IT mires one in expending energy on useless mental machinations*, thought Leaper. How he hated getting stuck in his own brain.

After the night he had, his life's work as a SEAL seemed somewhat…anticlimactic for the first time in his life. Here it was morning, and he was actually at work again, and surprisingly, he found he wasn't spending every waking minute thinking of his next step, or his Teammates, or the Teams in general.

*What's that about?* Instead, Dr. Kerry Hamilton, with all of her infectious joy and her tight, luscious body, was a lot more fascinating. His body tensed in a pleasant way, and his mouth formed a grim line. Was his life changing after such a brief time? Hell, it was too soon to know. It was just… His life felt like it was moving in slow motion.

He shifted inches to the left, just barely out of the way of a bird that had flown too close.

Standing on the beach in front of the Amphibious Base, he swatted at the overzealous bird who did a second fly-by. "I'm not prey, not a bug or a crab," he said to the bird, which landed two feet away and stared at him for several minutes before it gave up and flew off. "You cannot change your nature, and I suppose neither can I."

Leaper knew he was more of a predator in the food chain and humanity's hierarchy, yet he felt different around Kerry, as if another side of himself actually existed. Was that true? Could he have two parts to his nature, one as a warrior and another as something else? It was a strange thing to consider, and yet the hope felt good.

He shifted his weight and sighed. How he'd hated leaving Kerry again this morning, especially after their frolic in the water, but he had a duty to perform and he always showed up. His mind drifted toward home for one more quick thought: tucking Kerry into his warm king-size bed after their swim. Hours had passed, albeit too quickly, when his phone alarm buzzed, reminding him of his 5:00 a.m. date with a boat full of trainees, and now here he was.

Mmm, how he'd tucked the covers around her decadent body and watched her curl into a tight ball, without him by her side to keep her warm. It had taken all his strength to leave her and to not call in sick, but in truth he was worried about his boys. His gut told him that if he didn't stand with them through this test, most of them, if not all of them, were going to get over their heads and ring out.

Looking at them now, he could see how exhausted they were from their night in the boxes. None of them looked like they were prepared for their next fresh bit of hell, but they'd shown up, so Leaper wasn't going to disappoint them. Given an actual choice—without any possibility of losing their spot in training—every trainee would choose bed. *Well, at least, we all have that in common—except I wouldn't be sleeping.*

Leaper rocked back and forth. Adrenaline surged through him. Hell, he felt downright energized. Who needed sleep after marathon lovemaking?

One of the instructors on loan from the Army Rangers, Kendall Frock, sidled up to him with a smile on his tough-guy face. His worry lines were so shocked by the change of expression that it looked as if his face were about to crack his skull open. "Lefton, I heard you had a real-time rescue. A hot number: Curvy. Tiny. With a sweet bod—" The man's words stopped as he took in Leaper's face. "Uh, my bad."

Leaper nodded and signaled with his eyes that the man should go back to his boat of trainees. He wasn't in the mood to talk.

"Yeah, uh, catch you later for a beer. On me," said Frock as he hot-footed it back to his group. In truth, the Army guy was a good man, married to a Navy diver who had rescued the Ranger and signed on for a lifetime tour of marriage, love, and children. They'd have a chat sometime and smooth it over.

Leaper felt another presence nearby, and he crossed his arms over his chest. "Don't poke the bear."

"Poke. Poke. Poke." Declan Swifton—his swim buddy, best friend, brother, and current Commanding Officer of BUD/S—laughed. "Hell, Leaper, even I heard about the hottie in the drink. Here it is. I had to come all the way out here and give you some shit before you left, but it sounds like I might as well be talking to the wind."

"Yeah, yeah, up yours," said Leaper with a grin. He shook hands with Declan and then gestured at his friend's new leg. "Damn, that thing looks bionic. Probably has a better brain than you."

"It does," said Declan. "As long as it doesn't take over in bed with my wife, I'm good with that. So, you might not want to hear this, but I've seen you on a day after, and you usually look like someone kicked your ass." He put his arm around Leaper's shoulders and quietly said, "This one is different, isn't she?"

"Yeah. Maybe. I don't know." Leaper scrubbed his chin with his fingers, wishing he'd had time to shave. "Let's see how it goes."

Declan nodded. "When you're ready, we're here. You know how the wife feels about you. The sooner you can bring your new lady over, before the whole affair gets discovered by my better half, the better."

"Understood." Leaper lowered his voice. "Uh, how did it go with Zoxt?"

"Formal reprimand. Currently at Balboa talking to the shrinks about his actions, and I recommended his next duty station be helping our science groups in Antarctica. Let's see if the cold weather improves his Napoleon complex. Thanks for the text. I would not have been happy to be blindsided by that bullshit." Declan held Leaper's gaze for several seconds, and they both nodded.

The other instructors had the trainees shouting their names and dropping to the sand for fifty squats after each name. When everyone had sounded off, was accounted for, Leaper looked at Declan. "I better go drop my crew in the shark tank."

"Nice. Have fun." Declan winked.

Leaper smiled and then crossed the sand to his trainees. He spun one finger in the air. "Load up."

The trainees ran to the boat as if their lives depended

THE POWER OF A SEAL

on it. They hustled aboard, two of them holding the boat still in the waves for Leaper to climb aboard. It didn't bother him that he was already wet to the waist. He'd once been stuck in a hide with three men who all had food poisoning for six long days. A little moisture was a cake walk.

"Shove off," Leaper ordered.

Several of the men pushed off and jumped aboard. Then they all paddled, hauling ass until they were free of the current trying to drag them to shore and the hurdle of the underwater sandbars. It made for good muscle strengthening.

Leaper turned on the engine. He pointed the boat toward San Clemente Island.

Out of the corner of his eye, Leaper could see the men whispering among themselves. "What?"

Watson made his way to Leaper. "We wondered what was about to happen."

"You'll find out. You need to get used to the fact that every experience, like every operation, has factors of unpredictability." Leaper looked at Watson and gestured with his head, instructing the trainee to sit.

The men looked worried. Quite frankly, he didn't blame them. He wasn't doing the trainees any favors by spoon-feeding them ideology. They needed to sink or swim on their own merits—literally.

The closer they drew to San Clemente Island, the more clouds filled the sky until a marine layer hung over them like a giant gloomy shroud. Earlier, the night sky had been filled with brilliant, winking stars. How quickly the weather changed when you lived near the water.

Leaper knew these waters by heart, and he slowed

the boat to the perfect spot and cut the engine. He could hear the other boats doing the same around him, even if he couldn't see them clearly.

His words were succinct. "Over the side."

"What?" asked Watson. "But—"

"Take nothing with you. Go over the side or I will toss you in myself." Leaper wasn't fond of the stern tone, but he couldn't mollycoddle the recruits. If he said "Duck," he wanted them on the ground before he finished the word. It was about trust.

The men acted quickly. Several leaned backward and fell in, two of them lowered themselves over the side, and Watson flat out jumped. The splash was huge.

"What a fucking idiot," murmured Leaper, looking at the ripples in the water and knowing that boy might shortly regret his action.

Heads bobbed to the surface of the inky ocean. He could see their expressions—everything from cold to outright fear.

Next would come the real surprise.

Within minutes, shouts came from around them. Recruits from other boats were experiencing the glory of the San Clemente water's inhabitants.

Leaper spied the first dorsal fin. Super. It was a lemon shark. Oh, correction—four of them. Well, that was a piece of luck. He didn't particularly want to dive in and rescue anyone, though he knew the recruits would likely face worse in their time in the Navy, if they stayed on their current path.

Without taking his eyes from the trainees, Leaper reached into the utility box and felt around. He pulled out an extra Ka-Bar and strapped it onto his leg. Tying

THE POWER OF A SEAL

his signature bandana around the strap, he closed and secured the box and took up his previous position.

Several splashes close to the boat brought Leaper down to his knees. "Watson, don't hold on. You've got to let go."

"I…please…" Watson's jerky movements emphasized his panic. Damn, the boy didn't know what he was signaling to. Water has a way of telegraphing…

Leaper took a different approach. "Tell me, Sherlock, do you want to be a part of Special Operations?"

"Y-y-yes." Watson's teeth were chattering now, his whole body shaking.

"Good." Leaper leaned over the boat, tipping it toward the trainee. "Then chill out. Get this lesson now, or you aren't going to survive the night. So, I'll ask you one more time. Are you ringing the bell, or are you facing that damn fear?"

"I-I-I…"

The lemon sharks were moving off. That wasn't a good sign. The trainee's panicky movements were attracting other creatures. Big fish. Predatory ones.

He'd never live it down if one of his trainees got eaten on his watch. He sighed for a count of three, briefly loathing the actions he was about to take next. Not because he was afraid of whatever lived in the dark, deep ocean, but that water was fucking cold! Still, he'd walk through the very fires of hell to protect his men.

God bless the thick, cloudy marine layer. Leaper took off his shirt and shoes and slid soundlessly over the side of the boat. He treaded water beside the trainee. "Watson. Listen. Breathe with me. In and out."

Watson gulped in air. He couldn't seem to slow his

breathing. The frantic movements he had been making in the water only gained momentum.

*Fuck, I want these guys to succeed.*

"Look me in the eye and tell me you can't do this." Leaper knew it was too hard to ask a trainee to look him in the eye with this weather, but he was doing it anyway.

"Sir, I can't see a damn thing. What if—"

"What if! Who gives a shit about what-ifs? Shut off your damn panic button. You have other senses. Use them." Leaper lowered his voice, so only his guys could hear him. "Listen up, all of you. Sometimes life is scary. You don't know where danger is coming from.

"Instead of panicking, settle down. Be calm. Take in your surroundings. Hear the sound of your own breath and that of your Teammates. Find peace in the ebb and flow of the water around you. Allow yourself to act and react as needed. When you feel something come toward you, something you know in your gut is not friendly, face it. Respond accordingly and with the force necessary to defeat it.

"Sometimes you need to punch a shark in the nose to realize that fear isn't being paralyzed; it means acting with intention and awareness, with an appropriate amount of force and then you must reset yourself for the next event. Being calm, logical, and ready, with an instinctual ease, is the key to survival." That was the life lesson of the day. If these men got this message, they might survive some of the crap coming their way.

Leaper's crew seemed to take the words to heart as they stilled in the water. Leaper felt the change. Instead of using energy fighting themselves and their own fear, his boys were floating, relaxing. "Bravo Zulu," he said softly, which means the job is done well.

Moving methodically around each recruit, he reached out and touched them, moved them, or signaled to them until they were following him at an easy, effective pace. When they resumed their original position, everything had changed.

"Now you understand one of your most important weapons: inner calm. If you need to strike out, make sure your aim is true." With that, Leaper turned suddenly and slammed his fist into the nose of a tiger shark, landing an elbow in the eyeball as the creature turned away in startled, pained frustration.

"Awareness and inner calm are important states of mind, and crucial tools for survival. It protects you and your Teammates," Leaper said as he swam back to the boat and heaved himself up and over the side. He lay on the floor of the boat, catching his breath and staring up at the heavy marine layer.

He reached for his shirt, mopped his face with it, and pulled it over his head.

"I'm getting too fucking old to be teaching life lessons and wiping asses and pampering them with diapering," he murmured to himself before he hauled himself into a sitting position to resume watching over his flock. "Okay, men. Now, for the next step."

---

At the Marine Mammal base of Operations, Kerry's morning was busy with vet checks and preparation time in the feeding shack. She divided her ingredients into piles for a healthy, digestible dolphin meal. She sliced and diced and laid out the rest of her bounty. Then, stirring sheets of gelatin into hot water, she watched them melt. It was all rather soothing.

Her mind wandered for a few seconds. Last night with Leaper... Goodness, it had been mind-blowing. The sex, the companionship, the connection. He was seriously rocking her world.

Her fork pinged against the side of the tin as she stirred, reminding her to check on its progress.

The mixture was almost complete. Touching the side of the tin, she gauged the heat level and added a small amount of cool water before she added the fish.

It didn't bother her in the slightest that he'd had to leave in the middle of the night. Somehow it gave her time to think and be present in his space, like a free pass to explore and absorb without observation or comment.

Now all she had to do was sniff her arm and she could smell his soap on her skin. It was a nice reminder to carry through her day, especially for her libido. But it was work time, and she needed to concentrate on what was at hand. There were issues to be dealt with and mysteries to solve.

Kerry was concerned about one of the older dolphins. Merry, who was blind and deaf, was exhibiting signs of a kidney stone. If Kerry could find the right dietary mix, it could ease her symptoms.

Merry had spent most of her life as a member of the program, and she was one of the sweetest dolphins they had. Even without two of her primary senses, Merry still enjoyed activity and responded instantly to any vibrations in the water. She was often bouncing her favorite toys around her pen and was happy to have someone join her in a game.

Sometimes a kidney stone could become stuck, and Kerry and the workers would do their best to aid in its passing. Adding several drops of oil to the gelatin mixture as a home remedy, Kerry stirred everything one last time before placing it into the refrigerator. She added a label with Merry's name and the time it was supposed to be given.

She planned on taking two blood samples today too. Their laboratory wasn't picking up anything unusual, but Kerry had a strange feeling something was wrong, and she planned on sending the second sample out to another facility to see what they came up with. Her gut told her the dolphin was not well.

As she cleaned up her mess, Kerry heard someone walk up behind her. A voice spoke hurriedly. "I've got ten minutes before I have to give my next tour. With three interns out with the flu, I'm in charge today, and let me tell you, I've got stacks of paperwork to catch up on. Now, give! Share the details about that deliciously hot man who dropped you and Juliet off at the dock and returned the boat."

Kerry smiled secretively. She turned to her closest work friend, Emme Marie Stanley, and shook her head. "Can you be more specific? I couldn't possibly share everything in ten minutes."

"Seriously, Kerry!" Emme said exasperatedly as she towered one foot taller than her friend. "Get out more and we wouldn't have to do these info dumps. Being married means I'm living the single life through you, though it's more like *Friends* or *New Girl*."

"All right, I get it," said Kerry as she pulled her friend closer. "You have to promise that you won't tell anyone else."

Emme stomped her foot. "Nine minutes and counting. Spill!"

"I took Juliet out to give her a bit of exercise and to try out a new set of auditory signals. The wild dolphins, the ones I call the bad boys, came around and took Juliet out. I freaked and tried to follow her by diving into the water. The current caught me, and I ended up four miles from the boat. This…amazingly sexy man dove into the water and rescued me, and I can't stop thinking about him. He has so much personality. I find myself smiling, just 'cause." Kerry sat down on the nearby stool and sighed.

"Well, well, I'm upping your status to Rules of Engagement. I'm happy for you, my friend, but be careful you don't set yourself up. Don't let your hormones lead the chase instead of your heart and brain, unless all you want is a bit of bump and grind. Never anything wrong with that, as long as you're sexually safe."

"Ugh, Emme!" Heat rose in Kerry's cheeks. "I'm a grown woman. Can't you think about anything besides sex?"

Emme checked her watch. "Nope. So I still have a few minutes left. Tell me more."

"He's totally my type: athletic, tall, lean, and muscular. And his smile…man, it makes me grin too, just thinking about it." She arched her back. "Between us, I even pulled out my favorite lacy bra-and-panty set. It's in my bag." Waving a hand in front of her face, she added, "Your point is valid. I don't know a lot about him. Maybe I should slow things down and get to know him better. My libido is not thrilled with that idea, because his kisses could melt the polar ice caps."

"Kerry, just think how much better it will be with more information. You fall too quickly. You tend to think every man you date is a keeper, and in truth, they're pretty much all visitors, not 'the one.' Think about it. They check out the goods, take a sample, and keep on moving." Emme checked her watch. "Okay. I have to go. Time to give a tour. Stay strong, girlfriend."

"Wait, Emme—don't you think you're being a tiny bit cynical? Leaper didn't strike me as that kind of guy." Kerry felt in her gut that he was different. *But maybe I'm being biased. We barely know each other. I don't want to build him up in my mind, make him into a paragon, and then be disappointed when he falls from the pedestal.*

"With a name like Leaper, I'd imagine I'm dead-on with my description." Emme patted Kerry's back. "Hang in there, Kerry. I could be wrong." She paused at the door. "Oh, my brother is arriving from New York City today. Let me know if you want a hookup there."

"No, thanks." Kerry swallowed the knot of indecisiveness in her throat. "Have a great night."

"You too." Emme departed, the door banging closed behind her.

Kerry rushed her actions, and her mixture squirted her in the face. "Yuck." She wiped her face on her sleeve.

"Fine. I will take my time and go *somewhat* slower." Kerry's shoulders slumped. Nothing about that declaration was pleasing. Her gut churned with discontentment. "Well, hell, even my body is discouraged by the pace. But it can't be helped. This *is* for the best."

The rest of the day was uneventful, though she helped Special Funding Director Joshua Boscher carry four large boxes to his car. He was helping her seek money for several pet projects, and Kerry was happy to lend him a hand.

"What do you have in here, rocks?" she teased.

"Something like that," Boscher acknowledged with a slight smile as he secured the boxes in his vehicle. "We should be hearing about several of your applications any day now." He slammed the lid of his trunk shut. "Just remember, if you need help with anything else, please don't hesitate to ask me."

"Thanks. I appreciate the help you gave me on the forms and proposals," Kerry said. "I hope the Department of Defense and several of the sponsors think my projects are worthwhile."

"They'd be fools not to," said Boscher grimly. "Have a good evening, Dr. Hamilton."

"You too." Kerry watched the Director drive off, wondering what Boscher did in his free time. He was a friendly guy, but he never spent time with any of the staff outside of work. Maybe he had a family or other pastimes. Checking her watch, Kerry realized Leaper would be on the way to her condo soon. She had to hustle.

She turned the engine over, pulled out of her parking spot, and headed home.

~~~

Her condo was very close to water and Kellogg Beach in Point Loma. It made the commute to work short and sweet. Kerry cued Aretha Franklin's "(You Make Me

Feel Like) A Natural Woman" and stripped off her clothes. She danced around as she straightened the clutter and put on clean sheets. Then she took a shower and shaved her legs, knowing it would increase her odds of having sex. Who was she kidding—Leaper would probably have sex with her even if her body was stinky and her legs were stubbly.

*Ugh! Gross.*

She picked out a casual outfit with an adorable bra-and-panty set for underneath and got dressed, deliberately adding only a touch of mascara and lipstick. She pursed her lips as she looked in the mirror. "That works. Now to finish straightening up."

Fetching a handful of disinfectant wipes, she hurriedly dusted the apartment. Heavens, she wished she had more time to straighten before Leaper arrived. There were piles and stacks of research material everywhere, which suggested a strategy. Most of what she'd learned in life came from books. Could she approach a relationship in the same way? Research it and plan it, plot out a perfect romance in a step-by-step manner? This was a new concept to consider.

Kerry walked over to the bookcase and reviewed the contents. She had an entire shelf of how-to books on romance, and the rest of it overflowed with murder mysteries. Pulling several books from the pile, including Walsh's *VAK Self-Audit* and Chapman's *The Five Love Languages*, Kerry sat down on the floor and paged through them.

"Okay, show me your power."

Her phone buzzed and she looked at the emails. Two different groups—one in Japan and another in Russia—were offering her a job as the director of their marine programs. She couldn't take either one. Leaving the creatures here… It was too much. She loved her dolphins, and now there was Leaper to think of. Wasn't that how things happened? One minute life is quiet and normal, and then it explodes with activity.

The books fell from her lap. She picked them up and resettled herself to peruse them. *Right*, she thought. *No more work. Think about relationships and men.*

———

To quote Kerry's mother—and most etiquette books—"Punctuality is a sign of good manners." Leaper arrived precisely at the scheduled time, and she had to smile. Wasn't it a sign that he was excited to see her too?

"Welcome to my condo." It was a tiny one bedroom, but it fit her perfectly. There was a small patio out back, and being on the ground floor was wonderfully convenient when it was grocery day. "How was your day?"

"Better than I anticipated. My trainees survived." Leaper pulled her into his arms and kissed her. "Yours?"

"Busy. Good." She appreciated that he was a man of his word. Keeping someone waiting was so disrespectful. She stepped back from him, knowing that if she stayed in his arms for too long, she wouldn't have the willpower to stick to her plan.

He looked at her, puzzled. She could feel his eyes tracking her to the small open kitchen. "Kerry, I like your place. Water theme. Nice. There have to be at least a hundred shades of blue and white in here." Spying the stack of books on the floor, he zeroed in on the only messy spot in her home: her beloved bookcase.

"Can I get you anything? Would you like something to drink?" she asked, standing next to the open refrigerator.

"Water?"

Kerry took two bottles out and closed the refrigerator. She walked back over to him and handed him a bottle. "What do you think of my treasures?"

He raised an eyebrow. "Should I be concerned that you're going to murder me in my sleep or rope me into a relationship?"

"Hopefully neither. I believe in free choice." Kerry tucked an errant strand of hair behind her ear. "But…I do think we should get to know each other better. I, uh, have some questions I'd like to ask you."

"And you think these questions, undoubtedly from these books, will make the difference," he said skeptically.

"It's a place to start." She touched his arm. "For me. Please, Leaper."

"Sure." Leaper nodded and sat down on the far end of the couch. It gave him an unobstructed view of the front door. It didn't surprise her that Leaper was one of those men who didn't want to be ambushed from behind. She'd remember that next time they ate out.

"Hit it. I'm ready."

"Thanks," she said. The stress that had twisted her gut into knots all day long began to slowly dissipate.

Sitting down next to him, she kicked off her shoes and tucked her legs beneath her, shifting her body so she was facing him. She picked up a pencil and a pad of paper with her notes from all of her research and smiled.

—⁓—

What a bust! She knew she'd been too clinical in her approach to relationships and romance. Sure, she learned a few things, but there was nothing natural about the information process. She could have been taking a history before his prostate exam…not that she was *that* kind of doctor.

"What's the verdict? Do you know me better now?" Surprisingly, Leaper wasn't mocking her. He'd answered her questions honestly and without hesitation. Now she just felt like a jerk for pushing the idea.

"Uh, somewhat." She sighed. Frustration at herself filled her tone with drawn-out, elongated answers. "Communication, you respond optimally with the application or use of physical contact versus abstract or direct direction. You like quality time rather than any material possessions or gifts, and you prefer auditory stimulation versus visual and that's most likely how you learn best." Kerry tapped her pencil against the pad of paper she'd been taking notes on.

"Makes sense. We use physical touch when we're drawing closer to a target and use hand signals quick a bit. And, I've always preferred phone sex to, ah, porn, but I'll amend those words if the striptease was someone special and happening in person." Leaper's mouth drew in a slow grin. "Just thought you should know, full disclosure and all."

She could feel the blush start in her toes and practically burst out of her cheeks. The heat was intense and spreading to several wonderful places.

He winked, then tapped his head and pointed at her.

"Right, my turn to sum you up. Let's see, you prefer acts of service to positive reinforcement or affirmation, and quality time to gifts. I'm guessing you're a visual learner, not auditory. By the look on your face, I believe I nailed those observations."

She couldn't fault him. He'd gotten to the heart of it.

"Do you want to try out my auditory learning?" He inched closer. "Talk dirty to me."

She laughed. Placing the pencil and pad on the coffee table, she held up her hand to stop his movement. Then, thinking better of it, she crawled toward him. In her best sultry tone, she said, "I'm hungry. Are you?"

"Always," he replied, reaching for her. "Wait, do you mean for food?"

"Yes." She laughed. "Let's get out of here and go get something to eat." She kissed his chin and nose and then nuzzled his cheek. "Feed me."

"Uh-huh." He stood up and offered her a helping hand. She took it, and he pulled her to her feet.

He held her close for several seconds. It was so warm, seductive, and flat-out nice.

His voice ruffled the hair near her ear as he spoke. "Just for the record, this was interesting, but I'd like to state that I believe the best way to get to know someone is to spend time together. Throw in a few unexpected experiences, and that's a pretty thorough learning curve."

She nodded her head. "You're right." Her body leaned into his. The impact was delicate, tender, and oh, so pleasant. Oh hell, why did she want to forget her promise to herself and just hop back on the proverbial horse?

*Look at him! Of course I want him.* Shaking herself with the renewed determination, she stepped away from this tall, sexy man and walked to the door. "Ahem. On that note, are you coming?"

"Not yet, but I hope to later." His smirk said it all.

She couldn't stop a giggle from escaping her lips.

*Me too.*

---

Dinner was unconventional, sitting on the dock next to Juliet's pen and eating Chinese food. The night sky was overcast as the marine layer slowly moved in, and only a few stars shone through now and then.

Was it odd hanging out on the dock? Kerry wasn't sure, as she spent most of her time with the dolphins. Time took on a different meaning, as if being with them was the only way she knew her life had purpose. Days off were filled with menial tasks such as laundry, cleaning, food shopping, and paying bills. Only when she was back here did her existence seem real, as if time started ticking again.

Studying the man next to her, she wondered if Leaper fell into the same pitfall with his work. Right now, his body was turned toward her, but his head was facing the mouth of the bay and the ocean beyond.

She tapped his foot. "Sometimes you get this faraway look. Then, suddenly, it's gone and you're back to normal."

"Sorry. It's a habit of mine. I get lost in my thoughts."

"No, it's fine. I guess I wish you'd talk to me about what's on your mind," Kerry urged. "Communication is the cornerstone to…well, everything in life."

---

*Yes. Not very subtle, Kerry*, Leaper thought. He could appreciate her gentle approach. He did want her to know him better. He could only imagine how tender and kind she was with the marine mammals. She must be an amazing vet. Even now, her comment was sympathetic, implying she was attempting to be nonintrusive, and yet he knew she wanted more information. Hell, he'd known that someday a woman would ask it of him, but he hadn't perfected an answer as to why he zoned out. It was one of the questions he just never wanted to answer, along with how many people he killed and why he continued putting himself in the line of fire.

He gave her a half smile. "It's nothing." His avoidance was instinctive. "Dark night, huh? Wish we could see the North Star."

"Leaper, trust me. Please." Her earnestness was compelling. "I want to know you."

*No, you don't*, he thought. *It will change everything. How you see me. How we interact. Why would you want to kiss a man—make love to a man—who leads this life?*

Her fingers sought his, settling on top and squeezing. Those slim digits were so tiny and deft. Was she fragile or strong? Could he share his life? Would this be too much to ask of her?

He shook his head, attempting to dislodge the question. If she knew... "There are places you shouldn't go. Think of it as a Do Not Enter sign. Once that door opens, it can't be closed. There are things you can't unknow."

"I get it. Truly, I do. But how am I supposed to understand or connect with the real you if you won't let me in? Am I supposed to settle for the good-time guy that's sitting here, making goo-goo eyes and being superficial or take the bold step and dig deeper?" She was quiet for several seconds. "I like you, Leaper. A lot. When I'm with you, I feel connected in a way I never have been before…not with a human being, let alone a man."

"So you reserve your heart for marine mammals."

Tears filled her eyes. She quickly wiped them away, but they continued to fall. "Yes. I…I don't trust easily. Locking my heart from others keeps me safe. There's a lot I haven't shared."

He pulled her into his arms and held her as she wept. It was over quickly. As he moved his head so he could see her face, he said, "You're not a crier, are you?"

"No. What gives it away?" She mopped her face on his T-shirt, leaving wet spots behind.

"The burst of emotion." He touched his lips to hers in a gentle caress. "I'm glad you don't milk it. I don't handle bullshit and manipulation well."

"I don't either." She cleared her throat. "I'm very straightforward, and I promise I will share my inner self," she murmured against his lips, "if you do so with me."

"Damn." His mouth tightened. "I'm not an angel. They don't call SEALs when there's something gentle that needs to happen. We're… We do things that need to be done, eliminating threats and completing tasks even when the odds are stacked against us. We use bullets, knives, bombs, lasers…"

"You're evading, Leaper. Rip the tape off faster. Say whatever you need to say."

He took a long deep breath and exhaled slowly. "I'll give you an example." He folded his hands together, needing them to be occupied while he visited this memory. "I was on my third tour. We were watching a group of insurgents who were targeting a large family who were American sympathizers. We knew these bad guys were slowly killing this family one member at a time. We wanted this family to stay safe, so when we received Intel that the bad guys were going to strike the family and wipe them all out, my Team was sent up to 'handle' the situation."

He licked his lips. "It was the driest time of the year. Being in the desert was like sitting in a clay oven and baking from the outside in. We'd broken into four groups—two-man Teams—and my Teammate was shadowing me. A group of nomads was approaching, and there wasn't much cover. We'd found a decent place that had some shade from rocks, and when we dug into the sand and earth. Thankfully, it was slightly moist. We were probably better off than most of the Team, so we radioed in and hid for the day. It took a while for the nomads to arrive, and when they did, we identified several insurgents. These terrorists stopped about fifty feet away. They took a shovel to a spot that revealed a hidden well-spring, where they replenished their water supply and refreshed themselves.

"I speak Arabic, French, Spanish, Latin, and Russian, and I could understand them as they spoke about the group of boys with them and how they were going to pick the oldest for his 'act of glory.' Fuck, how it filled my blood with ice! When they called him up, they joked around with him. His name was Gabir, and he was twelve. They told him that when the bomb exploded, the charge would go forward, and only the infidels would die. Because he was a child, his life would be spared from the explosion. This is the reason they design a charge like this, and all Gabir had to do was to walk to this place and stand very still, facing a compound. They told Gabir he would live in glory for his action. And this boy"—Leaper's face contorted momentarily, and then his features smoothed as he regained control—"agreed readily and laughed along with the men, oblivious of the fact he was going to die. Gabir smiled broadly, a big toothy grin. He stood tall as they strapped explosives to his chest, and he just didn't care.

"The whole night, Gabir strutted around proudly as they celebrated and offered praises. The other boys looked on with such outright anger and envy. The men sang songs about death and its glory, about how little life here on earth meant. They said living was nothing—absolutely zero! Their power was, and is, their willingness to embrace death when others are so scared of it." His knuckles were white from squeezing his hands together. "There were forty insurgents. We didn't have enough ammo to take them all on, and we couldn't make contact with the rest of the Team, without someone hearing either our movements or our words. As the boy was finally sent on his way and the elder keepers lay down to sleep, and the rest of the group settled down too, we could finally ease out of our hiding place. We crept forward and dispatched as many as we could with our Ka-Bars, and then we followed the boy. We needed to stop him before he reached his goal. We ran like our pants were on fire until he was in our sight.

"We were closer than I thought, and I must have made a noise, because Gabir spun on me. He looked at me sharply, and his lips twitched at the corners as if to say 'Gotcha.' But before he could pull the trigger, my Teammate had thrown his knife and speared Gabir's kidney. It forced an inhalation, making it impossible for the boy to cry out. I was at a different angle, but I had thrown my knife too—it was a reflex—and it entered Gabir's heart up to the hilt. This small boy crumpled." Leaper's voice wavered, full of emotion. "The bomb did not go off. I rushed forward and dismantled the explosives." He cleared his throat and his voice steadied. "I took what I could and deposited it in my pack so they couldn't use it on another kid. Then I lifted Gabir into my arms, and my Teammate and I took him back to the rendezvous point to meet up with the Team."

Leaper looked off into the darkness. His mouth was dry, and he could nearly smell the dirt and sand—the scent had filled his nostrils. It suffocated him even now, scratching at his throat and clogging his senses. He coughed hard to stop the sensation. "I buried that boy and said a prayer, one that I haven't repeated since I was his age."

Leaper's eyes sought Kerry's. "A child raised on dogma that values death above life. How do I handle that? His life was ending that night, whether it was by our hands, the elder keepers, or his own. The politicians in his country blame the lack of religious education and children's gullibility, but whether that's true or not doesn't change the reality. I live with events, hundreds of moments, like snapshots in time. Even though I do this to protect my country and the people in it…it scars me."

He exhaled slowly. "Despite what the media wants you to believe, soldiers and sailors, we are human beings. I'll never be this perfect, untouched guy who can walk through life without taking all this…along with me." He rubbed his temple with his thumbs. "The moral code where one life is sacrificed to save the many… It often haunts me."

If Leaper could have cried, he would have. Had emotion been buried too long to provide any release? He knew the answer and wasn't sure why he'd even posed the question. Christ, perhaps this was his punishment, his burden to bear.

Kerry. Sweet, beautiful lady.

Her face was equal parts horror and sympathy, and her body was turned partially away. As she turned fully in his direction, he let out a breath he didn't realize he'd been holding. He truly cared what she thought of him. So how could he bring his issues to her? Why would he want to burden this amazing woman?

Was he making a mistake, revealing his darkest inner self? He'd never done this before, and for the first time in years, he felt…vulnerable.

"Leaper…" She lifted her hand slowly, bringing it toward his face. He didn't know what to expect, but he didn't flinch away. Instead, he waited, prepared to take whatever justice she felt he deserved. Her fingertips were cool and gentle as they stroked his brow and his cheeks.

"I will never know how vast or deep your pain is… I just want you to know that I will bear it with you. I accept it. I accept *you*. Please don't be afraid of it or me. I'm stronger than I look." Her intense hug emphasized the strength of her message. "Our country demands sacrifices from us. Sometimes that sacrifice is a piece of our sanity and our souls." Her smile was understanding as she leaned forward and kissed him. "Just know that none of us are without…regrets."

Leaper was shocked. Was this woman real? Was it possible she could truly accept him? If he believed it, this would change everything he thought to be true about relationships.

His eyes searched hers. He could see the sincerity of her emotion. Nodding his head, he accepted her message. It was powerful, and he felt as though an actual weight had lifted from him.

Leaper unclenched his hands. He stretched his fingers and then reached for her. Gently, he lifted her onto his lap.

She pushed her hair away from her face and snuggled closer.

His emotions surged as he leaned in and kissed her. The intensity of passion shocked him, and she matched it with her own. For long moments they kissed, a heated exchange.

"Thank you," he murmured against her lips. "You have no idea what this means to me."

Her hands cupped his face. "I do. Truly, I do." The kiss was unbridled, and each of them explored the other as they sought more intimate contact.

Remembering they were on a dock, he broke the contact. "Is there someplace more private we can go?"

She nodded. "Follow me."

Cold air tickled his skin as Kerry left his lap. They made quick work of gathering their dinner remains and disposing of them, and then they walked along the dock.

"How do you act so…jovial?" she asked, looking up at him.

"It's a choice. If I lived in the pit of my pain, I would have ended things a long time ago. I feel I owe it to my brethren who have departed this earth to enjoy my time on this planet. I'd want them to do it in my memory, so I do it in memory of them. I live like every day is my last on earth. One of my goals in life is to feel as much pleasure as possible before I die," Leaper said candidly.

"Does that mean…you want to have sex with every woman in sight?"

He laughed. "Hell no! It means…I want to laugh. I want to be happy, and whoever I'm spending time with, *they* have to want to be happy too." He scratched his chin. "I'm not being superficial. As I mentioned, I've seen a lot of fucked-up things. I've watched brothers die, seen limbs blown off, and I've watched people in relationships struggle with the most trivial things, because they've forgotten the point of life: to be happy. I want that for myself, and for whoever I'm with."

"Whomever," she replied.

"That too."

"I like it. I agree." She sat down and stretched out on the dock, legs extended, and propped her hand under head. "It's hard to find someone who's living a life that brings them pleasure. Believe it or not, there are people working in the Marine Mammal Program who complain. This job…it's, like, the coolest experience in the world. There are so many fascinating programs, I just don't know how someone could be unhappy. Maybe that's judgmental. I know some people start out wanting to enjoy a job and it isn't a good fit, but I've found a few individuals who are absolutely determined to be miserable no matter what. In my opinion, happiness starts inside of you and branches outward to the rest of your life." She sighed. "Oh God, I warned you that I'm an eternal optimist."

He edged closer to her until their mouths were only a foot apart. "Can I kiss the optimist? I, uh, kinda like that about you."

"Yes," she said breathlessly.

Their lips met in a tender kiss. Water sloshed over the side of the dock and wet their shoes, and they drew apart. Leaper looked in the direction of the water. Kerry laughed.

The dolphin below them was taking advantage of the rub rope, which was exactly what it sounded like. Leaper nodded. "Looks like a good idea. Is there anywhere here we can…uh…?"

"Do you mean away from the cameras and the guards? If so, the answer is yes." She took his hand and led him farther along another set of docks. She continued to the far side of a metal building, where a cramped office was tucked behind a small alcove. There was no ceiling, and the stars twinkled above.

He shut the door behind them. "Will the guards come in here?"

"As long as we're quiet, they'll stay out. The nickname is the sex shack, not that I've ever, uh…"

"Really? Well, virgin territory, then." A wicked grin settled on his lips. "Challenge accepted." His arms pulled her in tight. "You seem tense. Are you okay?"

"Claustrophobia. Let's distract me from the sensation of the small space."

"I'm good at that. Close your eyes and imagine yourself in a wide open field. The smell of lavender and wild flowers fills the air, and the brush of long weeds tickles your bare legs and feet…"

She smiled. "You've had some experience with this."

"Uh-huh. Auditory guy, remember," he murmured, kissing her cheek, her chin, and her neck, working his way downward. "It's a vastly difference experience distracting you than a Teammate dealing with a panic attack before an airplane jump."

"Heavens, I can only imagine." Her breath quickened as his hands played down her back to cup her backside.

---

His touch was magic, Kerry thought as he caressed down the length of her body and then back up again. Dang, Leaper was going to make her scream with delight. His hot trails of passion made her feel weak in the knees. She completely forgot about the small shack and her claustrophobia. Instead, the sensations his fingers—those long, tapered, and tantalizingly strong digits—left behind made her breath catch. As his hands played over her clothing, his mouth wooed her, inviting her tongue to come out and play.

Kerry obliged, allowing the kiss to deepen. Her arms wound around his neck as his hands tenderly opened her blouse and made their way up to her bra. He expertly released the clasp, and her breasts filled his large hands. He toyed with the nipples, bringing gasps of pleasure to her lips.

When her back arched and she felt the first climax slide through her body, he broke the kiss. "May I?" he whispered.

She nodded, watching as his head disappeared, kissing a path over skin and clothing all the way down to between her legs. His ardent kisses left damp patches before he gently pulled the leggings off and buried his head in her most private of parts.

"Yes," she sighed.

Leaper's tongue lapped at her clit, sending waves of intensity zipping through her until her breaths released in small, short pants. Again and again her body clenched as he brought her to the peak of pleasure, only to begin again before the sensation faded. Just when she thought she couldn't take it anymore, he replaced his mouth with a very agreeable alternative that filled her sheath to capacity.

She kissed the sweetness from his lips, drinking the delightful tang of her own essence, and then kissed along his ears and neck as he set a fast pace. Twin climaxes hit them, and they cried out together in satisfaction.

Sea lions and dolphins joined in, a cacophony of sound that echoed around them.

"I guess they approve," said Leaper.

"Ha-ha," said Kerry. "Oh, shit. Do you hear footsteps?"

A knock sounded on the door. "Uh, hello. Is everything okay in there?" asked a security guard from the other side of the thin wooden barrier.

Kerry gulped, horrified and embarrassed. She covered her eyes with her hand. "Yes, Fred. We're fine. We'll be out in a minute."

"Is the, uh, gentleman okay too? Sorry, I need to ask that."

"Hell no! She just drained the life out of me," replied Leaper.

"Leaper, shush!" Kerry hissed.

"No rush, ma'am," Fred said. "I understand." With that, his footsteps retreated down the dock.

Kerry liked that he helped her dress first and then took care of his own needs. When she was fully clothed, she swatted at him.

He was buckling his belt, but he dodged. Damn those SEAL reflexes.

"I have to work with these people, you know," Kerry said. "Good Lord, what will my friend Emme say?"

Leaper caught her around the waist and pulled her to him. "Bring it on, baby. I love it when you get fiery."

"In for a penny…" She sighed and rolled her eyes before giving into his antics. This was Leaper in all his glory, and she couldn't stop wondering what was coming next.

# Chapter 4

*UNDERSTANDING THE SOUL IS LIKE PINNING DOWN A BUOYANT spirit. You have to catch it, crush it, and analyze it before you understand it—but then it's changed forever.* Leaper mused on that heavy thought as he hummed the lyrics of Thirty Seconds to Mars's "Kings and Queens." The music cried of the ache in the soul, as if Jared Leto had looked into Leaper's darkness and pulled out his struggles. Leaper agreed with the song. Even in full light, something lingered, a shadow that fell on the soul until the light could burn it away.

His head rocked in time to the song. Leaper knew he saw the world differently than most people, but the fact that musicians touched him so deeply made him aware of the kindred spirits out there. Was Kerry going to be one of those? He hoped so. If he was wrong about her, well, he'd already revealed too much, too soon. Why had he done that? Wasn't it easier to stay closed off and apart from the world? That was his usual modus operandi.

His movements slowed until he was completely still, mired the quicksand of his worry. Sitting cross-legged on a wooden desk, where one wrong move meant a splinter in the ass, was a prickly experience. Leaper closed his eyes and attempted to meditate, approach it from a Zen prospective. "Oh-um."

Offices in the BUD/S building reminded him of grade school—the stale smell of the air, the chalk dust.

Windows were few and high off the ground so you couldn't look in or out, and the walls were long and heavily fortified. Most of the doors opened to a large, flat playground area called the First Phase Grinder. There were outlines on the ground of Churchill fins for recruits to put their feet on when they lined up. A giant creature from the black lagoon, a gift from a graduating BUD/S class, watched as the trainees went through their calisthenics, were given announcements, etc. The area wouldn't have been complete without the iconic brass bell, where trainees had the choice to ring-out and leave the program.

Leaper knew his share of guys who'd stayed in training and plenty who had rung out. But there were always reasons for a choice, two sides to every coin. He had always been glad he stayed, even on his worst days. Unfortunately, today he was feeling like he was about to get shot in the ass, and he didn't know how to avoid it. "Ohh-uuummm."

"Hell's bells, what crap has landed on my desk?" boomed a deep baritone voice.

Leaper cracked an eyelid and focused on the figure in the doorway. The man's body was so large, it filled the frame, blocking any sunlight from creeping through. "My god, you are mammoth! Have you gained weight?" Leaper asked Declan.

"Bastard!" Declan closed the distance in three strides and clapped his hand on the back of Leaper's neck. Instead of clamping down and bestowing a nerve-cramping block, he pulled Leaper in for a hug. From beneath the massive arms, Leaper said, "Your pits smell like moldy cheese."

A chuckle turned into a guffaw as Declan sat down in the old, squeaky chair about a foot from the desk. "Your breath smells like a camel's ass."

"You should know." Leaper uncrossed his legs and hopped off the desk. He located another chair and pulled it closer. "How's the leg?" He pointed to Declan's prosthesis. "You're limping more than usual."

"Yeah, I might need another surgery, but it's good enough for now. It gets me from here to there." Declan tapped his temple. "How's your skull? Still whacked?"

Hanging his head, Leaper clasped his hands together and hunched his shoulders. "Perhaps. I don't know. The doctors think so, and oddly enough, today I actually want to talk. Do you have time?"

Pursing his lips, Declan got up from the squeaky chair, walked to the door, and closed it. He sat again. "You have my full attention. What's going on?"

"Gabir." The name alone spoke volumes. Declan had backed him up that day. He was Leaper's best friend, swim buddy, and Teammate, and the experience tormented them both. It had been years before they could handle talking about it. Leaper wasn't sure why he had told Kerry about it, but it couldn't be taken back. He scrubbed his nails over his scalp and then clasped his hands together again. "I talked about it. Other than you, I've never…"

"I've shared with Maura. I told her about a year ago." Declan shrugged. "I was holding our daughter in my arms, and the waterworks started. I couldn't turn them off. Maura came in and found the two of us wailing, and she wrapped her arms us and starting singing 'Amazing Grace.' Both of us stopped and listened. After we put the baby in her cradle, I took her outside and told her about Gabir. She didn't judge me or offer advice. She just listened." Wiping a hand over his face, he added, "Must be a special soul, this lady, if you shared."

"She…isn't the reason I'm here."

Declan leaned forward. "What is?"

"Declan, I'm worried that I'm broken." Leaper slapped his palms on his chest. "Something's snapped in here. I know I've avoided talking to you about my last Op, but everything is hitting me, and I can't seem to fix it. You know me, I'm the man with a plan. I'll follow the steps or wing it and get to my destination. But where am I going? My whole life has been the Team, and I don't know who or what I am outside of it."

"Yeah, I've been there, buddy. One option, you could contact the Honor Foundation and apply to their program. It's an amazing foundation. I've heard it makes the transition for Spec Ops Warriors significantly easier." Declan frowned. "But I think you'd have to be close to retiring to do that. I'm considering applying when I'm ready." He lifted his hand and then dropped it. "You're not retiring, are you?"

"I don't know. It might be time for some kind of change," sighed Leaper. "But you, my friend, are never retiring. They'll have to physically remove you from the base to get you to go."

Declan chuckled. "So true."

"Honestly, I don't think I'm ready to leave the Navy. I just don't know if I can continue to do all of this, or even if I'm…functioning right." Leaper shrugged.

"Nah, I don't buy that 'functioning' bit. Sure, you pissed off a lot of docs and most of the officers in the area, but what the fuck is new about that?" Declan swatted Leaper's arm affectionately. "Frankly, if you weren't questioning yourself, I might be worried. If you were up to your old antics—lacing the coffee with scotch bonnets, replacing the cushions with pudding in all the commanders' chairs, or taking the Spec Ops dogs on a group serenade to SOCOM... Shit, I'm glad those days are behind you, Leaper." He tapped his fingers together. "What makes you think your mind is on the fritz?"

"For years, we had this theory that we can get through everything, as long as we keep moving. A month dealing with doctors had me so twisted that by the time I was free of 'em, I almost bungee jumped from the Coronado Bridge. And yet a few of their questions penetrated my protective wall. Sometimes when my emotion gets too raw, hitting that dark place, a new piece of the puzzle shows itself." Leaper let out a long, slow breath. "It fucking scares me. What it reveals is too...vulnerable. I fucking hate that feeling. I know that I cannot keep moving forever. I will have to stop, and then what? Who am I?"

"Join the club. That's being human. Looking for purpose. Just because we do extraordinary and dangerous things doesn't mean we don't have normal concerns or feelings. We eat, sleep, fuck, make love, laugh, pay bills, fight with our mates, try not to mess up our kids, and keep a roof over everyone's heads at the same time we keep the family happy. That's not easy stuff." Declan leaned back in his chair, and the poor piece of furniture creaked as if it were going to split in half. "We've been through the grinder together, and we've come out the other side. You know, my swim buddy, that leaves scars. You watched me break down when the shit hit the fan with my leg, and it still rubs me raw that it was the mental aspect—not the physical challenge—that busted my balls as I literally found my footing. At the time, I had this image of what I needed to look like and who I needed to be, and that expectation nearly killed. Took me a long time to let go and accept myself. Emotions can tie you up in knots. The main thing to remember is, there's no such thing as good or bad when it comes to life and memories. Judgment doesn't change any facts; it only hangs a target on your survival and longevity. The best course of action is to just watch, listen, and let the world teach you. Take what works and let go of what doesn't. Then fucking forgive, and release the negative energy."

"Pretty Zen of you. I was practicing my best pose on your desk there." Leaper gave Declan a sheepish smile. "So you're saying this is…useful. That I should see what my brain says—if it gives me info I need to share—and then do so. Take a life lesson if that works, or let it go." Leaper bobbed his head. "Brother, I'm still a fuckup. Why did you want me here, at BUD/S?"

"Leaper, I've been requesting your presence for the past two years. I wouldn't do that if I didn't think you have a lot more to say and a ton more to teach these trainees. Hell, most of these guys never make it out of the gate. We've had several black classes, and it's tough to not see anyone make it to graduation. You give trainees the lesson along with the challenge, and they get something more out of it. I wish more of the instructors did. Besides, I lose instructors every rotation, because some guys go on massive power trips and squash spirits instead of teaching important techniques. I know you.

You are *very* different, my friend. You have no ego."
Declan patted Leaper's back and left his hand there for
several seconds. "You've got a ton of crazy, that's for
sure, but in my book that's a good thing. Trust your
instincts, Lefty. Your ideas are worthwhile."

Leaper slapped away Declan's hand playfully. "Aw,
stop wooing me. I'm here, aren't I?"

"I knew life with you was going to be unusual when
you admitted how much you loved music, and that if
you had to choose a theme song it would be the Pixies'
'Where Is My Mind?'" Declan threw his hands up in the
air. "Who defines himself by a song, let alone *that* song?
Damn, Leaper."

"Well, hell, everyone should soundtrack their life."

"Grapevine says you've got more than *some*one in
your life. I'll say it again: How am I the last to know
the details? Tall? Fat? Short? Skinny? Blond? Brunette?
Red? Or a combination of all of the above?" Declan
frowned. "Thought I was your best friend, man, your
brother, and this is how you treat me. I don't know shit."

Leaper rolled his eyes. "Yeah, yeah, cry me a bucket
of tears while I pull out my teeny violin and play along."
He touched Declan lightly on the arm. "Fuck off, Dec.
I'm just getting to know her."

"Maura will have a few things to say if you don't
bring her by the house soon. You think *I'm* being a
drama queen? She freaks when she's the last to know
about something happening in your life. Don't make her
hunt down your lady and drag her to the house." Declan
sniffed loudly, goofing around. "You'd think you were
her kid or something, the way she dotes on you. Might
make a certain husband jealous now and then."

"Uh-huh. Well, man, when you've got it—" Declan tackled Leaper then, cutting him off. Swim buddy love! The chairs fell over with loud bangs, and the wooden desktop cracked as they landed on it. They hit the floor with twin thuds, mock wrestling each other. Not that this was a standard approach, but this was private and they were closer than brothers. Besides, the odds were fairly even. Declan was big and strong, but Leaper was wiry and fast. Best case scenario: both of them would be going home with bruises. Worst case: one or both of them would be stopping at medical for touch-ups before they returned to work. It got the blood pumping and the men laughing, and after a few minutes they called it a draw.

———∿∿———

People stood in long lines, waiting to eat. The diner in Point Loma was rocking fifties music cranked at maximum volume. The waitstaff was dressed in costumes to match the tunes, and the smell of burgers grilling and bacon frying made Leaper's nostrils flare. He scanned the room looking for Kerry, who had chosen a booth in the dimly lit room against the far wall.

Sliding in next to her, he whispered. "The food is great here, especially the milk shakes, but it's murder on my ears. Mind if we ditch for somewhere else?"

She nodded and placed her menu back on the table. He stood and offered his hand.

Kerry took it. As he pulled to her feet, he could see the edge of her white bra strap. If only they could substitute food time for another type of delight and satisfaction. Kerry must have read his mind, because she raised her eyebrows and brushed her chest against his before they maneuvered out of the tight enclosure. Together, they slipped out the back door and walked hand in hand.

"Let's take my car," she said.

"Sure." Leaper didn't feel like weaving around traffic right now, so it was probably for the best that they took her vehicle. He sighed softly. Though he appreciated Declan's advice about not allowing images of what he should be to get in the way of what he actually was, adding a lady to the mix was another matter entirely. Shouldn't he put his own life in order before getting closer to Kerry? There was all this minutia, this indefinable gobbledygook, that clogged his brain. God, maybe he was being silly. Kerry was awesome, and this was the first time he'd really connected with a lady like this.

Damn, this was frustrating. Why couldn't someone just give him some answers?

"In-N-Out?" Kerry suggested. Her bright smile calmed him. Even the sound of her voice was soothing. He didn't want to lose her, or whatever this was. "I like their grilled onions on burgers. Don't ask me why, but I have a craving." She unlocked the car, got behind the wheel, and buckled up.

"Sounds good." He took the passenger's seat. His mind was spinning in ten different directions as he buckled his seat belt. If only he could turn off his thoughts for a little while. He just wanted to enjoy this moment with Kerry.

Tracking the landscape as they headed for the burger joint, he listened to her talk. His mind drifted back to something one of the doctors had said. "Regardless of when you want to deal with issues, they will arise and demand attention. Keep that in mind as you walk out of here without taking advantage of all we have to offer. The backlash could be significant."

*Significant how?* he wondered.

Kerry's voice cut into his thoughts. Had she just asked him a question? He looked back at her blankly with no idea of what to say.

"Okay," she said, "what's going on? I've been babbling for almost twenty minutes." She tapped her fingers on the steering wheel. "It's too late to get out of line. We're boxed in. Since we're up next, what do you want to eat and drink?"

"Chocolate shake, fries with cheese, and lettuce wrap double-double plain with grilled onions." Leaper rattled off his favorite items. This was a rare day, as he usually ate seafood, salads, and drank protein drinks and tons of lemon water, but when in Rome, or in this case, San Diego... Even the name In-N-Out usually made him smile, though his mood was subdued today.

"Please let me treat you." Leaper handed her a twenty, watching her pause and wrestle with the thought. If she was thinking that hard, he'd already fucked up somehow.

She pulled through the line, paid using his money, gave him the change, and collected the food. Finally, she parked in front of a large billboard ad.

He watched her grab a small tub of disinfectant wipes from the backseat. She used one and gave one to him. When their hands were clean, she distributed the food and drink. They ate silently for several minutes.

Kerry broke the silence. "It's okay if you don't feel the same way about me, but I like you. The stuff we've shared means something to me. I don't want to lose that."

"Me neither," Leaper agreed, holding her gaze. *Please don't give up on me.*

"Let me take a guess. You're feeling vulnerable." She nodded. "I can see I hit the right answer. Fine. I get it. But don't take your frustration out on me because you overshared. I shared my feelings too, and that was as honestly given as your sharing." She folded up her napkin, spilling part of her burger.

He caught it and handed it back to her.

She placed it on a clean napkin. "Thank you."

"Kerry, I'm sorry. I'm not good at this stuff." Leaper put his hands on her free one, stilling her action of toying with the napkin edge.

"Who is? Dating stuff is mostly weird in the beginning, or so I'm told."

He gave her a half grin. "You're just…too easy to talk to, and I like…spending time with you."

"So are you, for the record. You're easy to chat with, to kiss, and to overall be with." She opened the napkin, holding her burger and stuffed cheesy french fries between the meat patties. "I still can't believe we went nighttime free diving and made love in a boat. Who does that?"

"Me. I love the water. And I know you do too. We…click on a lot of levels. I need to let go of my… trepidation."

Kerry sighed. "Would it make you feel better if I bared my soul right now?"

Leaper nodded. "Maybe. But I have to tell you," he said, cracking a smile, "I can appreciate the fact you called me on my shit. You've got guts, lady. Any SEAL worth his salt admires fortitude in a lady." Nailing the truth, being able to spot an evasion and get to the absolute heart of a matter, was a personality trait most good SEALs had. This lady had serious gusto, and he admired it, even if he was massively uncomfortable being on the hot seat.

"Goodness. Thanks." Kerry narrowed her gaze. "Guess I must really like you. Okay. Here it goes. This is a seriously embarrassing moment. When I was ten years old, I was stacked. I went from flat chested to a B cup practically overnight, and I was very self-conscious. So I did silly things like wear oversize T-shirts and walk with my shoulders hunched. The next year, my cup size changed to a D, and I was horrified, so I tried to strap my boobs down with an Ace bandage. During gym class, it came unwound, and I was hugely embarrassed. The boy I sort of liked made a grab for my breasts in front of everyone. I knew he was trying to be a big man, but I was furious. I decked him. From that day forward, they called me Combat Kerry."

"Good for you for decking him," said Leaper with an appreciative grin. "Standing up for yourself is important."

"Right! I thought so too." Her smile was huge. "I got suspended, but it was worth it. From then on, though, I never wore big shirts or hunched my shoulders. I never hid anything about my body or personality. People either liked me or they didn't."

"I never would have guessed you were ever awkward or shy. Confidence is a useful tool and a serious turn-on," said Leaper as he toasted her with his milk shake. He took a long sip and then placed it back in the cup holder. "Okay. My turn. If you decide anything I say isn't up your alley, I'm cool with us shaking hands and parting. Well, hell, that's not true. I'll be hurt, but I'd get it. Okay?"

She nodded. "Just rip the bandage off."

"To be up front, so that you know what you're signing up for…I'm dealing with some issues from combat." He said the words quickly.

"You say that like you're plunging a knife into your gut. Is it that hard to talk about?" Kerry asked, concern written all over her face.

"No. Maybe. Yes." Leaper held up both of his palms in a "stop" gesture. "I've never really talked about *any* of this stuff. So everything is…new territory. I chat with my best bud, Declan, but…not in depth." He dropped his hands into his lap. "I'm not sure when or how it will come up, but if I need space, I'm going to ask for it, and I won't justify it. If I want to talk, I hope you'll want to be there and listen."

"Got it. What are the rules of engagement? How do you want me to proceed? Do you want me to prod you or just see where things go?" The thoughtfulness and respect in her tone caught him unaware. Kerry was a gentle soul.

"The second. Listening is good."

"Thanks for the heads-up. Consider me briefed." Lifting the burger to her mouth, she took a giant bite. Grease dribbled down her chin.

Turning his attention to his own burger, Leaper lifted the lettuce wrap and chowed down. Sometimes, the succulent taste of good quality food really hit the spot. If it didn't, well, the grease would help it all slide through in the end. He laughed at his unspoken joke as the atmosphere in the car lightened.

His phone beeped. He turned off the alarm. "Listen, I have to bounce. My boys are facing live fire today, and I have to settle some logistics before I put them through the ringer this evening. Can we meet tomorrow?"

"Maybe. I have to work tomorrow, but I'm off the day after. You're welcome to come by whenever. If I'm not home, I'm running errands, which usually don't take long." She leaned toward him. "I don't have a lot of patience for shopping."

"Bummer. I love the stuff," he teased.

She threw her hands in the air. "Good to know. Then you are the designated shopper in this couple."

"I like the sound of that." Strangely, Leaper did. He was part of a couple. There were still a lot of unknowns that cluttered his emotions with doubt, but Kerry's being open, their being a couple…he enjoyed those facts tremendously.

⌁⌁⌁

At the Advance Training Center, or ATC, down the Silver Strand from the Amphibious Base, Leaper and the other instructors were working on several scenarios for the live-fire exercise. Leaper had been leaning against the wall of the bunker for twenty minutes while the other instructors tossed around suggestions. Finally, his legs began to protest—he needed to move or sit down and take the weight off—so he spoke up. "If I'm understanding the point of this exercise, the recruits will experience live fire for the first time, and we are gauging their reactions. That's it. They don't need to move from point A to point B or perform any show-pony tricks."

All eyes turned to him.

"What? I'm just summarizing." Leaper shrugged his shoulders. "I read the announcement about the live-fire exercise on the Advanced Training Center base being conducted between 0900 and 1000, as well as boat maneuvers pending in late afternoon. Hard to believe they actually provide a URL for complaining. I wonder if it encourages or discourages feedback."

"Lefton's got a point. Not about the complaints, but about the action." It was Zebbison "Zebbi" Davids, an instructor on loan from the British Forces. "The laddies need to do something. We have our guys play a mock capture-the-flag game for their first live-fire action." Zebbi was a stocky man with a tense tone, a wonderful sense of humor, and even better taste in whiskey. Not that Leaper was drinking these days, but once upon a time, he'd joined Zebbi's crew for a few nights out.

"I'm with Zebbi," Leaper agreed. "If the men have something to do—moving from this room to that room and carrying their packs with them, or tending to a mock-wounded man—it will force them to engage a different part of the brain. Task action versus fear reaction." Leaper smiled at Zebbi, who nodded his head. "At least they'd get something out of it, rather than just being scared shitless."

The rest of the instructors considered those thoughts for a few more minutes.

Leaper pointed at his watch. "Time is running out. We have less than twenty minutes to prep now. Decide. I'll be standing next to the ice plant." He walked out of the old, shot-up bunker and stood near the large outcrop of ice plant.

A few minutes later a hand slapped his back. "We

won, mate." Zebbi's lips clenched a half-chewed cigar. It was unlit, and Leaper knew how much the man wanted to light it, but there was a regulation about that on this new base too. Leaper sighed. When did the world develop so many rules? Would they be telling him how to use his cock next? In his mind, that was a lady's choice—the right lady, of course.

*Brrrupt!*

"They decided. Let's fetch the lads." Zebbi said loudly over the sound of gunfire as he led the way around the hill toward the waiting recruits. The men looked nervous. Leaper didn't blame them in the least. There was no doubt in his mind that this would be a crazy time.

———

A signal alarm sounded, announcing to the residential area beyond that this was a live-fire exercise. The chaotic sounds of gunfire commenced.

Next to him, Zebbi made the sign of the cross.

"Do an extra one for my guys, would you?" Leaper added.

Zebbi did.

Standing on top of the hill overlooking the bunkers, Leaper watched the recruits in Building A scatter to the corners like cockroaches when the lights are turned on. In this case, though, there were bullets piercing the walls, and the trainees had to carry out several tasks before making their way to Building C. The test would not be over until all the trainees had gathered together. If anyone got left behind, Leaper knew the instructors would keep going…at least until the ammunition was gone.

Leaper located his men. This was good—they were sticking together, helping each other out. Several of the guys hyperventilated, and Watson was belly-crawling to another Team leader, trying to get him out. Without Parks, his group was at five members. It meant the usual two by two couldn't happen. They would have to figure out a new buddy system. He hoped his trainees had hashed out that concept already.

"Use your knife to open the box," whispered Leaper under his breath—not that his guys would hear him from this distance. He was sort of praying for a Yoda-Skywalker moment.

Watson smashed the box with his fist and removed a document from inside. He put it inside a watertight envelope and pushed it down his shirt. Then he crawled back to his crew.

Captain Kirk was hyperventilating, and the rest of the group was calming him down. They were losing valuable time, but they were acting as a one unit, and that was reassuring.

The other Teams were already working their way toward the door. Leaper's group was the last in Building A.

"They've got a lot of work to do. I'd be surprised if the last two hugging the wall don't ring out by the end of day," said Zebbi.

"Room for improvement can be a good thing," said Leaper as he walked with Zebbi along the ridge to watch the recruits in the next building. "I noticed that your trainees split off and lost their buddy and their group. I'll take my guys over yours any day."

"We'll see." Zebbi's jaw tensed, and he looked at

Leaper for several seconds before he headed down the hill.

Leaper paused. The vantage point was useful. It gave perspective…about his guys and where they were in the training process compared to the other groups. Oddly enough, it also provided a little insight on life. Beyond the buildings, the waves crashed on the shore. A few SEALs with the day off were surfing with kites, sliding up and over the waves. The current picked up as the waves drew the water ever closer to the shore. The ocean was alight with white peaks and sun-ray diamonds sparkling on the surface.

Outlook. Positioning. Point of view. If only the recruits could see today as any other day, without the fear and panic. Then they'd have clarity of mind and perform better. Wasn't that a hard truth about war—that somewhere in the world the sun was shining, people were laughing, and the world was continuing to spin on its axis, even if you were ass deep in blood, horror, and bullets? One man bleeds as another celebrates. Life was a double-edged sword, and what you saw and experienced depended on whether you were facing the razor edge of that blade.

———

After the live-fire scorching, everyone headed back the Amphibious Base. At BUD/S, Leaper stood outside the door with the other instructors. They were observing their trainees.

Leaper scratched his neck as he leaned against the wall outside the classroom where the men sat. He could hear their comments, even in their hushed tones. He didn't recognize the voices, but they were definitely worked up. It was enlightening to listen to them.

"That was nothing like TV or the movies."

"Yeah, it wasn't cool or exciting."

"It was disorienting. I was frozen. I couldn't stop thinking about where the shots were coming from and how to deal with it."

"I kept thinking, 'Fuck! I'm fucking this up!' My dad did this, and he'd want me to handle it differently than I did, but all I'm doing is fucking panicking."

"It smelled hot. Does anyone else think that?"

"I didn't know it would be like that...the air full of plaster, dust, gunpowder, and just freaking *intense*."

"I'm embarrassed. I wouldn't be surprised if they decided to roll the whole class back."

"Don't fucking say that! You don't want to give them any fucking suggestions. Got it!"

Leaper knew someone had to get into that classroom and ease these trainees back into the game before they started fighting one another out of pure nervous exhaustion.

Besides, if they completely lost faith in themselves, they'd have a hard time recovering for the next hurdle. He wanted them to stay or go on their own terms, not because the live-fire exercise went sideways from both the instructor's and trainee's points of view.

"Let's get going. Who's first up?" Leaper wanted to suggest they have a quick game of rock, paper, scissors—or, in SEAL terms, Ka-Bar, fin, mask—but this was an extremely grim lot. "So, they fucked up," said Leaper softly, turning toward the other instructors next to him and breaking into the discussion. "What happened the first time you dealt with scorched earth?"

One of the instructors gave him a half smile, and the others frowned.

"I get it. My trainees panicked. Maybe they were worked up, or maybe they were not. This is all new. That's why we practice, practice, practice. I'll work with them, and they'll either get it or ring out. That's why I'm here as an instructor. In the meantime, none of your trainees were stellar either. In my opinion, we need to give them the mental and physical tools to work through the situation, rather than just dump them in and see how they do." Leaper was frustrated with this group of instructors. It was the first time he'd been at BUD/S where he felt like most of the instructors were unprepared and unwilling to push themselves as hard as they were pushing the trainees.

In Leaper's mind, everyone at BUD/S should give 200 percent or not bother showing up. If some of these instructors didn't improve, hell, he'd talk to the Commanding Officer of BUD/S about it. Having his swim buddy as CO gave him an in. Besides, everyone should be open to feedback; it fostered improvement. Wasn't that one of the powerful messages the Teams taught? The Team mandate was that all voices be heard, from enlisted to officer. All input is useful, and contingency plans are a must.

The other instructors gave a series of shrugs and nods.

*Crap! Way to show enthusiasm.*

*Fine*, thought Leaper. *If these instructors are so constipated that they can't get over a few rough patches, they're never going to survive getting these recruits to the next phase.*

"Okay, I'll take one for the Teams. I'll go in and talk

first. Give me an hour, and then one of you can cycle in." Leaper didn't wait to see if they agreed. He put on his best tough-guy face and walked into the classroom.

The tension was so thick you could sail a kite, and Leaper wrinkled his nose as he caught a whiff of urine. *Poor souls. I've been there.*

Leaper was tall and he had no trouble reaching the latches for the small, high windows. When they were open, he walked slowly through the aisles between the desks, making his way to the front of the room. "You fucked up. All of you hit the skids and did a crap job. That happens! The first time I heard an authentic 'in combat' machine gun ripping into a wall inches from my head while I was on a mission, I shit my pants. I admit it. I didn't trust my training at the time, and though I had made it through the entire BUD/S process, graduated, and gone off to save some soul in the middle of nowhere, I should have kept my mind on the task and not worried about the fucking noise. Because that's what fear is. It's noise—shit talk—that's rattling around in your head and distracting you."

Leaper looked at the trainees. "So when I finally got my head back on straight and focused on the mission, I learned two things in that moment: First, that MRE beef stew doesn't agree with my digestive tract, and I shouldn't wolf down a ton of heavy food before I need to be in action, because having the runs and puking is inconvenient during a rescue. On a personal note, I eat high-calorie bars to make it easier on me. Second, and this is the important lesson, awareness is the key to success.

"If you are afraid, emotion is blinding you. It is all you can taste, swallow, and piss. But if you are calm on the inside, then the world is alive with an incredible amount of information." Leaper held out his hands. "Everyone take a deep breath. Hold it for a count of four. Exhale for a count of four. Inhale for a count of four. Let's do this four times." Leaper waited while the trainees followed his instructions, and the atmosphere of tension changed to one of incredible calm.

"My favorite instructor, Gich, used to call those alligator breaths. He talked about the need to operate in any kind of circumstance: rain, mud, lightning, bullets, mortar fire, torture, you name it. Being calm is your optimal choice. Make your brain your friend. The body will follow the mind and the mind will follow the body. Flow with it. And, if you think you can be become desensitized to everything, hell, that'll take your whole life and it's unrealistic. Instead, consider the idea that everything coming your way is a challenge to handle— nothing more or less. Live in that moment. Get to the next one, and then the next one, and deal only with what's happening in your present. Stay in the now. Deal with what's happening and then let it go and move on. Fear is a choice like any other emotion, but logic and awareness are some of the most useful tools of success."

"For my next trick, I can teach you how to change fear into fuel." Leaper heard a murmur of voices from the recruits. He caught a few words and phrases, including *Rambo* and *looking like a coward*.

*Crap! These guys aren't worried about the sound of live fire; they're worried about their egos. Now that's a shame! Here I am giving them pearls on how I handled my first real-time event, telling them how they can move through the trauma and stay aware and alive, and they don't give a crap. Well, fuck! Do I have to remind them to be Clark Kent and not Superman?* His anger pricked him, but Leaper ignored it.

"Raise your hand if you have an image in your head of what you need to be and how you need to act in order to make it through BUD/S." Leaper tapped his foot, waiting. "Be honest."

Slowly, every single man raised his hand. At least they were stepping up to the question. If they hadn't answered honestly, Leaper had considered taking them outside to do two hundred burpees. Seeing trainees do these deep squat thrusts and rising quickly into a standing position made him happy. But the trainees avoided that fate…for now.

"Okay, okay. You can lower your hands." Leaper waved his hand in front of his nose, indicating the amount of body odor released in the room with this many armpits open to the air.

"I'll be honest with you," Leaper continued. "This image of a SEAL or some kind of Hollywood version of a Spec Ops operative—from television, books, comics, cartoons, games, or whatever your entertainment of choice is—is a false expectation. This bullshit is designed to trip you up, to provide unrealistic hurdles. Let's face it, kiddos, it's something you *think* you need to be, this Hollywood hero. It's a creation outside of reality, and it will not serve you. Let go of any and all expectations and choose reality.

"So…" Leaper began pacing back and forth at the front of the room. "Can you imagine if every time I wanted to kiss a woman, I needed to do twenty push-ups, six lip puckers, and turn in a circle four times?

This is bullshit expectation—what you *think* needs to happen to make a goal—and it's all a fantasy. Whatever your dad or your mom or social media said, *fucking let it go*!

"Enter this training process with a *clean slate*. Don't dwell on yesterday's memory, or what may come tomorrow. Be here. You need to be here and now. Get your shit together, be aware, and react. By leaving behind these mental distractions, there'll be more room in your mind for action and response. Remember our adage: 'The only easy day is yesterday.' So today is brand-new, unknown, and waiting to be conquered."

Leaper paused and tapped his temple. "Do societal expectations count when you're holding a 9 mm a foot from a bad guy's face? Are you thinking about being a big hero or getting out alive with your Team intact and the mission complete?" When there was no response, Leaper added, "Are you going to answer my question?"

"Yes, Instructor. Getting out alive."

"Good." Leaper nodded. "Any unfocused calisthenics of the mind are useless. Keep your mind as clear and razor sharp as your body. When you are holding that gun, it's shoot or don't. Are you going to pull the trigger, knock him out, don't pull the trigger, or let him go? Fuck, you need to make a good decision. Which choice will keep you alive and your Team safe? Do you know the answer? Hell, you better! But none of that will happen unless you are awake, aware, calm, and *present*."

Leaper rolled his fingers into fists. "Being part of a Team means letting go of the individual expectation of self; learning your physical, mental, and emotional

limits and how to move past them; and in its place building an understanding of what you're truly capable of,
what your Teammate is capable of, and how to success-
fully complete your mission. Can you swap expectation
for capability—dream for reality?"

"Aye, aye, Instructor," the sailors in the room swiftly
replied.

"Good. Let's get to work. Clean slate." Leaper nodded.
There was enthusiasm in the eyes of the recruits again.
He could see smiles, albeit somewhat reserved ones,
on several faces, including those of his men. Good.
These trainees were back, and they were eager to learn.
"Tonight's event was a fucking fiasco. The next time
we have a Life Fire event, there will be improvement—
warriors doing their fucking jobs."

"Aye, aye, Instructor," replied the trainees.

Next, Leaper gave them several pointers on how to
improve their techniques and told them how he set the
bar for himself. He challenged each of them to improve
where they were weak and hone where they were strong,
and then learn to maximize both actions. "Break it all
down. SEALs use the 'chunk it' process. Make each
action a reflex and commit it to muscle memory.

"Now," Leaper continued, "an assignment for tomorrow. In your notebooks, write a list of each of your problem areas and where you excel. After that, you will know
how to proceed. Being in Special Operations means constantly improving your reaction time, your capability,
and your capacity for achievement. Got it?"

"Aye, aye," the trainees said again.

Leaper's eyes scanned the men in the room. "Before
we move on to the next set of comments, I'm dismissing

you for"—Leaper checked his watch; he had thirty-five minutes before the next instructor came in—"thirty minutes. Be back before then. Dismissed!"

The men filed quickly out of the room as Leaper continued to speak. "And may none of you experience the intense diaper rash I did. Seriously, I have scars."

The men were gone before he could offer to drop his drawers. Not that he would have. Well, maybe. It had been a long day, and mooning someone might have been a hoot. Christ, he needed a breath of fresh air.

*Oh, Leaper, you ole sweetheart. You might be making a decent impact on these lives.* Knocking his fist against his chin, he murmured, "Aw, shucks."

Yeah, he felt good. Now, this was a good way to kick off the live-fire chat. He hoped the other instructors stepped up and gave a few useful words too.

He wondered what Gich would think of him now, a trainee who became a SEAL who was teaching trainees now. Guess this was the circle of fucking life. Frogmen forever.

Whistling to himself—Hoyt Axton's "Joy to the World," a.k.a. "Jeremiah Was a Bullfrog"—Leaper walked out of the classroom and onto the First Phase Grinder. He placed his feet on top of a pair of white-painted fins, a place where he had stood as a trainee and so many others had stood before him. He stared up at the sky, wondering what else the next few hours would bring. One moment at a time. Be present. Keep moving.

He continued whistling softly to himself as his eyes tracked a seagull circling above.

She paced around and around the living room. Waiting for a lover was nerve-racking. Kerry had cleaned and primped and checked the mirror about ten times before she began her nervous pace and now she was forcing herself to sit down. Her mother had once told her that eagerness in a lady is not a pleasant sight, and yet she couldn't quell her natural exuberance.

Leaper had agreed to spend the night at Kerry's condo, and she could barely contain her nerves. It wasn't as grand as Leaper's home, but the bare necessities worked for her. When the doorbell finally rang, she sprinted to the door and greeted him. She wore a form-fitting T-shirt, a lacy thong, and a smile. Screw it! She was happy to see him.

Making a show of leaning her arm slowly against the doorjamb for a sultry effect, she said, "Are you coming in, or are you going to spend the evening out there, staring at me?"

He gulped. "Let me lift my tongue off the ground and I'll be right with you." He stepped inside and closed the door behind him. "I'm like the wolf from one of those old cartoons—my eyes are popping out of my head, and my tongue is dragging along behind me. You're the pinup doll that I'm drooling over."

Heat climbed Kerry's cheeks. "Leaper, I'm not even wearing lingerie."

"You look good in everything, Kerry, and especially beautiful when you're out of it."

"That's sweet. Thanks." She took his hand and led him to the small patio. There were light rattan shades down on the sides, and though it was easy to see out, no one could see in. Pulling her T-shirt over her head, she said, "I have a few naughty fantasies. I'm going to play out a few of those tonight, if that's okay with you."

"I'm yours. Do with me what you will, as long as it doesn't involve needles or blood." He sniffed childishly. "I get squeamish."

"Really?"

"No, but I don't need my recruits asking any weird questions about my wounds." He winked at her. "Bite marks, on the other hand…I can handle those."

"Cheeky," she said slyly. "Are you hinting?"

"Come find out."

She pushed him onto the lounge chair and climbed into his lap. After wrestling his shirt over his head, she ran her hands up and down his muscled torso and his thick biceps. She could see his pulse thudding in the side of his neck. "You like it when I touch you, don't you?"

"Yes." His eyes had a mischievous twinkle, and she liked it.

She unbuttoned his pants and pushed them down over his hips, wiggling them all the way off until he was naked on her lounger. She'd read somewhere that SEALs don't wear underwear because of the fabric twisting and torquing their tender parts into painfully odd and sometimes dangerous angles. She was glad he was commando; it was a pleasing and titillating sight.

Kerry climbed back into his lap. His skin was warm against hers, and she wiggled her nether regions against his.

His hands caught her hips. "Kerry."

She raised an eyebrow. "Is that a warning tone?"

"I want to be able to entertain you for a long time."

She leaned in. "Maybe that's not what I want.

Maybe I want it hard and fast, so it takes my breath away and I…"

He caught her mouth, and she didn't get to finish her sentence. His tongue pushed through her lips and pillaged her soft recesses. Then he lifted her, his fingers playing over her clit with delicate strokes that brought her breath in short pants of excitement. His touch brought her to the edge, and then he slowed. He did it again and then pulled back.

She broke the kiss. "Fuck me, Leaper."

His cock pierced the softness of her sheath, filling her almost to bursting. The pleasure and pain line played back and forth until her body was shaking with mini climaxes. Just as she was about to climax, he lifted her and turned her around so she was facing away from him, and then he lowered her back onto his waiting cock.

Her back arched as she took him deeper, her body trying to hold him in one place. But he lifted her hips, setting a frustratingly slow rhythm. "Faster. Please, Leaper."

She was hungry for him, but she could feel his smile as he kissed her shoulder and neck. "Watch outside. See what I see. Give in to the cool salty air, listen to the sound of people outside. Use your senses to feel every inch of my cock pulsing in and out of your body."

Doing as he suggested, Kerry slowed her desperate want and her mind stretched, alive with additional sensation. She wanted to tease him too. Show him that turnabout was fair play.

Pushing her bottom back, she rotated her hips and heard him sigh. She did it again, changing the rules. This time she set the pace.

He took his hands from her hips, and she saw him

grip the armrests on either side of the lounger. His fingers held tightly as his knuckles went white.

"Come with me," she whispered as she gyrated on his cock, her fingernails lightly grazing the inside of his arms for added sensation.

"Kerry," he ground out, his voice rough and jaw tense as he came.

The explosion of juices brought her to a huge climax. Her body shook and shuddered, milking him dry.

He wrapped his arms around her as if he planned to keep her there, perched on his cock.

She leaned her head back and said, "I suppose we both had our wicked way."

"I can think of a few more ideas."

"Do tell," she said. "Curious minds want to know."

"Thank goodness, satisfaction will always bring the cat back."

---

The sun was still slumbering, but the happy couple was awake. Even after a full night of lovemaking, neither one of them wanted to sleep. They enjoyed each other's company as they sipped coffee and gazed into the darkness.

"I've never been with someone who enjoyed long silences as much as talking," admitted Leaper.

"Me either." She tilted her head. "It's companionable, like I can share all the silly stuff in my brain without criticism."

"Yeah. Speaking of which, I've been mulling something over. Do you want to help me with a little unsanctioned plan?" asked Leaper as he drank deeply of the rich brew.

"Oh, this sounds good. Of course! Lay it on me." She shifted her body toward him.

"In the early days of the program, it was customary for Frogmen—the predecessors of SEALS—and rescue swimmers to work with the Marine Mammal Program. I'm not sure when that all changed, but I can't see what harm a simple exercise would do. Matter of fact, I'm hoping the programs will start working more closely together again. They had huge successes in their work."

"Yeah, I've read about a few of the operations," she said.

"Well, I know that demonstrations are done regularly at the Marine Mammal base for all sorts of groups, and we could consider it along the same lines, except you bring one of your dolphins to meet my trainees."

She pondered the request, biting her lower lip, and then said, "My only rule is that it doesn't endanger the mammals."

"Agreed."

"Great. I'll ask one of the dolphin trainers if they have time to do a demonstration, something basic like Swimmer Invader. Can I text you with a time and place?" Kerry checked her watch. "Let's keep this demonstration on the down low, being unsanctioned and all."

"Yeah. I get it. I appreciate this. I know I've talked your ear off this morning about my trainees. They just need to see something else to push their dedication to the next level—they need more real-life experiences. Witnessing something like a dolphin capturing an invader would be useful. I can try out some of our new camera tech, too. It's easy to drop over the side of the boat and film underwater."

"We have something like that. It takes video and stills. We use it for training, like for athletes, so we can see where we need improvement." Kerry took a sip of coffee. "If a dolphin doesn't perform, it's the trainer who takes the heat, not the mammal. So we repeat actions in certain orders over and over again."

"Yeah, practicing," said Leaper. "That's a SEAL thing. You'll hear that word associated with us a lot. It's probably a holdover from when SEALs—well, Frogmen—ran the Marine Mammal Program. The owner of the guesthouse, the one I live in now, was a Frogman and part of the Marine Mammal Program when it was in Hawaii. If he and his missus weren't on vacation in Japan, I'd introduce you. Maybe when they get back."

"I'd like that." Kerry added, "I think the program was over at Kaneohe Bay, Oahu, back then."

"One of the places, 'cause I think they were all over the coastline, but that name sounds familiar." Leaper stood and scratched his chin. "Sorry, I'm itchy. I need to shave at some point. The stubble fairy has visited me. Do you have an extra razor?"

"Medicine cabinet, top shelf. There's shaving cream too, if you don't mind smelling like coconuts." She watched his muscles ripple as he stretched and moved. So sexy.

"I like coconuts. Remind me to tell you about the time I spent doing survival training on an island—what a blast. Coconut is delicious, but too much can do funny things to the body unless you add water into the mix. And, uh, thanks for helping me out with my guys. I've learned that veering away from the lesson plan can be useful at times. It can provide extraordinary insight for trainees."

He leaned over and kissed her. His mouth was just inches from hers as he spoke. "Who would have ever dreamed that making plans is best when done naked?" Leaper gently nipped at her shoulder. "I'm done talking. What about you?"

She stroked his chin. "Oh, baby, I'm not. I still have a lot to say. Come here."

"I'm itchy. My stubble will scratch you."

"I can tough it out, if you can."

He smiled and caught her lips and laid an intensely sexy kiss on her mouth. "Kerry, I like what you have to say."

"We have to be quick. I want to get to work early and do rounds. I'm taking the afternoon—well, most of the day—off."

He touched a button on his phone, and music filled the air. The Violent Femmes sang "Please Do Not Go."

"Mmm, good song. That's one of my favorites," Kerry said. "Sweet hands, Leaper."

"Mine too." Leaper dropped the phone on the floor, and then he lifted her and took her back to the bedroom. He laid her on the bed, ignoring the blanket and sheets.

Kerry squealed as he pulled her underneath him, kissing and caressing his way down her body. As he reached the junction between her legs, she said, "I love where you are…staying…" Then she sang softly to him, "Please, please…" Too soon, the rest of the lyrics were lost as she sighed with pleasure and arched against him. *Oh, Violent Femmes, you are amazing…*

The sun was just barely over the horizon, but the bases on Coronado were already buzzing with activity. Cars filled the lanes and moved in long lines, pouring into parking lots as personnel hustled to their duty stations.

Leaper had gotten word from Kerry on his ride over that the dolphin demonstration was all set. He asked Declan for two hours of free time with his group for a special outing. Leaper had gotten an "I don't know what you're doing, but have fun," and that was good enough for him. He didn't want to put his buddy in a bad spot, so he'd fall on his sword if he had to. Not that it should be a big deal. The Marine Mammal Program did unofficial demonstrations off the Ferry Landing in Coronado all the time. As long as everyone kept it low-key, it would work out.

He'd woken his crew hours before their usual time, given them power bars and water, and loaded them into the boat. Leaper had contemplated Tang and Pop-Tarts, his favorite breakfast growing up, but the trainees were working muscles and burning calories like crazy, so he ventured down the protein-and-hydration path.

Leaper enjoyed being up before dawn, and life was even better if he could feel the spray of water in his face and taste the salt on his tongue. He could function on as little as four hours of sleep for several months. It wasn't optimal, but he'd learned he could get by. If he was on a mission and had to doze, he woke himself up and put himself to sleep over and over again, staying tuned in to his environment.

New mothers often did it subconsciously, listening

for their babies during the night. When he'd been stuck going to therapy, he'd read several psychology magazines on sleep cycles, including a great article about a single father who was raising a newborn. He would hear her from the other side of the house and be at her bedside before he was fully awake. This man also claimed to understand the type of cries his daughter made and whether she needed a diaper change, food, or comfort.

Leaper wasn't sure if he would ever be able to distinguish such sounds. In his case, sounds meant potential enemy and discovery. If discovered by an enemy, it meant kill or be killed. The primal core of his nature tapped into this area easily after so many years of honing this skill set.

He sat in the boat with his trainees, waiting. He'd already pointed out several landmarks and shared water-based facts. If only he had a fishing pole, he could catch dinner. He really needed to get out in his boat and take advantage of the opportunity to fish before the season was over. What use was a license if he never used it?

His ears picked up the sound of a boat coming toward them.

The unofficial dolphin/invader event would take place in a small alcove on the far side of the Amphibious Base, on the Bay Side. To be specific, it was off the Discovery Bridge near the Silver Strand. The water was just deep enough to be useful, and it was beyond the boat and ship traffic.

"I've always wanted to swim with the dolphins," said Captain Kirk.

"Not that type of event. It's a watch and learn," advised Leaper. "If you want to swim gleefully with dolphins as part of a program, visit SeaWorld. In the wild, dolphins are very unpredictable, as I mentioned before. The bottlenose dolphin we'll meet today will be somewhere in between these two extremes of captivity and wild, because the Marine Mammal dolphins function and work in the wild, but they live in a safe environment where they're cared for by human beings. There's a distinct difference, and we need to follow the rules, so hands in the boat."

"I want to pet one," added Watson.

"What did I just say? Do you think this is a freaking petting zoo? Eyes only." Leaper shook his head. Had these guys not had coffee? Or perhaps they forgot to bring their ears to this event.

The Marine Mammal boat rounded the corner. Finally, they had arrived.

His trainees rocked the boat in their eagerness to see the dolphin. Several attempted to stand, and Leaper knocked their feet out from under them. "The next person who stands will be sent into the drink for a morning dip. Chill out."

Leaper looked over at the Marine Mammal boat. Kerry met his gaze and smiled at him.

He nodded back. After five minutes of waiting, he signaled to her with palms facing up and hands spread to the side, the universal "What's up?"

She shrugged.

Leaper checked his watch. He needed to get the recruits back to the Amphibious Base within the allotted time frame. A short field trip was fun, but there was still an afternoon schedule in place for his trainees that must be adhered to.

He waved at Kerry and tapped his watch.

She nodded. She got his signal now.

He saw her speaking with a tall, muscular, balding guy. Leaper might have been jealous, but with the wedding ring on the guy's hand and the way she kept glancing across the water, it was obvious who she liked—Leaper.

Leaper was too close to the Amphibious Base's Officer Country to shout. He knew training wasn't Kerry's area of expertise. The dolphin trainers were in charge. He noticed from their body language that there was one trainer bossing around two helpers, and Kerry was off to the side observing. She was possibly higher up on the food chain at the Marine Mammal Program, as the trainer appeared to defer to her now and then.

Taking his cell phone from his pocket, Leaper put it in a dry-sack and stored it in a locked toolbox. Then he pulled his shirt over his head and dove into the water.

He swam to the Marine Mammal boat and pulled himself aboard. "Can I be of assistance?" He extended his hand to the balding man. "Leaper Lefton."

The man grabbed it and held tight for a few seconds. "Duckie Summers. Sorry for the delay. We were supposed to have a combat swimmer, but he hasn't shown. Must be some kind of emergency. He's usually very reliable. Do you want to reschedule for tomorrow?"

Leaper's lips thinned. "Today was the only day we had some flexibility. Can I be the swimmer?"

"You need a tank. There's a weight with the strobe-light clamp, and we, uh, don't want you to drown." Duckie picked up the device and showed Leaper how it worked.

"I'm a combat diver and I free dive. I can hold my

breath for a very long time," Leaper said. He knew he could do it. The water wasn't that deep off the coast of the Discovery Bridge near the Silver Strand. Hell, he could swim to the Base Commander's house from here. "Give me a shot."

Kerry added. "I can vouch for him. We swam together. Besides, he's a SEAL and a very strong swimmer." She tucked strands of hair into her ball cap. "C'mon, Duckie, if Leaper says he can do something, I trust him."

"Don't get litigious on me if this goes butts up," said Duckie. "I still think you need a tank, because this device normally attaches to a tank."

"Understood." Leaper nodded. "So, let's pretend I have one. How does this work? Can you explain the process? What do I do—just swim under the boat and the dolphin will put the contraption on me?"

"Yes, that's about it. Though I'll reiterate, this device has a strobe light, and I'll attach the lead so we can grab you if there's a problem. So here's the breakdown of steps: the dolphin bumps the diver, releasing the device so it will clamp onto the diver's tank. The strobe lights up, and we send combat swimmers to fetch the enemy. The lead is short so it doesn't get snagged easily, but if there's an issue, someone can dive in and grab it—just another way to provide a safety measure."

"Okay. Can we do this demonstration under my boat, so my trainees can see with my cameras?" asked Leaper, pointing over his shoulder.

"Sure. Why not?" Duckie pointed to the two assistants, who opened the side panel on the boat and encouraged the dolphin to slide into the water. "I'll wave at you when we're ready to begin."

"Great. Give me five minutes to prep." Leaper swam back to the boat and briefed the trainees on how to use the cameras. He watched them drop the cameras properly into the water so nothing got tangled in the mounts, and then he gave them an idea of what was going to happen. "My one request is that all of you stay in the boat, no matter what. Understood?"

"Aye, aye," they replied.

"Look, the dolphin's in the water," said Watson. "Too cool."

"Right. Nothing can go wrong here," murmured Leaper as he got back in the water and swam a few feet away. He turned back to the Marine Mammal boat and gave them the thumbs-up.

Duckie waved.

Blowing air out of his lungs in short bursts and repeating it several times, Leaper then took a slow, deep breath, filling his lungs to capacity. He dove under the boat, hamming it up on the underwater camera. He pretended to be sabotaging the prop when something hard and heavy clamped onto his ankle. It felt like a vise.

His reflex made him kick out, and the impact landed on the dolphin's body.

The bottlenose turned quickly and lightly bumped his snout into Leaper's abdominal. Half of Leaper's air whooshed out. *Dolphins give equal or stronger force to meet whatever is given to them*, he thought as he looked around for the dolphin. He didn't want to get blindsided again, and he sure as hell wasn't going to respond.

Clamping his mouth shut, he held tight to the rest of his air as the dolphin pulled on the lead attached to the mount. Something was wrong. Dolphins were not supposed to directly engage the enemy. The dolphins' main jobs were to identify enemy divers, tell their trainers or handlers, and point out sea mines.

Leaper was still one moment, on the move in the next. The dolphin was taking him for a ride.

He flailed his arms, trying to reach the mount. Leaper didn't make it as the dolphin pulled him swiftly away from his boat and toward the Marine Mammal boat— and if they went farther, into the direction of the open shipping lanes. He was fucked if he made it all the way out there.

All hell broke loose as recruits dove into the water. When Leaper looked over his shoulder, he could see them. The water was clear, and their activity attracted the dolphin's attention. It circled back to the trainees, dragging him along.

Dumbasses! They'd done the one thing he didn't want them to do—dive in—and this was the dolphin's environment. She had the upper hand, and several of the recruits belatedly realized that as it knocked them around with her powerful snout and tail. Several trainees gave up and paddled for shore, while others attempted to get into the boat, which the dolphin had conveniently flipped over.

Soon, those still in the water swam aimlessly about as the dolphin circled and played with them.

*Fuck!* At least the dolphin had abandoned him. Leaper managed to release the strobe-light mount.

Perhaps he was too quick to celebrate as he watched more of the dolphin fiasco along with the Base Commander and his wife, who both stood on the grass in their backyard, pointing at them. He could hear their shouts of concern, and for a brief second, Leaper wished he had drowned.

The Marine Mammal boat pulled up behind him.

"The lead didn't work. The dolphin liked it too much," Leaper choked out as he looked over at Kerry and saw that she had covered her eyes with her hand.

"What a bust!" She was shaking her head with a look of tense frustration. "I don't know what happened."

*Maneuvers gone wrong* splashed across his brain in neon letters. So much for unsanctioned events! Leaper doubted they would ever get permission to train together again.

He handed the mount to Kerry.

"I'll call you later."

"Sure," he said flatly. "Thanks for trying. I have to handle…all this."

She nodded, and then the Marine Mammal boat took off. The trainer signaled for the dolphin, who eagerly responded and loaded onto the boat.

Leaper watched the Marine Mammal group depart and then swam back to the trainee boat, flipped it, and hauled himself on board. Then he picked up those recruits still in the water and steered the boat toward the shore to get the rest of his group.

"We never leave anyone behind," he grumbled to himself as he lifted and secured the prop engine and then beached the boat on the lawn of the Base Commander's home. This was Officer Country and an Admiral's home. His trainees had made the worst choice ever, to aim for this place as a landing zone. They literally had signs posted outside the area warning individuals not to enter unless their reasons directly related to something of personal or vital importance to the officer residents and their families.

Putting his feet firmly on this hallowed dry land, Leaper gave the trainees in the boat a stern look to stay and then made his way up the perfectly manicured lawn, where several of his trainees were already gathered. These guys were actually wrapped in towels, drinking lemonade and eating cookies too. He was so frustrated, he couldn't stop the litany of swear words in his head long enough to choose just one.

At least it looked like the trainees had the good sense to stay silent as the Base Commander's wife plied them with treats. She was definitely one classy lady, but the Commander was striding toward Leaper with a furrowed brow and a deep frown and was undoubtedly going to give him an earful—or worse, a formal reprimand. Who could blame him? Who wanted a bunch of fumbling trainees, young men drenched to the bone and lapping up groceries like a pack of hungry dogs, standing on his back lawn, especially in front of his wife?

*What a goat fuck!*

*Think fast*, Leaper told himself. *Think very, very fast*.

# Chapter 5

LEAPER'S MIND SPUN WITH EMOTION AS HE REMINDED himself, *Anger is a powerful feeling fueled by bruised ego, indignation, frustration, and exasperation. If I cannot do anything useful with a bomb of this magnitude, then the best thing I can do is to get far, far, far away from humanity and find a very quiet and peaceful refuge to reboot. Alone was the operative word.*

"Hey, Lefton. Hold up!" shouted a familiar male voice.

Leaper was in no mood. He didn't want to talk to anyone. His long strides moved him swiftly toward his hog and an easy escape from the Amphibious Base. The Base Commander had handed him his ass, though the story Leaper had concocted about developing a new program for SEALs and Marine Mammals did stimulate the Base Commander's interest somewhat. Of course, making shit up on the fly was Leaper's favorite thing to do, especially as he explained that the dolphin outing was a test of his idea before he presented it to the higher-ups. It helped Leaper slide by; using his brains and wit was definitely his talent, but he had still endured a harsh lecture and load of crap from the rest of Command. It could have been worse, though.

"Lefton, fucking stop. I need to talk to you," shouted Poshen.

The rest of the BUD/S staff wanted to know the

intimate details, and they weren't going to get any. Leaper was a private person and he didn't share his trials easily.

*Fuck off, man! Take a hint and leave me alone.* Leaper had only been trying to give his guys a taste of something new. *Doing nice stuff can bite ya in the ass. Well, fuck this. I'm done with this day. I need to get out of here fast or I'm going to deck someone.*

Setting a hard pace behind the Quarterdeck of SEAL Team ONE, Leaper ignored the person attempting to flag him down. He wasn't in the mood for bro time or comfort time or any other diversion. When an arm snaked out and grabbed his, Leaper spun around ready to fight. *Prepare to die*, thought Leaper in his best Inigo Montoya voice.

Parker "Posh" Poshen, head of the instructor staff, looked mighty flustered, as if he'd wet his pants if Leaper took a swing. "Talk to me, Wild Man. I heard the Base Commander got ahold of you."

"What do you care? What the hell do you really want, Posh?" Leaper snarled. Using one of Leaper's nicknames wasn't going to do a thing. His second nickname was Bug Eyes. With over twenty years in the Navy, it was rare that Leaper lost his temper anymore, but getting reamed by the Base Commander sucked hind tit, and Leaper wasn't sticking around the base while his temper climbed up notch after notch to full steam ahead. He'd learned when to stay and when to go; he needed to go. Stewing in pain led to fistfights and all sorts of dumb-ass shit—at least it had in the past, and he didn't want to test the theory in the present.

The best thing Leaper could do was get the hell out

of Dodge and cool down. He knew just the person he wanted to let off steam with too, and it wasn't this hairy monster standing in front of him. Seriously, the man had fur pushing out every side of his tank top, and he sounded like a wind-up toy on helium.

"Don't do it. Don't leave. Those trainees need you. It's my fault. I know I gave you a fucked-up crew, but you've helped them achieve so much. It's beyond anything anyone could have imagined. Even the CO is impressed." Nervously shifting his weight from foot to foot, Poshen added, "If you walk, the recruits will see you as ringing out, and you know the ethos—failure is not an option. So suck it up and get back to it."

Leaper gave the man a long, hard stare. "I'm not fucking leaving, you dickhead. It's my day off. I came in this morning to do something special for the trainees as a courtesy. Now I'm taking a freaking break from all of this, unless you have a problem with that. And if you do, well, I'm going anyway." Leaper took two steps back, and then he turned and looked over his shoulder. "By the way, those fuckups are my people. They're great. Ask Gich. I was the biggest nutjob to go through training, yet I survived and thrived. I was practically the mascot of the Goon Squad, I was on it so long. And for the record, my success rate on missions is pretty damn high, even when I get myself shot to shit. Only two shit storms under my leadership in over forty missions, which I know is two too many, but I'd take the place of those lost men in a heartbeat."

"Oh, I know. Sorry, Lefton. I didn't realize you were just off for the day. And you're right. Your crew is pretty damn lucky to have you instructing them. If they turn out anything like you, they'll make superior operators."

"Damn straight." Leaper nodded and made a beeline for his motorcycle.

Posh just stood there and watched. There was nothing more to say, yet the man just stayed put.

As Leaper mounted his hog, inserted and turned the key, and felt the engine roar to life, he let out a long slow breath. The corners of his mouth pulled into a grin. Under his breath he added, "Of course Command is going to fucking hate anyone turning out like me. Isn't that just peachy fucking keen!"

He triggered the Bluetooth function on his phone and it linked to the stereo connection in his helmet. Picking a song, the Lumineers sang "Ho Hey" as Leaper gunned the engine and took off like a bat out of hell. His eyes were glued to the road ahead as the band sang about living life.

The music and the confrontations with the Base Commander and Poshen triggered a windfall of other issues, pent-up feelings he'd shoved deep inside of him, including the root of all of his frustrations: *Where do I fit in? Was it possible these strange hurdles were arising because he needed to change his tack like a sailboat being pointed into the wind?*

He wove in and out of traffic, his body on autopilot as he fought the deluge of doubts.

–––∿∿∿–––

Pulling up in front of Kerry's condo, Leaper cut the engine and his tunes. His mind immediately silenced. She was so captivating. Standing by her car outside her condo, she was unloading grocery bags. Wearing a short dress with worn cowboy boots and a matching aged leather jacket, she was a vision even doing such a mundane task.

He waited, watching her. The way she moved was elegant, as if her every movement was part of a larger ballet. If he choreographed dance, Kerry would be his muse.

When she spied him, she walked over with a grin on her lips. "What a wonderful surprise! How did you know I'd be outside?" She kissed and then gestured to the bags of groceries she was unloading from her car. "You can guess what today is."

Leaper held her for several seconds before he reluctantly released her. He admired Kerry's forthrightness and her abundance of energy, like that little bounce in her step. His small sweet dancer. "I just knew. Intuition."

"*Right*." She cupped his cheek with her hand. "Chore day isn't fun, but it's a necessity. Sorry that the demonstration didn't go as planned."

"Yeah, me too. Thanks for the help." He cleared his throat. "Do *you* need any help?"

"Nah, I've got this. What's up with you today?"

"Playing hooky and wondering if you'd like to join me." Gesturing with his hand, he motioned toward his Harley Davidson. "Want to climb aboard? We can drive up the coast or play in the ocean. Maybe fish or free dive."

"Oh, yes! Boy, you know how to show this girl a good time. Water *is* my element." She gave him a darling smile. "You know me so well. Give me ten minutes and I'm all yours."

Her eyes were alight with happiness as she turned away. She slammed the trunk of her vehicle, beeped the automatic lock, lifted the grocery bags from the ground, and dashed into the house. As the door shut behind her, he looked at the blue sky. The sun was shining, and the whole day was theirs for the taking.

Somehow, she'd melted away his frustration and anger. It just…couldn't exist in the same space as she did.

Checking his watch as she ran outside and took the proffered helmet from him, he noted it took her less than six minutes. She was a spitfire.

As she slung her leg over the seat and snuggled up behind him, he turned the key. The engine roared. He lifted the kickstand and set them on their path.

*Okay, Day, we're coming to claim you.*

———∿∿∿———

The ocean breeze slapped salt spray all over his face as he slowed his boat and cut the engine. *Perfect, the Pacific is calm and gorgeous today.*

His phone was playing Norman Greenbaum's song "Spirit in the Sky." He stretched his arms over his head and sighed with pleasure. "The sun's shining. We're in a boat several miles off Dana Point. It's the middle of the week and off-season, so there are no tourists lingering about. Nothing to disturb us, except each other." Leaper raised an eyebrow at her and then turned his attention to dropping the anchor. Leaning over the side, he made sure the anchor was secure before laying out the fishing rods and bait cooler.

Kerry pulled her sweatshirt over her head, revealing a pink bikini top. "It's a gorgeous day."

"You're the one who's gorgeous. Do you go to work like that?" Leaper gave low wolf whistle. "Not that I have a right to comment on fashion choices."

"Often!" She batted her eyelashes playfully. Sitting in one of two chairs at the back of the boat was blissful. "You know how my patients like to drench me. Sometimes they're not fond of me taking blood from their dorsal either, so I get a few extra splashes. I also swim with them to see how they're moving and progressing." She plucked at the center of her top. "I usually wear one-piece suits, but I have to admit, today is laundry day. Instead of bra and panties, I have this. Remember, I still have chores to do. Though I noticed a washer and dryer at your place."

"It's yours. Use it anytime. And don't forget I offered to bring in the groceries, but you wouldn't let me." He bit his lip. "I could happily wash all your delicates by hand, if you like." Leaper leaned toward her. "I mean that respectfully."

"Thanks. That's sweet. I'll think about the washing. I know several wives who would jump at the chance for their husbands to do a load, and quite frankly, I think I'd be insulted if you didn't notice I look hot in this suit. I was saving it for our next swim date. Today was just lucky. Well, that and...laundry day." Her smile lit something inside of him. He liked the way she made him feel at ease. Usually he was awkward around women, but Kerry was different.

Leaper chatted about the tides and the weather and the possibility of their catch. When he was settled in his chair next to her, he asked a question he had been pondering for a while. He wanted to know about Kerry's expectations, her wants and desires. "Any dreams?"

"Gosh." Kerry laughed loudly. "There are so many. The highest priority is taking a trip to the Amazon. The river is supposed to contain three subspecies of pink dolphins in their natural habitat. I've read several papers, and I can't help wondering if their diet and lifestyle contribute to their health."

"How so?"

"The river is murky, acting like a natural sunscreen, yet they still get tons of Vitamin D. There's a direct link between D and bone health and kidneys. Also, they can digest small furred animals as well. Bones and all, which is a type of protein I hadn't considered before and would like to understand better. Lastly, I believe they, uh, mate often. Sex can be good for, well, the entire system." Kerry blushed.

"Lots of sex and good food for a healthy life. Makes sense to me. Why are they pink?" asked Leaper as he threaded a rather substantial hook on the end of his line. He knotted it and secured the bait.

"The males, who are usually significantly larger than the females, often battle each other. It brings a pink hue to the top of their skin, like overinfused capillaries that are permanently damaged by wounds. Oh, and don't get me started on the properties in their blood." Kerry leaned toward him. "What *also* blows my mind is their echolocators, you know, in their snout, which are huge—larger than a bottlenose dolphin's. With this biosonar, I can only imagine how the world opens to them. Learning more about that function alone could significantly improve our knowledge in mechanical replication, with applications as varied as helping impaired animals or humans to improving sonar on submarines and ships." She blushed. "Too much? I get really excited about the possibilities."

"Please. Get excited." Leaper winked at her.

She wrinkled her nose. "Oh, Leaper."

"Nah, I'm serious. This is very interesting." Leaper tipped the end of the rod backward and then cast his line, allowing plenty of line to release with it. "Just to remind you, our goal today is to catch either yellowfin tuna or nothing. We grill or we pick up food on the way home." He stretched his legs out in front of him. "It's a good day to be off duty."

"I agree." Kerry's cast was nothing short of amazing. She'd obviously spent a lot of time fishing before, and Leaper was impressed. Not that he was going to tell her. At least, not yet. He preferred to keep her guessing about some of his admiration. "This beats cleaning the rugs at my condo."

Leaper grinned at her. "I'll help you pound those rugs." He wagged his eyebrows.

"You're on," she replied with equal delight. Yet they sat in companionable silence for a time, just enjoying each other's company. It had an easiness that was remarkably calming. "Uh, I hope you don't mind my bringing up a subject. The other night I heard you talking in your sleep about someone named Hissop. Let me know if I'm prying, but you seemed really upset."

Leaper opened his mouth and then closed it. After several seconds, he spoke. "Hissop was killed on my last mission. It's hard to talk about. I just... I hate taking green operatives on a complex mission, and I should have asked to pick a group of old-hats, but I let Command dictate." Scratching his nails along his stomach with his free hand, Leaper made several long stripes on his skin and then stopped himself, realizing it mimicked the angle that Hissop had been sliced on. Leaper hunched over.

"I know shit happens—they always use that fucking line to make someone feel better—but it doesn't do justice to losing someone," he continued. "It's fucking horrendous. A piece of myself died with him, and I'd gladly give my life ten times over to get him back." A few tears spilled out of his eyes. "I know crying is the body letting pain out, but I can't remember the last time I wept. I just… I hardly let go." He took a long, ragged breath. "I don't want any more of my guys to die. And the memories keep coming back faster and faster. When does it stop?"

Talking made the tears speed down his cheeks. He wiped his hand under his dripping nose. "Fuck."

God bless her, Kerry didn't say a word. She didn't reach for him or try to comfort; rather, she just let him be. So he kept talking, letting the words spill out with his emotion.

"The doctors asked me questions. When I didn't answer, they called it the 'fog of war,' which basically assumes you can't remember what happened. But I'll never forget, and on some level, most warriors remember every heartbeat of tragedy, like a metronome ticking away in their heads. Click. Click. Click." Leaper squeezed his hand into a fist.

"Telling Hissop's widow about her husband's bravery, assuring her that he didn't suffer, that it was quick— it's the worst pain. I can't even describe it." Leaper swallowed the lump in his throat, choking momentarily before it went down. "I signed up knowing the possibility of bullets and shrapnel slicing me up. I knew it could happen and most likely would, but this…"

He unclenched his hand, wiped the tears from his face, and offered his open palm to her. She put her fishing pole in the holder and took his hand, squeezing it.

"This is the main reason I keep moving, so I don't have to think, to face any of this pain and loss." Leaper looked out at the ocean. "I know it's always there, lingering on the horizon like a tsunami waiting to strike. But the last few weeks, it's like… I'm understanding that conflict comes whether you want it or not. Out here with my boys, training and teaching them, I get that they are learning, fucking up, correcting, getting back on board with new attitudes and knowledge, and then they go through the whole cycle again. So if conflict is in everything, why not allow myself to have silence too? What happens if I let peace inside? What if I stop moving? Will my world explode, or will I heal?"

Kerry kissed the back of his head. "In pain, we heal. In healing, we experience pain."

"Duality." Leaper pondered her words. His mind could see so much so clearly right now. "I get caught up. It's easy to get lost in the job. The missions, they take every ounce of your concentration and commitment. You have to be *in*—100 percent—for your Teammates' safety and for yours. Sometimes it's like living in constant chaos, beautiful and frightening, and yet when you return to civilian life… Christ, the slow, plodding pace feels odd and unnatural. My mind screams—where's the uncertainty, the adrenaline, the extremes? And my body is…confused. It wants options."

Leaper scratched the back of his neck and then rubbed the spot hard with the pads of his fingers. "My buddy Declan once asked me who he is outside of the Teams, and I didn't have an answer. That was when his leg got blown off and he had to face the big questions. Well, I didn't have anything other than a smarty-pants reply. 'Yourself. You are yourself every damn day of your life.' I was an ass!" He turned his head and looked at Kerry. "But I think I get it now, why he asked that particular question. He wanted to understand the civilian version of himself. When you're operational, you don't need that answer. But as you slow down or phase out, being prepared for stopping is a fucking necessity. It's like the concept of peace is so foreign it's almost scary. Even during the so-called quiet times in the world, there's conflict. Someone is dishing it out, and someone is responding. It's hard to fight human nature and territorialism. There's always more happening out there in the world worth understanding...and knowing that someone has to deal with it. Always."

"I never thought of it that way. When all you see on a daily basis is the usual stuff that happens here in San Diego, I guess you don't think bigger picture. You've been ass deep in conflict, and there's just always more out there. I get it." Kerry nodded her head. "Sorry that's all you've seen. So do you think that you are staying or leaving the Navy?"

He pursed his lips, considering it. "I don't know. That's the million-dollar question, or in my case at a base value, $125,000, give or take bonuses, and shit, I'm a saver. My body isn't as flexible as it used to be. I don't bounce back like I did during my first decade in the Teams. And politics have an effect on things. Different leaders want different types of Ops, and they impose crazy regulations that are impossible to uphold while keeping everyone alive and fulfilling a mission. If everything stayed the same, the same standard I came into the Navy with, then yeah, I'd stay in for thirty years, or until they booted my ass."

He sighed. "But that's not reality. I feel like…I need to know who I am outside of the military. I'm circling the concept of peace in my life and wondering if I'll ever be able to…let go. It's like life is banging on my door, and that knock is getting louder and louder every day. If I open it up, who or what will I find on the other side? I just don't know."

Kerry nodded her head. "As a civilian consultant, I'm rounding twenty years in a few months. I'll get half pay at my retirement." She touched his arm. "The dolphins aren't a job to me. They're…family. I know some of these creatures on a deeper level than I do my own family. I can't imagine ever leaving them. There's so much need right here. Besides, where does a nephrologist specializing in marine mammals go?"

"Research? There have to be grants."

"There are. I guess I could be interested in trips, but I'd want to come back here…to these special creatures. Do you think I'm nuts? Is this a weird way to live life?" Kerry wound her hair into a bun and tucked the strands together to keep them in place.

"No. It's who you are. I like your dedication. It's rare these days." Leaper closed his eyes. "I feel the same way. The Teams are my family. But, what else is too." The boat rocked back and forth, calling on him to rest.

Quiet stole into his consciousness, pulling him under, giving him something he hadn't felt since he was a small boy: tranquility and restfulness.

Sometime later, the sound of Kerry's voice reached into his solitude and pulled him back, slowly bringing him into present.

"Leaper. Wake up. Do you see that?" She sounded concerned.

The worst options raced through his mind, and he was on his feet before Kerry finished her question. His eyes scanned the horizon for threats. "Uh, I see…a collection of nets bobbing on the surface of the ocean. Shit! I know what that is." Rushing to the toolbox, he opened the lock and pulled out a Ka-Bar and a bandana. He attached the knife to his leg and tucked the bandana into one of the straps. Leaper grabbed two masks and two sets of flippers before he secured the lid of the box. "How are you at whale whispering?"

"Oh God!" Kerry's face paled. "Is that…a whale caught in nets?"

"Yes. You can stay here if you want, but I won't let that creature die." Leaper held a mask and a set of flippers out to her. "You don't even need to get that close. Just stay off to the side and speak in soothing tones. I'll take care of the rest."

She grabbed the equipment and sat on the edge of the boat. After donning the swim fins and mask, she held on to the mask and slid over the side and into the ocean.

"That's my lady," said Leaper as he followed her actions and joined her in the water.

Cold water smacked at his body. The Pacific water had that cold edge—something that most trainees hated but Leaper usually preferred. It kept his senses awake, aware, and alive.

"Didn't I just read about this problem in an NPR article?" asked Kerry as they swam with steady strokes toward the creature. "Wildlife getting caught in abandoned nets; it's so awful."

"Yeah, I read it too. Sickening. Human waste and neglect is horrific." Leaper looked at her. "Sorry. I get a bit passionate about the topic. I've seen a lot of this. We rescued a small pod off the coast of Greenland, but one of them beached the next day. Too tired to continue."

"That's awful!" Kerry readily agreed. "Get as riled as you want on this topic. Just so you know, I have your back."

"In the Teams we call it having someone's six—and I've got yours too." Leaper playfully reached out and tickled the small of her back.

She smiled at him.

He turned back to watching the whale's movements, which were frighteningly slow. "He's tired. This could be dicey. Keep in mind that you can turn back anytime. A wounded mammal is very—"

"Dangerous. Yeah, I'm familiar." She swished her mouth with seawater. "Remind me to tell you about my thesis project someday."

"You got it," said Leaper as he pointed toward the side. "I'm going to eyeball it and figure out the best approach. I'm a free diver, so I can slow my heart rate and oxygenate my body beyond normal capacity. As soon as you start talking to it, I'm going to prepare my body and go under."

"If there's a problem…" Kerry's voice was high and nervous. He could see the worry written on her face.

"There won't be."

—⁓—

She hugged her arms around her middle, knowing that she was about to do something very, very stupid. *Well, hell, passion makes us do insane things that we struggle to survive.*

As she swam into the whale's proximity, she spoke softly and steadily to the creature. "Hi, I'm Kerry. I'm a marine-mammal vet, and I can see that you're stuck. Can I help you out of that net?" The hump-back was approximately sixty feet long and probably weighed over forty tons. The intelligence in its eyes struck her—as did the pain and exhaustion. "We'll get you free."

The whale's gaze tracked her. She could see its breathing was labored and changing to match her body's movement.

*No! Can it be?*

"I'm going to work on that loose part of the net and see how far I get." Seeing a break in the edge of the net, Kerry swam closer to the whale until she was touching the creature. She patted her gently as she began untangling the net from around the whale's face. The net moved backward as Kerry loosened the ropes, until she felt the whale's belly move, confirming her suspicion. What a time to be right.

"Leaper," she said, softly but firmly. "Stay back there and get those nets and ropes off her belly and tail immediately. Don't speak. Don't argue. This whale is pregnant, and I think the little one is trapped. Her stress has most likely brought on an early labor. Let's attempt to keep both of them alive."

A hand extended with a thumbs-up before he disappeared under the water.

Kerry moved as quickly as she could, shifting the net backward, working diligently until their joint efforts freed the whale from the mishmash of ropes and nets.

Kerry held her hands on the whale's belly and felt movement. Diving below the surface, she was just in time to see the little one slide out.

The mother bellowed, the vibration traveling through the water.

Surfacing next to Leaper, Kerry shouted to the whale, "You did it. Well done." But she could see the whale was tired, too tired to catch the calf and bring it to the surface for its first breath. "Oh God, the calf is sinking. Help me bring the calf up," Kerry said to Leaper, diving into the ocean's depths.

Leaper was next to her in an instant, and together they guided the calf upward. They brought it to the mother's head, and she nuzzled it affectionately.

"How is the whale going to care for her calf, given the exhaustion?" Leaper whispered. "Wait, I know a sand bar. It won't beach her, but she can rest for a short while." He pointed to a spot several yards away. "I have no idea how we can get them there, though."

"I do," said Kerry. "The calf. Move the calf slowly, perhaps a few feet at a time, and the cow will follow. Let's try it. The best we can do is encourage the mother to rest and eventually feed, and that will help her regain her strength, but it's ultimately her choice to survive. Just so you are aware, bossing around a forty-ton creature is…not something I've ever done before."

"You do just fine bossing around a tall SEAL," he teased.

"Ha-ha," she replied, but his attempt at levity actually made her feel a little better. She was worried for the whale and its babe.

Slowly, they urged the calf forward. The cow watched them wearily at first, but then she closed the distance. As they neared the sand bar, the mother turned and dropped into a deeper crevice of water. Bubbles floated to the surface, and she came up from underneath, mouth open.

"Is that a good sign?" asked Leaper as he distracted the calf, which was so enormous, it was longer than their small boat. Pushing and guiding it was like urging an elephant to water. It was a chore.

"Yes," said Kerry with a smile. "It's great! She's eating krill. Thank God. This will help her get her energy back." She stroked the top of the calf. "It's the second best news of the day."

Kerry took advantage of the babysitting opportunity to gently run her hands over the calf's skin and play with it. How often does a vet get a chance to examine a wild whale calf?

Leaper was getting splashed by the calf now and then, though it was nuzzling him too. Guess the calf knew a quality guy. When he chuckled at its antics, Kerry knew Leaper was having fun too.

She was glad that they were staying with the newborn as the mother fed. Treading water and stroking the back of the calf, she willed her calming energy into the child. Already it had been through so much. And there was even more to face, with giant predators in the wild ocean depths and a dangerous trek to reach the safe haven in Mexico where there was a protected birthing ground. If they made it, the calf would have an opportunity to get stronger and the mother would have others to help her. Until then, this humpback adult would need all her faculties to protect this wee one.

What seemed like minutes later, but was actually at least an hour, the mother returned. It was promising to see her shoot water through her blowhole and use her tail again.

The mother called to her calf and then gently nudged Kerry and Leaper away. Before the mother left, she stared at Kerry, as if thanking her. It was impossible not to well up with emotion and wish that they survived their journey. As the mother and child headed down the coastline, Kerry put the last of her energy into swimming back to the boat. It was a long trek as the current pushed against them. In the end, Leaper ended up cajoling her, so the last part of the journey was fun, if not thoroughly exhausting.

"This day has blown my mind. We saved two lives," said Kerry breathlessly as she hauled herself into the boat and wiped away a few remaining tears of exhaustion and emotion. "I can't believe this whole thing happened." She sat down and took a long swig of water. "I'm going to write about this. The Marine Mammal Foundation will find it really interesting, as will a journal on veterinary medicine. Gosh." She took another drink and then handed it to Leaper. "Want some?"

"Thanks." Leaper drained the bottle and placed it in their recycling bag. "You did a good thing today."

"We did it together." Kerry went to him and hugged him tight. His arms were strong and warm, and they felt so good around her, as if her body was protected, safe, and forever cherished.

"We're an impressive pair, aren't we?" Leaper kissed her before she could reply.

She smiled as they kissed. Boy, he could say a million things with each touch of those gorgeous lips. Every kiss spoke volumes, and each was as unique as the last. "Sometimes when we're together, I can't stop smiling," Kerry admitted.

"Is that bad?"

"No. It's…unexpected. It's never happened before." Heat rose in her cheeks.

"I love it when you blush." He kissed her again once, twice, three times. *Mmm*.

"For me, it's your kisses. The way you kiss my upper lip and then linger on my lower lip before you kiss the center, as if each inch is to be treasured." She sighed.

"If I had to list all the things I liked about you, well, we'd be in this boat for a very long time." Too soon, he pulled back from the embrace and put a little distance between them. "Let's head back to shore. We have a special date. I have a few people I'd like you to meet. Important ones."

"Now I am curious. Are you showing me off?" Kerry giggled. "You're making me feel like a schoolgirl who's about to meet your parents."

"Hell yes, I'm showing you off. Declan's the closest I have to family." Leaper pointed at her head. "You might want to take the seaweed out of your hair."

Kerry felt around the back of her head and pulled off a large clump of seaweed. "Bend over," she told Leaper, dangling it between them. "Wait until you see where I'm going to put this next."

"*No!*" He danced out of reach.

She wasn't going to let him off that easy. She had a burst of energy and she was ready to play.

—⁓—

Small pieces of green ocean plants swirled around the shower drain. She'd lost the seaweed battle, but she knew she'd win the war.

Hot water bathed her skin with blissful, seductive pulses as Kerry lathered her hands and ran the suds over her body. She could have stayed in here for hours, but she didn't have that luxury today.

The scent of sandalwood filled her senses as she rinsed her body, standing under the heavy spray until the last possible second. Being at Leaper's home was luxurious. She wondered if he knew how lucky he was. People paid millions for this view.

Out of the corner of her eye, she saw Leaper enter the glass shower stall just before she stepped out. He flipped a switch that sent water to three additional showerheads, creating the sensation of being in the middle of a waterfall. The look in his eyes was heated and wickedly sensual.

She loved it.

"Excuse me, ma'am, I'm with the soap police, and I noticed you seemed to have missed a few places. Can I help you with that?" His voice was thick and gravelly.

She nodded her head eagerly and placed her hands on the wall of the shower stall, turning her back to him. She wiggled her bottom, teasing him.

Leaper's large, sudsy hands ran up and down the length of her back. She slid in and out of his reach, making him growl with desire.

As he made his way to the front, he cradled her large

breasts, gently teasing the nipples. She found she didn't want to escape anymore.

Kerry pushed her backside into his touch, craving his ministrations.

Nudging her thighs wider, he tenderly pushed his cock against her opening. As he rubbed it back and forth, Kerry could feel herself climbing that incredibly sexy climactic mountain. Her body tightened and released, pushing her higher and higher until she shuddered with intense pleasure.

Standing on her tiptoes, she lowered down onto his hard cock. Her slickness welcomed him inside even as her sheath attempted to capture and hold him captive.

It was the most intimate thing in the world, when he tucked his head next to hers and whispered, "You are the most beautiful woman I've ever known. Sexy. Vibrant. Smart. Sassy. Sweet. And delicious." His words punctuated each thrust until her body was on the verge again. Her sheath tightened, and she came with a shout. Multiples orgasms cascaded through her as she panted and shook.

"Kerry," he said as he leaned his weight against her momentarily. "Are you okay?"

"Amazing," she sighed. Indescribable joy filled her as he held her tight. She barely had words to describe how she felt.

He pulled out and tenderly rinsed her under the water. Leaper treated her with such delicate ministrations that she felt cherished and adored. After they got out, he bundled her in towels and carried her to the bed, and Kerry couldn't stop the smile that was radiating from her heart.

"What?" he asked.

"Nothing," she said, shaking her head. She wasn't ready to share everything that was bouncing around her head. Seeing the clock, she said, "Wait. Aren't we supposed to be somewhere?"

Leaper craned his neck to look at the clock. "Shit. We need to go. So much for making love again."

She kissed the tip of his nose. "Later?"

"Hell yes." Leaper jumped off the bed—sans towel—and strode hurriedly around the room, pulling out clothes. She couldn't help but admire the view. Yes, Leaper had won their seaweed battle, but her body reminded her that she was the victor, in all the right ways, of the war.

———

Does chaos beget chaos? Where does order come in? Kerry knew she shouldn't laugh at Leaper as he rushed around his home, but hadn't he known that showering and, ahem, celebrating each other's bodies was going to put them in a time crunch?

After they docked the boat, they'd driven to her house and picked up her makeup bag, shoes, and dress and then come back here. She'd known they were going to have sex. Hadn't he?

As he stalked toward her, now fully clothed, he said, "If you continue to lie there naked, I'm canceling the dinner date with Declan and Maura."

She gave him a mock salute.

"Smart-ass."

"Indeed."

He ran his hands over her naked flesh. "I guess I could share a few instructions from the Navy, if you could share a few things about discipline too."

"Fine, I'll get moving." She scooted out of his grasp. "Don't you start sweet talking me, or we *will* be canceling tonight's festivities, Mr. Lefton."

"Bummer." Leaper sat down on the bed and sighed. "What a handful you are, Dr. Hamilton. If only we could play doctor a little more. I want to show you where it hurts and have you kiss my…"

"I thought we were playing marine biologist, discovering new outcroppings and such," she said as she flicked her towel at him.

"Damn," he said, smiling. "I am a blessed man."

He triggered the app on his phone, and music filled the bedroom. The Rolling Stones sang "You Can't Always Get What You Want."

She had found exactly what she needed, and maybe that was better, because she could never have imagined someone as incredible as Leaper.

---

Riding a motorcycle in a dress as it sped down the Strand was extremely challenging. Kerry squeezed her legs closed and held on for dear life, trying to keep her heels from slipping off the footrests. There wasn't much to her blue silk dress either, and if the material snagged on anything, she was going to arrive in her bra and panty set.

Luckily, the trip was short, and they arrived in the Coronado Cays without too much upheaval. Kerry smoothed her dress into place and fluffed her hair as Leaper wedged the bike into a small parking spot.

Together, they walked up the short walkway to a large one-level modern ranch home. She rang the bell, and Leaper laughed at her. "I'm family. Just walk in."

"No way... I don't even know..."

The door opened, abruptly ending the discussion and revealing a tall woman whose belly preceded her by at least a foot.

"Hello, Mrs. Swifton." Kerry presented a bouquet of sunflowers. "I'm Kerry Hamilton."

"How lovely! Thank you. Please, call me Maura. Come in." Maura stepped back to let them in and almost tripped over a small toy drum.

Leaper caught her elbows and steadied her. "Easy does it." Leaper hugged her. "You smell so much better than Dec."

"Of course!" Maura smiled at Leaper as she patted his shoulder. "Well, don't just stand there, let's head to the back." She waved a hand. "Ignore the mess and just step over whatever you can. I can't even bend down anymore, so this mess is waiting on Declan to play housemaid."

"Does he wear a push-up bra and frilly skirt?" teased Leaper.

"Nope, it's too distracting for me. But I give Declan high marks—that man knows how to use a feather duster," quipped Maura.

"Too many details," Leaper muttered as they moved farther into the room and faint strains of music became audible.

"Really? You're playing Marvin Gaye's 'I Heard It through the Grapevine'?" Leaper threw his hands in the air. "I get it—I should have introduced Kerry sooner."

"I knew you'd catch on. Guilting Leaper with music is very effective, Kerry. Remember that. It's better than a fight or a two-hour discussion. I say that as a surrogate sister and good friend." Maura changed the track to the

Young Rascals' "Good Lovin'." "Speaking of loving, Declan has terrific skills." Maura looked up from the stereo and winked at Kerry.

"Ew! It's like seeing your parents kissing. No one needs to see that action." Leaper cleared his throat. "Hey, I'm usually getting attacked about now. Where's the little one? Not that I'm trying to invite an ambush. I was hoping to avoid a Pink Panther scene, since my lady friend is here."

Kerry wrinkled her nose. "Wait…the scenes where Cato attacks Inspector Clouseau…that's hysterical."

Leaper nodded. "Until you are being body slammed by a giant Swifton *and* a little one. Those odds aren't fair. I just get creamed, and there's no one to heal my wounds."

"Good heavens, someone get the world's smallest violin and we can play you a pity ballad, Leaper." Maura rolled her eyes.

Leaper sniffed dramatically. "I'm so abused."

Kerry giggled softly. This was adorable. She'd never seen this side of Leaper before, and it was darling. Did he know how cute he was being? She wasn't going to let on…otherwise his ego might swell so big, they couldn't drive the motorcycle home.

"Who are you kidding, Leaper? You adore it. Though there's no ambush tonight. Declan's putting her to sleep now. *Oof!*" Maura stopped and rubbed her belly. "Now, that was a serious kick. They are going to be linebackers." She panted briefly and stood up. "Only three more weeks until my boys are due. I can hardly wait to see them."

"Two. Incredible. I hadn't heard." Leaper leaned down and scolded Maura's belly. "Now you guys lay off Mom. You can play with Uncle Leaper once you both land on your tiny feet, but until then, remember: she's precious stuff."

"As long as they aren't biters." Maura shivered. "Leaper, you're such a sweetheart, God love you. Kerry, he's been a lifesaver. Declan calls our soon-to-be-born babe Lefty."

"After me. Isn't that flattering?" Leaper tapped a finger against his mouth. "Leaper Lefton is a mouthful. I still can't believe I'm a godparent and future guardian."

"Hell yes, and you get them both if, God forbid, something happens. You and my parents will share custody. Good luck with that. You know how my folks can be."

"Maura, I'll fight dragons for those babes, and your parents love me. They'll stuff them with food and I'll run them around until they're out of energy. It's a great combo."

"I know. Having you in our lives is a blessing." She turned to Kerry. "Sorry, I didn't mean to be rude and exclude you from the conversation. Leaper's been gone so much, it's nice to have him home."

"No problem. I don't think I've ever met friends that are so close," said Kerry.

"The Teams change friends into family," added Leaper.

"Definitely," said Maura. "The camaraderie is hard to explain, but once you've experienced it, you will never be alone again."

"I meant to tell you, your house is lovely. Do you like living in the Coronado Cays?" Kerry said as she reached for a toy. She picked up the items within reach and dumped them into a large open trunk. The control freak in her sighed with relief.

"Bless you, Kerry," Maura said. "I appreciate the help. By the by, visit the small cabinet by the kitchen sink for our drinks. We've got every kind of liquor imaginable, or the fridge has about twenty kinds of iced teas and juices. Declan made the pink and green ones from scratch." Maura eased herself onto a stool and sighed. "Leaper, he loves that gift. How did you know?"

"It was a given. What do you purchase a man who is 50 percent health nut and 50 percent gearhead? A juicer." Leaper laughed as he took two waters out of the fridge and placed one aside for Kerry. He took a long drink, placed it on the countertop next to hers, and then helped Kerry rectify the toy explosion. Just as they were finishing, Declan walked in.

"Now that's service. I still read three bedtime stories every night." Declan shook hands with Leaper. "And you must be…"

"Kerry. Nice to meet you," she said as she shook the hand of the giant, bearlike man. Next to Leaper, who was all muscle and lean height, they were an odd pair.

Leaper smacked Declan on the back, and the two hugged each other.

Watching them banter made Kerry laugh. "You're a monkey." "Fine. Watch me scratch my ass." "That's my ass, not yours." Their verbal play was so close to that of Abbott and Costello that she couldn't stop several giggles from escaping.

"They are a pair, aren't they?" Maura nodded at the men. "It's like having two more toddlers running around. I wouldn't trade it for the world, but don't tell them that."

"Let's sit on the deck," Declan announced. He leaned

THE POWER OF A SEAL

down and adjusted something on his prosthetic leg, then pointed outside. Taking control, he pushed a prepared giant cart of food and drink toward the large open deck on the water. It was charming the way Leaper was right by his side, quietly lifting one end so it glided seamlessly over the threshold of the sliding door. Kerry could tell these two were close. They didn't even seem to need words.

The outside deck extended the beautiful medley of Southwestern colors and charm. There were two couches and a fire pit next to the gate leading down to the water and a dock. Closer to the door was a giant professional-looking grill and a cream wrought-iron table.

"Please sit," said Maura. "Tell me about yourself. What do you do?"

"I work for the Marine Mammal Program as a vet. That's about it. I heard that you own a gym in Imperial Beach and you have some wonderful programs that help kids." Kerry scooted her chair closer and took a sip of water.

"Yes, I love it. There's no end to the number of kids coming through the gym, so I can bring the little one to work. We've set up several parkour programs, and our membership has skyrocketed in the past two and a half years. Time flies by quickly." Maura fanned herself with her hand. "Can you please pour me some iced tea? Being pregnant and having hot flashes does not lend itself to easy movement."

"Absolutely," said Kerry as she reached across the table and poured a glass for Maura, then one for herself, Leaper, and Declan.

"Take my advice," Maura said, "and travel while you

can. Once you have babies, it's harder to get away. The amount of support they need…it's almost mind-blowing. Are you planning any trips overseas? I'll live vicariously."

Kerry opened her mouth and closed it. There were a few opportunities on the table that she hadn't told Leaper about yet.

Maura took a long sip. "It's unsweetened. If you'd like sugar or the fake stuff, check the small bowl next to the salt and pepper."

"I prefer it this way," said Kerry, taking a small sip and then another. "Is that mint combined with black tea? It's delicious."

"Yes, I like brewing all sorts of concoctions." Maura looked at Kerry, her gaze shrewd. "I hit a nerve with that travel question. You're tea talk is deflective, a serious giveaway."

Kerry eyed the two men at the grill. She leaned forward and said softly, "I was offered a job in Japan. But…it just doesn't feel like the right position for me. I'm too attached to my dolphins, and it's too far from… I have another offer to work with a Russian group, and that doesn't feel right either. Also—"

"Leaper," said Maura knowingly. "I get it. He's in your life now. You know, you are the first female he's ever brought over. Sure, he's dated plenty, but he never gets close to them. There's something unique about you, or you wouldn't be here." She took a sip and put down her glass. "Declan was like that for a time, sort of a playboy. Work and women. For a long time, the only thing that really mattered was his work."

"I want to travel. I have a ton of dreams, places I want to go and species of dolphin that I'd like to meet.

But how could I ask that of Leaper?" Kerry shook her head sadly.

"You might be surprised at what Leaper decides to do. When he's all-in, he jumps in with both feet. He's that kind of spirited soul." Kerry looked over at her husband and smiled. "They have that quality in common."

Declan came over and placed a plate of grilled shrimp and lobster tails on the table, along with a giant grilled salmon with large wedges of lemon and lots of fresh dill doused in butter. "Help yourselves," he said. He must have caught the last of their conversation, because he added, "When you meet the right woman, the whole world changes." He kissed Maura on the top of her head.

"Japan, huh? Russia too," added Leaper between mouthfuls. "First I'm hearing of those offers."

"Boy, you have good ears." Kerry shrugged. "Doesn't matter, though. I'm not taking the jobs. For me to leave here, it has to be…ideal. The ultimate excursion." She laid her hand on his and squeezed it. "And I don't want to cut ties with the Marine Mammal Program here."

Leaper smiled at her. "Good to hear. But if it is something you want, I hope you'll share it. I want to support your dreams."

"Ditto."

They dug into the food. Silence surrounded the group as they devoured the meal.

Leaper sighed. "Excellent grub, Declan. Five stars. Beats those tarantulas we roasted on the deck of that carrier. Ugh, that was awful."

Declan chuckled, a deep rumble. "Even I had to convince my stomach to keep that meal down. But when you're starved—"

"Everything tastes like survival," finished Leaper. "Yeah, I know. I still can't look at rats and squirrels the same way." His eyes met Kerry's. "Don't ask."

"Daddy! Daddy! Wet! Wet!" yelled a tiny voice from inside the house.

"I knew I shouldn't have given her a second glass of water. My bad." Declan exchanged a long look with his wife and set his napkin on the table beside his plate, sighing. He'd obviously lost whatever nonverbal discussion they'd had. He pushed his chair back, hoisted himself onto his feet, and headed inside to deal with the crisis.

Kerry was impressed. "Now, that's a man."

"Here, here," said Maura, toasting her husband and taking a long sip of her iced tea before she went back to fanning herself with her hand. "Good Lord, soon there were will be more of them too."

"Reinforcements are right in front of you, if you need 'em." Leaper picked up the empty plates and stood. "Ladies, if you'll excuse me, I'm on KP—kitchen patrol, a.k.a. dish duty—where I'll be making some extra suds."

"Do you need help?" asked Kerry. She smiled at his suds reference. It reminded her of their showers together.

"Nah, I'm good. You enjoy yourself." He disappeared inside. After several more trips, the table was cleared and it was impossible not to appreciate the silence.

God, Leaper was good. That man was changing her life in more ways than she could list, and it was only for the better. Looking up, Kerry felt oddly at peace as she studied the sky. The sun was setting, painting streaks of red, pink, and orange above them.

"I'll never get used to the view," said Maura. "The beauty of Southern California is astonishing."

Kerry nodded her head. "It is lovely. You must spend every evening out here."

"Most of them," confirmed Maura. She shifted uncomfortably in her chair. "While we're alone, I want you to know that we've enjoyed meeting you. Leaper means a great deal to us. He's more than a friend; he's a precious part of our lives. Don't, uh…" Maura faltered, as if she couldn't bring herself to say the words.

"I won't. It would hurt me if I hurt him," Kerry assured her. "Leaper, he's special. I've never met anyone like him. When we're together, we fit so well. It sort of freaks me out. And when we're apart, I can hardly wait until I set eyes on him—until I can hold him in my arms and smell his essence mixed with that crazy sandalwood soap," Kerry blurted out. She covered her mouth, trying to stem the flow of her blathering. She opened her fingers and said, "Sorry for the overshare."

Maura grinned. "It's perfect. You said it exactly the way I hoped you would. If your lover doesn't ring that fantasy bell to the hundredth degree, then it's not the right soul. Girl, we're going to have fun talking. Let me tell you about my first naked experience with Declan. I was on this paddleboard when the current caught me, dragging me to sea. Long story short, he was stripping me naked and putting me in a tub of water. Boy, did that get my juices going."

# Chapter 6

SEXY, SENSUAL, AND ROMANTIC SCENES—THE STUFF OF dreams and stories—bloom in organically bounteous moments. Tonight was a time like that, where the moon slid behind a bank of thick clouds, drawing away all remnants of light and leaving the couple shrouded in darkness. The air was just cool enough for them to sit close together as even the shadows suited intimacy, cloaking them in privacy.

"What a great night," said Kerry with a contented sigh.

"Uh-huh," replied Leaper, whose home was just behind them. The ocean was before them, lapping languorously on the shore, and the rock and sand were just beneath them. The night with its dark mantle wrapped them in seductive seclusion.

Birds skirted the water mere feet away, scooping up their midnight catches. The last of the moonbeams had drawn those fish to the surface, and the absence of light disoriented them now, making them easy prey.

Nature was so primal. Want and need. Fulfillment and satisfaction.

Kerry snuggled closer to Leaper. "Thank you for an amazing day and a wonderful evening. I like Maura and Declan. It'd be great to spend more time with them." Kerry sighed. "That meal was delicious too. I'm stuffed."

"Glad you like them. Declan's one helluva good

cook." Leaper wasn't prepared to tell her that his swim buddy had given his agreement during kitchen duty—a thumbs-up in terms of Kerry being in his life, that is. Not that Leaper needed the confirmation, but hearing from his best friend reinforced what he already knew. Leaper hadn't even realized he wanted to know what other people thought. Then again, Declan and Maura were special.

Leaper nuzzled her neck, and she leaned into his caress. He knew Kerry was one of a kind, and he wanted to spend more time with her. His friends' validation just made him more sure.

Wind blew in soft gusts as the lapping of the ocean waves soothed him like a lullaby, yet nothing could cool his desire. In his arms was a rare beauty. A tiny honey blond with a lush and lovely body. *Ah*.

"Leaper, are you thinking up mischief?" Kerry asked as her fingers rubbed along his shoulders. Her voice was sensual and sweet, even when she was roaring with emotion, and he liked it.

"Maybe." He grinned as he buried his nose in her hair and breathed in the scent of the salty ocean and Kerry's sweet honey scent, as if she bathed in it. Oh, he definitely loved that idea. He was putting it on the top of his to-do list.

He felt her hands slide down his chest and toy with his bellybutton. He liked her boldness. Passion could draw a man the way a flower does a bee.

"Leaper," she sighed as she stretched her body along the length of his.

He sat down on a rock—an outcropping that reached into the ocean—and softly kissed along the pulse of her neck until he reached her lips. Slowly, oh, so slowly, he kissed her with a teasing passion. The touch made her lean in for more. Nothing could make him rush this moment.

Holding her close made all of his senses sing; being with her made him feel alive. That observation shocked him. She affected him the way an Op with his SEAL brothers did, with one exception—he didn't want to get naked with them. But her… She was a flesh-and-blood siren who lured him, sang to his soul, and made him want to drown in her body.

She had a gorgeous smile and an air of freedom, as if she lived the life she was always meant to, and everyone in her presence should do the same. It was irresistible.

"Kerry." He murmured her name against her lips, a breathy caress.

Her tongue darted out, as if she couldn't bear his leaving her lips. "Leaper," she sighed as her hands dug into his back. "Please…don't make me wait. I want you. Now."

"Say my name again. I like the way you say it."

"Leaper." She drew the syllables out as if each one was a succulent, saucy caress.

He smiled against her lips, his grin wicked and hungry, and then slanted his head slightly and gave her exactly what she craved, kissing her with a passion he'd held in check for most of his life. The floodgates opened, and waves of sensuality poured over him as he gently lowered her onto his lap. She was a treasure, a fragile creature who must be worshipped with tenderness.

She shifted in his lap and straddled him boldly, and it was obvious she had other plans. Who was kidding—he adored it! He craved a woman who was his equal in bravery, pluck, and passion. Was Kerry the one? From all he'd learned about her, she was smart, courageous, and lived life with gusto. She was an incredible soul who wreaked havoc on his senses in a way no else ever had.

A wicked grin played on her lips. Her body vibrated with need as she moved deliberately over him. Her hands stroked his face.

For a moment, he almost lost control like a love-struck teenager. Then the self-discipline that made him a superb operator in combat kicked in, and he was in command of his body and emotions again. He stroked his fingers along her back, her hips, reaching in front and brushing his fingertips over her breasts.

"Yes," she sighed as she pushed into his touch.

His hands cupped her breasts. He sighed. Her skin was so tender, so soft, like silk. "Luscious."

"More." She pulled her shirt over her head and pushed up his own shirt. "I don't want anything between us."

Leaper nodded. He set her on her feet.

"Keep your eyes on me." She turned slowly around on a low, flat rock and then stood still as she disrobed.

He watched with an eager gaze as she stripped off her clothing. Her every movement made his blood boil until he was pulling his own clothes off in a rush, trying to alleviate the heat building inside him. He tossed the clothes behind him, heedless of where they landed.

Water splashed their feet as she crawled onto his lap. She put her hands on her hips and slowly lowered herself onto him.

His cock could feel each glorious pulse of her vagina as he moved farther into her achingly slowly. When her muscles gripped him hard with a climax, he had to struggle not to come immediately. *God, she's incredible!*

His eyes locked with hers. When she began to move, he lost all capacity for speech. He had to gulp in air so he could hold his ground. With his pulse racing and his heart hammering, pleasure laced through every part of him until nothing else remained.

Moving together in a rhythm as ancient as time, they became a solitary being. They were living, breathing, shuddering, beating, reaching, arching, and making love as one unit.

In that moment, the moon revealed itself, leaving behind the thick clouds and bathing the couple in moonlight. Beams of light danced across Kerry's hair and naked body as Leaper's gaze took in the vision of her glorious form and the riveting place where their bodies were joined.

As his gaze shifted back to her face, he could see her eyes were alight with delight, those twin glints of enchanting mischief, and it pushed him over the edge. He struggled to speak. "I…"

"Me too," she said, her voice strained. Her back arched as she cried out in pleasure.

His body had climbed as high as it could, and he came with a mighty roar as his body plunged with hers to completion.

Their bodies shook, spent.

They held each other, arms entwined.

His forehead touched hers, and they kissed intermittently. Neither wanted to let go, and they clung until they both began to shiver.

Leaper reluctantly lifted her up and placed her on her

feet. He bent down and grabbed her clothes, wet from the water on the low, flat rock.

Grabbing his shirt, which had actually landed on a higher, dry rock, he held it so she could slip it over her head and put her arms inside. The hem hung to her knees. She looked adorable.

She laughed. "It smells like you."

"Great. Sweat," he said critically.

"No," she said with an equally serious tone. "Like a warrior. A lover. Like a man who is mine."

"Our scents smell good, mingled together." Standing naked before her, he kissed her tenderly and said, "What is mine is yours. My body. My heart."

Her breath caught. "Leaper…"

"Kerry." His body was hard, needing her and aching for her. His lips found hers. Passion swept through his body.

She broke the kiss and took his hand. "Follow me." In her free hand were her wet clothes, and it reminded him to grab his shorts. He pulled them on hastily.

They walked along the sand dune in front of his home to a small stone wall. His body was taut with need.

With the tide out, the beach stretched farther. It would be an hour or two before the tide came in and they would need to climb to safety. For now, the rocks gave them some privacy. Plenty of time for what he wanted to do…

He reached for her hand, so tiny, yet capable. It tucked into his large one, and he curled his fingers over hers, protecting her delicate digits. His instincts told him he was getting too close too fast. He didn't care. Kerry was worth the risk, and besides, his name was Leaper. Sometimes you have to live the true meaning of your name.

---

The sound was as unique as a thumbprint.

She laughed seductively, her voice low and throaty, as she broke away from Leaper's touch. "My turn. Lie down."

Playing in the sand on the rocks was incredible. Being in nature took on a whole new meaning for him. He obeyed, lying with his butt toward the sky and his privates hidden in the sand. He looked over his shoulder and winked. "How's this?" He laughed. He'd had enough sugar-cookie drills to make sure his shorts were over him before he pulled that "dick in the sand" move. No one wanted a sandpaper ride, not him and especially not her.

"Leaper!" She smacked his ass, sending a reverberation of pleasure through him. "You like it. I can see it on your face. Damn. What have I started?"

Slowly, he rolled over…so his cock was directly below her pleasure zone, and then he lifted himself to her. "I like a lot of things. Let's explore that. But… ladies first."

"Chivalry. Hmm, that's nice. Manners are not lost on you, Mr. Lefton. You're earning brownie points."

"Points, huh? I have several 'points' I'd like to make. Like this." His hands reached, caressing the tops of her thighs and her hips, fingertips brushing lightly. Then he cupped her breasts as his thumbs played over her nipples, making her breathing quicken and her body move. His cock was trapped beneath her movements, and it was an exquisite torture.

He moved his hands with long, gentle sweeps

between her legs, teasing her. Then he cupped one of her favorite spots and stroked the smooth skin of her nether lips. She purred with delight.

Kerry pulled her T-shirt over her head and stared down at him, no longer the siren. Now she was like the radiant Celtic war queen Boudicca, about to quell her chattel.

And Leaper was ready to do her bidding. His eyes were locked on hers.

Parting that glorious entrance with his fingers, he touched the top of her clitoris. She lifted her hips upward, giving him better access. This was what he loved…her deep-rooted sexiness, this glorious self-comfort, and the confidence it gave her to open up and enjoy a beautifully hedonistic experience. This was the greatest aphrodisiac on the planet.

The two fingers of his free hand gradually slid into her, reaching into heaven one centimeter at a time. The inside of her body was supple and slick.

Her muscles moved, locking tight on him. They pulled, wanting more.

Slowly he pulsed his fingers in and out. He let her set the rhythm, feeling the exquisiteness of her juices as they wet his hand. With his other hand he could feel the pulse of her against his thumb. "Yes, sweetness. My Kerry. That's it."

He turned his fingers slowly, creating an erotic rhythm to take her higher. She responded immediately to the intensity.

"Oh God! Leaper!" Her thighs clutched the sides of his hips with incredible strength.

"Go, darling. Go. Enjoy the freedom."

She tossed her head back, her hair flying in the wind like a sensuous queen's, and she rode his fingers until she cried out in pleasure.

Still he did not stop. His hands played over her nether regions again and again until at last she cried out for a final time and wept with the power of her release.

As the tears fell on his chest, he withdrew. He lifted the discarded T-shirt, wrapped it around her, and opened his arms to warm her further.

She snuggled tighter, wrapping her body tightly against his. So sweet.

He held her close. His cock was thick, pulsing, and hard. He wanted her so much. He could have rolled her underneath him and made love to her for another hour or two.

Being inside of her was beyond description, indefinable on the pleasure scale. Yet, as her breathing settled into a rhythm and her body relaxed, this moment was full of such intense emotional bliss, he didn't dare move. As a SEAL he was used to physically "toughing it out." Holding her like this—well, he wanted to cement it into his brain so he could draw on it again. This would be a golden moment he'd drag out when he was waiting in the woods somewhere. In the movies and media, they never talk about those long, boring moments when you're shitting in a bag and rationing your water until the call to move out comes through.

Kerry moved restlessly as she slept, pushing the T-shirt onto the sand. The final barrier was gone. They were heart to heart. Her bare breasts were on his naked chest. She purred sweetly, sounding content.

He willed his warmth to envelop her. He knew he

was a furnace on most nights. He hoped it was enough to keep her comfortable until she woke naturally and he could take her inside and tuck her into his bed. Having her in his home made the place…better. Was it strange to enjoy the sight of her panties on his chair or her hair band on his countertop—and best of all, of her at his kitchen table and in his bed?

Her breathing came out in soft steady puffs, a darling purr.

*Kerry*, he thought as he wrapped his arms more tightly around her. *I'll hold you, dear lady, lost in pleasure— yours and mine. For you, I can wait forever.*

—∿—

Kerry smiled at him. "This is like…instant transport."

"Really? Are you clicking your heels and arriving at your destination by the third beat?" asked Leaper as he avoided an eager paddleboarder who was inexperienced and veering dangerously toward the shipping lane. Waves radiated from the boat, forcing the paddleboarder to lie down on the board and head back toward shore.

"Close enough. Being taken to work by boat is pretty snazzy treatment," said Kerry as the wind blew her hair in swirls around her. She could feel the eyes of her man watching her. "A lady could get used to this white-glove taxi service." She shook her rear teasingly. "By the by, I can't believe Glorietta Bay has so much morning traffic. San Diego definitely has a busy port." She looked over her shoulder at him.

His eyes moved upward to meet hers. "Hey, sexy lady, do you think this trip is free? I'm planning to take my wages out in sexual favors." Leaper's grin was alight with pleasure.

She wanted to see what other parts of him could salute too. She knew she was being bad, but he brought out the vixen in her, and she loved it. Coming around to the back of the boat, she snuggled up beside him and teased her fingertips along the inside of his thighs.

"A little to left," requested Leaper. "To quote Beyoncé, 'To the left, to the left…'"

She smacked his back. "Leaper!"

"Oh yeah, that's the spot. Do it again." He wiggled his back against her without losing control of the boat. She could attest to the fact that the man had many, many skills in both the boating and bedroom department.

"You're incorrigible," she teased.

"The engine's loud." He pointed to his ears. "Encourage you, you say? Absolutely! I'm happy to. Just say when."

She shook her head and stood as they neared the dock. "When." She stuck her tongue out at him and jumped onto the dock. Her landing shook the boards with a slight vibration, but she didn't fall on her butt. Success.

"Don't tease me, or I'll take that as an invitation to French kiss you in front of all your colleagues." Leaper cut the engine.

She squeaked, "Don't you dare."

"As you wish. I won't take it as a knock on my abilities or my manhood, rather that you'd prefer to pillage me in private."

Kerry laughed. "I adore you."

"Have a wonderful day, dear lady." He bowed to her.

"And to you, handsome man." She blew him a kiss.

As the engine fired up, she couldn't resist looking back at him and waving. He returned the gesture, and a wave of butterflies fluttered around her heart.

Kerry took a deep breath. She couldn't remember the last time she'd felt so happy and relaxed. Having a sex life was doing wonders for her, especially in her off-hours. Considering she was a die-hard workaholic, this change of pace was unexpected and wonderful. She was even considering canceling her standard massage appointment. Why did having the right person in her life make her world seem bigger?

She hummed as she walked down the dock, adding a skip in her step now and then. As she walked up the gangplank and went through the security door heading toward the office, it took her a few seconds to realize she was humming Village People's "In the Navy."

She smiled. *How appropriate!*

She waved to the security guard posted near the double doors and let herself into the main office. Taking a hair band from around her wrist, she wound her hair into a bun and secured it in place. Time to switch into doctor mode.

There was a stack of mail for her in her postal slot. She sorted through it, looking for a particular packet of information. She'd sent a blood sample of Merry's to a secondary laboratory for verification, and the results were bound to be here. Sure enough, she spotted an envelope from the lab.

Stuffing the rest of the mail back into her cubbyhole, she took the packet back down to the docks and sat next to Merry's pen. She ripped open the envelope and read the numbers. Then read them again. Staring at them wasn't changing the reality. There were several high and low values, and none of it matched their current lab results. This wasn't just bad—it was a nightmare.

Her happiness washed away. This news frightened her, and at the same time, it completely frustrated her. How long had the lab been giving false results? Heads were going to roll for sure, but that wasn't her main concern. It was the dolphins. They were the ones at risk and the creatures she promised to watch over.

Her eyes traveled down the length of the dock and marked all the dolphins housed there. She wondered if any of them were in danger.

Her stomach twisted. *Dear Lord, please don't let any of them have the virus the wild dolphins have. Please, please, please.*

She tucked the results back into the envelope and secured it in her waistband. She needed to think, come up with some kind of plan. But first she had to calm down.

Lying on her belly on the dock, she stared into the water. Her reflection showed a miserable and distraught woman with eyes full of fear. She dangled fingers over the side of Merry's pen and gently wiggled them in the water.

Merry arrived in record time. Her skin slid against Kerry's fingertips. The dolphin rolled onto her side, giving Kerry her fin and waiting for loving strokes.

"You're so precious, Merry." Emotions clogged her throat. She choked out the words, "All of you are," before her eyes flooded with tears that fell into the pen below her.

Merry nudged Kerry's hand with her snout. She rubbed several times, and it was as if the peace of the marine mammal was being transmitted into Kerry's very core. Worry was replaced by determination as if at the flip of a switch. "I understand. You're right, Merry. Time for action." She stroked the dolphin one last time, and then she steeled herself for the battle ahead.

Pulling out her kit, she took samples from Merry and worked her way down the line of dolphins, gathering skin, saliva, and blood. Kerry was going to use her skills to solve this problem.

---

Nobody likes fights or confrontations. People react to accusations with "fight or flight." Not that any of the lab techs were interested in exerting even an ounce of energy. Their "hang loose" attitude made her want to stuff them onto ecofriendly scooters and toss them off the base, but that would probably be a reward, especially with a good surf report today.

"What happened to integrity in the workplace? Doesn't anyone give a rat's ass about doing a job well?" Kerry spoke the thoughts aloud, but she could have been screaming them from the top of the building for all anyone cared. The lab was empty. At first attack, the techs had scattered, and she was left with an empty room. Their supervisor was conveniently on vacation for two more weeks.

Putting the samples from the marine mammals into safe storage and locking the cooler, Kerry decided to do something that she hadn't done since she was a child. She walked over to the recycling bin and kicked the shit out of it, screaming, "Fuck you!" at the top of her lungs and tossing the few papers onto the floor. When her energy was somewhat spent, she cleaned up her mess and sat down on a stool and waited. Surely someone who knew how to work some of this equipment would come in.

It seemed like an eternity until the door opened and sunlight streamed in. She saw one of the vet interns, Dilly, who had an armful of extra sample kits. "Hi, Dr. Hamilton."

"Hey, Dilly. You can store the sample kits in the far shelving unit."

"Sure." Dilly put away the extra kits and then took the stool next to Kerry. "What's up? How can I help?"

"Can you refresh my memory on how I access the digital readouts on the lab equipment versus the reports generated on the computer? They are separate, right?"

Dilly nodded. "Yeah. They've changed the system, and they're supposed to be linked, but there was a problem about six months back, before that big display of dolphins in Georgia." She walked over to the machine. Picking up the manual next to the machine, she paged through the text until she found the right code. She punched it into the keypad, and thousands of numbers sped by. "Wait." Picking up the portable printer, she hooked it into the back and then entered the code again, followed by a print order. The machine spat out page after page of readings.

Kerry was relieved. It was one thing to follow her gut and shout to get a response, but when it fell on uninterested souls…she knew she was sunk. At least until Dilly came along and produced the exact data she needed.

"Doc, this is going to take at least six reams of paper. I'm going to run up to the office and grab a case."

"That's great. It'll be a lot to sort, but it'll be worth it." Kerry nodded. "Thanks, Dilly."

"Oh, and if you find yourself taking a dolphin out, I'd like to go sometime. If that's cool." She waited, biting her lower lip. What a sweet, brilliant soul. Dilly had a full ride to Stanford and was taking a semester off to be at the Marine Mammal Program, helping out wherever it was needed. She was a trooper.

"Consider it done," replied Kerry. *Unless I get fired for stirring up all of this crap.*

Gathering the first batch of numbers, Kerry accessed the information she had for each of her patients, starting six months ago. Her heart sank as she confirmed the facts: the lab had been changing the numbers to clear the dolphins. Someone high up had had to approve this action, because the techs wouldn't have done it for a lark. As much as she'd had a tantrum five minutes ago about their lack of assistance, she had known many of the techs for years, and they were basically decent souls. Except for this. But if their jobs had been threatened, could she understand their position? Work in the marine mammal field was tough to find, though she knew she'd rather quit than hurt any creature.

Kerry was sick to her stomach. "Morals just aren't in vogue anymore. How am I going to fight an unknown enemy?" She shook her head. "I have to try."

After spending the entire morning running from the lab to the office and talking with over twenty staffers, techs, and trustees, Kerry was on the verge of blowing another gasket. She was stressed beyond her capacity for keeping it in check, and she wasn't leaving this fight until there was an action plan in motion.

"Can you repeat the course of events?" asked the
Chairman of the Trustees. "I have Admiral Walter Dale
on the line."

Kerry pursed her lips to stop the string of curses bub-
bling inside her. She took several calming breaths and
launched into a shortened rendition. "I am Dr. Kerry
Hamilton. During a routine examination, one of our dolphins exhibited unusual symptoms, and I took a blood
sample. Our lab said everything was normal, but my gut
disagreed. So I took a second sample and submitted one
sample to our lab and the same sample to a secondary
facility. The results do not match. When I questioned
our lab techs, they would not give me a straight answer
and claimed I'm bullying them. I took the decision to
our Director, and we've been on the phone with all par-
ties involved ever since.

"There's something going on. I don't know if someone decided to ignore the unusual values so our dolphins could travel, or who made that call, but someone
in a position of authority had to do it. Before I went
on my own hunt, I took new samples from all of our
dolphins, and I have submitted them to two different
laboratories to confirm what I believe is the problem."
Kerry couldn't keep the frustration out of her voice. It
practically screamed. "Do something! Anything!"

There was a buzz of muted conversation on the other
line. Kerry tapped her foot impatiently. "Listen, I have
been on a roller coaster of bureaucratic red tape this
morning, and while all of you might feel perfectly fine
twiddling your thumbs and waiting for the dolphins'
deaths, I'm not! I'm concerned! Our entire dolphin
population might be infected with a virulent disease.

The time to act is *now*." Kerry slammed her hands on the desk, and the painful sting made her fingers and forearms vibrate. The conference phone jiggled before it settled on the wooden surface. "What are you going to do?"

"Miss—"

"Doctor," she corrected through gritted teeth. "*Doctor* Kerry Hamilton. Would you like me to come to wherever you are and explain in more detail?"

A second voice responded. "This is Admiral Dale. We appreciate you making us aware of the issues surrounding this problem. We will take all necessary steps to resolve it quickly, and we will keep you in the loop."

The Chairman of the Trustees added, "We'll get back to you, Dr. Hamilton."

The line went dead.

Kerry balled her hands into fists, resisting the urge to throw the conference phone through the Director's tiny, claustrophobia-inducing, barely usable office window. She turned on her heel and marched out of the office, knees high. She could have been a freaking majorette. Passing by several of the interns, she waved them off and headed to the docks.

Why hadn't she taken those jobs in Japan and Russia more seriously? Would they accept her calls now? Oh, she was too furious to even think about dealing with any boards, trustees, directors, admirals, or command structure of any kind.

"Kerry. Wait, I need to talk to you." Emme's voice penetrated some of Kerry's brain fog.

"What!" Kerry counted to ten in her head. "Sorry. What's up?"

"Don't you think you're going overboard with this whole virus thing? They're not human. It's not that big of a deal." Emme towered over her. For all the times Kerry had thought her friend cool and sophisticated, it was horrifying to hear these comments.

Kerry's mouth dropped up. She stuttered. "I-I-I can't believe you said that. Those are my friends down there in those pens. I spend more time with them than I do with humans, even my own flesh and blood. I love them, and I'm going to fight for them. Bottlenose dolphins are also a critical part of our ecosystem. If the subspecies dies out—or the entire species of dolphins and whales—what do you think happens to our ocean? Besides, we, the human race, probably poisoned them with pollution. Regardless, it's up to us to fix the problem." She pointed her finger at Emme. "If you want to be part of the solution, then help, and if not, then stay out of my way."

"You're crazy," said Emme, her cheeks flame red.

"Maybe. But if being crazy solves this problem, bring it on."

With that, Kerry stomped away. She swiped her badge at the gate on the gangplank and rushed the rest of the way down to the dock. Pacing back and forth in front of the dolphin pens, she knew she was too upset and frustrated right now. She had to calm down and develop a plan of action.

Hadn't her mother told her as a child that she was methodical—that this was one of her greatest strengths? At the age of five, Kerry had made a lemonade stand and earned forty-six dollars to buy her father a new fishing pole for his boat. If the powers that be weren't going to give her any answers, she was going to use her methodical ways to get some. "Right. Back to basics."

Just then, two figures caught her attention.

"Hey, are you two busy?" Kerry asked. "If not, I'm taking an RIB out." Without even giving the two vet techs, Clay Jones and Dilly, a chance to answer, she shared a small part of her plan and roped them into her trip.

All of them loaded into an RIB with her favorite travel medical bag and headed out to sea. "If I'm going to fight this virus, then I need samples. I hope you're both prepared to wrangle a few uncooperative wild creatures, because we're not going back until we get these samples."

"Uh…" Dilly looked at her, stunned. "I have a date, but I suppose he'll wait."

"Of course he will. Look at her." Clay nodded.

"Thanks, Clay," said Dilly.

"Grab a set of binoculars, Dilly, and look for birds feeding, or any sign of a pod or dolphin activity." Kerry held a set to her own eyes and was already scanning the horizon.

Clay drove the RIB into the Glorietta Bay Channel, heading toward open ocean waters. "Hey, Doc, I heard that the waves were breaking up around the Coronado Islands. Want to head out there? We might find a few surfers."

"Absolutely. Wait, I have an idea. Let's make a pit stop. Over there, the tenth house from Naval Air Station North Island Base." Kerry led them to Leaper's place. She pillaged his stash of paddles and paddleboards, along with several vests and three lightweight helmets, masks, sets of fins and gloves, and a knife. At the last minute, she grabbed his bait bucket, which was oddly half-full. She sniffed it; it wasn't too bad. Hungry dolphins would eat it.

Loading it all aboard, she nodded to Clay. "Take us to the Coronado Islands, Clay. Dilly, please keep scanning for signs of dolphins. I'm going to write out a few contingency plans." In her mind, a song was playing over and over, Debbie Harry and Nigel Harrison's song "One Way or Another." She was determined to get what she needed.

Taking a pad of paper from her bag, Kerry laid out the options. Tucking the pad back into her bag, she prepared several fast-filling syringes along with bags for skin samples and saliva swabs. She duplicated the process several times and soon had ready-made kits at her disposal.

"Anything, Dilly?" Kerry asked, standing up and stretching her cramped legs. She hoped she wasn't being rash. She didn't want to lead the interns into danger, but it was either bring them or go it alone.

"No," Dilly said, sounding frustrated. She lowered the binoculars and frowned.

"It's okay, Dilly. Let's give it a rest for a few minutes while I explain the test kits to you. I want you to assist me. Does that work for you?" Kerry saw Dilly's eyes brighten.

"Yes, it does. Thanks. I won't let you down." The girl practically glowed with joy at the prospect of doing open-water work. The ocean could be a contemptuous force of nature. Kerry hoped it was in a good mood and would give them a few breaks today.

Kerry touched Dilly's arm. "I know you won't. Let's glove up. Remember, these creatures are wild, so if it's between getting hurt and doing your job, I want you to protect yourself."

The waves smacked the RIB hard as they got closer to the Coronados. Kerry explained the test kits to Dilly, and then they watched the sky.

"Will it storm?" asked Dilly, looking uncertain.

Kerry reassured the techs. "One dark cloud, bolt of lightning, thunderclap, or any other weather issue and we're heading back to home port. Okay?"

"There!" shouted Dilly as she pointed to a feeding frenzy off their port bow. "Dolphin sighting."

"Fantastic! Great sighting, Dilly," Kerry said. She pulled on a safety vest and hooked one line to herself and the other to a secure ring on the side of the RIB. Dilly did the same. When both of them were as ready as they could be, Kerry said, "Clay, take us in slowly. When we're about ten feet from the feeding frenzy, cut the engines."

The RIB inched into the fracas until they achieved the right distance. Clay cut the engine and the birds screeched, wings beating against each other, splashing as they dove in and out of the water.

Kerry laid her first kit next to her. She tapped her fingers on the hull of the boat in time to the rhythm of the water.

"Dilly, start dropping the bait," Kerry ordered. Dilly dropped small chunks of salmon next to the boat. A dolphin poked its snout out of the water, and seconds later it opened its mouth, wanting more. "I've never met a dolphin that didn't love some Alaskan salmon," Kerry said.

Dilly brought the dangling bait toward Kerry, who

quickly swabbed the dolphin's open mouth, took a skin sample, and even lured it onto its back so she could get a blood sample from its tail—all while it was happily eating salmon. When she was finished, Kerry wrapped up the kit and handed it to Clay. "Mark it female, adolescent. The wonderful part about dolphins, especially bottlenose, is their innate curiosity. I bet we have a few more...and here they are." Kerry pulled out two kits and moved from one to the other as Dilly fed the two males. Luckily they were already fairly well fed or they might have gotten aggressive and swamped the RIB, taking whatever they wanted from the bucket of fish.

Kerry was relieved to have three dolphin samples under her belt when she saw a larger male on the other side of the boat. He seemed to be waiting for her. Was he sick? Was there a problem? As she bent down, she could see extensive scarring from fights with other predators, probably sharks. His skin was still healing in places. "Clay, can you get the green tin from my bag?"

Clay handed it to her, and Kerry rubbed a salve onto the wounds. She could tell it eased the dolphin's pain. "That should help you, big guy." When she touched her hand to his stomach, the dolphin rolled for her. Though dolphins are playful creatures, this move could take years to perfect in captivity. As her palm moved over his liver, Kerry could feel the distension. "You're sick, aren't you? Do you have this virus or something else?" Kerry kept talking as she took a blood sample. When she finished, she pointed at the cooler in the center of the RIB. "Give me a half—the center cut."

Dilly handed Kerry the thick chunk of fish.

Kerry eased the big dolphin onto his belly, took the

fish from Dilly, and gave the dolphin his treat. He took it in his mouth and swallowed it. The expression in his eyes as he stared at her…it struck her to the core, it said so much. It was a cry for help, of need, for anything to make things better. She knew it as surely as she knew rain would fall in San Diego in February. Rubbing her hand over his dorsal fin, she said, "I'll do everything in my power to help you. I promise."

Sitting back on her heels, she watched the big dolphin dive down into the ocean. She shook herself and said, "Let's get one more set of samples."

Dilly stood. "Over here. I think it's a female."

Moving to the other side of the RIB, Kerry slowly leaned over, careful to keep her weight balanced. "Good call, Dilly. It is."

Clay opened a fresh sample kit.

Kerry swabbed the female's mouth and gave the approximate weight and length to Clay, who wrote the information on the labels. Then she took a quick skin sample. The last thing was the blood sample. Holding the syringe, she attempted to coax the female onto her back, but this lady wouldn't budge.

"I don't blame you, missy," Kerry said to the female dolphin. "I get a little shy now and then too. But you're doing this to save your species. Not just bottlenoses, but everyone related to you."

A tail slapped the water and Kerry made a grab for it. The syringe fell into the boat and Kerry was pulled into the cold Pacific water. She came up sputtering, and the female dolphin's face was inches from hers. Her mouth was open, and she laughed at Kerry.

"Gee, thanks." Wiping the water off her face, she saw

the large male surface beside her. Then she witnessed something miraculous: the female turned on her back and gave Kerry her tail. That kind of trust usually took years to cultivate.

Looking over her shoulder, Kerry could see Dilly holding out a syringe. Kerry gently took the sample and handed it back to the tech. Then she noticed that the dolphins were not a random grouping. From this vantage point, she could see this was a family. On some level, they knew what was happening. "I hope we didn't do this to you." Emotion flooded her, knowing that all creatures were connected in some way. "Regardless, it's up to us to fix it. I won't stop until I do."

She returned to the boat and hoisted herself over the side. Lying on the floor of the boat and looking up at the sky, she took a few seconds to breathe and center herself. Then she unhooked the line, removed the life vest, checked that the samples were secure, and gave the order. "Back to base."

The engine roared to life as the boat made a wide circle and headed back to Glorietta Bay. The wind had grown colder, and without a change of clothes, Kerry hunkered down on her haunches and wrapped her arms around her legs.

She studied the two vet techs who were chatting excitedly about the experience. She was relieved that the trip had paid off and they were returning with something to work with. But concern about the road ahead was nagging at any sense of hope. Even with this small sampling, it could take years to develop a vaccine. Worse yet, the devastation could be dramatic enough to cause a domino effect. What if…

Kerry put her head in her hands and tried not to cry. She was growing more cynical, and she had to keep telling herself to believe.

Someone else has to be out there working on answers. She couldn't give up.

———~~~———

Arriving back at the Marine Mammal base, Kerry left the boat carrying her treasured samples. "Can you dock and clean the boat?" she asked, hoping Dilly and Clay would agree to help out. She wanted nothing more than to focus all her energy on the samples and work in the lab.

"Yes," said Dilly, who was familiar with the process. She frowned as she picked up the trash in the boat.

"Thanks and, um, you're welcome to come help me in the lab afterward, if you'd like. But you're not required to."

Kerry watched Dilly's eyes light up. "I'll be there," Dilly said. "I appreciate it. Thanks. This is very informative."

"And off the record," Kerry reminded.

"Right."

"Oh yeah, what about your date?" asked Kerry.

"There are other nights. How often do I get to work with you?" Dilly said took the garbage and dumped it into the trash bin.

Kerry smiled. She was pleased that Dilly was so committed. As she headed down the dock, her eyes scanned over the dolphins in their pens. She took mental notes on any changes in their skin or behavior. She walked up the gangplank slowly, protecting her bounty. She let herself through the gate and then headed for the tech tent. It was empty.

Pulling on paper booties, a gown, a paper shower cap, gloves, and protective eyewear, she let herself into the sterile environment through the double-door entry system.

She claimed a large table for her project and laid out the treasure. The samples came from five different dolphins. They'd managed three males and two females, and Kerry was excited to see what information the samples could provide.

Dividing each sample into four portions, she labeled and documented every task and what needed to happen with each one. She would send blood, skin, and saliva to two different laboratories, store one sample, and run the data herself on the last sample. The logical part of her personality was thrilled to have a set of checks and balances, but the emotional part was too spent to even contribute to the conversation. That part was ready for the work to be complete and the answer to be in front of her.

It wasn't going to be that easy. She put all the samples in the refrigerator and found the proper shipping containers. Writing out instructions and the packaging for the two sets of samples took the better part of two hours.

Then she repeated the tasks with the samples from her own dolphins. As she finished the tasks, a wave of exhaustion hit Kerry. She steadied herself and pushed on. Her need to help the dolphins was going to carry her through these crucial tasks.

Dilly came into the sterile field dressed in appropriate attire as Kerry finished up and watched her efforts. It was like having an eager kid dogging her steps, but if it made Dilly a better vet, it was worth it.

"Ask questions," Kerry reminded her. "I'm open to answering them."

"Why did you choose two different laboratories? Won't they produce the same results?"

Kerry cocked her head to the side. "In theory, yes. But it's possible that their instruments are gauged differently or that there's something wrong with the sample or its prep, *or* something happens in transit. Basically, I *want* the results to be the same. Redundancy is good in this case, but I have to be prepared for it not to be."

"Are you running the same tests here for the same reason?" Dilly sat down on a stool. There were circles under her eyes, the goggles making every line look more pronounced. The poor girl looked tired. Maybe Kerry was working her too hard. Then again, Kerry never asked more from anyone than she required of herself.

Though Kerry could honestly admit that she too was running on fumes. "The tests I'm performing now are going to be used as my personal control data. I'm setting my levels here."

Dilly yawned. "Sorry."

"Don't be. I'm exhausted too. Why don't you knock off? You could drop off the samples at the shipping company before you go home." Kerry pointed to the refrigerator. "You'd be doing me a great favor. The sooner they're on the move, the sooner we get our results."

"Happy to." Dilly opened the refrigerator and took out the two shipping boxes. "I'll text you a picture of the shipping information."

"Thanks. See you tomorrow." Kerry stopped Dilly before she could leave the sterile environment. "You did really good work today. You kept your head in the situation, especially given a set of strange working circumstances, and you excelled at your tasks. Well done."

Dilly's face lit up with joy. Bright eyed and wearing a toothy grin, she looked as if she'd won the lottery as she bounced on the balls of her toes. "Thanks, Dr. Hamilton. That means a lot."

"Kerry. Call me Kerry." She knew she was letting her guard down, but she wanted to be able to rely on at least one other person at work. Having that individual be a woman who strove to follow in her footsteps was a bonus, and it bolstered Kerry's spirits. "Good night."

"Okay, Kerry. You too. Have a great night." Dilly went through the double door and into the regular part of the lab tent. Kerry tracked Dilly's progress until she was alone.

Sometimes Kerry preferred things this way…just her and her work. What else did she need? A small part of her brain nudged her, reminding that she should call him. *Later. I'm on to something here.*

And then she got lost in the data, a world of numbers that meant so much more than they expressed on paper.

———~~~———

The sterile environment was empty and as close to silent as was possible at the Marine Mammal base. The dolphins vocalized and chatted with each other, and the sea lions communicated too. Kerry had determined over the years that the sea lions always wanted more food, and the dolphins adored playing more than anything else — they wanted to engage.

Finished with all of the tests, Kerry sat down heavily on the stool. She ached in places she didn't think it was possible to ache. She looked up at the clock and saw that it was two hours past the time she was supposed to call Leaper.

She sighed. "I'm a rotten girlfriend. He'll understand, right?"

Methodically, she stored the leftover sample materials in the refrigerator, making sure they were properly labeled, and then she cleaned up the table she was using. She took her flash drive, printouts, and notes and left the sterile environment through the double-entry doors. The *whoosh* of the doors was oddly reassuring, and the noise from the mammals was a welcome cacophony. Happy chatting was a good sign.

Stripping off the paper garments, she stuffed them in the appropriate bin and located her phone. She dialed Leaper's number. It connected after the second ring. "Hey. Sorry."

"No worries. I figured you were working." Leaper was calm, and she was relieved he was so laid-back. One guy she had dated a few years ago had freaked out when she didn't call at the specified time. Was it any surprise that someone like that wasn't going to last in her world? Work was a completely engrossing experience for her.

"Yeah. I'm still here." She rubbed her forehead and felt the paper shower cap still on her head. "Dang, I'm tired." Whipping off the cap, she walked back to the correct bin and shoved it inside.

"Do you need help?" His offer was so sweet, but there wasn't much more left to do.

"Thanks. No. I don't have that much left." She bumped her hip accidently on the table and almost lost her balance. Suddenly she remembered the equipment she'd borrowed from his house. "I meant to tell you... I robbed you earlier today. I took a few things to help with my excursion."

He chuckled. "Yeah. I know."

"How?"

"Trackers. They're on everything I own. I think there might even be one on my butt." His chortle made her laugh.

"I'll check for you, next time I'm down there." Smiling felt so good, especially after the day she'd had. "Thanks for the loan. I'll load it into my vehicle and—"

"No need," he said. "When I saw the stuff was at the Marine Mammal base, I figured you were either using it for fun or work, so I swung by and saw Clay unloading it. He briefed me as we loaded it into the boat. I'm glad it worked out."

"Me too." She rubbed her eyes, trying to coax them to focus just a little longer before they required sleep.

"He only gave me the basics. I'd like to hear the whole story."

"I'd be happy to share it. My work is almost complete. I have a few more things to do." Kerry picked up her purse and the data and walked to the lab tent's exit.

"No rush. I'm here. Come over when it suits you." Leaper was so easygoing. She adored that about him. How did she get so lucky?

"Great. See you soon." She hung up.

Kerry took her flash drive full of information to her car. She had run tests on her dolphins several times now, and the results were the same. Adding the data from the wild dolphins made her even more certain. The same illness was in both groups, and it would kill them unless something changed. Her heart hurt at the thought. She just couldn't let that happen.

She took her laptop from the case in the backseat and loaded the data onto the hard drive. Using her phone as a link to the internet, she logged into a private website for marine mammal research, recovery, and relocation. Without disclosing her place of employment, she made the data as generic as she could while maintaining the integrity of her sampling, and then she uploaded the data with her name attached.

Since she volunteered for a number of facilities such as aquariums or water-themed marine mammal parks throughout the United States, her client would stay hidden unless she decided to reveal it. At this point in the process, Kerry was hanging on to that fact in case she needed a bargaining chip with the trustees. Sure, it might cost her this beloved job, but it would save her dolphins—her friends— and that meant more than any paycheck ever could.

Reviewing results from other researchers, she located a research scientist and doctor in Greenland who had encountered the same virus and was having positive results with a vaccine he'd made. He based his chemical compounds on a study done by the National Oceanic and Atmospheric Administration, or NOAA, who said the virus was being named the morbillivirus infection, which "resembles a measles infection; in addition to bottlenose dolphins being at risk, porpoises and whales are too."

*Shit! This is frightening news.*

Kerry sent him a private message with a link to her data. Tapping her fingers, she wondered what time it was in Greenland.

His response was quick, so she guessed the time difference didn't matter. She read on, and he was extremely generous with his offer. He included a copy of all of his findings as well as the formula for a vaccine.

She could hardly believe her eyes. Loading his data onto her thumb drive and taking a picture of the formula with her phone, she was eager to talk to the trustees and her fellow doctors. She wrote a quick note to her fellow staffers and sent a copy of the formula, and she copied the message to the Director. She prayed they were as eager to help the dolphins as she was.

She pressed the heels of her palms against her eyes, which throbbed with overuse and exhaustion. Sending a second message to the vet in Greenland, she thanked him for his information and told him that she'd keep him in the loop.

She turned off her computer and put it back in her computer bag, taking it with her when she locked up the car. Heading back down to the dock, she texted Leaper: I'm too tired. Can you come get me in the boat?

His reply was swift. I'm on my way.

She let herself through the security gates, waved at the guards, and headed slowly down the dock. Her gaze lingered on each dolphin. She knew them better than her own sisters.

She sat down on the dock next to Juliet's pen, not daring to close her eyes.

Sleep sucked her under just as she heard a boat pull up to the dock. Kerry was vaguely aware of the strong arms that lifted her, tucked her into a corner of the RIB, and wrapped thick blankets around her. Distantly, she heard Leaper's voice and wanted to thank him. But when the boat began its journey home, the movement lulled Kerry into a deep, deep sleep. Darkness took her fully away to a place where dreams didn't dare intrude.

# Chapter 7

PANIC GRIPPED HER. RACING PULSE, RAPID HEARTBEAT, AND cold sweats overloaded her senses as Kerry fought to wake up. When she did, she didn't know where she was. She couldn't even remember going to bed. She panted as she tried to calm down.

A hand touched her shoulder, and she practically flew out of bed.

Backing up too fast, she hit the wall hard and slid down to the floor, landing in a shivering heap.

"It's me," said Leaper, switching on the light. He came over to sit beside her. "Bad dream?"

"Don't know." She was rocking. "Disoriented. So much…fear. I don't know how, where the time went." Her breathing was growing strained. She was on the verge of an anxiety attack. "You and me, coming here… How did that happen?"

"Kerry, slow down. Breathe with me and I'll explain everything." Leaper had her inhaling and exhaling on a four count until she could feel the terror lifting.

"Thanks," she said softly. "I'm better."

He nodded. "You texted me and asked me to come get you in the boat. You were asleep next to Juliet's pen, the place where we had a dinner date. I picked you up, brought you here, and tucked you into bed."

"Right. The text. I remember that." Kerry looked

down at her body. She was wearing a T-shirt and panties. She raised an eyebrow. "Did you undress me?"

He nodded, like a pup that was happy to see his owner. "The first thing you always do is take off your bra, and I didn't want you to get cold, so I put my SEAL Team FIVE shirt on you, which you fill out better than I do."

She rolled her eyes. "And I slept through the whole thing."

"Like a babe. I was gentle and respectful."

Kerry didn't doubt that for a moment. "Sorry I got freaked out. It was such a long and overwhelming day."

He stood up and offered her a hand. "C'mon, I make a great cup of hot cocoa, if you want to tell me all about it."

Placing her hand in his, she nodded. "I'd like that." This was precisely what she needed, to unwind. "Are we having marshmallows or whipped cream?"

Leaper pulled her to her feet. He held her close for several seconds, and then he kissed her nose and led the way into the kitchen. "I'm a professional. We're using both."

---

The boat skipped over the frothy waves as if it were giddy to be cutting through the ocean at full speed. She'd spent three grueling days producing the vaccine correctly, per the instructions of the Greenland vet, and she was praying that it would work. Going into the vast ocean to find a pod of dolphins was like hunting for a yellow needle in a stack of loose hay, but they were still going to do it. One look at her man and she knew his determination matched her own.

She breathed deeply. The fresh air was so sweet,

she practically gulped it in as she stared at the horizon. Kerry knew she would always choose the outdoors to being cooped up, no matter what the weather was like, though she also preferred having control. Mother Nature rarely allowed human beings that privilege.

A cool wind smacked her face hard, whipping her hair into her eyes. Kerry pulled up the hood of Leaper's sweatshirt and cinched it tightly over her hair. She couldn't stop herself from winding her fingers into the dangling strings and chewing on one of the giant string notes until her inner turmoil became so heavy, she finally blurted out, "Are you sure?"

He glanced at her and said, "For the fourth time, yes. Kerry, please relax. Fidgeting isn't going to make this go any faster or any better. Just take some time to review your tasks and chill and then face the situation; do your best, and go home. It's all any of us can do."

"I bet you say that to all the trainees."

He raised his eyebrow and made a noise.

"Yeah, you're right. I get it." She rubbed her cold nose and tucked her hands into the giant front pocket. Underneath the soft sweatshirt, her body was encased in a wetsuit and her core was toasty warm. In truth, it probably wasn't even that chilly out, but her concern about the vaccine was seriously getting to her. If someone put the fate of an entire species in your hand, wouldn't you be nervous?

Glancing over her shoulder, she review their supplies. They'd laid down waterproof camp mattresses in the back of his boat, because this was a risky endeavor—heading into the ocean to find a wild bottlenose that would allow itself to be captured and tagged—and if a human being didn't use it, then they could hoist a dolphin into the boat. Seriously, she was glad to have him with her.

Tucked between her feet was a bag of dry clothes, a large thermos of coffee, breakfast bars, salty snacks, potassium treats, and bottles of water. In back was a massive first aid kit and the doses of vaccine were split between two coolers. There was even an empty cooler for samples. What more could she do?

As Leaper chomped on a breakfast bar, she threw him a wry look. How he could eat was beyond her understanding or capability. She was more likely to heave than swallow food. Her adrenaline was rushing, and she was too keyed up to devour anything. *Of course*, she thought, looking at him, *I do have a special kind of hunger for him*. That thought made her smile.

*Dang, he's right. I need to loosen up.*

"Are we heading to San Clemente Island? We took our samples from a pod near the Coronados. Can we head there?"

He nodded his head. "Were you near the breakers?"

"Yes. I don't know if we'll find the same pod, but I want to try."

The night was dark and there wasn't much light, except for the stars and moon above and their boat. Leaper turned the boat downwind, and for several seconds they were airborne. "I'm not sure if I'll find a place to anchor in that area. There are deep caverns. Tell me when to stop, and I'll see what I can do."

Kerry stood up and pointed. "Over there, about fifty feet."

Leaper slowed the engine. The boat passed over the

area several times. He looked over at her and held her gaze. "Don't look so upset. You knew it would be a long shot."

"Yeah, I know."

He hugged her.

She broke the embrace and paced the length of the boat. "I want it—this—to matter," Kerry said, angrily slamming her foot against the toolbox.

Leaper approached her slowly. He opened his arms. "You matter to me."

"Thank you, but that's not what I mean." She allowed herself to find comfort in his embrace again. "I need to leave my mark. I entered this world and I helped someone, something, specifically the dolphins. I can't let them die." Her body shook as she wept.

His hands rubbed her back, soothing her. "Let it out."

She pounded her fist on his chest. "What's the point of having all this education and experience without putting myself on the line? I need to save the dolphins. How can I look my patients, my friends, my *dolphins* in the eyes, knowing that I wasn't willing to risk every ounce of my life for them?"

"I get it. Honestly, I do." Leaper's words were gentle. "We're not giving up. Are you willing to give my spot a try?"

She nodded. "Yes."

Leaper escorted her back to her seat and then drove the boat away from the breaks. He brought it to the far side of the island. The water was calmer here.

It was nice to be out of the screaming wind.

Out of the coroner of her eye, she caught sight of a fin. "There!"

Bringing the boat into a small grotto that was protected from the wind, Leaper cut the engine and pulled up the prop. He said, "We have about eight to ten minutes before we can haul her onto the sand." The boat drifted slowly toward a sandy beach.

Kerry's eyes scanned the water. She tapped her fingers against the boat, hoping the pod might recognize her. No one came. "Crap." Frustration was welling inside of her.

Several heads popped out of the water. Kerry recognized the older male. "It's them. Yes, yes, yes! Thank goodness!" Pulling off Leaper's sweatshirt, she placed it next to the thermos and prepared to lower herself into the water.

"Not so fast," said Leaper, grabbing her arm. "Take a breath. You need your vaccine and your tagging equipment, *and* you're not going into the water without me."

"You're right. I'm rushing. I'm excited. I can't help it." Kerry sat down and counted to ten before gathering her tagging equipment and the vaccine. "Leaper, am I a monster for wanting to do this? Individuals who don't quarantine and follow specific protocols can run the risk of unleashing something horrific into the ecosystem." She shook her head. "Maybe I've watched too many zombie movies."

"Kerry, you're not a monster. I'm not a monster. What you're doing in attempting to save an entire subspecies of dolphin takes kindness, love, and respect. Cut yourself some slack." Leaper squeezed her knee. "Besides, didn't that guy in Greenland test the vaccine on the dolphins in the Atlantic? It's already in the ecosystem. If it had negative repercussions, wouldn't they already have happened?"

"Good point. Let's go for it. And if this is a giant mess, it's on me."

Leaper lowered an anchor, securing the boat in the deeper area, and then dropped lights over the side of the boat and secured the lines to cleats. The entire grotto lit up, and they could both see two different pods in the area. "I see stingrays in the sand, a lot of them, which means you cannot put your feet down under any circumstances," Leaper said.

"Thanks. I try to be aware of them." She'd seen a man wearing a wetsuit who was pierced through the chest by a stingray. The wetsuit had barely slowed down the stingray. It was horrifying. "Why don't you go in first? You can be the safety. Let's hang by the boat for five minutes and see what happens."

"Sure thing." Leaper was attaching several knives, bandanas, and a spear gun to his person. He put the fins on his feet, then splashed water into the mask, dumped it, and put it on. He was in the water before Kerry was done gearing up.

Kerry attached the tagging equipment to her dive belt and then tucked the injectable vaccine into a pouch. Grabbing swim fins and a mask, she lowered herself beside him.

They waited patiently. When none of the dolphins came near, Kerry signaled to Leaper to stay, and she swam toward the older male dolphin. The rest of the members of his pod scattered, but he stayed put.

Stopping a few feet from him, she put out her hand.

He came forward and nudged it with his snout. He allowed her to rub down the length of his back. When her hands were on the fluke where she would normally take blood in an examination, she dove underneath him, gave him the vaccine, and quickly tagged him.

The dolphin didn't seem to notice she had done anything. If he had… Well, dolphins can stop the blood flow to parts of their body, and she definitely did not want him to do that. So she continued to rub him and caress him until she had to go to the surface for more air.

*Poor guy. His lymph glands are horribly swollen and misshapen. I wish I could do more to ease his symptoms.*

Taking breaths as deep as she could, she replenished her air supply and made her way back down to him. Where was he? She turned in a circle looking for him.

Leaper pointed above her. It was nice having him there with her. He'd come closer to help her when she was clear of the dolphin. What a thoughtful soul.

Kerry smiled and stroked his arm.

A creature nudged her thigh.

She spun.

The dolphin was in front of her, and then he danced to the side. He was playing hide-and-seek with her. Well, he had to be feeling better. Should it be that instantaneous? Who knew? This was all so new.

Running her hands over the dolphin again, she noticed that the swelling on his body was reducing. The inoculation was definitely helping. The elation made her skin tingly with excitement, and she couldn't stop smiling.

Leaper had backed up yards to give her room, and he gave her a thumbs-up.

She nodded at him and pointed to the boat. As she swam, she contemplated what this meant. A cure could change everything. Oh God, please let this be true. Surfacing near the boat, she wiped her hand against her chin, dislodging a small piece of seaweed. She didn't care. She'd become a sea hag, if it could save the dolphins.

"What are the details? How did it work?" Leaper asked.

"It's amazing, Leaper. I've never seen a dolphin heal this fast. Where there was distension when I first touched him, it's halved. This shot was meant to be preventive, a vaccine to help the body produce antibodies to prevent the disease, and yet it's acting as a cure. An actual cure." She put her hand on the side of the boat. "It's better than I'd hoped. I wish we could get this male in the boat and take him home, but the pod might follow, and I don't want them getting hurt or trapped in the bay. Human beings have very little awareness of what's swimming underneath their water transports, and everyone wants to manhandle the dolphins. Bet human beings wouldn't like to be treated that way."

Leaper nodded. "Wild dolphins tend to freak out in captivity, don't they?"

"Sometimes. Wounded ones do okay for a short time, but if they're in too long, it does something to their spirit. Of course, the dolphins raised in captivity prefer the pen, because it's home and they are safe and well cared for and tend to live longer." She was anxious to activate the tracking equipment. "Let's get going. If I need to come back here or go find him, I have the right tools."

"Great. Let's go. You have my full support," Leaper finished. "Back in the boat?"

"Yes, please." Kerry was happy when one of Leaper's strong arms pushed her straight up into the air and onto the boat. Man, he had *serious* muscles.

He hauled himself up beside her. "You know, there's

a cave system we can stop at on the way home. We can visit all the glowworms inside."

"I've heard of it, but never been. As long as we only go partway in." Kerry was so happy that she would have agreed to walk on hot coals.

They stored their gear on the boat. Leaper pulled up the anchor, secured it, and lowered the prop into the water. He drove the boat slowly out of the grotto. The lights were still hung over the side, and he was able to avoid hitting any dolphins with the prop. When they were in deeper water, Leaper motioned to Kerry about the lights. She gave him a thumbs-up and pulled up the lights. She turned them off, securing them in the toolbox.

"Ready," she announced.

"Onward ho," Leaper said with a smile.

He touched a button on his phone and music filled the night air. The song was "Come Together'" by the Yesteryears. Listening to Leaper sing along made her laugh.

*Oh, Leaper*, she thought. *You're a great partner in crime, and thank you for bringing so much levity and love to my life.*

---

*Do I love her?*

*Do I romance with my eyes or my heart? Does every touch set my world on fire?*

*Dang, is it possible to qualify what it means to spend time with someone?*

Leaper pondered these questions as he dropped the anchor. When he touched Kerry, his mind drifted someplace else, and he didn't even *want* to force it to function.

The boat was off the coast of La Jolla. The ocean waves were small, and the wind had died down. The water looked peaceful, almost glassy and calm. He made sure there was enough battery charge to keep the lights on. There was, but not enough to drop dive lights over the side. He placed the dive buoy and flag in the water and tied it to a cleat on the boat. "Can you grab flashlights?" he asked Kerry.

"Will do."

He checked the knives, which were still securely strapped to his thighs. He watched Kerry take flashlights, swim fins, masks, and snorkels from the toolbox.

She handed him gear. Their fingers grazed, sending sparks through his system. He wondered if he'd ever get used to it. Did electricity fade, or would their connection only grow stronger? "Thanks, Kerry."

"You're welcome, Leaper. I'm glad you choose this cave system. It's big enough to drive a Mack truck through the center of it. I'm a tad bit claustrophobic, so this place works for me on multiple levels." She leaned over and scooped water in her mask, then dumped it out. "Last one in is a rotten egg."

Leaper donned his gear and slid quickly over the side of the boat. It took a second for his eyes to adjust and locate Kerry, and then he switched the flashlight on. A bright beam of light illuminated the area around them.

A hammerhead shark veered into the edge of the light and then changed course. Leaper had swum with a variety of marine life and found that if you didn't bother them, you were often left alone. But if something invaded his personal space, the gloves came off, and Leaper would end the fight very quickly.

Kerry pointed ahead to the cave entrance. He took her hand and they swam side by side underwater, using their fins to propel them. As they entered the caves, they came to the surface.

Leaper blew water out of his snorkel and removed it from his mouth. He pointed his waterproof flashlight at the ceiling and walls. "Right there, in the upper corner, you'll see glowworms. There are only a few, and I think their presence has something to do with the limestone deposits." He swam under a drip of water. "This is fresh water. If you open your mouth, you can taste it."

Kerry laughed. "I don't have a cast-iron constitution like yours. I'll take your word for it. How did you learn about glowworms, by the way?"

"I was on a mission, and we stopped off in New Zealand. Declan and I visited Waitomo. Now, there's a spectacular sight, and one I'd like to see again, if you're game." Leaper moved his light to another spot. "Over there is a type of fungus that some people call cave flowers."

"This cave has so much life in it." Kerry swam closer to him. "Is that a ledge?"

He nodded. "Want to take a break?"

"Okay."

Leaper gave Kerry a boost onto the stone ledge. "How's the view?" He pulled himself up beside her.

"Lovely." She turned to him, then leaned in and kissed him. "There's no one around, right?"

"Not unless the Coast Guard stops by. My diving buoy and flag are out, so we should be okay for a little while. What did you have in mind?"

"How about some hanky-panky?" Kerry said softly

as she wiggled out of her wetsuit and removed her one-piece bathing suit.

Leaper was already stripped down to his bare skin by the time Kerry finished. She was so free-spirited, confident, and beautiful, and the way her eyes sparkled with mischief…it was intoxicating. "I have my panky, but I think I left my hanky in the boat."

"*Leaper*." She drew his name out in long, sexy syllables that echoed around them.

"That's some echo. Keep in mind there's a walkway above, probably with adults and kids."

"So what?" Kerry shrugged. "It'd take them a while to get down here, and we'll be done by then."

"So this is a quickie."

She pointed at his cock. "No. That's a longie."

He chuckled and reached for her. Kerry dodged out of his grasp. Then she lifted her tush in the air and wiggled at him. "Come and get me, big boy."

Leaper didn't need to be asked twice. His mouth zeroed in on her clit, and he delighted in her sighs as he played a few of his favorite rhythmic movements against her most sensitive spot. She was dripping with wetness.

He got on his knees and teased the tip of his cock over her entrance.

She pushed back into him. "Leaper." Her tone was annoyed. "I want you. Now."

"As you wish." Leaper thrust his cock into her wet, waiting sheath. Enveloped in warmth and pure delight, Leaper remained very still while she arched her back and came just from the sheer size of him.

Kerry's breathing returned to normal. That was his cue to thrust in and out of her slick, blissful warmth. Her body continued to reach for him, urging him to go faster and harder, until they moved as one in a powerful union that took them both over the edge.

They cried each other's names in unison. Their names echoed around them.

Kerry laughed, and Leaper joined in. It wasn't every day that coital sounds were amplified at this volume.

Leaper sat down on the ledge and pulled Kerry into his lap. He kissed her, their tongues teasing and tantalizing. He could feel his body priming again, but he pulled away when water splashed his feet. "We better scoot. The tide's coming in."

Kerry nodded. She pulled on her bathing suit but struggled with her wetsuit. Leaper dressed with ease, and by the time she turned to him for help, he was already ready to go. "How did you get your trunks and wetsuit on so quickly?"

He shrugged. "Practice." The water was splashing around their ankles, and they needed to get out of the cave before the waves filled the entire space. Leaper helped Kerry tug on her wetsuit. "When we get in the water, I'm going to tie my utility belt to your wrist and connect it to mine. It's been a while since I've been in these caves with the current rushing in so fast, and I want us to stay attached."

"Thanks," she said. "I'm a decent swimmer, but this flow looks strong."

Leaper removed his utility belt. He tied one end of the strap to Kerry's wrist and the other to his own. Then they sat down on the ledge and eased into the water.

"Brrr." It was cold and gave him one helluva wake-up call.

"You're not kidding. So much colder in here than it is out there."

"It's deeper—all those cavernous tunnels and ledges."

He turned on their flashlights and gestured for her to do the same. He took slow, deep breaths and watched as she mimicked him. Then he counted to three, and they dove downward, swimming toward the entrance.

The undercurrent was pushing sand and loose plants into the water, and it was hard to see more than a few feet in front of them. Leaper skinned his knee, but he didn't stop. He plunged ahead, fighting through the current and tugging Kerry along behind him.

His muscles strained as he battled through the water until suddenly he was through the worst of it and could swim more freely. He surfaced and brought Kerry up beside him, using the belt as a safety lead. She coughed and sputtered.

"Are you okay?" Leaper asked.

"Yes," she managed. "I'm glad…you connected us. The force of that water was intense."

"It certainly was. I think our timing might have been a bit off."

Kerry touched a finger to his lips. "Your timing…is remarkable. Nature just has other plans sometimes. That was a beautiful experience."

He rolled on his back and tugged Kerry on top of him. Using his fins and leg muscles, he propelled them toward the boat.

She laughed. "This is wonderful. You make a delightful flotation device."

"Wait until you see what I can do with my cork…talk about buoyant."

She splashed water in his face and giggled. "Let's pop that cork sooner rather than later."

He laughed. "Aye, aye." His head grazed the boat. With a single arm, he thrust Kerry up and into the boat and followed her in.

The boat rocked from side to side. He pulled her close and kissed her.

"Shall we untie the belt?" Kerry asked, holding up her wrist.

"Let's see how much fun we can have, being attached." He nipped at her bottom lip.

She rubbed her body against his. "Now that's a pleasure I haven't tried before, and I find the idea quite appealing." Her lips tugged at his as she hugged him closer. "Show me how it's done."

He growled with excitement. His body was primed to tangle. He could hardly wait until they were both naked again, just Kerry and him engulfed in glorious waves of passion.

---

The sun beat down mercilessly about a mile and a half off the coast of the Amphibious Base, Ocean Side. Sweat dripped down Leaper's clean-shaven face, and his shirt was soaked all the way through. He shook his head, and sweat droplets flung out in all directions.

He looked over the trainees. Work, work, work.

Two groups had performed terribly during the live-fire exercise—Poshen's group and his. The main reason had been lack of teamwork, and Leaper knew just the exercise to help the trainees work together. It was an old-school routine that Gich had used on his BUD/S class.

The official training had dumped the exercise, because it was hard to find a boat that was slow enough to grab a man from the water without causing harm. But Leaper had tweaked this boat's engine so it ran slower, and he'd gotten permission from the Commanding Officer of BUD/S to give this Team-building exercise a try.

Leaper watched his trainees fall one by one into the water. He was putting his group in the drink first, and Poshen's group would follow.

Leaper watched as his trainees spaced themselves out in the water fairly evenly.

At the helm of the boat was Poshen's crew. Their job was to pick up Leaper's guys, and then they'd switch. Watching the red-haired Seaman at the helm of the boat, Leaper knew this was going to be one seriously long day. This trainee knew nothing.

Leaper leaned over and said, "There are more than two speeds. Consider the purpose of each one. If you come in at full speed and try to pick up someone from the water, there's a possibility of harm. We don't want any dislocations, broken bones, ripped rotator cuffs, etc. So I would suggest using your slowest setting."

The red-haired helmsman was startled. "It's my first day at the controls."

"Interesting. My crew has already been doing swift-boat-driving maneuvers. Why haven't all of you done it?"

"I don't know."

Leaper closed his eyes and pressed his hands against them in frustration. "Who's been driving your boat the past few weeks?" he asked, then held up his hand. "Wait. Don't answer that. It was Poshen." Forcing himself not to raise his voice, Leaper gave the Seaman a swift lesson in boat and wave dynamics. "That should be enough to get through the day without running over anyone. That's your goal: don't knock out your classmates."

"Aye, aye," he replied.

Leaper briefed the entire crew. "Before we pick up the members of your class who are treading water in the drink, let's review what's going to happen. The helmsman will drive a 180—that's a semicircle, for those who don't remember their geometry. He will maintain his speed while two people at the back of the boat handle pickup. One will hold the loop and fish, and the other one will roll the sailor out of the way so the next person can get on board. Watch your weight distribution so we don't flip the boat. Any questions?"

Poshen's trainees looked at each other nervously.

"I'm serious. I'd rather you ask me now than have a problem later," offered Leaper.

Every trainee raised a hand. Questions shot at Leaper like BBs from a BB gun.

*Crap!* He wanted to smack his head and then each of theirs. What had Poshen been doing with these guys? Obviously he hadn't been teaching them—just torturing them.

Did this mean Leaper had to go over each of the basics? Poshen's trainees needed to know this stuff, or they wouldn't be able to handle boat-to-boat tactical evasion.

Leaper glanced back at his crew. They looked relaxed enough, treading water or floating. Geez, each of his men was already interested in studying ocean-floor composition. He could pick on any of his men, and they could describe in detail every patch of sea floor from Mexico to Alaska.

Leaper sighed. "Okay, ask me your questions one at a time."

<p style="text-align:center">~~~</p>

*Perseverance means hanging in there, and never, ever throwing in the towel.* Leaper's trainees had taken those words to heart and excelled today. He was proud of them. But there were issues to be dealt with outside his Team.

Leaper liked to give people the benefit of the doubt. When he'd tried to call Poshen from the boat, the man had said, "It's my day off. Fuck you," and hung up.

Leaper didn't get angry. He was just sad for Poshen's trainees.

Being on call 24–7 was part of the process. Leaper always had a phone or beeper with him. The trainees knew they could contact him, and he'd rather they called him than suffer or ring out.

Some individuals made fantastic teachers. They prepared their students with a macro and micro world perspective, including mind-set, physical skills, and tactical awareness. Others couldn't be bothered to teach more than what was at the end of their noses. Narrow perspectives could endanger lives.

Leaper didn't want to have to call someone on their shit, but honesty was a big part of Team dynamics. The ability to dish it out and to learn from criticism was vital. Feedback was a core principle of the learning process.

Leaper's large boots sank into the sand as he climbed the dune that separated the beach from the parking lot on the Amphibious Base. What did it say about his day that the very best part was taking Kerry to work on his

boat and receiving that delectable goodbye kiss? Maybe
he'd surprise her and stop by after work.

After stomping his boots on the parking lot's asphalt,
he brushed the sand from his pants and walked at a fast
clip to BUD/S. He flashed his ID at the gate and headed
for Declan's office. He hated to be *that guy*, but Declan
needed to know what his instructors were doing. Most of
the instructors were doing an okay job, and a few—like
Zebbi—were performing wonderfully.

But Poshen... Well, he was a lazy fuck. It would be
surprising if any of his guys made it through another
week. They'd been so hungry for information that
Leaper's men had treaded water for over forty minutes
before they were picked up. Not that it was tough on
them. Their water skills were very strong.

Watson had floated on his back most of that time.
That kid definitely brought joy to Leaper's heart. He
was a good sort.

Walking through the large space of First Phase
Grinder, Leaper saw that Declan's door was open. He
knocked on the door.

"Leaper, what's up? Oh, great, you have that look on
your face...like I'm not going to like what you have to
say." Declan pushed back from his desk and stood. His
chair squeaked. "Come in and close the door, and give
it to me straight."

Leaper pulled the door closed behind him and sat
on the edge of Declan's desk. "I'm here to share a few
words of wisdom about teaching techniques."

Declan sat down in his chair. It protested loudly. "I
knew I wasn't going to like what you have to say, and
that's not me being psychic."

Leaper picked up a globe paperweight, tossed it in the air, and caught it. "Good to hear. Declan, my friend. We're going to lose good people if a few things don't change. Did you know that there's a whole boat crew that hasn't learned or performed swift-boat maneuvers? That's one of the most important skills; it's up there with evasive driving techniques on land. Let me give you a brief of what's going on…"

—∿∿—

*I need a cheat sheet to understand my own motivation.*

Kerry sighed. Did she ever wonder if her body knew something was about to happen long before her brain caught on? All the fucking time!

Somehow Leaper did that to her. Made her anticipate him so that her body was primed for his appearance.

Her heart pounded as she looked up. There he was, just outside of the Marine Mammal gate. The sight of him made her knees weak. She couldn't stop herself from rushing into his arms and reaching her mouth to his for a kiss.

As his lips met hers, something in her spirit sang loudly and joyfully. Had love ever felt like this? She didn't think so. Of course, there was always the possibility that she was experiencing that intense emotional connection for the very first time, as if he completed her energy and spirit. Not that she planned on ever giving up her independent lifestyle, but she was willing to make compromises for the right man—well, for him. Leaper was special, beyond description.

The kiss deepened as her tongue met his, sending sparks of electricity zipping through her body.

"*Ahem.*" Someone nearby cleared a throat.

Kerry didn't care who witnessed their public display of affection. She was happy. But the throat clearing turned into a full-blown cough, and her curiosity was piqued. She cut the kiss short and looked over her shoulder. Well, crap, she hadn't expected to see this sailor at the Marine Mammal department.

Standing in front of the gate was Admiral Dale. With gray creeping into his hair and sideburns, and deep lines etched into his forehead, he was a debonair yet forbidding presence. The Admiral looked like he was going to smile at Kerry, but then his gaze took in the companion to her right. "Lefton."

"Admiral Dale, good to see you." Leaper was all kinds of jovial, and Kerry was learning that this meant there was history between this person and Leaper.

But still, Admiral Dale rarely came down here. Maybe Kerry was getting fired. A sinking feeling hit her stomach like a ton of bricks, though Kerry guessed this could be a social call. Hadn't Emme been trying to date this guy? Right, right, right, she remembered now: Emme had given him a call.

"Are you looking for Miss Stanley?" Kerry asked attempting to be polite.

"No. I came here to speak with you, Dr. Hamilton." His tone was unreadable, his face a mask devoid of emotion. They must teach that at "fork and knife" school— otherwise known as officer's training.

Her heart sank. "What can I do for you?"

"Is there somewhere we can speak privately?" Admiral Dale looked around. "The docks are swept, correct?" Kerry nodded, and Admiral Dale added, "Let's head down there."

Kerry grabbed Leaper's hand and pulled him along behind her. Admiral Dale stopped at the gate and looked at Leaper. "He's coming too," Kerry insisted.

They walked past the double doors leading to the Marine Mammal Office and down to the gate on the gangplank. Kerry scanned her ID and opened the locked gate. Leading the way, she headed for Juliet's pen.

As she sat down on the dock, Leaper settled down next to her. It was such a supportive gesture; she gave him brownie points.

The Admiral seemed to contemplate the fact he was in uniform and then he picked up a bucket, flipped it over, and sat on a fairly clean bottom. The proximity was close enough to give them some privacy. "Our phone call…"

"Admiral, I'm sorry about that," interrupted Kerry. "I was upset. I practically accused everyone except myself of messing around with the numbers. I shouldn't have jumped the gun so quickly, and I'd like to apologize."

"There's no need for that." His face softened. "Dr. Hamilton, I'm not here to reprimand you or to fire you. Your passion for these animals and your expertise are two reasons we appreciate you being here. That said, you raised the alarm on an extremely important problem. I'm here to brief you, to give you information."

"Me?" Kerry was shocked. She closed her mouth and attempted to regain her composure. She had never thought there'd be a day when an Admiral reported information to her. It was always the other way around. "Go ahead, please."

Admiral Dale nodded solemnly. "A while back, we had Special Funding Director Joshua Boscher, and we were able to trace the current situation back to him. He was using the program to springboard himself into a few private government contracts using different types of marine life. He was the one who fudged the numbers and changed the protocol listing for the lab techs. He also used legitimate projects to cover his siphoning of funds, like your tank project. He took off with a third of your spending. Since no one had oversight over Boscher, no one questioned it. Boscher seemed to be in charge when it came to these projects, and the techs thought this was standard procedure."

"Boscher...really?" Kerry considered the man. "I don't know him very well, but he was always nice to me. He didn't spend much time here, if I remember correctly. He was mostly in Washington, DC. And when he was at the Marine Mammal base, he offered to help everyone. I—I just don't get it. Boscher?"

"Yes," confirmed Admiral Dale. "He was working with several groups who were lobbying on his behalf too. A lot of this circles back to money. Unfortunately, he got away with over $10.5 million."

Kerry whistled and then frowned. "Wait, what type of marine life was he working with?" She grabbed the Admiral's arm. "I think I know. Let me guess— Boscher's working with sharks."

The Admiral nodded. "But what makes you say that?"

"Like attracts like." Kerry nodded. "I'm right, aren't I? He went for cold-blooded rather than warm-blooded."

He took a slow, deep breath. "Roger that. I assigned several sailors to retrieve Mr. Boscher, but there was little to retrieve. It seems he was a victim of his enthusiasm."

"Ugh, the sharks ate him," said Kerry, swallowing a sudden rush of bile in her throat. "Not a good way to go."

"We found several fingers embedded in the dock—they had his DNA and some hair. Since the Navy has no one to prosecute for this crime, we have to close the case. But we know there are still outstanding issues, and we want to do the correct thing for our marine mammals. They serve selflessly. So I'm here to ask what you need." The Admiral spoke succinctly, as if he'd rehearsed his words. Most likely he had. According to Emme, the Admiral was a very precise man. He preferred everything just so.

Leaper nudged her as if to say *Tell him what you've done so far*.

It was Kerry's turn to take a deep breath. "Okay. So I've been chatting with a scientist in Greenland who's had excellent results with a new vaccine he developed. I made a batch and took it to a place where I knew there were sick dolphins." She lifted her hands and spoke quickly. "I didn't want to do it this way, but I knew that the Foundation would balk at me using our dolphins as guinea pigs. The funny thing is…the wild dolphin went from lethargic to energized very quickly. I've never seen such a fast turnaround. Since this was such a positive response, I was going to ask to speak to you, the Director, and whoever else will listen about testing it on one of our own."

"Kerry has video she recorded," added Leaper.

Admiral Dale leaned forward and looked at Leaper. "I suppose you were in on this wild-dolphin mission?"

Leaper grinned.

Admiral Dale nodded. "Well, I agree that I don't condone sticking a wild creature without knowing the results. It could have caused horrible effects." The

Admiral rubbed the back of his neck. Kerry could almost see the wheels in his head turning.

"She knows that," Leaper said. "I do too. There are hundreds of contagion movies out there, warning about the dangers of jumping into the unknown with a chemical concoction. But I stand by her, and the dolphin rallied very quickly." His voice was calm and steady.

Kerry's eyes misted. She was impressed and touched that he was standing up for her. Rubbing her shoulder against his, she added, "If what I did in the ocean is a criminal offense, I cannot let Leaper take any blame. It's all on me."

"I should have figured the two of you would find each other. Stubborn is as stubborn does." Admiral Dale stood and brushed specks of dirt from his uniform, finally giving up when he noticed a large streak down one leg. "Pick a dolphin and quarantine her. Follow the strictest guidelines of protocol, and then go ahead with the vaccine."

Gratitude flooded Kerry. She stood at once and shook the Admiral's hand passionately. "Thank you, Admiral. If the results are as dramatic as I believe, our dolphins will be back to normal very, very soon."

"Keep me informed. Daily reports." Admiral Dale stepped away. He tilted his head to the side and said, "Lefton."

Leaper nodded.

The men seemed to communicate nonverbally, which completely baffled Kerry. As she watched the Admiral walk away, down the dock, and up the gangplank, Leaper's arms wrapped snuggly around her waist. He squeezed her tightly against him.

"You did it, Kerry," he whispered in her ear.

"*We* did it," she replied as she hugged his arms tighter to her body. She closed her eyes. Relief was easing through her, lifting all the weight from her shoulders. After such a long adrenaline rush, her body was exhausted. "I need rest."

"Let's go to our home. The morning is a good time to start this project. Sleep will heal your brain, and I will work on your body." Leaper kissed the side of her neck.

She sighed. He was right. There were a ton of things she would need to prepare. First thing in the morning would be the best time.

"Have I sparked your interest?" he murmured against her neck.

She tapped her feet. "I'm clicking my heels, but we haven't arrived home yet."

He chuckled. "Maybe you're not clicking in the right spot. Let's try that again when we get back to the house."

Together, they walked down the dock and up the gangplank. Letting themselves out of the ID-controlled gate and then the main gate, they headed for her car, which Leaper had brought over for her during the day. When Kerry was tucked behind the steering wheel, he said, "Give me a second and I'll follow you."

She started the engine, her eyes tracking him as he walked to his motorcycle. Suddenly it hit her: he'd called his house "our home." Her mind spun through twenty different interpretations of his slip, unless it wasn't a mistake. Was this how he really felt—that the two of them should live together? Wow, that they would have a *home* together?

Leaper flashed the light on his motorcycle, requesting she take the lead.

Kerry backed out of the parking space. She drove to the main checkpoint of the base and turned right, leaving work behind. A part of her psyche—her ego, to be specific—was over the moon with delight at the notion of their being together on a permanent basis. Only a small, cynical portion told her to take it slow.

Her mother had told her time and again, "Never make big decisions when your emotions are high or low. Wait for those steady moments of calm, so you can see all the perspectives and decide wisely."

Kerry knew her mother was right. If only she could harness her hormones…but nothing could keep them in check. The rush of chemistry was intense, and her body was already primed. She stroked her index finger along her bottom lip, imagining Leaper's touch.

She directed the car toward Coronado, toward his home and the place they spent most of their time together. Kerry was eager for Leaper's kisses and caresses, and she squirmed in her seat, anticipating his body fitting perfectly against hers. Skin against skin, hearts beating hard, pulses racing as they brought each other to completion. *Oh God,* Kerry thought, *I can hardly wait. Oh, the things I want to do to Leaper and have him do to me.*

# Chapter 8

THE BEST-LAID PLANS OFTEN GO AWRY FASTER THAN IMAGINED. Oh, how true that was! Their roles switched, and now she was following Leaper to his house, when his motorcycle began spewing dark smoke.

Pulling her car over to the side of the road, she followed Leaper's lead into the small airport parking garage. Kerry kept her lights on, as the overhead lights were not very strong. After about fifteen minutes of his toiling with the engine, he pulled out a part, locked up the bike, and got into the passenger's seat of her car.

"Sorry about that. A part gave out. I have a spare at home. Just need to swap it out, and I'm back on the road. I'm constantly fixing this thing, but it's hard to give up the wind in my hair." Leaper sighed.

"You could buy a convertible," she teased.

He smiled. "Gee, thanks."

She pulled the car out of the parking garage and turned onto the main road. Driving was relaxing. Kerry's hand held the steering wheel gently as she turned the corner. Sometimes, when she was feeling sad, she drove to lift her spirits. On the flip side, her friend Emme was notorious for being an angry driver. Personally, Kerry never understood why; extreme emotion tended to exacerbate situations. She'd tried to communicate that fact to her friend, but it never sunk in. But maybe being happy was an extreme too.

Tonight, Kerry knew she had every right to be bouncing off the walls, but her habit of being peaceful in the car was still comforting. She gave in to it and relaxed. Leaper was scraping the edge of his motorcycle part and blowing on it.

Her mind was spinning with too many thoughts at once. She needed to slow down and give herself time to digest and then prioritize her actions, to make a list and construct a plan.

Kerry's mother had always teased her about needing to be in charge. Maybe her mom had been right. Management of her faculties was a big factor in Kerry's life. She rarely drank more than a few sips of wine or beer, and she was a stickler about doing things in a *certain way*. Looking at the man seated in her passenger's seat, she could honestly admit she was having a hard time processing her emotions about him, other than knowing…she liked him a lot.

A phone beeped loudly.

"Hey, I just got a text from Command," Leaper said, interrupting her thoughts. "Admiral Dale thanks me for my help with the Marine Mammal Program. Told me to keep up the good work." Leaper did a little happy dance in his seat.

"Don't look so smug and self-satisfied," Kerry teased. "You are not Mr. Perfect."

"Aw, you're just jealous because I got 'snaps' and you got nothing." Leaper sniffed. "I may not be perfect, but I'm right most of the time."

"Really? You think so? Well, Mr. Right-Most-of-the-Time, I got the best reward of all—the Navy offered to help to heal my dolphins. Nothing can top that," she said, sounding smug and satisfied. Kerry turned her head as she spied activity in the water. "Wait, do you see something going on over there?"

"Polar bears—the people, not the actual bear." Leaper waved his hand at them. "It's colder in the bay at night, so the people start their preparation in San Diego and work their way up the coast. Slow down, and you can see their bathing caps—there's a polar bear on it."

"*Brrr*. I'd put on a wetsuit."

"Yeah, they don't. The Council told them they had to wear bathing suits or shorts or something to cover their, uh, private parts while they swim in San Diego. But there are many stops on their coastal tour where they swim with nothing on." Leaper chuckled. "As freeing as that is, I can name a few places I wouldn't want my willy hanging out for something to nibble on."

Kerry laughed. "I can imagine. I didn't expect to see them. I guess sometimes a banana is just a banana or a cigar is just a cigar." She pushed on the accelerator and the car shot forward as it climbed to the speed limit. They zipped along the streets, taking the back roads along the water. They passed Midway and Seaport Village, the Hyatt and Marriott; they passed the convention center and the Hilton and then sped over the hill and across the trolley tracks to take the Cesar Chavez on-ramp onto the Coronado Bridge.

"Don't monkeys eat bananas… Well, monkeys and me."

"You're bananas," she quipped.

"No, you are." Leaper mimicked a monkey, banging his chest and scratching under his arms with his fingers.

Kerry couldn't help but laugh again. "Leaper, you're

better than cable." She blew him a kiss. "I mean, thank God you're completely bonkers. Never a dull moment."

"Hooyah to that." Leaper put the motorcycle part on the floor mat in front of his seat. "Don't let me forget this."

"Sure thing." Kerry added, "So you have a stockpile of parts for your motorcycle?"

"Yeah, I practically have three-quarters of another one, if I'm honest. I've a habit of helping other Team guys with their hogs."

The car sped onto the Coronado Bridge, where there was hardly a car in sight. At night, the bridge was even more intimidating than during the day. The lampposts highlighted patches of the bridge and left other places in shadow. Beyond the sides were long, long drops through the inky darkness into the cold Glorietta Bay.

"Do you see that? There! Someone's running. That's dangerous." Leaper pointed at a person running along the bridge. "Wait! I know that gait and that hair. Fuck, it's Watson. Put on your hazard lights and block the lane. Something's going on. Watson wouldn't be up here unless there was shit going down." Leaper looked behind them. "No one's coming. Trigger the lights now and keep them on."

Kerry pushed the button and brought her car to a halt. She picked up her phone. "I'm calling 911."

Leaper didn't hear her. He was already out of the vehicle, running after Watson.

—⁂—

"Hey, Watson. Hold up." Leaper gained on the group leader, clamping a hand on the trainee's shoulder and encouraging him to stop. "This is the worst place to run. You could get killed. What gives?"

"It's not me," he said, his breath coming in short puffs. "It's Worthington."

Loosening his hold, Leaper scanned the bridge, looking for Quentin Kirkland Worthington, the trainee that he'd nicknamed Captain Kirk. "Where is he?"

Watson looked around frantically. "Fuck! I had him in my sights. He's so damn fast. Wait!" He pointed. "Up there, on the edge of the railing."

Leaper spotted Quentin. *Shit! There he is. One wrong move and it's toes up. Hell no!*

"C'mon, Captain Kirk. Stay with me." Leaper wasn't going to let the boy jump. He took off at his fastest pace. "What happened? How did he get to this point? Brief me as we move."

Watson barely kept pace with Leaper as he managed to say, "Anxiety. Hiding medication. Didn't know. Until today…'cause he had no more meds." He sucked in air and continued. "Think he was rationing the stuff."

"Damn. Anything else?"

"Yeah, Quentin talked to his dad. Discussion was bad. The Admiral said not to come home if he rung out of BUD/S." Watson struggled to keep up. "Quentin was crushed, and then he wanted to run along the shore. Didn't know he was heading for here."

"Cold news from a parent." Leaper weighed his options. "Okay. Go back to the car, get inside, and wait with Kerry. She's my girlfriend, so be polite." Over his shoulder he added, "Dude, you're on Goon Squad until your stamina is better."

"Thanks." Watson shook his head. "Wait, shouldn't I help?"

"This is how you can help. Leave it in my hands. One sniper, one voice, one shot."

Watson paused. "Is he…going to be all right? I feel responsible for him."

"Go," said Leaper gruffly. "Let me do my job." Without turning to see if Watson was following his request, Leaper closed the distance until he was less than six feet from the recruit. "Hey, Captain Kirk. What's going on?"

Quentin was shaking like a leaf as he straddled the railing and hugged the nearby utility pole. "Don't… don't come any closer, or I'll jump."

Oddly enough, Leaper knew this part of the bridge well. As a recruit, he'd scaled it several times. There had been a heavy metal safety fence underneath this portion. *God*, he prayed, *let it still be there*. He hopped up onto the concrete edge of the bridge and wavered for a few seconds before he found his balance. "Hey, Quentin, I'm just going to hang out with you. We can talk…or not." Leaper lowered himself to sit on the edge of the bridge. His feet dangled over the side; if he fell right now, he'd most likely die. Of course, he couldn't think about that right now. His full attention had to be on getting this recruit off the edge—literally. Time to change tactics. "Trainee, sit. It's an order."

Quentin actually sat down. It was slow going, watching the boy move, but he obeyed the order. This had been a test and it was a good start.

"Talk to me." Leaper used his firmest voice. "I need to know what's happening. Sit rep."

Quentin nodded, licking his lips. "I'm not… I didn't want to do this. My father wants me to be like him, but I'm not. I need my music and I live for making art. But I had to do this." He squeezed the bridge of his nose. "I don't like the smells—coppery blood, gun powder, grit and grim caked in your sinuses, and the noise. So much screaming. I can't do this anymore."

"What do you want?" Leaper scooted closer. He was near enough to Quentin to pull him backward onto the concrete, but that was a last resort. If the trainee could talk everything out of his system, maybe he'd relieve some stress and be less likely to attempt something like this again.

"I like my friends and the boat stuff. Even the shark thing was cool." Quentin's hands shook as he rubbed them over his face. "But I can't kill anyone. I won't."

"What do you see, when your finger's on the trigger?"

"Me." Quentin slapped his hands on his thighs. "I see me. I'm shooting myself if I pull the trigger, and when I hear shots being fired, it's like everyone is attacking me." Tears washed down his face. "I can't be what they want me to be."

"Who's we?"

"My parents. Well, I guess it's just my dad. He'll never accept me." Quentin's body was racked with sobs.

"The only thing that's important is that you accept yourself. It's your life. You need to decide how to live it. And there are ways to let go of other people's voices in your head. Trust me—I've been through some serious shit storms." Leaper put his arm around the recruit, and Quentin leaned into him. Using his momentum, Leaper turned them and took them both off the edge of the bridge. They landed back on their feet on the concrete roadway.

Leaper waved off the police officers who had been gathering at either end of the bridge and walked Quentin back to the car. There would be a lot of paperwork to file in the morning, but if Leaper could just get this guy into the car and off to medical, it would be a win. Leaper typically hated dealing with doctors, but in Quentin's case, he knew medical intervention could be the start of a special relationship that could save the recruit's life. The boy had a long road ahead of him, but Leaper would keep tabs on him, let him know he wasn't alone. He wondered how the father, the Admiral, was going to take it all.

From what Leaper knew of the Admiral, he was a good guy. Did he really pressure the boy, or was this all in the recruit's head? Hopefully, it could get resolved.

As Leaper opened the back door of Kerry's car and clipped a seat belt over Quentin's shaking body, he made a mental note to talk to Watson. He didn't want another recruit going off the rails. This event was nobody's fault. Sometimes people snapped. What mattered was how the issue was resolved. Luckily, everyone here was safe.

Leaper closed the car door and headed back to the center of the bridge to speak with the police officers. They weren't going to like what he had to say, but they'd deal with it. This was life and death, and this recruit was going to be submitted to Balboa as soon as possible. Spending time in a jail cell was not going to help anyone.

Offering his hand, Leaper began. "I'm Leaper Lefton, Instructor at BUD/S. I'm taking him to Balboa for medical care. You can follow, if you like, and I can give you a full statement of this evening's events. Also, I can be reached at this number for any further questions…"

⁓

Words had deserted him.

Standing on the patio of his home, Leaper looked out at the bay.

Having Quentin committed to the psych ward took less than twenty minutes. Talking his way out of the cop situation took over forty minutes, but they finally gave way when Leaper mentioned the need for pharmaceuticals and that the boy might have a seizure without them. If the cops hadn't let Quentin be transported to the psych ward, it would have been a serious violation of his right to seek medical attention. It also helped that Declan as Commanding Officer of BUD/S showed up to back up Leaper.

It had been one hell of an experience. What Leaper cared about most was that Quentin received the support and help he needed.

Damn, but it was true that Leaper would rather face a dozen terrorists than watch someone's mind crumble before his eyes. Healing a mind was tough stuff. He should know; he was still dealing with his own. Of course, his issues were a walk in the park compared to Quentin's.

Listening to the water was calming. The night was still overcast, and the rhythmic sound of the waves against the shore lulled him. How strange to think that despite the chaos that had just taken place on the bridge, the earth continued to turn on its axis.

Kerry wrapped her arms around him, hugging him tight. "Are you okay?"

"I suppose. Are you? You were white as a sheet when I finally got back to the car."

She leaned her head on his shoulder. "I nearly wet myself when you jumped up on the railing of that bridge. My heart was in my throat the entire time you were up there." Kerry held her hands over his heart. "I'm glad it all worked out."

"Me too." Leaper sighed. "Honestly, I was winging it. I find that if I trust my instincts, the situation resolves more organically." He turned in her arms and kissed the top of Kerry's head. "That kid's going to need a lot of therapy. He's probably going to get a medical discharge from the Navy, if it's anything more serious than a case of the jitters. I suspect there's some serious stuff going on that makes him manic, with extreme highs and lows. Just a suspicion."

"The Navy will help him get a good diagnosis and treatment, won't they?" she asked. "I've heard good things about Navy doctors."

"Yes. They're well versed and pretty thorough. When he gets home, though…that's not going to be a fun experience. To have a father that would rather you didn't come home, unless you stayed in the Navy—that's some cold stuff." Leaper shook his head. "I couldn't give someone I love an ultimatum about how to live life."

"That's one of the things that makes you different, Leaper. You encourage an individual to live boldly, to enjoy who they are on the inside. Very few people celebrate the inner child as a part of the adult."

"I'm all kid."

"No, you're not. You're mindful and awake, which makes you aware of yourself on a soul-deep level. You're comfortable and happy with who you are. If only more people could accept themselves…" She looked away sadly.

"I'm learning…about where I belong in this next phase of my life and what I mean to me. This is a hard journey. I know I struggled with it during BUD/S—getting to know myself and understand my place in the Teams, making the decision that I was going to fight each and every day for my country and my Teammates and myself. What I'm discovering right now has to do with how I relate to myself and the outside world for this next phase of my life. It's a necessary evolutionary process." Leaper took a deep breath. "I understand what Quentin is going through, with one small exception. I wanted to become a SEAL—it's my life's purpose—and he's doing it because he thinks he has to live up to some grand plan. Someone's purpose or reason for going through training can make or break them. I've said it a hundred times: it's never pretty or easy. The mind is complicated, and it will oftentimes stop us when we walk to the edge of the abyss and look in." He swallowed and coughed. "I'm grateful Watson was there and we got there in time, and that the kid is safe. No one should feel like they're out of choices."

"I agree. Please let me know if you think there's any way I can help." She touched his cheek.

"Thanks. Letting me talk, being with me, that helps a lot." He laid his hand on hers. "Being with you, it's peaceful."

She nodded.

He gathered her in his arms. They held each other, just being together, until she noticed that their hearts were beating the same rhythm.

"How do you do that? Chase away the world until it's just the two of us?" Kerry looked into his eyes earnestly. "It's a gift. You know that, right?"

"Well, you inspire me. I've only been able to do this with you. Enjoy the silence." He shrugged. "Maybe it's happiness."

"Fascinating. Leaper, I cannot imagine you being unhappy."

"That's part of my internal struggle, what fills me with joy, out here in the real world." Wagging his eyebrows, he said, "Of course, I can think of one or two things that give me instant pleasure. Things you've told me I'm good at…"

She swatted a hand playfully at his chest. "Leaper."

He drew her closer and tenderly kissed her cheek. Then her neck. "A little bliss here." Working his way down, he slowly disrobed her, kissing his way down to nirvana. When his mouth was tucked tightly between her legs, he lapped at her clit, making her breath catch and her pulse race.

"You should give master classes," she stuttered out.

"Are you trying to loan me to others?"

"Never!" She pushed his head back to where it was. "Don't stop, Leaper. Heavens, please don't stop."

"Right-o." His tongue worked over her clit in a way that pushed her over the edge. Heat and hunger zipped through her body as pleasure swept her senses. A full-body orgasm caught her by surprise and made her shake and shudder.

She sighed, "Leaper. Leaper. Leaper." As his tongue waged war again, he sent her climbing to the highest peak again until her body climaxed. She couldn't wait any longer. She craved his touch, needed him inside of her. "Please."

He trailed his hands down her body, and she felt him

gently climb on top of her until his cock was snuggled at her entrance, thick and hard. She longed to taste him on her tongue, and yet she needed him inside of her. "Take me now."

Leaper thrust into her, and all her thoughts disappeared. There was only the two of them and the marvelous sensation of how fully he filled her. Her body held him, cherished him. Her back arched as he moved, opening herself wider to his ministrations.

Her sheath shivered with the intensity as the pleasure built.

She slanted her mouth, welcoming him. Their tongues played, teased, and tantalized each other with strokes and touches as he plunged in and out. Her hips met the rhythm easily, urging him to go faster and faster. The climax built to an incredible pressure.

"Kerry," he shouted as he came. "Oh God, Kerry!"

It was a gush of pleasure so intense that it brought her climax too. For several seconds, it actually took her breath away as Kerry's heart slammed hard in her chest. Her body had never felt so aware. Making love was an affirmation of life, a way to honor the trek of getting up and fighting to survive the pain.

Her hands stroked over his skin, tracing the scars on his back. She'd kissed, caressed, and rubbed those places. Did she reach into him as deeply as he did into her? She hoped so.

Intimately connected like this, she felt safe and protected in his arms. She'd never felt that way about anyone. If only she could keep the rest of the world away and stay here with him forever. But she knew it wasn't possible. She'd have to leave the comfort of Leaper's embrace to deal with reality, and that sadness lingered at the back of her mind as he pulled out and tucked her close to him.

Staring into the darkness, she knew she wasn't going to sleep, not tonight. And she watched the clock and wondered how long it would take before he fell asleep and she could sneak away. Until then, she'd lie here and worry about all the things she needed to do, making mental lists to help save the other creatures she loved: her dolphins.

*Love.* Had she really used that word when thinking about Leaper?

She smiled to herself. The night was full of revelations, wasn't it?

---

Leaper noted the sounds: running water, the shower turning on and off. Then he watched Kerry dress in the dark. His eyes adjusted to darkness very quickly. They should have, after years of wading through pitch-dark horror shows.

Honestly, Kerry could have turned on the bathroom light to help her bathe and dress. That would have ruined his night vision for several seconds, but the woman deserved to protect her toes, which Leaper had just watched her stub.

She looked over at him. He didn't move. She thought he was sleeping, and he didn't want to disabuse her. It appeared to be important to her that he rest. He presumed it would make her feel better if he continued with the pretense.

*Have a good night, Kerry, and Godspeed in figuring*

*out the correct protocols for the vaccine test*. He willed the message to her as he watched her feel around in the dark for her purse and phone. She slipped out the door, locking it behind her. As if a thief would be dumb enough to break into a SEAL's home.

Swinging his legs over the side of the bed, Leaper wiggled his toes in the carpet. He loved those plush fibers. It beat mud caked under his toenails, feet so cold that frostbite was a dire concern, or sand so hot that it seared your skin.

All the things he didn't have when he was away from here were luxuries. Was a girlfriend a luxury or a necessity? He didn't want to answer that question.

Leaper reached for his pants and pulled his cell phone out of his pocket. He checked the time, but it didn't matter to him; it had only been two hours since they arrived home, and it was still the middle of the night. Leaper knew he could call Declan at any hour. He pushed the autodial.

It rang only once.

"Hey, Leaper. What's up?" Declan yawned.

"Did I wake you?"

"Hell no. Maura's had a craving. I'm making bacon burgers on the grill. Want to come over?" A sizzling noise filled the line. "I made ten of them."

"Can you bring me one?" Something in Leaper's gut didn't want Kerry to be alone at the base this late at night. He could have brought it up to her before she left, but he didn't want to give her an opportunity to say no. This way, he could show up with Declan, and they could hang out while she worked.

Of course, Leaper knew there was security at the

base, but after the incident on the bridge, and the fact that he was so jumpy, he knew he'd be happier if he was close to Kerry. Having his swim buddy, Declan, guarding his six was another plus. If nothing came of the excursion and this odd feeling in his gut, at least Declan would have a nifty tour and Leaper could blame his nerves on something else. Maybe he'd blame it on the hamburger he was going to eat, though Declan did make a great burger. The key was the crisp bacon and the three different types of cheese stuffed inside. When you took a bite, the cheese just oozed out with all the yummy meat juices. Leaper's mouth watered just thinking about it. "Put ketchup on mine."

"Sure thing. Give me five minutes before I hit the road." From the sounds Declan had been making, which Leaper had heard a hundred times before, he had closed up the grill, locked the back door, wrapped the burgers, and dumped the dishes in the sink.

"Good. I was hoping you might be up for an adventure. I've got this bizarre feeling that I can't shake." Leaper pulled his pants on and slipped on his shoes. "It could be boyfriend jitters. Damn, I can't believe I just called myself someone's boyfriend."

"Not someone's—Kerry's. You're Kerry's boyfriend. Pretty cool, Leaper. I'm happy for you." Declan cleared his throat. In a low tone, he added, "I trust your instincts. They've been right more times than I can count. Do I need gear?" That was their code for weapons, usually being two 9 mms, a Ka-Bar, and some additional hidden toys.

"Nah." Leaper picked up his shirt and pulled it over his head. "I'll meet you in front of the Marine Mammal base entrance."

"Roger that." The phone clicked off.

Leaper pocketed his phone and grabbed the keys to his scarred and battered backup hog, the one he held in reserve to scavenge pieces off of, if the occasion should arise. Right now, it just looked like a beat-up hunk of junk, but it functioned. Maybe he had more in common with it than he let himself consider.

The night air was cool, and it smacked at his face as he drove the motorcycle down First Street, onto Orange Avenue, and over the Coronado Bridge. The path was well-worn, and his motorcycle seemed to know the way as it sped along.

There were very few souls who would meet at any hour and at any place without a lengthy discussion. Declan was there, no matter what. They were brothers. Teammates. It was a bond more vital than anything Leaper had ever known.

Though Kerry…was coming very close. Her presence in his life was turning his personal rules of engagement upside down. He had never let a woman into his head and heart this intimately.

What would his friend say to this information? Leaper chuckled. Most likely, Declan would say *About fucking time you fell for someone*. And fuck it all, he was probably right. Perhaps Leaper was finally ready for the straight-and-narrow path, just like a regular, ordinary guy, which is something he never considered himself. As a SEAL, Leaper was prepared for all manner of issues, whether it would be by sea, air, or land. But this… Was he ready for full-time Kerry and full-time togetherness? The boat was still out on that question.

# Chapter 9

NIGHT WAS AN IDEAL TIME FOR MISCHIEF. EVEN THE FISH were sleeping, or at the very least not biting yet. The world slowed down in the darkness. Clouds filled the San Diego night sky, obscuring whatever existed above, and only a few souls partied privately until dawn.

Morning was still several hours away, and the wee hours of the night were very quiet, especially on the bridge connecting Point Loma to nearby San Diego's Lindbergh Field. The water below was still and the air smelled stagnant.

A skinny man scratched his nose and adjusted himself. He pulled out his phone, chose the phone number with the label *StpUp*, and sent a text. This moment is dedicated to you. Without your help, we never would have known where to go, how to enter, or what to do. I'm honored you chose me and I have this opportunity to lead others. Power to the People, as each of us chooses to willingly Step Up. He snapped the cover shut. Before he concealed the phone in an airtight, waterproof case, he wondered if he should ask his source who he was and why he was helping them. In the distance, he heard the call of a mockingbird mimicking a ringtone, and he shook off the brief moment of doubt.

The main purpose was that citizens take up the fight and act. Right? He nodded his head, answering his own question. "Time to begin."

Holding a webcam at arm's length, he spoke softly. "This is Octavius 'Tavi' Ploke, and we're about to shake things up for the Navy." He turned the camera toward the water. "Over there is the Marine Mammal base, and we're going to 'free Willy.' Just kidding. We're releasing dolphins and sea lions back into the wild."

Pointing the camera at a piece of wrinkled paper, he said, "This is the note that began it all. It reads: 'Here's a challenge for those whose hearts are worthy. Open the cages at the Marine Mammal Program and let our aquatic friends go free. If you require help, open this bottle.'" He pointed to a blob of lines on the note. "This is a map to this very bridge. Now, I'm going to strap this camera to my head, and my friends and I are off to do some good."

*Darkness suits the night's events*, thought Tavi as he secured the webcam to his head mount. *It's doubtful the moon will make an appearance tonight.* Tavi wore dark-blue board shorts and a black T-shirt sporting the phrase *Saving It All* in silver. He waved to two women and four men who stood in the shadows, urging them to walk onto the bridge.

A waterproof backpack was secured to his back with broad straps across his waist and chest. This was the first time he'd have a chance to use his gear, and Tavi was very excited.

He waved again, this time more frantically, and the small group moved in concert like lemmings, hurrying along the walkway of the bridge until they reached the far side. Only then did they catch their breath and wait for the next step.

Several cars approached. Their lights were overly

bright, and Tavi was tempted to flip them off because they didn't turn off their high beams, but he stopped himself. *One battle at a time*, he told himself. *No sense calling attention to yourself.*

"Look at the stars, Tavi," said one of the women to him as she approached.

He sighed. Her name Lonettia, and she was not very good at being inconspicuous. Her blond hair was died black, and it was obviously a temporary color. It bled down her cheeks, following the path of her sweat. And her erratic movements screamed *Pay attention to me*.

A police vehicle sped by, going toward Point Loma. Luckily, the officer didn't even slow down to see what this group was doing. Tavi liked the current state of affairs. Every citizen was on hyperalert and scared to confront anyone. They just made a mental note and sped by, afraid to comment or interfere with anyone else's personal "freedom of expression." That meant his pursuit of activist events went uninterrupted. Did society know how perfectly it was setting itself up? Not that he was complaining.

Tavi checked around the bridge to make sure no Coast Guard or Coastal Front Security boats were lurking about. When he was sure they were safe, he shattered the closest streetlight with a well-aimed rock. He then tied a rope ladder to the edge of the bridge railing and dropped it into the water. The dark color of the rope blended into the dark night.

Gesturing with his hand, he urged the others to descend.

Smiling, he watched the others climb over the railing and down the ladder. It was a proud moment for him. His opportunities to lead had been few and far between in his life. His father had told him constantly that he'd never inspire confidence. If only the old tyrant could see him now.

"Tavi," snapped Lonettia from the water. "Hurry. It's cold."

He sighed. He knew they were waiting in the darkness beneath the bridge for him to join them, but he wasn't moving until he was ready.

His fingers checked the fasteners on the backpack, making sure it was sealed, and then he hoisted himself over the railing and quickly moved downward until his body was submerged in the Glorietta Bay water.

"We need to sabotage the pens and get the dolphins moving from their cooped-up area into the ocean," he whispered. "I want everyone on the dock until we see how many we're dealing with, and then we can divide and conquer. From this point forward, no talking." They nodded in confirmation, and Tavi led the way. They swam single file toward the Marine Mammal base.

Tavi could hear the dolphins vocalizing, and he wondered what they were saying. In his mind, they cried for help. He believed wholeheartedly that the creatures were being tortured, and he wanted to set them free. This was the point of the endeavor, to release them into the wild. Boy, would these dolphins thank him!

They neared the far end of the dock. Tavi knew from months of observation that the guards would be shifting position and that there would be a rather long break before they resumed their posts. Smoking in the parking lot seemed to be their preferred activity. He guessed they got reprimanded if they puffed around the mammals.

Here it was. The moment. Tavi watched them walk

the docks and head up the gangplank. He pulled himself onto the dock and waved his group forward.

Water splashed on the dock as the activists mounted it. Tavi frowned at them and put his finger to his lips, signaling them to be quiet. "There are more pens than I thought," Tavi said quietly. "You three work on freeing the dolphins from this pen, and you three the next. I'm going around the side and work on the last one. We're hidden by the shacks for now, but keep your ears open for those guards. I have the only bottle of the special potion, and it should make our job a lot easier." He looked over his shoulder at them. "What are you waiting for? Move it!"

The four men and two women hurried off. Tavi rounded the corner and reached into the water to slice through some netting.

Heads bobbed to the surface.

It shocked him. He'd never been this close to a dolphin before. He had an odd, childlike urge to get in the water with them and play.

Several young dolphins looked at him quizzically. They bumped his hand. Tavi slapped them away and they poked at his hand with great force. "Ouch!"

A larger dolphin appeared suddenly, herding the young ones into a far pen.

Tavi hadn't realized the pens were connected in this manner. When he followed the creatures to the far pen, he reached down to grab a hunk of netting. A larger dolphin came out of the water like a bullet and knocked the knife from his hand. It sank into the water.

"I'm trying to help you," he whispered angrily. A tail smacked the water, splashing water all over him.

Tavi was drenched. His anger climbed. "We can do it the hard way."

Unclipping the straps over his waist and chest, he lowered the backpack to the ground and released the watertight seal on top. He reached into his bag and withdrew a small blue bottle. The only legible wording on it was HP 1020.

"A few grains of potion and you'll be easy to take out to sea," Tavi said. "I have this info from a good source who told me exactly how to do this." He held the bottle tightly as he wrestled with the top.

Voices made him freeze. He hadn't been able to remove the cap, but they didn't need to know that. His heart was beating so fast, it felt as if it was slamming out of his chest. What was he supposed to do now? Was he going to be caught? It didn't matter. This was only one of many plans. His source was a genius who was going to free all the marine mammals, even if this operation didn't work.

Tavi squared his shoulders. *I'm tough*. He was prepared to do battle, and if it went horribly wrong…well, he wasn't going to give up his source, no matter what they did to him. He'd take that name to the grave.

~~~

"Leaper, I heard something. One of our mother dolphins was using her angry tail slap. Let me just check on her." Kerry's hands were still covered by thick gloves, one of the protocols for the vaccine study. She was unprepared as she turned the corner and came face-to-face with a skinny man holding a strange bottle over one of her beloved dolphin pens.

"Roger that," said Leaper.

"Stop!" Kerry shouted. "I don't know what that is, but please don't hurt it. She's pregnant."

"Where's the other voice? It sounded like a man." The strange man looked nervously over her shoulder. He frowned as his eyes scanned for his friends. "Hey," he whispered anxiously. "Where are you guys?"

"Ah, hi. Who are you?" Kerry inched toward the man. "I'm Kerry. What's your name?"

"Tavi." His gaze ran up and down her body. "I can take you in a fight or I can be a martyr if you like; either way, it won't matter. We will be victorious, even if I go down," he said through gritted teeth. "Just remember that I warned you. To avoid further wrath from me and my friends, you need to let these dolphins out of captivity. I'm only going to warn you once, and then I'm going to dump this into the pen." He tapped his head and added, "Just so you know, I'm recording you. Smile for the camera."

"This is their home," Kerry argued. "You see how strong and clever they are; they can let themselves out with one leap. They're happy here. No one is holding them against their will." She could see Declan and Leaper coming toward them from the far side of the dock. Both of them dripped with water, yet their steps were silent. The look on both of their faces was deadly, and it almost distracted her. She knew she had to keep this guy talking. "I see something in your hand. What is it? Can you tell me what you're holding? Please, I'm a doctor…a veterinarian."

"You're a vet! You should know better. These dolphins need to be in the ocean, swimming free. You're a horrible person for keeping them penned in." The man's arm shook. "That's why you're wearing gloves. You're performing some kind of horrible test on them, aren't you?"

"No, I'm not! I'm trying to save them. The wild dolphins have a virus, and it's infected our group. We are testing a vaccine that's shown great results, and it could save an entire subspecies, possibly the *entire* species." Kerry hadn't meant to tell him so much, but she was flustered. If only her gloves were looser, maybe she could wrestle that bottle from him. "You should know a few more facts. The bottlenose dolphins in this pen were raised here. This mother's mother was a rescue, brought here after she'd been hurt in a storm. She was nursed back to health and eventually gave birth to a female. We love our dolphins, and they get the best care. Out there, in the ocean, they would most likely die. Is that what you want—to see them dead?" Kerry hoped her words would make him understand how damaging his actions could be. "Please, tell me what's in the blue bottle."

"I don't have to. I'll show—" The man's words were cut short as Leaper tackled him. The blue bottle of carfentanil flew into the air and Kerry caught it. She sighed with relief. The top was still tightly sealed.

Declan secured his arms and legs with ropes. "Secure," he said. "I subdued the other activists. The rest of group is, uh, tied up."

"Pat everyone down for bottles. On the outside of their clothes," Kerry advised. "This stuff is toxic."

Declan's voice carried from around the corner. "No bottles. Just screwdrivers and plastic bags full of small fish. Stinky, but not illegal."

"Phew. I'm, ah, going to deal with this." Hurriedly, she took the bottle into a small hazmat hut, closed the door behind her, and placed the bottle inside a tri-container containment. She stripped her gloves and clothes off and put them in a secondary hazmat container. *Please, please, please protect us all.* She took the coldest shower of her life within the self-contained hazmat system. Why hadn't the program sprung for a small water heater? It felt like her body was being washed with lye and frozen at the same time. Her skin was red, her goose bumps were layered with more bumps, and her nerves were completely fried.

Doing the math in her head while she was in the shower almost gave her a heart attack. Carfentanil was a deadly sedative used on elephants, and even a small amount could kill thousands of people. If the whole bottle had been dumped in the bay, there was no telling how much marine life or how many human beings would have been affected. She gulped, imagining the horror of it. This stuff should be banned from entering the country.

*Breathe, Kerry.* She sucked in air too quickly and coughed.

She looked at the receptacles. The bottle was sealed and contained, and she was pretty sure nothing had leaked out. But when there was an alert to all medical professionals across the country about the potency and danger of carfentanil, she'd rather err on the side of caution. Dogs couldn't even be trained to sniff for it—they could die instantly.

Standing there naked and shivering where no one could see her was triggering her claustrophobia. "I can do this. I will not panic." She took a long, slow breath.

Kerry was pretty sure that she was the first person to use these hazmat facilities in the entire history of the program.

*It had to be me, right?* She sighed. *I can do this. I'm tough.*

Another what-if slammed into her brain, testing her resolve. If Leaper hadn't invited Declan over to the Marine Mammal base for a private tour, what would have happened? Could she have managed all of these activists on her own? No. Would Tavi have dumped that bottle? Yes. Thank heavens, Tavi had been the only one with a bottle.

Her heart raced, but she wouldn't let her fears spin out of control again. "Just breathe."

From outside she could hear movement, voices, and all sorts of interaction. She listened intently.

"Hold him steady," someone yelled.

There was the sound of skin hitting skin.

"That's for scaring the shit out of my girlfriend." Leaper's voice was low.

"I'm a rescuer," shouted Tavi. "They're calling me. The dolphins need me. Let me just swim with them and commune. I can speak their language. Why don't you understand?"

"My girlfriend is in a hazmat shack, and you're telling me that substance you had isn't lethal?" Leaper's *voice* sounded lethal, like a sharp blade cutting through the bullshit.

*That's my man. You go, Leaper!* she thought.

"I didn't know! Someone gave it to me. I thought the dolphins would just be a little calmer and easier to take out to sea," Tavi shouted as he was led away. "I didn't know! You have to believe me, I didn't know."

"Get him…the fuck…out of here," growled Leaper.

Kerry heard the whole exchange. She anxiously looked around for something to put on. Paper gowns were not going to cut it, this close to the water. One wave and the gown would dissolve like a tissue.

The door opened abruptly and Leaper poked his head in. "I thought you might need this." He handed her a change of clothes from her bag.

"Thanks," she said, relieved. "I didn't want to go out there naked." Kerry took the bag from him and found some warm clothes.

His body blocked any view from the outside as she dressed. "Darling, I want to come in there and show my appreciation for all that beauty, but I'm guessing that having half of the Feds in San Diego listen to our foreplay might be a buzzkill."

She laughed.

Leaper lifted both hands. "Not that I don't want to, because I do." His smile was soft and gentle, matching the tone of his voice. "You are so very beautiful."

"Thanks," she murmured. Heat rose in her cheeks.

"Uh, just out of curiosity, what was that stuff in the bottle?"

"Carfentanil," she replied. "It's flooding the black market, because it boosts the power of opioids. Drug cartels are sourcing it from overseas and using it to cut their heroin, but even a small amount is too much, and the death toll has been enormous. No one really understands how deadly this stuff is!"

"Damn. That's messed up." Leaper gave a low whistle. "Is there anything I can do to help you? Did it get on you?"

"No," replied Kerry, shaking her head. "Leaper, this is all…so crazy and disturbing. Why here? Why…carfentanil? Who is this terrorist? Did he know that he was about to commit mass murder on one of our most important species? I've never been this close to an event of this magnitude. This wouldn't have been a rescue—this would have been an act of terrorism." Finally warm and dressed, she hugged Leaper tightly, grateful for his presence. Tears surprised her as they fell down her cheeks. "If that top had opened and the wind had caught one grain… Oh God, if it had touched you…" She choked.

She let the worry out and pulled herself together. Her shock and the talk of what-if must have made the tears spring from her like a fountain, but she wasn't one given to emotional outbursts. Her mantra was empower and power through, show of strength over shrinking-violet syndrome. "I don't know what's wrong with me," she said.

"Kerry, it's okay. I get it. Trust me. Bad situations can hit you upside the head in unexpected ways. Just remember, you're okay. We're okay. The mammals are okay. We survived it. You're my superhero lady. Who else grabs the evil mojo juice and runs into a hazmat facility?" He kissed the top of her head. "I'm proud of you. You think quickly on your feet. And Declan and I rounded up the bad guys, so the MPs have them in custody. Their night isn't over yet, though. I'm sure at least two different government agencies will want to chat with them."

Leaper opened the door wide and escorted her into the fresh air. She breathed deeply. It eased her, the smell of salt comforting and familiar.

"Hey, you can see them there, up near the office." Leaper nodded in the direction of the terrorists.

She followed his motion. There they were…the group of terrorists. They looked nervous as they attempted to loudly talk their way out of their handcuffs. It didn't look as if the military police were budging on that point.

"When I told them you dashed to hazmat, the MPs called Command, who requested the Coast Guard, the CDC, and a Terrorism Task Force from the FBI." Leaper's voice was matter-of-fact, as if he dealt with dramatic events every day.

She knew the authorities had handled worse. Something about that fact eased her further. The situation was in hand. Procedures would be followed. All she had to do was give her statement, and the authorities would take over.

"The Coast Guard's Cutter from Naval Station San Diego is docked over there. I'm pretty sure someone from the CDC will arrive within the hour." He craned his neck. "And I see gold letters. The FBI is here. So let's get this chat over with. Ready?"

Kerry nodded.

As they walked, the moon slid out from behind the thick clouds, casting bright rays of light into the pens. Seeing the dolphins moving around was a godsend. They exuded peaceful vibes.

She looked at Leaper, and her heart sped up. She smiled at the realization that she loved him. It was as clear as the bright moon overhead. Though the clouds threatened to slide back into place, she didn't care. There was clarity now, both in the night sky and in her own mind. There was no cynical voice to point out her doubts. There were only two very clear facts: Leaper had risked his life for her and she would risk hers for him. Love was a fierce emotion, its protective instinct made even sharper by the possibility of loss.

Leaper took her hand and tenderly kissed the back of it. It pulled Kerry out of her reverie. She smiled broadly at him. "Thanks."

"Of course. I have you, and you have me. Team dynamics, remember?"

"Your Teammate—that's a big honor." She bumped her shoulder into his. "Speaking of… Where's your other Teammate?"

"Declan? He went home. They'll talk to him in the morning." He whispered in her ear, "He was like a big kid when we took those activists down. He enjoyed the action. When he learns about the substance, though, it'll hit him hard. They live on the water. He and his daughter play in the bay almost every day—kayaking, swimming, canoeing, sailing, tubing…"

"Yeah, that's what shook me up so hard, that innocents would be killed. It's still a lot to take in."

"I agree. Now, let's wrap this up and go home."

Straightening her shoulders, she pursed her lips and mentally prepared herself. The good news was that if the camera on the man's head had survived the takedown, the entire event was on film. This would probably be one of the few times in history that cameras were a plus.

Kerry and Leaper walked toward the two waiting FBI agents who stood on the other side of the locked, chain-link gate. Their badges were out and their jackets flapped in the breeze. She knew that once the world learned about the blue bottle of carfentanil, this place would be swarming with even more personnel. This would be seen as a terrorist event. The Navy was going to have a hard time containing the media, once they learned about it. And there was no doubt that the entire Marine Mammal group would be moving locations again, to someplace even more secure. But that wouldn't be so bad. She was ready for a change of location.

This had been one of the scariest nights of her life. Tonight's events would haunt her for a long time and most likely affect the entire Marine Mammal Program, like the ever-widening ripples when a pebble is dropped into the water. But she had courage, and she'd wear that bravery like armor.

Kerry pulled open the gate and walked through. Leaper was right behind her, and she knew she could lean on him. But for now, she was going to stand up and make her voice heard, starting with the fact that carfentanil needed to be banned. There were other drugs that could be used on large animals, safer ones. No one needed this event to be repeated.

"Gentlemen, I'm Dr. Kerry Hamilton. Let's get started. I came to the docks to work, and my boyfriend and his Teammate stopped by. Little did I know that the Marine Mammal area was being invading by individuals determined to release our dolphins, which, for the record, can leave anytime they want by simply jumping the edge of the pen. These invaders, for lack of a better word, could have endangered the lives of our dolphins, because some of them require medication to stay alive and healthy. The invaders had malicious intent, as they intended to release a deadly toxin into the water that could have killed marine and human life. Questions?"

The federal agents' mouths dropped open in surprise. A variety of voices rose, wanting to know more. Yep, this was just the reaction she'd thought they'd have.

———⁓———

The air in Leaper's home was stifling. Kerry craved fresh air. She couldn't remember this small place ever feeling so closed off and confined, and she tugged at the neckline of her shirt. Glancing at the clock, she knew she would only be getting a few hours of sleep before she made her way back to work, but she didn't care. Being away from the base for even a short time was a reprieve. The FBI and the CDC were still there, and some of the brass, as well as the director of the program, were sticking around too. She needed a breather, a little time to regain her equilibrium.

So why was she so crabby, like she needed to move or act on something, and yet so exhausted? Was it the adrenaline rush? Could she still have one? Maybe she wasn't fit for company, but she couldn't bear hurting Leaper with her moodiness. Yet she was loath to leave here.

Her eyes tracked Leaper as he moved about the room. Clothes spilled out of his hamper, and several pairs of pants hung on the back of a chair. Had he always been this messy, or was she seeing evidence of it for the first time?

Music grew in volume as Louis Armstrong sang "All of Me." Normally, she loved that song, but at this moment, it was fraying her last nerve. Why was that? Didn't she want someone to take "all" of her?

She gritted her teeth against the song, the banging cabinet doors, the shoes being tossed nonchalantly into the closet and slamming against the back wall before they fell, and, to top it off, the squeak of the bathroom door. When she couldn't stand it anymore, she ground out in an angry voice, "Stop! Just stop, please. I can't take it anymore."

Leaper froze. "What?" He turned toward her and came to the bed. Getting on his knees, he reached for her.

She batted his hands away. She couldn't deal with being touched at this moment. "I need some space."

"Do you want me to take you home?" His eyebrows were drawn in tightly, and he looked concerned. She wanted to smooth those lines away, and at the same time, she wanted him gone. She didn't know why she was so frustrated. "Should I leave?" he asked, his expression growing more puzzled. "C'mon, talk to me. I know you had a rough night."

"That's an understatement," she mumbled grumpily.

"Right. Ah, I believe you're having a reaction, a type of posttraumatic-stress-induced moment." His tone was firm, but soft. Thank God he wasn't placating her. She would be kicking his butt right now. Of course, what he was saying rang true. Emotionally, she was very out of sorts.

"How so?" Kerry asked.

"Your fight-or-flight response was triggered, and nothing's turned it off yet. You're still running and fighting, and now you're turning those emotions on me." He tapped his finger on his chest. "You can take it out on me. I'm tough! Though I'd prefer if it didn't become a habit. It might be a teensy bit hard on my fragile ego to handle it daily."

"Fragile, my ass," she scoffed.

THE POWER OF A SEAL


"And what a beautiful tush it is," he quipped.

"Thanks," she said flatly.

"Kerry, what can I do to help? Talk to me or don't. Whatever works for you is fine with me. I can even leave you here alone, if that makes you feel better. I can go sleep in the boat or at the Bachelor's Quarters on base—"

She touched her finger to his mouth to silence him. "Thank you. I don't know what to say. How do *you* handle it?"

He nodded and opened his arms. "If I'm lucky, I can hold someone special. If not, I work out, like swimming and surfing, until I'm too exhausted to feel anything. Sometimes, I talk. There's no right or wrong method."

She crawled into those big strong arms, and her body relaxed slowly. She didn't know how much time passed, but at some point she started talking. "The marine mammals… I'm so glad the dolphins are accounted for and safe. This event didn't seem to rattle them. The techs checked them over, and another vet stopped by to double-check. Just receiving their texts made me feel better. But…but…" Her lips quivered. "I still feel like I failed them, because I didn't protect them from strangers getting onto the docks in the first place. These invaders… It's like they came into my home and violated my safety. I've always been safe at work, and now I'm going to be searching the water constantly, looking for the enemy. I'm angry."

Leaper held tight. "Kerry, you have every right to feel violated. But remember, security isn't your job. Healing and helping is your forte. You can't blame yourself over responsibilities that aren't yours. Also, the Feds said that the activists, these invaders, had a very specific note with directions and a map. It was a planned endeavor and most likely it was an inside job. How could you have known about it? It could have been a disgruntled employee, someone who's antimilitary, or someone who doesn't believe in the program. Few souls are aware of the marine mammal rescues the Foundation sponsors or that you promote longevity and a family atmosphere for the creatures. Regardless, no creature or human was hurt, and everyone is accounted for. The base is locked up tight and has extra security. No one is getting in there now. So what do you think about that?"

She nodded her head. What could she say?

"It's going to take a while for this emotion to process. I've heard that the more you talk about it, the more it'll loosen its grip." He sighed. "Dang, I sound like a shrink. Sorry, I don't mean to…unless it helps."

He was right. This was going to take a while to work through. She wasn't the type of person to sit and fret. She was more fearless warrior than stagnant weeper. She acted.

Her eyes met his. "Fight," she murmured.

"What?"

His arms rocked her gently.

She pushed out of his embrace. It was as if a flip had switched inside her. Her eyes lifted to his. "I'm going to fight. I'm not going to let criminals stop me. If I have to choose between being afraid and being fierce, then I choose the latter."

Leaper's mouth pulled slowly into a grin. "That's my lady." He lifted one of her hands, opened her fist, and placed a kiss inside, and then did the same thing with the other one. "When I've had to face fear, look it in the eye, and tell it to go take a flying leap, I've asked one thing of myself—to be calm. When you're calm in the face of the unknown, you can see everything clearly, endless possibilities and outcomes, and the best moves to make. So next time you get scared, try to calm yourself and see how it changes your experience."

"Thank you. I will." Kerry bit her lip. "Along those lines, I have to say something. This is really important to me. I've been scared to tell you how I feel. I have to be true to myself and to my heart." She leaned toward him until their faces were inches apart. "If I had died, or you had, without telling you this important thing... Leaper, I love you."

He smiled broadly. His eyes were warm, liquid pleasure. "Good choice. I'd rather that emotion than hate."

Closing her eyes, she leaned her forehead against his. A wave of joy filled her heart and a surge of adrenaline filled her body. "I know you *love* me." She grabbed the front of his shirt and nudged his body with hers. "Not the random words that people string together to get laid or whatever. You know that I'm the *one*, and no other person can fill those shoes. It's only me."

"Yes," he said softly. "I admit it. You're right. I love you, Kerry."

The words were drawn out slowly and sweetly, and they stuck in her mind, obliterating all other thoughts. Waves of joy swamped her, and she grinned at him.

His arms crushed her, holding her body so tightly, she could barely breathe. "Every day, I can hardly wait to have you in my arms again," he said. "The moment you leave them, I wish you were near."

Her hands were trapped between them, but she didn't care. She could feel his breath against her neck and hair. The caress of his hands along her body was exhilarating, and his message, those three little words, rang loudly in her heart and head. Not the "you're right" part, though that was nifty to hear, but "I love you." She'd waited her whole life for a declaration that made her melt inside.

"It's like I tell the recruits: Choose your life and career carefully," Leaper said. "Do not make decisions lightly. Be in Special Operations because you cannot imagine any other way to live. Be with a partner because you can't imagine living without them. I...I cannot imagine living my life without you."

Tears streamed down her face, dripping onto his shirt. "Me neither. Damn, I didn't think I had any moisture left in my body." She reached up to brush his cheek and felt moisture there too. "You, too! Aw, man. What now?"

He stood, picked her up, swept her into his arms, and carried her to the bed. Lying down beside her, he said, "I'm going to make love to you. I'm going to praise every part of your anatomy and listen to you come before I enter you."

"Maura was wrong. Music isn't the best way to communicate with you. *This* is." She kissed him with every ounce of her love and emotion.

"Kerry," he sighed.

Her breath filled with the images of them physically connecting. "Love me, Leaper. Love me until I cannot take any more."

She watched him as he delicately removed her clothes and lowered himself onto the bed next to her. As his fingers stroked her belly, her eyes fluttered closed.

*Oh, the pleasure those hands bring. This man certainly knows how to push my buttons and how to focus rhythmically on just the right one. Mmm, again and again.*

# Chapter 10

*ORDINARY DAYS ARE PUNCTUATED WITH ROUTINE AND STANDARD stuff, but after a cascade of crap and chaos, what's a lady to do?*

Kerry pondered the question as her eyes tracked Leaper around the room.

He stood there—tall and strong and naked—all lean muscles and caged energy, ready to pounce. The sun had just begun to rise, and long sunbeams stretched across the bay, leaving a trail of glittering, diamond-like sparkles in their path. It was gorgeous and slightly surreal in its picturesque glory.

Kerry gave up her musings. She couldn't resist coming up behind Leaper and wrapping her arms around him. Being in the nude, skin to skin, was a titillating experience. She wanted nothing more than to spend the entire day making love. Could she do that? She kissed his back. The skin was soft and warm and smelled of him. "Good morning," she murmured.

He turned in her embrace and kissed her. That single touch of lips was magical, as if it spoke directly to her soul. "I appreciate your morning attire. Any chance we could go back to bed for a few hours?"

"I was just thinking that." She wiggled in his embrace. "We need to get moving, if you're still interested in having your men see a Marine Mammal sea lion demonstration. I have a text from Topper's trainer, Adam Forrest, and he wants to schedule it for 0800."

Leaper looked at the projection clock next to the bed. "It's 0600. That doesn't give us much time." He frowned. "I'm skipping the quickie, but tonight, we're having a longie."

She chortled. "As always." She danced out of his reach and into the bathroom. "I'm calling dibs on the shower." She turned on the water and stepped inside.

He opened the door. "There's a water shortage, ma'am. I'm afraid you have to share your shower time."

"Oh no," she said in a movie-worthy mocking tone. "What will I do?"

Water pelted her skin as he pulled her close. His kisses set her on fire as his hands blazed a path of glory to between her legs. As his fingers found her clit, her breath shuddered out. "Leaper."

"I'm not making love," he said, his voice low and gravelly. "I'm just making sure that certain places get… squeaky clean."

"Yes," she sighed, leaning into his touch. Her pleasure heightened as the sensations climbed and climbed until her sheath tightened and her body shook with the power of her climax.

She leaned on him for several seconds, wishing her legs didn't feel like gelatin. He held her steady, and then he reached for the soap and played bath boy as he gently moved her about, covering her with suds and rinsing them away. It was such an erotic shower, she wished it didn't have to end. But soon enough he opened the shower door, wrapped her in towel, and deposited her on the bed, only to disappear back into the bathroom for his own morning routine. She knew she had to get moving or she'd be late.

Kerry prided herself on not being rude. Since the sea lion trainer was doing her a favor, with Command's approval, she needed to be there early. Besides, she wanted to have extra time to check on her dolphins.

Rushing around his bedroom, she dressed quickly. She wrote him a note and left a lipstick print at the bottom.

*See you at 0800 under the bridge, Coronado side. xxoo Kerry*

The morning sped by practically in a blink of an eye. Kerry checked on all of her dolphins and provided additional hydration instructions to Clay and Dilly. She sat beside Juliet's pen and allowed herself a few minutes to relax. Opening Juliet's care kit, she withdrew a toothbrush and paste.

Her hands smelled like fish, but she didn't care. It was such a relief that the dolphins were eating well and that none appeared to be succumbing to any further viral infection. She could wait until the end of the day to wash her hands with lemons. The oils from the lemon skin could penetrate even the worst odor.

Juliet nudged Kerry's hand, and Kerry brushed the dolphin's teeth and tongue. Then Kerry stowed the mouth-care items and obliged her by tossing a ball into the pen. The ball smacked the water, and the dolphin was under it in record time. Under and down the ball was tossed, then pushed and rolled, spun and poked, until Juliet was lost in her own game.

"I completed the task list you wrote. The extra hydration on Buckeye and Delores really perked them up." Dilly nodded at the dolphin. "How's Juliet doing? Has the vaccine had any effect on her?" She sat down on the dock beside Kerry.

"Hard to tell. Her blood test confirms that she has the virus, but she doesn't have any symptoms." Kerry tucked her legs underneath her.

"I don't understand." Dilly scratched the tip of her nose.

"Think of it this way," explained Kerry. "Two kids get the measles or chicken pox. One child is covered head-to-toe in a rash or spots. The second child doesn't have a single sore. Immune systems will vary, depending on genetics, diet, rest, stress, environment, and the state of your health at the moment you become ill. In my opinion, our dolphins receive significantly better care then they would out in the wild. They eat regularly, play often, socialize with each other very well, and have every medical option open to them. All of this happens without the constant daily threat of predators or the need to find food or shelter or safety. That takes a lot of stress off a creature."

Kerry wiggled her fingers in the water, and Juliet brought the ball to her. Kerry tossed it in the air and the dolphin volleyed it back. "Oh, if you think of it, could you please remind me to visit the lab? I ran a few tests on Juliet's blood to gauge the progress of the vaccine and its effect on the disease. In the wild, the effects were practically instantaneous, but it was with an older male who had an advanced infection. I want to see how these isolated blood cells react to varying doses of the vaccine."

The ball came soaring through the air.

Kerry caught it and rolled it on top of the water, watching Juliet leap out of the water and dive over it before she came up from below and bouncing it into the air. "I love how she plays. She's such an inspiration, putting playtime as a priority. A few weeks ago, I would have observed and enjoyed Juliet's antics. But now, having someone in my life who likes to get out and explore, I think I understand how vital and important time off is for mental, emotional, and physical well-being."

"He's built, your guy. Tall, too. He has an easy smile." Dilly observed.

"Yeah, he certainly does." Kerry noticed the sea trainer, Adam Forrest, was walking purposefully in their direction. When he picked up an ordinary rope, smiled at Dilly, and gave her a small wave before he left, the intention was obvious. "Since you're done here, do you want to observe the sea lion demonstration? Adam's running it."

"I'd love to, but I'm volunteering at the sea lion pens in an hour. Next time." Dilly clapped her hands together and stood. "Thanks for thinking of me."

Kerry nodded. She wondered if Dilly would ever pick up the hints from Adam; his interest was clear. It was funny how a trained observer saw other worlds but never her own.

The dolphin aimed the ball at the departing Dilly, but the tech wasn't prepared, and it bounced right off her head and landed back in the pen. The dolphin nodded her head up and down, squeaking and clicking, and Kerry could have sworn Juliet was laughing.

"I'm Adam, and this sea lion is Topper. The primary tasks that our marine mammals perform are identifying and alerting us to enemy divers and sea mines. The marine mammals are not trained to engage or attack the enemy," said Adam Forrest. "But these mammals do have a mind and motivation of their own. They can be unpredictable."

"What do you do when they are acting out or misbehaving? Do you punish them?" asked Trainee Parks.

"No," said Adam. "We ignore aberrant behavior and reward good conduct. Though it's fascinating to note that, just like a human child goes through the terrible twos, there are periods in a sea lion's growth and development where rebellion is part of the learning process. We use this time to teach a way to communicate, so we can instruct them, share commands, and know if they need something. The name of this game is patience, kindness, and positive reinforcement—and then even more patience. Sea lions and dolphins are very aware of positive and negative emotions. So I save my frustration for private reflection or activities such as surfing, kayaking, or paddleboarding. As a trainer, I work with sea lions every day. They are more than my friends. It's like they're my children. The more loving I am to them, the happier they seem to be."

"How strong are they?" asked Watson. "Topper looks like he can take on at least two of us."

"No doubt." Adam looked at Topper, who was watching the discussion with avid attention. "Sea lions are very strong and intensely smart. They don't like to be pawed, but they will wrestle with human beings if the opportunity arises. Biting is part of both their affection process and their defensive reactions. Markings that leave a small ring or barely break the surface are considered playful, while biting off large chunks shows aggression."

"Is there a daily routine?" asked Coates.

"Yes. You brush your teeth. We brush their teeth. You eat breakfast. They eat. We check their physical state regularly to make sure they are fit. You get medical checkups. They love to play, and I imagine that all of you do too." Adam nodded. "Right then, let's have our combat swimmers—Mestor and Soq—in the water, and we'll begin the process."

Leaper barked out instructions. "As Adam prepares, let's drop our lights and cameras over the side and record this process for further discussion."

The trainees took out the requested equipment and secured it to the cleats on the side of the boat before lowering it into the water. Watson checked that the anchor was still secure, and then he caught Leaper's gaze. "All set."

Adam released the latches and lowered a small portion of the side panel of the boat. Topper jumped into the water, and the combat swimmers hopped in after him.

Pointing to the tennis ball mounted at surface level, near the open side hatch, Adam said, "If Topper sees something, he will surface and touch this ball with his nose." Just then, the sea lion broke the surface of the water and rubbed his nose on the tennis ball. "I give him a float—it's like a buoy, but smaller and more of a flagging device." Adam showed them an example. "Like this one. The sea lion takes this float over to the spot where he sees an enemy swimmer or a mine and leaves it there.

"Just so you can understand a portion of how important

this is… Divers can spend weeks, months, or even years hunting for mines," Adam continued. "Dolphins and sea lions can locate them in mere minutes. Their ability to understand their environment and decide what fits and what doesn't is remarkable." Adam gestured toward the surface of the water. "If we were out patrolling somewhere, and Topper did just this—touched the ball, received a float, and marked the spot—then our combat swimmers would explore what was down there."

"What's the history behind the Marine Mammal Program? When did it start?" asked Watson.

"The program originated in 1960," explained Adam. "Bottlenose dolphins were the primary focus back then, but sea lions joined the program shortly thereafter. We work with female dolphins and male sea lions. We can trace the effectiveness of the mammals' contributions all the way back to the Vietnam War, where they saved thousands of lives by alerting us to underwater mines and enemy swimmers. The marine mammals have served in the Persian Gulf and additional areas that are currently classified. What I like is that I can take Topper here on just about any type of transportation, from a van to a plane, to a train or a boat. As long as I can keep him cool and comfortable and hydrated, he's pretty happy to go anywhere in the world."

The combat swimmers surfaced and headed back to the boat. Topper was right beside them. "If these swimmers were the enemy, then Topper's flag would alert us to something we cannot readily or easily see or sense," Adam explained.

He called the sea lion into the boat. "People think we're the ones forcing the mammals to work for us.

That's not true. Topper was rescued from an oil slick as a tiny pup and he would have died if we hadn't cared for him. He was literally laying on his departed mother waiting for rescue. We saved one adult and two pups that day, and now, we are the ones who have the privilege of feeding him, loving him, and learning from him. The mammals are the ones who give the permission, and they have the option to relocate or voice their opinion. Dolphins hop out of the pen and sea lions can be clever escape artists. And, you don't want to be on the receiving end of a mammal's dislike. Biting is one of their favorite communication tools. You'll notice a few scars. You see, as I teach the sea lions, they also teach me. It's the best job in the world, and one of the most fulfilling." He chuckled. "So how many of you want to leave SEAL training and work for the Marine Mammal Program?"

"Adam…" Kerry admonished him.

Leaper raised an eyebrow at his men. If his guys preferred the program, he'd attempt to smooth the way, but from the body language of his recruits, they were determined to stay right where they are. "Good try," he teased.

"Hey, a guy's got to throw the option out there." Adam shrugged. "I know that demonstration was pretty basic, but I always start with something easy for Topper. What else can I do for you?"

"Can you walk my crew through the best method for interacting with sea lions, including both wild sea lions and ones that are part of the Marine Mammal Program?" asked Leaper. "We can even switch boats. When you need me, I can play a role in another scenario, such as the sea lion going from water into boat, so we understand how he loads in."

"Your funeral, man. He doesn't know you well, and sea lions, as I mentioned, they bite." Adam nodded. Leaper didn't bother giving a response. "Okay. Let's do this. You and Kerry go back down to the bridge. When I signal you, drive directly toward us at a normal approach rate, and I'll take care of the rest."

"You got it," affirmed Leaper. Turning his attention to the trainees, he added, "A reminder that the cameras and lights are deployed. If you need to move the boat, pull them and store them properly."

"Aye, aye," replied the trainees.

The two men switched places. The boats rocked precariously for several seconds before Kerry took the helm and steered it back toward the bridge. She hummed Simon and Garfunkel's "Bridge over Troubled Water" to herself until Leaper was whistling along.

From the smile on Kerry's face, it was obvious she enjoyed being with him and doing all that she did. The way he interacted with her coworkers put everyone at ease. He was glad Command had approved this demonstration and interaction. The more comfortable people were with the marine mammals, the more likely they would respect their intelligence and personal space. Yes, today was a much better day than the one where the Base Commander had yelled at Leaper—not that Leaper hadn't handled it with his usual aplomb, but a sanctioned experience opened the doors for illumination and absorption.

---

The humidity was rising as the sun climbed higher in the sky. Being on the water, Coronado usually stayed fairly cool, but in the hotter months the heat index could climb to ninety degrees and higher.

Kerry's shirt clung to her skin. She wished she could strip it off and dive into the water to cool off. But this wasn't the time to play. Maybe after they were done with the second part of the demonstration. For now, she'd have to settle for wetting her mouth. She lifted the glass water bottle to her mouth and drank deeply. As she was securing the top, something odd caught her attention. She turned toward a boat that was weaving in and around the pylons of the Coronado Bridge. As the boat came closer, she squinted at it.

Something still wasn't right.

It was a tourist boat, moving in an erratic manner. It was zigzagging and going so slowly through the water that it was practically crawling. The man driving it looked oddly familiar. "Where do I know that face from?" Kerry muttered.

"Are you talking to me?" asked Leaper, making his way toward her from the back of the boat. The folding side door, which the sea lions and dolphins used to get on board, had partially opened, and Leaper had been fixing the latch and making sure it wouldn't fail at an inopportune time. "I have binoculars."

He held them out to her, and she took them, holding the binoculars to her eyes. Her finger worked over the knob, bringing the images into sharper focus. "Well, I'll be damned. There's a dead man driving a boat."

"May I?" asked Leaper, holding out his hand.

Placing the glasses in his hand, Kerry said, "Unless I'm horribly mistaken, that's Boscher. What's he doing here? I thought he was dead."

"The guy that Admiral Dale said was responsible for placing the dolphins in harm's way." Leaper's lips thinned. "There's another guy in the boat, and he's… armed. Dammit, those are ground-to-air missiles. Now, where are they going with those?"

"Shit! It looks like Boscher's headed toward your boat crew, the combat divers, and our sea lions. Can we head him off?"

"We can. He's driving a dinky boat, rented from the marina. I recognize the colors on the hull. Do you see the sticker on the stern?" Leaper tucked the binoculars into the utility pouch behind the seat. He picked up the bottle Kerry had been drinking from. "Can I have this?"

"Yes. Don't ask me. Just do it." Fear laced her words. "But please be careful."

He picked up her other water bottle and said, "I'll replace this. I promise." Leaper emptied the water, drinking thirstily, and then he put the boat in gear and drove a swift course parallel to Boscher. His hand fingered the glass. As he neared their boat, he tossed the glass water bottle in a perfect spiral arc and it struck the head of the other man in the boat. "Now it's just Boscher."

"Amazing shot! That engine must be loud, because Boscher is still driving the boat, and he didn't even notice the hit." Kerry's pulse was thudding loudly, and not in a pleasurable way. She didn't want anyone to be harmed, and the hardware in that boat was not the friendly peacemaker type.

"Yeah, I once nailed a skunk that was eating my friend's irises. It didn't kill him, but he was knocked out long enough to relocate to better hunting grounds." Leaper slowed the boat slightly and veered to the right, so they were riding in Boscher's wake. "We need to switch places. I want you to drive the boat up to his, as close as you can. I'm going to jump onto his boat and subdue him."

"That sounds very risky," she said, swallowing the lump in her throat.

"Kerry, this is what I do. I take down bad guys. If you cannot handle it, we have a problem." His eyes were determined and forthright. "Are we good?"

"Maybe."

His eyebrows shot up. "No, this is important. You cannot sit on the fence. Please walk me through…whatever is happening in your mind."

"I get it. I understand what you are saying. I was looking at you as my boyfriend and not as a SEAL. In the same way I have the potential of being harmed in my job, so do you. Strong emotions can cloud the issue and can even cause harm. So compartmentalizing makes sense at times." She nodded. "I'll get better at this. My protectiveness is a reflex, but I'll get there. We're good, and if I'm not later on, I'll tell you."

He sighed with relief and kissed her cheek. "Thank you. You have no idea how that scared the shit out of me. I don't want to lose you, but I'm not ready to change my career either. Wasn't it Popeye who said, 'I am what I am'? Though his 'am' sounded more like 'yam.'"

She chuckled. "Leaper, you make me laugh. Keep doing that."

Out of the corner of her eye, she spied another boat, and her smile melted away. The driving was really strange. The person at the helm did not know how to cut through the waves and was in danger of swamping the craft.

"Leaper, is that another one of those tourist boats? Didn't the person at the helm just wave at Boscher? And why is it picking up speed and heading for Naval Air Station North Island?" Kerry pointed in the direction of the convention center.

"Can you contact Adam?" he asked.

"I'll try." She withdrew her phone from her pocket and found Adam's phone number. She dialed and put it on speakerphone, then handed it to Leaper.

Leaper steamrolled over Adam's greeting. "Head's up. We're following a boat with ground-to-air missiles on board. You have invaders heading in your direction—rental boat with a white hull, green trim, and a hotel sticker on the side. I don't know what else is on board. Could be weapons? There are several 9 mms in the toolbox. Watson can show you, if you feel you need them. All my guys can land their shots. I'm calling the Coast Guard."

"Roger that," said Adam before he rung off.

—~~~—

Leaper dialed the Coast Guard number from memory. He admired and appreciated the Coast Guard; being an authority on water was a tough challenge. "I don't know if I mentioned it, but I dated a Coastie who worked in the Command Center. It was a long time ago. She's retired and lives in Florida now, married to a helo pilot with twin boys. But I've never forgotten the Center's number." The phone connected. "This is Navy SEAL Leaper Lefton. I'm following a boat—white hull with green trim—and it has weapons aboard. A second tourist boat is heading toward NAS, and it's unknown what they have. My trainees and a trainer from the Marine Mammal Program lie in wait between them and their destination. My security number is Alpha Tango Whiskey Charlie 6 9 9."

Leaper rang off. He tucked the phone into Kerry's pocket. "Ready to go knocking at his backside."

Kerry put the boat into its highest gear, and it shot forward. She guided the boat to within three feet of Boscher's. Standing on the bow, Leaper jumped on board. The impact of his landing made the boat rock back and forth.

Boscher looked back. His face distorted from one of relaxed pleasure to intense anger. Pulling a weapon from inside the front of his shirt, he aimed at Leaper and pulled the trigger.

The shot missed, and Leaper ducked low to avoid being shot and belly crawled along the bottom of the boat. Boscher would have to either abandon the steering wheel or wait for Leaper to rise and become a better target. Both options gave Leaper the advantage.

"What's going on?" A slurred voice was attached to an arm with a steely grip, which had caught Leaper's leg. The guy who had been nailed with the glass bottle sported a large lump on his head, and his fingers were digging into Leaper's calf.

In response to the distraction, Leaper's fist snaked out, slamming into the temple and knocking him out again. No doubt, the man was going to need a CAT scan after this adventure. Leaper added several direct hits to the head and face, just to be sure, and the man stopped speaking and passed out again. Yanking his foot from the man's grasp, Leaper ran his hands over the missiles.

He found exactly what he was looking for: firing pins. He withdrew and pocketed them. The missiles were still dangerous, but they couldn't be used without these precious pins. Rising onto his knees, Leaper leaned around the seat.

A series of gunshots rang out, and Leaper got a good look at the gun. Unless Boscher had another clip hidden on his person, there was only one shot left.

Standing up, Leaper launched himself at Boscher. His body slammed hard into Boscher's, and they landed at an angle on the padded seats. Fists connected to skin as Boscher threw punches, and Leaper retaliated with several well-aimed gut punches of his own. He didn't want to continue this fight, so Leaper threw an elbow strike at Boscher's throat, which halted the man's resistance.

Grasping his throat, his face turning red, Boscher righted himself and stumbled forward, then propelled himself into Leaper, who lost his balance and slid off the side of the boat.

Boscher's maniacal laughter was loud as he pulled a pin from his pocket. Lifting a ground-to-air missile launcher, Boscher inserted the pin, aimed, and triggered the launch.

The missile soared through the air, landing less than twenty feet from the bow of the Coast Guard cutter. A huge geyser blew straight up in the air from the impact. The cutter, which had been heading toward Adam and Leaper's crew, changed course.

Before Boscher could lift the second missile launcher, Leaper hauled himself back on board, climbing a loose dock line, and rushed Boscher, tackling him to the ground. The launcher fell to the deck of the boat.

Leaper pushed it out of reach and then his fists pummeled the man's soft bits—diaphragm, gut, groin, and neck—and ended with a hard right cross to the jaw that felt like it broke some bones.

Boscher was hunched over in pain, coughing and choking, before he passed out. The man looked like a bloodied ass, and Leaper would never assume that this guy was out for good. Bad souls had a way of rising again.

Pulling the wet bandana from his pocket, Leaper tightly secured Boscher's wrists. Several fingernails had been previously yanked from his right hand. What sick fuck would yank out his own healthy nails to prove his death was authentic? Guess one that was trying to get away with a ton of money, the potential for devastating damage to the Navy, and, of course, murder. Bastard!

Tugging on the bandana to make sure that Boscher wouldn't be free anytime soon, Leaper located a tethering line to bind the hands of the other man, who'd suffered from the glass water bottle beating and the punches to the head. Leaper gathered the weapons, making sure all of the safeties were on. As he stood, he could see that the Coast Guard cutter was close enough to communicate with. He gave them a thumbs-up and yelled, "All is secure. I'm Navy SEAL Leaper Lefton. These two men were attempting to take out a ship at Naval Air Station North Island. Weapons are safe. In the boat behind me is Marine Mammal Vet Kerry Hamilton."

"Coming aboard," replied a stern voice belonging to a woman whose rank said Coast Guard Lieutenant. Her crew threw lines down to Leaper.

He caught them and secured the lines to the cleats.

Waving at Kerry, he urged her to bring the boat parallel with the other side.

"I'm Lieutenant Vy Zalais. We appreciate the call. Looks like this situation could have been worse." The Coast Guard Officer was dressed impeccably and was wearing a GoPro camera. She gestured to it. "Hope you don't mind. We're taping today, to help with training."

"Not at all. But speaking of training, my crew is up there. I'm responsible for those men, and I need to check on them." Leaper was anxious to see what was happening. The surface of the water looked calm, but over half of his men couldn't be seen, and that meant they were under the water. "Can you send an additional boat over there, while I lend my trainees a hand?"

"Yes," replied Zalais.

A loud groan came from Boscher, who was attempting to reach his pocket. Leaper stuck his hand in the man's pants and pulled out a cell phone. He'd taken enough explosive ordnance disposal courses to be able to understand the basics. "This looks like a trigger."

"Bastard," moaned Boscher. "Last word is mine."

"Not if this beauty stays closed."

"Dickhead." Boscher spit blood. "How do you know there isn't a timer?"

"Because you have a trigger."

"Aww, I have this sweet little device so I can make it go *boom* earlier. What do you say to that?" Boscher looked so smug.

"Where did you put the explosives, you prick?" Leaper gave the phone to Zalais and lifted Boscher off the floor of the boat and into the air. His arms didn't even shake with the weight. The man was suspended there, at Leaper's mercy, with his bloody grin and misshapen mouth.

Kerry shouted. "I saw Boscher weaving in and around the bridge. Could the explosives be there?"

Everyone's attention went to the bridge, which was packed with commuters. The lanes were filled on both sides. Some people were heading into San Diego, and others were driving to work on the base. This was a usual time for shift change, so a majority of those drivers would be military.

"Oh God, no. All those people," whispered Kerry. "You can't! Why…why would you do such a thing? What did any of us ever do to you, Joshua?"

"Dr. Ham'ton, you are one of them, following that crazy do-gooder dogma, and none of you would even consider my plans. I'm smart! Brilliant! So, fuck you all. I'm impo'tant. After that bridge goes down, they'll listen. The whole world will know how I do things." Blood welled out of his mouth as Boscher spit two teeth onto the deck.

Leaper lowered the man, and two strong seamen took Boscher's shoulders and hauled him onto the cutter. Cuffs were snapped onto his wrists, and zip ties linked his legs together. Leaper couldn't watch this anymore. He shook his head in disgust. "Zalais, he's all yours. Do you want me to call the Amphibious Base for our Explosive Ordnance Disposal?"

Zalais looked over her shoulder, and the Captain signaled her. "Our Captain just did. Go check your crew. When you're done, meet us at San Diego Naval Port."

"Roger." Leaper jumped the small gap and landed on the boat with Kerry. "Let's check on my trainees."

The engine was idling. Kerry changed gear and the boat lurched forward, gaining speed as she aimed it at the SEAL trainees and Adam.

"I count two of my guys in the boat. Where are the rest of them?" Leaper scanned the surface of the ocean. He spotted a change in wave movement. "Drive us closer to the barriers of the base."

Kerry cut the engine and hurried to the back of the boat to lift the prop. "Since the sea lion is familiar with this boat, I'm opening the side hatch and splashing some water on the heavy pad on the bottom of the boat, in case he needs to slide in."

A hand surfaced from the water and slapped the inflatable.

"Shit. I'm going in." Leaper dove over the side.

The salt water stung his eyes, but he kept them open anyway. He spotted his three trainees through the whirl-wind of sand and debris kicked up from the confronta-tion. His men were wrestling four invaders.

In a pile connected by ropes were four sets of sea mines. If these insurgents were able to place them near the ships, they would detonate as the ships attempted to dock or leave. The sea lion pulled on the tether, edging the sea mines farther away from the invaders' reach.

Watson took a punch to the hip, even as he lashed out with a kick to the invader's groin. It connected, and his opponent doubled over. *Way to go, Sherlock*. The trainee grabbed the invader and hauled him to the surface.

Tucker had an invader locked under one arm, and he was swinging his empty arm like a pendulum, attempt-ing to connect with the fourth invader, who was danc-ing just out of reach. Tucker's face was scrunched up in pain, and his eyelids were squeezed shut. Leaper could only guess that something had gotten in Tuck's eyes or that the salt was stinging the crap out of his eyeballs.

Coates's arms were on the shoulders of an invader, and the two of them were rolling, twisting, and tumbling through the water, like a deadly Viennese waltz. The invader shoved Coates's head against a rock, and they broke apart.

The sea lion came out of nowhere and slammed its nose into the invader's back. It hit him again with a body slam and a finishing flip of his fins.

Leaper grabbed Coates's body and took him to the surface. One of the invaders was already tied up in the boat. Watson was on board, catching his breath. One eye was halfway closed and he'd be sporting a nasty shiner in the morning, but he smiled.

Leaper handed Coates up to Wallace and Mesner, the trainee who had transferred to his group after Parks rang out and the groups were condensed into three semi-viable groups. Wallace pulled their Teammate on board and gave him mouth-to-mouth, helping Coates hack up sand and seawater. Leaper gave them a thumbs-up and disappeared under the surface again.

Leaper looked around for the fourth guy. Where was he?

Suddenly something struck Leaper's back, and he turned with his arm raised, blocking the next strike. Using his powerful arms, Leaper grabbed the invader and hauled him kicking and protesting to the surface. The trainees brought him on board.

Tucker and Leaper fought the last two invaders, striking them in the throats and watching their eyes open wide as they clawed for the surface and air. Following them to the surface, Leaper couldn't help pointing out to Adam that his sea lion poked at the invaders with that powerful nose thrust and even landed half a dozen bites.

Escorting the invaders to the trainee boat, Leaper gestured to his men to wrap up the situation. His guys were always eager to comply.

Mesner and Wallace hauled the bad guys on board and trussed them up tight. Tucker climbed on board and poured a bottle of spring water over his eyes. "Damn, that feels good. Felt like hot pokers were stabbing my eyeballs."

Leaper gestured at the invaders. "Keep an eye on them. I'll get the tourist boat." He swam over to the invaders' craft, snagged the docking line, and tugged it closer to the boat of trainees. Then he crawled aboard, where he found the two Navy combat swimmers, Mestor and Soq, lying on the bed of the boat. Checking their carotid arteries, he was relieved to find pulses. "Wake up." He gave them each a strong slap on the cheek, and they snapped to attention.

"What the hell happened?" asked Mestor. "Where did that lump on the back of my head come from, and why do I taste blood?"

"All I can taste is seaweed. Ugh." Soq spit over the side of the boat.

"There were a few nasty invaders who wanted to get up close and personal with you. We've got them. Can you hang here until the Coast Guard arrives?" Leaper helped the swimmers sit up. Over his shoulder he yelled, "Toss us a few drinks."

Four bottles of spring water were hurled into the

boat, and Leaper picked them up and handed them off. The swimmers splashed their faces and eagerly downed the water.

Leaper stood and quickly counted heads: five trainees (there were six, but Worthington was still in the psych ward), four invaders, two combat swimmers, and one gorgeous girlfriend. "Where's Adam, the sea lion trainer?"

A hand waved from the water.

"Are you okay? Do you want to come aboard?" asked Leaper, offering his hand.

"I'm going to load up with the trainees." Adam gave a low whistle and splashed the surface of the water. The sea lion popped up beside him. "Hey, Topper. Thanks for the help. Even though you aren't supposed to engage the enemy, I'm sure the trainees were grateful."

Leaper shook his head. "You talk to him like he understands you."

Adam smiled. "He does. His senses are better than mine, than ours, and I'm sure he knows a helluva lot more about what's happening at any given moment."

"Interesting," replied Leaper. "Hey, was that your hand on the inflatable?"

"Yeah, Topper and I were making sure nobody attempted to breach the perimeter of the base. You're going to find several chunks of flesh are missing from the idiots who decided they wanted to tangle with an adorable sea lion." Adam grinned. "Fucking amateurs. Looks are deceiving."

"You have some serious balls to work with sea lions and to take on those targets. This will undoubtedly be an experience they won't forget." Leaper shook hands with Adam. "I owe you for watching over my guys."

Adam nodded. "I'll collect. A single-malt whiskey is always welcome."

"Noted."

*Boom! Boom! Boom!* The water reverberated with the explosions.

Leaper was on his feet in an instant, moving to the end of the boat. He expected to see the Coronado Bridge falling apart. Instead, he saw the EOD crews clearing the explosives and detonating them in bomb barrels.

Shipping traffic was halted an appropriate distance on either side of the bridge. Coast Guard ships had temporarily halted its progress.

The EOD folks brought their barrels back onto their boats and waved an all-clear flag. The Coast Guard instructed the boat traffic to resume with several horn blasts.

A small Coast Guard powerboat pulled alongside them as the Response Boat stayed in deeper waters, providing support. "Are you Lefton?" asked a Coastie crew member.

"Yes, these are my trainees: Watson, Coates, Tucker, Mesner, and Wallace. That guy is a Marine Mammal Trainer for sea lions, Adam Forrest, and the woman on the far boat is Dr. Kerry Hamilton," Leaper said. "Hell of a day for a swim."

"Aye, sir," the Coastie acknowledged. "Do you mind if we take the extra boat and the invaders back to port? We can drop off your swimmers too. They look like they need medical."

"They're all yours." Leaper looked at his guys. "Trainees, help with the transfer of the detainees and our brave combat swimmers to the Coast Guard, and then take Adam and his sea lion back to the Marine Mammal base. I'll see you at San Diego Naval Port." He pointed across the bay. "And give the digital chip for the cameras to the Coast Guard. It should be part of their evidence chain, as it will document the invaders' malicious attempts to harm sailors, civil servants, and a marine mammal, and to breach the Naval Air Station North Island ship perimeters."

"Aye, aye," replied Watson.

Leaper dove into the water and swam to Kerry. He hauled himself on board.

She hugged him tightly for several seconds and then appeared to remember there was an audience. She cleared her throat and pointed at the water. "I could see the whole fight from here. It was a scene out of a thriller movie. When you got hit from behind, well, I almost dove in to help out. But I saw Adam and Topper, and it seemed like a better plan to hold the line with them."

"Good call," he said. "I got you wet."

Kerry laughed. "No big deal. You should see what I've been covered in. Wait! That would probably ruin the romance. Let's just say there are worse smells than rotting fish guts."

Leaper sat down, his body aching. "Two groups of terrorists were captured and a weapon was fired, but didn't find its target. If you hadn't set up this demonstration today, or if we hadn't noticed those anomalies… damn, the lives that could have been lost. This terrorism act would have impacted the Navy and the military and civilian populations of Coronado in a drastic and irreversible way." His eyes held hers. "There's a list of souls who should thank you, from the Navy and the

Coast Guard to the Terrorism Task Force. And me." He shook his head, sending a spray of salt water in all directions, and then he wiped his hands over his eyes. "You spotted Boscher. Kerry, I don't know if you realize what you've done."

She touched the side of his face. Using the edge of the bandana she'd tucked into her pocket, she tenderly wiped his eyes. Then she kissed his lips. "I understand. I do. We were in the right place at the right time. This is the way it was meant to happen. Besides, I can't take all the credit. You and your trainees kicked some serious butt." She couldn't resist adding, "The sea lion wanted to help more. Aren't marine mammals the coolest?"

"Yeah, I witnessed that 'helping,' especially when I saw the chunks of missing flesh from the invaders. Sea lions really are biters. I've got that highlighted in my mind." Leaper picked up her hand and kissed her palm. "You guided the Coast Guard in too, didn't you?"

"Yes." She nodded. "Knowing when and how to help a situation is important."

"Any time you want to guard my six, I'd be honored." He swallowed a knot of emotion. "I've never said that to anyone outside of the Teams before. I've offered to guard someone's back plenty of times, but never the reverse."

Kerry leaned into his arms. "I'm honored."

From his sitting position, he hugged her tight, his head landing just under her breasts. "This is nice."

She wiggled. "Audience. I keep forgetting. We should shove off."

"Agreed." Leaper released her and stood. "Would you like to drive, or should I?"

"Take the helm. I've had it for today. I'm ready for a break."

"Hooyah to that." Leaper lowered the prop and turned the engine on. He selected the gear, and the boat moved slowly out of the vicinity of Naval Air Station North Island. He wove through the traffic on the bay as the wind ruffled his hair and took some of the moisture out of his clothes.

The trip across the bay was short and uneventful as Leaper headed to a dock at the San Diego Naval Port. "What a morning," he said, checking his watch. "It's not even time for an early lunch. We're still in the breakfast phase." He smiled sardonically.

"What? Food? How can you be hungry after that?" asked Kerry. "I want a cup of chamomile tea and a cold compress. Yet *you* look calm and, dare I say it, pleased."

"Yeah. I am. I'm proud of my trainees. They acted quickly and decisively. They worked as a unit, a Team, and there were no casualties. That's a serious win in my book." It had been a while since Leaper was on the Coast Guard base. He hoped there wouldn't be too much paperwork. Thinking of breakfast—pancakes, sausage, eggs, oatmeal, and fresh fruit—made his mouth water. His eyes scanned over the large floats marking out a perimeter around a ship and he smiled.

"I can practically see the wheels spinning in your brain." Kerry touched his arm. "What gives? Spill it."

"Besides food? Okay. Do you know those giant inflatable flotations that mark a perimeter around the carriers? That concept came from a think-tank group discussion where an operational SEAL mentioned that the greatest chance of harm was a small vessel driving into the hull and exploding. The SEAL even wrote an article about this concept. Thus, when in port, these inflatables are standard precautionary measures, along with additional safety features including well-prepared snipers who watch everything that comes and goes. But the ground-to-air missiles…no one had ever contemplated such a thing. Boscher is a madman, for sure, but he also might have saved some lives by pointing out a weakness in our security."

"You have an idea on how to fix it, don't you?"

Leaper nodded. "I'd need to speak with a few of my retired and former brethren and see if their companies can handle the amount of materials needed to construct what I want, and then I'd approach the brass. Having a plan, along with a timeline for production and a cost analysis, will make an enormous difference."

Kerry smiled. "You and I are spending too much time together. I think I just read your mind. You're going to research and propose a giant net coming up from the inflatables and attaching to the top of the air tower on a carrier or the stacks on a refueling ship."

He laughed. "Damn, I'm glad I'm not a cheater. You *are* reading my mind. Let's see if you can answer this. What would this net do?"

"I'm guessing that it would nullify the charge in some way or splatter the charge across a larger mass to dissipate it." Kerry giggled. "I'm right, aren't I?"

"Nailed it. There's this company in Connecticut, entrepreneurs who developed armor clothing. This is light, wearable, flexible antiflak-type material that can repel gunfire, so let's crank this up to missile-repelling strength, and you have a new defense system that can sit tucked away at the top of ship. With the push of a button it deploys, and with another push it rolls itself back up." Leaper pulled the boat alongside the dock. He cut the engine and tossed the bowline at the waiting Coastie. "I can see it in my mind."

"Impressive," said Kerry as she stood at the ready in the stern and handed up the aft line.

"Got it," said the Coastie as he caught and tied off the line.

"Let's go up," said Leaper. When the boat was secure, Leaper gave Kerry a boost up and onto the dock, and then he joined her.

Boscher was being escorted by armed guards. His face was swollen, and his mouth was bleeding.

"Wait," said Kerry. "Please, I have to know. Boscher, you did Special Funding for the Marine Mammal Program. Did you believe in it, or was it all for the money?"

"You are so naive, Dr. Hamilton. I like that about you. It made you such an easy target to hide behind. I wish I could have stayed longer. I would have earned so much more." Spittle gathered around the edges of Boscher's mouth as he spoke.

"I don't believe that. I think you wanted acknowledgment more than you wanted any of that money." Kerry stepped closer.

Leaper caught her arm, holding her from getting too close. "It's not safe to get too close to him," he whispered.

She nodded and stepped back until her back was touching Leaper's chest.

Boscher spit on the dock, and there was blood in his sputum. "Perhaps, Dr. Hamilton, I wanted both recognition and the accolades and funds…at one moment in time. But I was misguided then, for there was a part of me that believed the government could change and the world could be different. But the DOD stripped me of my dream and didn't let me participate as I wanted to. Those activists were so convenient for me, as were my associates in the boats. What rejects me, I reject. It's as simple as that, really." His smile was pure evil, and his eyes were dead, pools of endless nothing.

"Then why did you help me?" Kerry shook her head. "You wouldn't have gone above and beyond to fight for my tank funding or offer to help with my projects without a deeper reason. That was a lot of work."

"Convenience, my dear. Nothing more." Boscher straightened his shoulders as much as he could in cuffs. He took several steps away and then turned and looked over his shoulder at her. "Good luck, Dr. Hamilton. I don't think you've heard the last of me."

Leaper cut in. "I do. That man is not getting out. He'll serve at least two lifetime sentences. The Navy, the FBI, Homeland Security, you name it, looks down on an individual or group committing acts of terrorism. Between the activists invading the Marine Mammal base and Boscher's admitted part in that, combined with the bombs strapped to the bridge and the missiles he was going to use on the naval ships, that man is never seeing daylight."

Boscher grew smaller and smaller as he neared the ramp off the dock. He never looked back as he walked up the metaphorical gangplank and disappeared inside the large double doors into Naval Headquarters.

Kerry turned to Leaper. "Am I blind? How could I not see that?"

"You have a good heart, Kerry. There's nothing

wrong with that, or optimism, and believing that people are doing things for the right reasons. Cynicism creeps in too fast with bad people and hard experiences. I should know. I've wrestled with evil for my entire career. It's real." He held her shoulders and looked deeply into her eyes. "Please don't give up that joy inside, even if a rotten apple tries to poison you. Spit out the poison and find your joy again, okay?"

Her lips thinned but eventually she nodded.

He hugged her tightly and felt her shiver. "Give it time, Kerry. There's no sense or reason to an individual's delusions. Don't look for it. Rather, I suggest you give this wound of betrayal...time to heal."

Leaper kissed the top of her head.

They stayed in their embrace and watched the activity on the dock as they waited for Leaper's crew, who were dropping off Adam and the sea lion at the Marine Mammal base before they docked at the San Diego Naval Port. Most likely, Adam would stop by later today and give a statement, or the Coast Guard would make a stopover there on their next patrol and talk to them. The Coast Guard was very good at doing its job, and they knew how to put together a significant and unbreakable paper trail that should frighten any criminal going to trial.

Kerry shifted her position. In Leaper's opinion, she must have felt somewhat better as she pulled out of his embrace after twenty minutes. She wound her hair into a knot at the back of her neck. She plucked at her sweat-soaked shirt. Even in disarray, she was still the most intriguing and beautiful woman Leaper had ever met. How many individuals could have handled a high-speed chase, gunfire, and multiple enemies? She was made of some powerful, strong stuff. He respected her for that and for so much more.

"You're staring at me," she whispered.

"It's...been such a crazy time. So much has happened, and yet here I am, still pinching myself that you're in my life. Sometimes, I can hardly believe how lucky I am." He kissed the top of her head, the sweet scent of her hair mingled with his shampoo. He loved how she smelled, those scents that were so uniquely hers and such an aphrodisiac that he had to remind himself that he was standing on a busy port dock.

She hugged his arm. "Ditto."

He rolled his eyes. "Now I get the 'ditto' comment."

Laughing, she whispered, "I can hardly wait to get out of these clothes."

"I can hardly wait to watch you," he teased.

Kerry lightly punched his arm. "Leaper," she chided, though the mirth in her eyes was a dead giveaway.

His trainees pulled into port and followed the docking procedures perfectly. Leaper nodded his approval.

Watson led them, and Leaper knew he was going to be a good sailor. The jackasses of the world might label his men fuckups, but Leaper knew the truth. These Navy men performed in the clinch, and he'd be proud to work beside any of them.

Leaper shook their hands. At Watson's side, he paused and stared into the man's eyes. "Bravo Zulu."

"Thank you, Instructor," Watson said, beaming.

Very few souls would be willing to dive into the unknown and handle whatever they found there. Leaper had seen men go into battle with a gung ho spirit, only to be compromised because they couldn't handle the pressure or surprise of the unknown. His men—the last five from his original group and his one addition—were all going to make it over the finish line.

In his heart, Leaper knew he would see these men at graduation someday. He'd bet on it. One or two of them might be struggling with physical strains and fractures. And if their bodies couldn't hold the standard, there was an option to roll for medical reasons. Then those trainees would be in the next class so they could finish the training and graduate.

Who knew what the next step would be for his guys, but whatever it was...they would work hard. These trainees were becoming warriors who kept fighting, willing their bodies to survive the physical conditioning and the mental games. All of them were learning that survivors persevere.

"I'm proud of you," he said to the trainees, looking each one in the eye and acknowledging his ability to stick with the fight and come out victorious. One glance inside the boat showed that everything was shipshape. There wasn't so much as a water bottle out of place. He was pleased. "Let's chat with Coastie Command, and then breakfast is on me. Move out."

The serious moment turned into levity quickly.

"Aye, aye," they replied in unison, looking relieved. He knew they must be starved. They could consume about 4,000 calories per meal and still be hungry.

Leaper's stomach rumbled as he took Kerry's hand in his. She leaned into him with a grin and pointed to his gut. "I bet you can't give *that* orders."

"Just watch and see. I'd bet breakfast on it, but I'm treating the trainees, and I don't want to lay that burden on you. I know how much they can eat." Leaper led the way down the dock to the Command Center.

"I have savings. I'll take that bet. And if you lose, then I get to choose the soundtrack for our next water adventure." Her eyes sparkled with joy. He could stare into them for hours.

He kissed the back of her hand. "Agreed."

Leaper looked over his shoulder to see the trainees following. He knew there would be a long road ahead of these men before they reached the finish line, but for now, time was in their favor. Training was a time to learn, hone, and master—to push yourself to the limits of capability, and then even farther. But the best part was that every day was a step closer to achieving those goals.

Leaper scanned his ID, and the door buzzed open. He held the door for Kerry and stepped inside. Cool air enveloped him as the subdued lighting eased his eyes. He blinked several times, adjusting to the dimness. There were several more doors until they reached their ultimate destination.

She squeezed his hand.

Leaper had to admit he had an incredible woman walking beside him and a confident and strong entourage behind. What more could a blessed man ask for?

# Chapter 11

LARGE CROWDS ALWAYS MADE LEAPER'S PALMS ITCH. Standing within one made him feel even taller and more separate. This was only one of the reasons Leaper preferred one-on-one time to organized group chaos.

Several months had passed since the Boscher attack. On a bright, sunny morning at the submarine base on Point Loma, next to the Navy Lodge, a ceremony with over a thousand attendees was being held in an annex area. Like a beehive, it was alive with noise and activity.

Leaper wore his dress whites, and he'd recently buzzed his hair. It was less muss in the water, but it made his cover, or hat, slide oddly around his head. He had to stand very still so it didn't slip off to one side.

He was so proud of his lady, and to be here watching the ceremony where Kerry was recognized for her work in Special Programs was pretty cool. If only the crowds didn't have to be so big. SEALs were rarely into crowds…too many people to watch at once.

Thinking about the passage of time, Leaper was happy that Kerry was contented. The Marine Mammal dolphins were doing great. Kerry had received approval for treatment with the preventive vaccine, which ended up being a cure too, and she was over the moon with the dolphins' response. The Marine Mammal bottlenose dolphins were going back to their regular routines, and Kerry was spreading news of the vaccine to the other facilities where she'd volunteered. She'd also published a series of articles on the entire process, from discovery to healing—with Command's approval, of course—and the doctor from Greenland had joined in on several of the formal discussions. He was up for several research awards for his achievements.

The loudspeaker squealed, making many in the audience cover their ears until it stopped.

"Sorry for the interference, folks. Now, for her outstanding work in the field of marine mammal preservation of life and her dedicated service in a time of crisis, we would like to recognize Dr. Kerry Rose Hamilton," said Admiral Dale as he presented Kerry with a wood-and-brass plaque. "Would you like to say a few words?"

Kerry shook hands with him and accepted the award. "I'd like to thank Admiral Dale, Navy Command, our Marine Mammal Director, and the veterinary staff. I'd also like to thank the Foundation, which continues to support research and a healthy marine mammal community. I couldn't have made such progress without the assistance of Dilly Quinn and Clay Jones. Ms. Quinn assisted with the sample collection, processing, and data analysis. Morbillivirus has had a devastating effect on our dolphin and whale populations, but with continued inoculations and a diligent Marine Mammal force, we will stop the progress in its tracks. The vaccine has recently been modified, and I'm pleased to say that it's now being passed on through shared feeding grounds."

Leaper's eyes caught hers. Her smile warmed him to his soul. His love for her made him feel both vulnerable and invincible, and he wouldn't trade those warring feelings for anything on the planet. Gich had once told him,

"True partnership checks off the 'risk it all' category so there's a lot more on the line emotionally and physically. It's the best and worst of extremes and experiences. But relationships—good ones—are a rare gift, and they're worth it. Hold on to the good tightly." Adding fidelity and chemistry to this blew his mind. Leaper couldn't agree more.

Kerry's voice carried out to the audience. "I'd like to extend my personal and professional gratitude to Navy SEAL Leaper Lefton for his support and to commend his foresight and intuition in contributing to the safety and well-being of myself and our marine mammals. I dedicate this award to him." She clapped one hand against the back of the plaque, and the audience joined in.

She sat down next to Admiral Dale as the Director of the Marine Mammal Program went to the lectern and called Adam Forrest forward to recognize him with a Merit of Excellence award. Next, the Director handed out certificates to the techs and volunteers. "Our plans for the future include a more widespread public-awareness campaign. We will have an active social media presence through the Marine Mammal Foundation to keep everyone looped in on important endeavors, such as our vaccine program, wellness efforts, and preservation of life and training processes. On behalf of the Navy, our marine mammals, staff, volunteers, and all of our supporters, we'd like to thank you for attending our program today."

There was loud clapping. A few hoots of support and a couple of cheers added to the jubilation.

Leaper's eyes followed Kerry as colleagues and coworkers surrounded her, offering words of praise. If the smile on her face was any indication, she was one happy camper. He was pleased for her. It had been a long road to this celebratory moment, and he had no doubt they would get through the trials and tribulations. He supposed that's what separated achievers from doubters: the will to persevere. The SEAL Ethos spoke of honor and courage and never quitting. Leaper believed in those values, and to have a woman by his side with the same moral dedication blew his mind.

Admiral Dale pulled away from the pack of people and walked toward him. "Lefton, you received the materials I sent you?"

"Yes, thank you, Admiral Dale. I have the packet, and I appreciate your assistance and your offer." Leaper said, somewhat formally.

"After everything we've been through, call me Walter." The "off-duty" part was understood.

"Walter. Call me Leaper." The men shook hands. "Hey, did you catch the Army-Navy game?"

"Yeah, Army kicked Navy's ass. Sad day for sailors everywhere."

———

The ceremony was fairly standard, the usual pomp and circumstance, but lovely all the same. It wasn't often that Kerry found herself the center of attention. She didn't need the recognition, though. The fact that the dolphins were recovering was the best possible reward.

Kerry squinted up at the sun, wishing she hadn't left her sunglasses in the car. She clutched the plaque under one arm so she could embrace friends and shake hands, but she was ready to put the event behind her.

She was more comfortable around Leaper and the mammals.

Relief flooded her as the crowd thinned. She didn't necessarily care for large-style events. It was another thing that she and Leaper had in common.

A familiar voice called to her. It was Emme. Kerry was shocked when her fickle friend approached her full of hugs and warm accolades. The last time they'd spoken, it had been to fight. She'd made a point of discouraging Kerry from making waves.

"Kerry, congrats, my friend," Emme said, "Hey, listen, I'm sorry for what I said about the dolphins. I didn't understand, not the danger they were in or your relationship with them. This is just a job to me. For you, it's, like, your whole world. I hope you'll forgive me."

"Yes. Maybe it's odd that work is a big part of what drives my spirit, but this is me. Why don't we just start fresh." Kerry knew there was redemption in making yourself vulnerable and reaching out. "Thanks for the apology. I'm not very good…with human beings."

"You follow your heart." Emme gestured at Leaper. "It looks like that personality trait is serving you well. He's around quite a bit these days."

"Yeah. He's a very special soul." She gazed at Leaper Lefton, the love of her life. He was so handsome in his uniform and even more desirable out of it. She smiled to herself, thinking of their naked time together. If someone had told her that she'd be walking around at home in her birthday suit and that he'd be chasing her around as if she were Aphrodite, she never would have believed it. They'd accomplished so much together too, both personally and professionally.

"I've got to run," Emme said, interrupting Kerry's thoughts. "I have a date with the Executive Officer of that submarine. He's giving me 'the tour.'"

"What about Admiral Dale?" asked Kerry. The man had begun to grow on her, and she had to give him credit. He'd certainly come through for the marine mammals.

"Walter? It didn't work out. He wants something more serious, and I'm not ready to settle down. I'm living the dream." Emme rocked forward on her feet, eager to get moving.

Kerry knew the single life wasn't the one she wanted anymore. Her life with Leaper was far better than anything she'd ever imagined. But she wanted her friend to be happy and to do what was right for her. "Have fun."

"Oh, I will." Emme waved. She headed for a sailor dressed in his formal whites, standing off to the side. The man's face was delighted. It was obvious he was already smitten with Emme.

"Go, Emme. Hope you find what you're looking for."

Kerry looked out at the horizon and pondered the events that had led to this moment. Leaper and Declan had taken down activists who had been instructed by Special Funding Director Joshua Boscher, saved San Diego and the surrounding waters from being eco-bombed by a potent and deadly drug, foiled the terrorist revenge plot of missiles and bombs by the disgruntled and not-dead Boscher, and actually received commendations from their bosses. Add in the amazing healing power of the dolphins, and all of those things had to be miracles.

Of course, there'd been quite a few mishaps along the way too, including Leaper's overshare when they first met and he confessed to the Gabir story, the crazy unsanctioned dolphin-invader scenario near the Base Commander's home, and the viral outbreak of the wild dolphins and its spread to the Marine Mammal dolphins. The search for samples, the contact with other labs, the vaccine/cure, the drama associated with everything… It was a lot to take in, especially in such a short time frame. Surviving had been a feat of sheer will, yet she'd go through it again. Kerry had known true companionship for the first time in her life.

How strange. She could never have imagined life unfolding this way.

Wasn't that how things happened? Everyday tasks and experiences moved from ordinary to extraordinary in the blink of an eye, and all the preparation in the world didn't matter in the least. There was no handbook for risking your heart or falling in love or challenging your preconceived views of your work and career. The best course of action for life appeared to be trusting your gut instincts and leaping. How appropriate it was that she was in love with a man who had *leap* in his first name! And if you landed on your ass, you dusted yourself off and tried again. Leaping into present possibilities was significantly better than sitting on the sidelines and dreaming of the future.

The dolphins knew the key elements to a joyful existence. They surfed the big waves, dove for fresh fish, enjoyed tasks and playtime, and sought camaraderie. Also, they were horniest bunch of marine mammals she'd ever seen in her life. But hey, primal drives are fundamental building blocks of life.

Kerry's eyes sought Leaper, who was chatting with

Admiral Dale. They were laughing. Raising her eyebrows, she wondered what they were talking about. She hadn't thought her man got along with the brass very well.

"Congratulations, Dr. Hamilton," said Dilly, grabbing her hand and shaking it. "You deserve this."

"Thanks, and it's Kerry, remember? Did you hear me mention your name up there?" Kerry asked. "Without those samples from the wild dolphins, I don't know if I could have trusted the vaccine data. But our results matched those from the wild dolphins in waters surrounding Greenland."

Dilly smiled. "I was touched by the accolade, and, uh, I think I have you to thank for the offer I just received from the Director of the Marine Mammal Program. If I want to stay on as a part-time vet tech, shadowing only you, I'll receive a wage with an option to extend the position into full-time after I complete my studies and residency."

Kerry nodded. "I admit it. I put in a good word. But it was your stellar work that earned your position. Anyone can take a job, but you're making this into a passion and a career. I told them they would be fools to lose you. Besides, by the time you're ready for full-time, I'll probably be dialing back to part-time…or perhaps pursuing a few other life options."

"You'll never leave the dolphins," said Dilly.

"No, but I'd like to make room in my life." Her eyes were locked on Leaper, who shook Admiral Dale's hand and was making his way over to them.

"Got it," said Dilly, following Kerry's gaze. "I'll see you next week, Kerry."

"Have a great weekend, Dilly." She waved at the vet tech. Kerry was glad the talented and resourceful tech would be staying on. Some people had a special gift when it came to creature connection, while others couldn't quite relate to the bond. Dilly was unique and a credit to her inquisitive mind, her family, and her school. Kerry had no doubt that Dilly's contributions to the Marine Mammal Program would be astounding.

"Hi, there." Leaper leaned in and briefly touched his lips to hers.

It was a quick kiss, yet electricity sparked her lips. "Are we ready to go home?"

"Almost. Only one more stop to make." He held out his hand and she took it, linking her fingers through his. They wove their way through the parking lot until they reached her car. She tugged him close and kissed him in a soul-searing lip-lock. It was heavenly.

He mumbled against her mouth. "We can skip."

"What?" she asked, pulling back.

"We don't have to go." His eyes were alight with heat, and she knew he wanted to get naked. There wasn't time for a quickie, though. They needed to be on the Amphibious Base ASAP.

"Yes, we do. The trainees are getting a Bravo Zulu too," Kerry chided him gently. "Tell you what—you get to pick the song as I race over to Coronado."

"Deal." He opened her door, and she slid behind the wheel. Leaper closed it behind her. His manners might be old-fashioned, but she loved it. To her, it was a sign of respect.

His fingers spun through his playlist until Journey's "Don't Stop Believin'" filled her speakers. She knew those intro chords by heart and sang along with the lyrics. Leaper's voice rose loudly with her own as they drove off the sub base and took back roads past the Marine Mammal base, over the bridge that the activists had used, past Lindbergh Field, and onto the I-5 until they reached the exit for the Coronado Bridge.

Her eyes strayed to the place where Leaper had talked the trainee, Quentin Kirkland Worthington, off the ledge. At their last visit to Balboa, the boy was still in a locked psych ward, but he'd seemed more aware of his surroundings. The stress of being a SEAL, a sailor, or any kind of military-inspired hero had lifted, and he seemed more at peace.

After spending his mornings in therapy and his afternoons in art therapy, he smiled more. He spoke of his mother visiting, and said that she lived only a few blocks away now.

A nurse had told Leaper and her that the Admiral—Quentin's father—had been sighted at the hospital twice. All of these things had been good to hear.

In Kerry's opinion, it was so rare to be able to catch an individual before tragedy struck. The line between what breaks us and what makes us stronger is a thin one, and knowing when to reach out for help is both lifesaving and empowering. If only our society rewarded awareness and acceptance of one's mental learning curve, perhaps more individuals would reach out before it was too late. Life is very precious.

Things could have turned out so horribly. She was grateful for the blessing.

*What did Leaper say? Know yourself so that others may count on you and know you too. It's a warrior adage that becomes the basis of being a useful operator and Teammate.*

*Do I know myself? I'm a type of warrior, a heroine of my own life.* She pondered the thought as they turned onto Orange Avenue. *Yes*, she decided. *I accept myself as I am, and I'm excited to explore and grow and enjoy being me.* She smiled as they zipped down the Silver Strand until they reached the Amphibious Base. The checkpoint was busy, clogged with bikers, walkers, and cars waiting for access.

Sailors in uniform directed traffic down to the grassy expanse where, Kerry had learned, many ceremonies took place. A podium, awning, and chairs were set up in an organized, military fashion, and Kerry was escorted to a chair in the first row as Leaper was led to the side.

A whistle sounded, and everyone took a seat. They were just in time.

The color guard approached carrying flags, and everyone stood. The pledge was spoken with great honor. Those who had served or were serving saluted, and the rest of the crowd stood with hands over their hearts. A prayer was read, and the speakers shared powerful and memorable messages.

Kerry's eyes kept straying to Leaper. He was so handsome as he stood at attention. It was obvious he loved being a SEAL and serving his country. Kerry wanted his happiness to continue and would support him in whatever manner he asked. That thought shocked her, because she knew she'd move anywhere he did and do her work from wherever she lived. Yes, she was dedicated to her dolphins, but they were healing and there was more work to be done throughout the world. She knew she would always maintain a strong link to those she loved, but she was ready for more…with him.

When Declan Swifton took center stage, Kerry's attention shifted to him. "I've been asked, as the Commanding Officer of BUD/S, to introduce our friends in the Terrorism Task Force: Michael Beckwith and Doug James."

Two men joined Declan. His voice rang out clearly. "They'd like to present Commander Leaper Lefton of SEAL Team Special Forces with this certificate and medal for his efforts in terrorism prevention."

Leaper approached. He saluted the brass and Declan, and then shook hands with the two men from the Terrorism Task Force. Accepting the proffered items, Leaper stepped aside as his five remaining recruits received small pins and certificates of recognition for their distinguished efforts.

Kerry liked the way Leaper looked on like a proud papa. He was nurturing that way. Her hand strayed to her belly for a split second. She hadn't thought about having kids, but with Leaper, everything seemed possible.

Too soon, the audience was standing and the group at the front was filing out. She watched the parade walk past, in awe of the beauty and symmetry of the Navy. As the audience moved toward an area with food, she joined Leaper, who was in mid-discussion with the two men from the Terrorism Task Force.

"This is Michael Beckwith and Doug James, and I'd like to introduce my girlfriend, Dr. Kerry Hamilton," said Leaper as he took her hand and brought her in closer. There was sweetness in his gesture.

She smiled at the men. "Nice to meet you, gentlemen."

"We're attempting to lure your boyfriend away from the Navy," said the taller of the two men. "But he's not biting."

"Didn't I see you at the Marine Mammal base with an FBI jacket?" she asked the shorter man.

"Yes, I'm Special Agent Beckwith. I'm assigned to the Terrorism Task Force. I didn't speak with you that night, but I was there. Good call on the carfentanil. That's nasty stuff." He leaned forward. "How did you know…about the man in the boat?"

She shrugged. "I'm sure you read the After-Action Report on the incident. The person in the boat was acting strangely. Leaper noticed it first. Also, our sea lions kept circling his boat. They have an incredible sense of smell. When I looked through the binoculars, I recognized Joshua Boscher, who was supposedly dead—killed by his own shark study—but there he was in a boat, alive and well, and with several ground-to-air missiles. It was pretty frightening."

"But none of you lost your cool," added Doug James.

"No," said Leaper. "We're all well practiced and trained to function effectively and efficiently under pressure. I knew I couldn't let those missiles be launched, so I acted, and Kerry was an excellent support. She's my rock."

"Without forethought to your safety, and with concern only for others," added Declan, joining the conversation. "That's a warrior. And with the commitment to never surrender or quit, and to bring everyone back home. No one gets left behind."

Leaper slapped Declan on the back and the two men shook hands. "Thanks for this. It wasn't necessary."

"Like I had any say in it. It was these bozos who wanted to recognize you." Declan laughed. "I'd just as soon buy you an ice cream with sprinkles."

"You know I only like chocolate chips. Colors taste weird."

"*You're* weird." Declan rebutted.

Kerry laughed. "You two should take your Abbott and Costello act on the road."

"That's what Maura always says," replied Leaper and Declan in unison. They chuckled loudly.

"Two peas in a pod," Kerry murmured affectionately.

"We don't want to hold up your celebration," Special Agent Beckwith interjected. "Thanks again for the help. We could use an instructor like you." He held out a business card. "If you change your mind, give us a call."

"Thanks. I'm okay where I am." Leaper paused and looked over his shoulder. "Though you should know I never play by the rules. I hear you guys are sticklers for going by the book. That's just not my thing."

"We are…very strict about the rules, for legal reasons," added Doug James. "But the offer stands." He nodded his head at Kerry. "Ma'am." Then he offered his hand to Declan. "Swifton, let's have dinner soon. My wife wants Maura's recipe for butterscotch brown Bettys."

"Sure thing. I'll let her know." Declan shook hands with both men and watched as they left. Under his breath he said, "You know that I'd never let them steal you, Leftie."

"As if you could stop me from doing something I want to do. *Pffft!*" spouted Leaper.

"If only I could bottle you and add you to our perfect sailor mix." Declan smiled.

"We'd get sour grapes," they said in unison.

"Seriously, though, I know you're probably going operational again. I just wanted to say thanks for helping us out." Declan nodded, his face tight with emotion.

"Anytime, my brother," said Leaper, adding levity to his tone and words. "Spending time with you is a vacation, though I might need a vacation from this break. Those natives were pretty restless—activists and disgruntled employees as well as enemy invaders and big, threatening bombs. Let me choose my own activities for the next trip to teach at BUD/S."

The two men held each other's gaze for several seconds. Kerry knew there was some kind of special exchange happening, and it filled her with happiness and warmth to know that her Leaper was deeply cared for, respected, and appreciated. Of course, she couldn't stop herself from saying, "Are you two going to kiss or what? I'm ready to get out of these heels."

The men laughed at her barb. It was the perfect thing to say.

They moved over to the buffet table to help themselves to food.

"Can you make me a plate?" Kerry asked Leaper.

"Absolutely."

She went to find seats for them, anywhere she could get off her feet and quietly kick her shoes off for a few minutes. What had possessed her to wear four-inch heels all day when she normally ran around in deck shoes or tennis shoes was beyond her! Her cobalt-blue dress wouldn't have hung correctly without the heels to lengthen her legs. That's what she got for being short and busty. It's amazing what a person goes through for fashion.

The guesthouse on First Street in Coronado seemed like such an ordinary place to Leaper, and yet the peace it had brought him over the years was immeasurable. He turned on the stereo and cued "I'll Love You Forever."

"Is that Davy Jones? Retro and totally awesome. His voice is silky smooth." Kerry hummed along to the song.

"Don't have a *Brady Bunch* moment on me." He smiled at her. "Okay. Go ahead."

She stuck her tongue out at him.

"Keep doing that and I'll take it as an offer," he added, raising his eyebrows. "Yeah, I run the gamut on style and taste. Glad you like it."

"Let me just finish folding the clothes while they're hot. I hate wrinkles. Then I'll come play."

He nodded his head, going back to his musing. Before Kerry, this small guesthouse had been a place to store uniforms, weapons, and toys like his motorcycle, kayaks, paddleboards, and his boat. Now, his needs and wants had changed, and this place was more of a quiet treasure, with his lady here. It didn't feel like a storage unit anymore. Instead, it fed the harmony inside of him.

It was home.

Leaper opened the french doors onto the patio and stepped outside. A cool, salty breeze was coming off the water, and the distinct ocean scent filled his senses. For years, he'd thought it was the water that eased him, the Teams that made him feel whole and grounded, and his love of life that gave his world spark. In reality, a part of him had been waiting for Kerry. With her, he'd allowed himself to share the darkest parts of his world and had learned more about himself.

He found a way to have perspective as he reexamined

and reevaluated the events of his life. Not because she asked him to. She wasn't intrusive in that way. Rather, she lived with a certain amount of freedom and self-expression that inspired him to search and grow too.

What would have happened if he'd never seen her that day in the ocean? Was it fate that brought them together? Or a dolphin with a greater plan? He didn't want to look too closely at it. He was grateful for the opportunity to know Kerry, and he wasn't going to let it go.

He breathed deeply, allowing the lap of the waves to calm him and melt away any tension. His world had changed so much with her in it. No longer the gawky comedian, he was Leaper Lefton, the man who loved, laughed, and lived. A SEAL. A lover. And a friend.

The wind picked up. In the distance, Leaper could just barely hear the sound of feeding time at the Marine Mammal Program. The cacophony was music to his ears in a way he'd never considered before.

As Kerry joined him on the patio, he turned toward her. Pulling out a packet of papers, he held it out for her. He knew his face would be a mask, unreadable.

"What's this? You look serious." She read the first page. "I don't understand."

The stereo system changed tunes, cuing Tom Petty and the Heartbreakers' "I Won't Back Down." The lyrics played softly in the background as she looked at the paperwork again.

"Yes, you do. It's a grant from the Navy to study pink dolphins in the Amazon for their sonar capabilities. Barring any additional emergency for the Marine Mammal Program, you're good to go after the virus is resolved." He grinned. "Because I know how you feel about your dolphins and need to know they are well and safe, that comes first. Then this paperwork gives you paid leave to pursue your research." Leaper watched her eyes scan the documents again.

"I can't believe this! I was ready to tell you that I'll follow you anywhere." Her hands shook as she clutched the papers tightly. Her mouth open. "Do you know how long I've dreamed of this opportunity?"

"Well, I know a few people in Space and Naval Warfare Systems Command, SPAWAR. I've been in Spec Ops for over twenty years. I explained your position, and they were interested. They're into communications research and they have the budget, so it fits." Leaper delighted in her jumping up and down and then throwing herself into his arms. He clung to her, loving this moment. He hoped she kept this fiery part of her personality for all time. He'd do his best to support it.

She kissed him passionately. "Oh, Leaper. This is amazing!"

"Wait, there's more. I'd like to officially apply for a position on your staff. Chief bottle washer or wrangler, or whatever you need. Home will be wherever our love will flourish."

"Leaper. I'm honored. I'd be thrilled." She squeezed him hard and then slowly pulled back from him. "Wait. That's *my* dream. What about the Teams? What about you?"

He tucked a strand of loose hair behind her ear. "I'm being assigned to you and your project for the next year or so, with an evaluation after that time to see if the Navy is prepared to continue your grant and the loan… of me. Though I'm pretty sure there are some brass who will be happy to have me off their backs for an extended period of time. I'm a bit of a pain in the ass."

"No!" she mocked.

"Really, it's true." Leaper kissed her tenderly. "My dream is to expand my horizons, learn, live, and explore. A trip of this nature is a good first step. Now, uh, prepare yourself." He placed her back on her feet and took two steps away from her. Then he dusted his trousers and got down on one knee.

Kerry's mouth dropped open. "What…what are you doing?" She dropped the paperwork on the nearby lounge and covered her mouth with both hands.

"I'm doing exactly what I preach: following my instincts. Will you seek pleasure with me…for the rest of our lives?" Leaper didn't know what he'd do if she replied in the negative. He couldn't imagine living another moment of his life without her. Never in a million years would he have imagined himself wanting a wife and family, but with her, with Kerry, it was special. "Kerry Rose Hamilton, will you marry me?"

"Oh God. You're serious! Like really, really serious! Marriage, lifelong commitment, my socks mixed with yours!" Kerry's voice rose higher. "Yes. Yes. *Yes!*"

He grinned as he pulled a small pouch from his pocket and released the contents into the palm of his hand. "I want this ring to start a new tradition, to be passed on through our family. I didn't realize it was important to me until I met you. I hope you like blue sapphires and pearls."

Joy filled Kerry's eyes with glittering tears. "Man, I'm turning into a serious weeper. I'd be honored to start a hundred traditions with you. I love it, Leaper. I love *you*." She held out her hand.

"I love you, Kerry. To us, forever together." He slid the engagement ring onto her finger. "A perfect fit. Just like us."

Leaper stood and pulled Kerry into his arms, kissing her with all of the passion in his heart. As she reciprocated, he knew that she was the perfect Teammate for him, his swim buddy for life.

# Author's Note

ROMANCE WITH A DASH OF ACTION IS THE SPICE OF LIFE. IT adds layers of meaning to the story and characters. This story—even as it weaves in real-life aspects of military life—is a creation of my mind and meant to spark the imagination and entertain. I took liberties with some of action and adventure elements, though I've been told by military friends that many aspects are extremely plausible.

The Marine Mammal Program is an innovative part of the Navy, and in my opinion, worth researching and supporting. My husband was a part of the program when he was a Navy SEAL. At that time, the program was located in Hawaii, and when it moved to the San Diego area, it was developed further with the assistance of the Marine Mammal Foundation. Their reach into preservation and protection is far-reaching.

The experts—vets, trainers, staff, techs, researchers, and volunteers—associated with this program are dedicated souls whose commitment to excellence for our marine mammals is a tribute to their roles, their education, their families, and humanity as a whole. They have saved many lives, including those of wounded, beached, abandoned, and sick marine mammals. Many of these experts deploy and are put in harm's way, and we honor their sacrifice. To those that have passed, we salute you and we thank you. Always know how dearly you are missed.

Please note that many wild dolphins are affected by morbillivirus, a type of virus that also affects porpoises and whales. Scientists, researchers, and vets are still working to combat its spread and aid in the wellness and/or recovery from this devastating virus. There is no known cure to date. There are several articles in the reference section about the virus, if you'd like to learn more.

Also, the research that the Marine Mammal Program and the Foundation are doing on kidney issues in bottlenose dolphins is significant and important to the field of nephrology. This is only a small part of how the Program and Foundation are working to protect our marine mammal friends and the ecosystems we share. For more information, please check out the links following this note.

Also, the drug carfentanil is an elephant tranquilizer and has been in the news often, as it's being used to cut heroin. The mortality rate associated with this drug is high and even an extremely small amount can be fatal. Do not touch it, inhale it, or get close to it. If you suspect that this drug is on, in, or near you, call 911 immediately or go to the hospital. Report any and all incidents to stop the use of this killer.

Lastly, but most importantly, suicide has reached an epidemic level for our military. If you suspect someone is tormented or in pain, the VA offers help and there's a veterans crisis hotline. Several cities are taking great lengths to protect our warriors by retrofitting bridges and buildings with suicide barriers, and we are grateful to see this. We hope our veterans know how much we love them and thank them for their service.

Many thanks to the fans who wrote me and wanted to read Leaper's story. It's a beautiful way to end the West Coast Navy SEAL series. I hope you enjoyed the ride, and thank you for taking so many wonderful journeys with me. This has been a precious experience that I will cherish for the rest of my life.

Hooyah and hugs!
*Anne Elizabeth*

# Additional Resources

*National Marine Mammal Foundation*
**www.nmmf.org**
   Mission: "To improve and protect life for marine mammals, humans, and our shared oceans through science, service, and education."

*The Honor Foundation*
**www.honor.org**
   "The Honor Foundation (THF) is a unique transition institute created exclusively for Navy SEALs and the U.S. Special Operations community. We provide a clear process for professional development and a diverse ecosystem of world-class support and technology. Every step is dedicated to preparing these outstanding men and women to continue to realize their maximum potential during and after their service careers."

*U.S. Department of Veteran Affairs*
*Veterans Crisis Line*
**www.mentalhealth.va.gov/suicide_prevention**

# References

Chapman, Gary. *The Five Love Languages*. Chicago: Northfield Publishing, 2004.

Dyer, Trey. "Carfentanil Linked to 19 Deaths in Wayne County, Michigan." DrugRehab.com, October 14, 2016. https://www.drugrehab.com/2016/10/14/carfentanil-linked-to-19-deaths-in-wayne-county-michigan/.

Goldish, Meish. *Dolphins in the Navy*. New York: Bearport Publishing, 2012.

Lee, Jane J. "What's Killing Bottlenose Dolphins? Experts Discover Cause." *National Geographic*, August 28, 2013. http://news.nationalgeographic.com/news/2013/08/130827-dolphin-deaths-virus-outbreak-ocean-animals-science/.

Leschin-Hoar, Clare. "Whales, Sea Turtles, Seals: The Unintended Catch of Abandoned Fishing Gear." National Public Radio, September 28, 2016. http://www.npr.org/sections/thesalt/2016/09/28/495777033/whales-sea-turtles-seals-the-unintended-catch-of-abandoned-fishing-gear.

Melendez, Steven. "How America Gets Its Deadliest New Drug." FastCompany.com, September 9, 2016. https://www.fastcompany.com/3063518/carfentanil-synthetic-opioids-heroin.

National Oceanic and Atmospheric Administration. "Morbillivirus Infection in Dolphins, Porpoises, and

Whales." August 28, 2013. http://www.nmfs.noaa.gov /pr/health/mmume/midatlantic2013/morbillivirus _factsheet2013.pdf.

Subbaraman, Nidhi. "Big Break in Dolphin Die-Off: It's an 'Outbreak' of Measles-Like Virus." NBC News, August 27, 2013. http://www.nbcnews.com/science /big-break-dolphin-die-its-outbreak-measles-virus -8C11014690.

Walsh, Brian E. *VAK Self-Audit: Visual, Auditory, and Kinesthetic Communication and Learning Styles: Exploring Patterns of How You Interact and Learn*. Edited by Ronald Willard and Astrid Whiting. [Print on demand]: Walsh Seminars, 2011.

# Leaper and Kerry's Playlist

American Authors, "Best Day of My Life"

Thirty Seconds to Mars, "Kings and Queens"

Village People, "In the Navy"

Pixies, "Where Is My Mind?"

The Lumineers, "Ho Hey"

Barry White, "Your Sweetness Is My Weakness"

Hoyt Axton, "Joy to the World"

Aretha Franklin, "(You Make Me Feel Like) A Natural Woman"

Marvin Gaye, "I Heard It through the Grapevine"

The Young Rascals, "Good Lovin'"

Rolling Stones, "You Can't Always Get What You Want"

The Yesteryears, "Come Together"

Louis Armstrong, "All of Me"

Violent Femmes, "Please Do Not Go"

Norman Greenbaum, "Spirit in the Sky"

Blondie, "One Way or Another"

Simon and Garfunkel, "Bridge Over Troubled Water"

Journey, "Don't Stop Believin'"

Davy Jones, "I'll Love You Forever"

Tom Petty and the Heartbreakers, "I Won't Back Down"

# Acknowledgments

With great thanks to my cherished husband—retired Navy SEAL, EOD, and PRU Advisor—Carl Swepston; to the outstanding retired Navy SEAL Thomas Rancich and his remarkable Liz; in memory of the incredible Rear Admiral and #1 Bullfrog Dick Lyon and with great love to his fabulous wife, Cindy; with thanks and joy to old goat roper John T. Curtis and his marvelous Miranda; to inspiring retired Navy SEAL Moki Martin and his family; for former Navy SEAL Hal Kuykendall and his lovely wife, Denise; to retired Navy SEAL Jerry Todd and his terrific Pete; for the wonderful Frank Toms (UDT 11/ST1) and his family; our dear friend John Baca, Medal of Honor recipient; Medal of Honor recipient Mike Thornton; the Vietnam Era "Old Frogs & SEALs" who contributed comments and stories; and *Hooyah!* to all of our operational friends.

Many thanks:

To Christine Feehan—you are a tremendous talent, a dear friend, and an incredible inspiration!

To Marjorie Liu—you are brilliant, witty, and insightful!

To Joanne Fluke and John Fluke—two wonderfully talented and amazing souls!

To Cathy Maxwell, Kim Adams Lowe, D. C. and Charles DeVane—sending endless love and hooyahs and hugs!

Cheers to amazing friends: Tamara Worlton; Liz LeCoy and her Walt; Mimi and Alan; Laurie De Salvo, a.k.a. Lia DeAngela, and Efrain; Jan Albertie; Suzanne Brockmann; Alisa Kwitney; Christina Skye; Angela Knight; Leslie Wainger; Dianna Love; Andrew and Megan Bamford; R. Garland Gray; Mary Beth Bass; Maura Troy; Domini and Chris Walker; Brian Feehan; Sheila and Ed; Sam and Zavier; Jo and Johnny; Jennifer; Maria R. and Joao; Maria M. and Frank; Maria N. and Emanuel; Jessica and Ryan; Kim and Paul K.; Jill and Carl H.; the Lynches; Brenda; Mary H.; Anne M.; Stephanie H.; Rose S.; Mic; Ginger D.; Nonny; Erika; Amy; Katheryn; Kat; Cindy; Lynn; Robyn; Lora; Traci; Trudy; Stacey; Kristy; Simone; Laura L.; the entire BB crew; and Sara and Lindsey Stillman, who are marvelous. A shout-out of love and joy to Craig, Sherry, Shae & Caden; to the fascinating Kathryn Falk, Kenneth Rubin, Carol Stacy, and Jo Carol Jones; and to my agent, Eric Ruben.

Thank you to the Sourcebooks crew—the talented Laura, Susie, Heather, and Earl, and to the marvelous Deb Werksman and Dominique Raccah.

With infinite love and respect to my parents—always!

# About the Author

*New York Times* and *USA Today* bestselling author and comic creator Anne Elizabeth has a bachelor's degree in business and a master's in communications from Boston University and is a member of the Author's Guild, Horror Writers Association, and Romance Writers of America. Her West Coast Navy SEAL series from Sourcebooks includes five books: *A SEAL at Heart*, *Once a SEAL*, *A SEAL Forever*, *The Soul of a SEAL*, and *The Power of a SEAL*. *A SEAL at Heart* was seen on the independent film *Hello, My Name Is Doris*, starring Sally Field, and on the sitcom *Mike & Molly*. Anne has stories in eight anthologies: Atria/Simon & Schuster's *Caramel Flava* and *Honey Flava*; Highland Press's *Recipe for Love*, *Holiday Op*, *For Your Heart Only*, and *Operation: L.O.V.E.*; Sourcebooks's *Way of the Warrior*; and the independently published multiauthor *Hot Alpha SEALs* megaset. Four of the anthologies donated funds to the military or military programs and organizations. She's also the author of the popular graphic novel series *Pulse of Power*, as well as *Zombie Power* and *The Hall of Insides*, and her comics have been seen on *The Big Bang Theory* nine times. She's written more than seventy articles and columns for *RT Book Reviews* and is the recipient of the L.A. Banks Warrior Woman Award and the Romance Writers of

America Service Award for Lifetime Contributions to the Romance Industry. Anne and her husband, a retired Navy SEAL, reside in San Diego.